WRECK & RUIN

Blue Angels Motorcycle Club

EMMA SLATE

Tabula Rasa Publishing

Chapter 1

"CAN I GET YOUR NUMBER?" the frat guy wearing a blue and white checkered shirt asked.

"Sorry," I said, shooting him an insincere smile. "I don't give out my number to customers."

The red-cheeked kid leaned over the bar and said, "I drive a BMW."

"I'm really more of an Audi girl."

He blinked at my response and then smiled. "You're funny. I like funny."

Shelly snorted from somewhere behind me.

"I can get you into the best clubs in Dallas," he said, trying again.

"But we're in Waco," I reminded him. "I don't care about Dallas."

He reached into his wallet and pulled out a fifty and slid it across the bar to me, his eyebrows raised.

"You've got to be kidding me," I sputtered. "Did you just—do you think I'll…"

Two men stalked into the bar, immediately drawing my attention. They were older than the usual crowd of college frat guys and douchey accountants in khakis. Mid-thirties if I had to guess.

One was blond and tall. He was lean, but I could tell he was in good shape.

The other…

The other was taller than his friend, muscular, swarthy, and *trouble*.

Both were tatted to high-heaven and I had to stop myself from swooning at the sight. I was a sucker for body art.

An idea popped into my head. "Excuse me a second," I said to the guy who'd just tried to pay me fifty bucks to sleep with him. "My boyfriend just got here."

I ducked under the bar at the service station and walked across the battered wooden floor, which was in desperate need of a refinish. With nerves jangling in my body, I sauntered up to the dark-haired man. As I approached him I realized he was taller than I originally thought. His jaw was covered with dark stubble and his brown eyes looked down at me.

"Hi," I said, wetting my lips in nervousness. When he didn't say anything, I took a step closer. "I need you to do me a favor. I need you to pretend to be my boyfriend so that prick at the bar leaves me alone. I'll let you drink for free tonight. You and your friend." I finally managed to glance away from the man who had yet to appear as though he'd heard anything I'd said. But the moment I took my eyes off him he decided to move.

His hands settled on my hips and pulled me toward him. His head dipped and his lips covered mine, his tongue sweeping inside my mouth. I vaguely heard his friend let out a low chuckle, but I was too consumed by the man who was kissing me. One of his hands left my waist to travel up my body and caress the back of my head. He angled his mouth as he gave me the most carnal kiss I'd ever experienced.

Excitement shivered up and down my spine as my nipples pebbled against the thin fabric of my black tank top.

Abruptly, he lifted his mouth from mine and stared down at me. His brown eyes were no longer blank. They seemed to be glowing, banked embers just waiting to be stoked into a fire.

The side of his mouth curled up, but it was in no way a smile. He looked away from me to stare at a spot over my shoulder.

"He's gone."

His voice was like velvet on naked skin.

He dropped his hands from my body, leaving me aching and wanting more.

I felt exposed and confused; I was supposed to be in control of the situation, but the fact that I wanted his lips on mine again told me I controlled nothing.

"We'll take two drafts," came his friend's voice. "Will you bring them to the booth in the corner, darlin'?"

I blinked, my eyelids feeling droopy and tired as though I had been drugged. I looked at him and nodded slightly before turning and walking back to the bar without saying a word.

As I ducked under the service bar, I caught Shelly's expression. Her mouth was hanging open, her eyebrows raised. "What the fuck did you just do?"

I grabbed a pint glass and began to fill it. "I think you saw."

"Everyone saw!" She took a step closer. "Do you know who you just kissed?"

"Yeah, I kissed a guy who scared off some punk kid who wanted to pay me for a night in bed."

Shelly shook her head, her honey blond ponytail sweeping her shoulder. "No, *you* just kissed a Blue Angel."

I set the pint aside as beer frothed over the lip of the glass and reached for another. "So?"

"So?" she nearly squeaked. "You don't just go up and kiss some random biker."

"First of all, I didn't kiss him, he kissed me. Second of all, I told him he and his friend could drink for free tonight if he pretended to be my boyfriend. What's the big deal?"

"You have no idea what you just got yourself into, do you? I grew up in a trailer park, Mia. I'm familiar with biker clubs. They were around all the time. And the last thing you want is to be on their radar."

"I'm not on their radar," I said in exasperation. "He did me a solid. It's no big deal." I didn't want to hear any more of my best friend's lecture, so I took the freshly poured pints and delivered them to the two bikers who were sitting in the corner booth.

They stopped talking the moment I approached. The blond smiled up at me and said, "Thanks."

"No sweat," I said. I set the pints down and began to turn with the intention of leaving.

"I'm Zip. Your boyfriend's name is Colt." His blue eyes twinkled with humor and I felt my cheeks heat.

"Ah, yeah, thanks for that," I said, shuffling from foot-to-foot, feeling awkward.

"And who are you?" Zip prodded, a smile blooming across his face.

"Mia," I said. "My name is Mia."

Colt said nothing, but continued to look at me with an indiscernible gaze.

"Enjoy your drinks."

I hastily made my way back to the bar. Shelly opened

her mouth to say something, but I held up my hand. "Don't."

Thankfully, a group of people entered and for the next few hours we were too busy for chitchat and the inevitable lecture that I knew was coming.

When the rush died a few hours later, I looked at the booth where the bikers had been sitting, but they were gone.

"I'm taking the trash out," I said.

"You sure? I can do it," Shelly offered. "You did it last time."

"I don't mind," I told her. I lifted the hefty bag full of empty beer and liquor bottles and maneuvered my way off the floor toward the back alley of Dive Bar.

I pushed my shoulder against the door to open it and immediately heard the unmistakable sound of knuckles striking flesh.

I dropped the bag of refuse when I saw a leather-clad biker fighting a khaki-wearing, ripped meathead. The two men were about the same size, and for a moment I couldn't tell who was winning the brawl.

My heartbeat accelerated at the scent of blood in the air and I gasped at the violence, frozen in place.

The two men fought like lions, bloodying each other as though they were battling to the death for territory, neither of them willing to back down. Grunts and guttural sounds filled the air and blood streamed from their faces when finally the biker knocked the muscled man off balance and kicked his legs out from under him. The meathead fell to the ground. When he tried to rise, the biker grabbed his hair with one hand and pulled his head back. Looking straight into his eyes, the tatted biker sank his fist into his opponent's face with all his might, ending the altercation.

A shaft of moonlight peeked out from the clouds to reveal the bloodied face of the man who'd kissed me just a few hours ago.

Colt's eyes blazed with intensity as he stared at me.

"Go back inside," he commanded. His voice was angry, rough.

A shiver of fear danced down my spine.

Fear, and something else.

I turned to leave.

"Wait," he called.

I glanced over my shoulder and Colt's eyes held mine for a moment before he stared down at the guy on the ground in front of him. The prep was unconscious, breathing heavily after being knocked out cold. His head lobbed to the side and a trickle of blood and drool began to form a puddle next to his face. I wondered if I should call an ambulance and tried to look more closely at him in the light.

Yeah, definitely calling an ambulance.

I thought Colt would leave, but instead he began to stalk toward me, causing my heart to beat in terror. I scrambled back, tripping over the garbage bag behind me.

I was about to fall, but Colt was suddenly there, and his hands reached out to steady me. Hands that were surprisingly gentle as they held me, when moments ago, they'd been used to inflict violence.

It was too late to escape, so I forced myself to have a tiny shred of courage. I tilted my head back so I could gaze up at him. "What happened?" I whispered.

His expression was dark.

Murderous.

But for some reason—some stupid, asinine, hormonal reason—I didn't truly believe that Colt would hurt me.

"Are you gonna call the cops?" he asked. His voice was heady, potent, unlike anything I'd ever heard before.

"That depends." I wet my dry lips, briefly realizing his gaze tracked the movement of my tongue.

He paused again, clearly weighing whether or not to let me in, wondering if it would cause more trouble than it was worth to explain it to me.

"He drugged a woman."

I blinked. "Excuse me?"

"He might be clean cut and built, but he's a rapist. He drugged a woman in your bar," he repeated. "He bought her a cocktail and she accepted. She got up to use the bathroom and that's when he laced her drink. That shit doesn't fly with me or my club. You don't hurt innocent people and get away with it."

"Oh my God," I said in horror.

"Zip noticed what was going on and we watched it unfold in plain sight. He stopped the woman from drinking whatever this fuck put in her glass and sent her home with her friends." His gaze wandered to the guy still passed out on the pavement. "Dickhead didn't like being accused of what he'd done and made the same mistake they all do."

"What mistake is that?"

"Choosing a fight with me out back over the cops."

I swallowed, but couldn't find the words I wanted to say. It didn't matter because Colt wasn't done speaking.

"He's damn lucky you showed up out here…"

"Were you going to—" I blurted out the words and then cut myself off before I said something that might put me in danger.

What was this man capable of?

Colt's lips pulled back into a smile, but it wasn't beautiful. It was demonic and vengeful. And the shaft of moon-light bathed half his face in shadow.

"He'll live," Colt assured me.

I felt him loosen his hold on me and relax. I was suddenly bereft and cold. I couldn't understand why I wanted a savage vigilante to touch me again.

But I did.

"Better get back inside," he said softly. He gestured with his chin to the passed out meathead. "He's got friends in the bar. Let them know you found him and they'll take him home. I'm pretty sure they aren't gonna call the cops."

With that pronouncement, Colt turned. A shaft of moonlight illuminated the logo on the back of his leather vest, a skull flanked by open angel wings.

He strode from the alley, becoming one with the darkness.

I crossed my hands over my arms, my fingers stroking the spot where he'd touched my skin.

After a few moments my daze cleared, and I got the bag of trash into one of the nearly full dumpsters.

I took one last look at the creep on the ground and then turned and went into the bar.

The next morning, my doorbell chimed. I shot up in bed, terrified, my heart in my throat. I'd been completely asleep, dead to the world, and the noise had sounded like it was playing on speakers directly in my bedroom. Cursing and sleepy-eyed, I got up, tripping on the comforter that hung off the side of the bed. I found a pair of pajama shorts before heading into the living room to the front door.

"You're a terrible person, do you know that?" I glowered at Shelly as she stood on the steps holding two coffees and a paper bag from our favorite bakery. We used to do our homework together at Madeline's. We'd sit in the back, sharing a chocolate croissant and a latte because that was all Shelly could afford. I always offered to pay, but Shelly never accepted charity.

"You look like hell," Shelly said. Her honey blond hair was pulled up into a messy bun and she was wearing white denim shorts and a pink sleeveless tank. Her toenails were a subtle shade of coral. The woman didn't ever look like she worked nights. No bags under the eyes. No pale skin from lack of sleep. Fresh as a spring daisy.

Always.

"I didn't get to sleep until about four," I admitted, waving her inside.

She handed me one of the to-go cups. "Why is that, I wonder?"

Shelly had tried to get me to talk about Colt and the kiss when we'd been closing up the bar. While we washed glasses, put the chairs on the tables, and swept the floor, she needled me relentlessly. I'd only managed to escape her inquisition because I'd volunteered to clean the bathrooms and then taken out the garbage. Not only did I want to escape her determination to find out how good the kiss was, but I also wanted to see if the guy Colt had beat up was still there.

He wasn't.

"You got away last night, but I need details. And I need them now."

"Why?" I asked as I walked into the kitchen to grab a plate from the cabinet. I took the pastry bag from Shelly and unloaded the pastries onto a plate. We both sat at the old Formica kitchen table from the 1950s. It was orange and hideous, but it had been my grandmother's favorite piece of furniture and I didn't have the heart to replace it. I didn't have the heart to redecorate her home at all, actually. Surrounded by the decor of my childhood, I kept the memory of my grandmother alive as best I could.

"Why?" she asked, mouth agape. She tore the croissant but didn't take a bite yet. "How long have we known each other?"

"Twelve years," I said.

"Right. I've been there for boyfriends who have become ex boyfriends, I was the first phone call after you lost your virginity, and not once have I ever seen the look on your face that I saw last night—after you kissed a total stranger. A biker, no less. I was trying to tell you about the whole biker thing and you wouldn't let me."

"Let you? We were at work. What was I supposed to do? Ask our customers to stop ordering drinks so you could give me the run down? I got the memo. Don't get involved."

She popped a croissant bite into her mouth and chewed. After she swallowed and washed it down with coffee, she replied, "You shouldn't have singled them out. You don't understand them like I do."

"You know the Blue Angels?"

She shook her head. "No, but I told you I know biker culture. My mom…" Shelly trailed off, not wanting to say more about the woman who'd given her life, but not much else. "Anyway, bikers are weird. They're like, oddly possessive of their women. But they fuck around *a lot*. Fidelity isn't big in their world."

"Okay? What does any of that have to do with me?"

"Just, don't get involved with this guy, okay? You're a good girl. A nice girl. You deserve more than some rough biker who won't come home to you every night. They don't have normal jobs, or live normal lives. They're not suburbs and white picket fence guys."

Normal.

Yeah, nothing about my interaction with Colt had been normal.

I forced a smile. "I think it's really sweet that you're trying to warn me off, but you're forgetting something. He just kissed me. I doubt he's even still thinking about me."

"That's what I was trying to explain to you. You may not want him, but he *definitely* wants you. For him to kiss you in public like that? It was basically him putting his brand on you."

I rolled my eyes. "That's just dumb."

She shrugged. "Like I said. It's weird, and as an outsider, it's hard to comprehend. Your grandmother wouldn't want you to end up with a guy like that."

"Please don't bring her into this," I said lightly.

"You're right. It's a cheap shot. But you have to swear to me that you won't get involved with them."

"I swear."

The vow was made easily and without an agenda to get her off my back. I truly had no desire to get involved with Colt. Even if it had been the best kiss of my life.

"Good. Now am I allowed to change the subject?" she asked.

"Please."

Shelly looked at me for a long moment and then stood up. She reached into her pocket and pulled out a sparkly ring and slid it onto her left ring finger.

"Oh my God." I jumped to my feet. "Way to bury the lead!"

"I knew if I told you I got engaged last night—well, early this morning," she grinned, "you'd want to talk about it. But I wanted to talk about your thing first."

I grasped Shelly's hand so I could get a look at her ring. "It's beautiful. How did it happen?"

She smiled dreamily. "I got home from the bar and walked into the apartment. Mark had lit candles and scattered rose petals across the floor leading to the bedroom like a walkway. I followed them and..." Her cheeks flushed. "He was down on one knee, wearing a tuxedo. He said he didn't want to propose on our one-year anniversary, so he proposed the day after. Even if that meant proposing to me the moment I got home from work. He said he didn't want to wait any longer to start our life together."

Tears misted my eyes and I launched myself at my best friend, who was a good six inches taller than me. "I'm so happy for you guys. You deserve all the happiness in the world."

She hugged me back just as fiercely. "Will you be my maid of honor?"

Laughing, I pulled back and swiped the tears from my cheeks. "Like you even have to ask."

Chapter 2

"You really don't mind finishing the rest?" Shelly asked a few nights later. "I took out the garbage and cleaned the bathrooms already."

"Go," I said, taking a sip of my Red Bull.

Mark stood at the end of the bar and eagerly draped his arm around Shelly when she was close enough. He was four inches shorter than her, but clearly it didn't matter to either of them. Shelly had finally found a good man who treated her the way she deserved and she loved him deeply.

"Dinner soon, yes? Our place," Mark called out.

I nodded. "I'd like that."

"I just got a new grill," Mark said, his green eyes lit with excitement behind his glasses. "I am the grill master!"

Shelly rubbed her hand across his chest. "Yes, you are."

"Please leave before I vomit and have to clean it up myself."

Shelly saluted mockingly and then she and her fiancé left. I followed them and flicked the lock closed.

After I swept the floor, I cleaned out the icemaker and then counted the till. I gathered up the cash and receipts and headed to the back where Richie kept the safe. When I pushed open the door to the office, I lost my hold on the paperwork, which fluttered to the floor. Red Bull was no match for true exhaustion. I hadn't slept well since I'd met Colt.

"Mia!" Richie exclaimed, jumping up from his chair.

"Crap," I muttered, sinking to the ground. I didn't spare him a glance. "Sorry. Thought you'd left already. Hey, can you open the safe for me?" Scooping up the derelict papers, I looked at Richie. His olive complexion was unusually pale and there was a sheen of sweat covering his long forehead. Slicked-back hair and beady eyes made my boss look like a weasel. His gaze darted from me to the corner of the room.

When I rose, the receipts and till in my hands, I realized Richie wasn't alone. His companion stared at me with ill-concealed interest. I was used to being leered at; I was a bartender. But I'd learned that most of the guys were harmless.

Not this man.

A salt-and-pepper beard covered half his face and his silver hair was pulled back into a ponytail. Brown eyes surveyed me, making me feel naked. His gaze stayed riveted on my chest a moment before he looked up. A slight smile curved his lips.

Something was off with him. Though only average in height and bulk, I knew he was dangerous. His leather vest didn't hide that he was packing. We were in Texas, so it wasn't a huge shock. I even had a pistol in the glove box of my truck.

"Sorry," I chirped, forcing a smile. "Didn't know Richie had company. I'll just leave all this here." I walked toward the desk and set everything down, wanting to escape as soon as possible.

"Thanks, Mia," Richie said, his voice strained.

"Mia," the stranger crooned. "That's a beautiful name."

My smile remained in place, but I attempted not to engage. The man wasn't having it. He strode toward me. He took my hand and brought it to his lips and I had to force myself not to pull it back.

"I never let strange men kiss me," I teased, calling on my arsenal of bartending flirting skills.

"Call me Dev." He kept my hand as his smile widened. "There. We're not strangers anymore."

I glanced at his leather cut, noting the president patch. Batting my eyelashes, I prayed he thought I was a ditz with a decent rack.

"You headed home?" he asked.

"Yup." I extracted my hand. With a quick wave, I skedaddled out of the office and closed the door. I grabbed my purse from underneath the bar and exited to the side alley. I found my keys, ready to head to my beaten-up, green and rust colored vintage Chevy truck, but the sound of voices through the air duct stopped me.

"She's a hot piece of ass," I heard Dev say.

"She is," Richie agreed.

Swine.

"Customers love her. She's fast and her till is never off," Richie continued.

"Is she smart?" Dev asked.

"I trust her with money, if that's what you're asking."

"You know that's not what I'm talking about," Dev said, his voice dropping in tone. All playfulness, all lightness had leeched out of him, and I heard the dominance, the strength in him.

It was terrifying.

"She doesn't know anything," Richie promised. "She doesn't know about our arrangement—"

"Good," Dev interrupted. "It better fucking stay that way. New shipment coming in tomorrow. I don't want any trouble."

"There won't be any trouble. She doesn't know. No one at the bar knows anything."

I'd heard enough. Whatever they were involved in, I wanted nothing to do with it. Backing away, I left the alley and got to my truck. I opened the heavy old door and climbed inside, wanting to get the hell out of there as fast as possible.

Richie's bar wasn't a biker bar, but in the last many days, two men from two different biker clubs had found their way in. Coincidence?

Doubtful.

~

"Have you heard from Richie? Or seen him lately?" Shelly asked three nights later.

I frowned. "Now that you mention it, no. I've been off the last couple of nights though."

"Hmm. He's usually here at the end of the shift to open the safe and put the till in, but he hasn't come in yet. I'm glad he finally gave me the safe combo so I can do it myself."

"Well, let's hope he shows up tonight," I said.

She held up a nearly empty bottle of tequila. "We're out of Añejo and I couldn't find any more in the store room."

"There's no way we're out. Richie orders that stuff by the case."

It took me a few minutes to find a rogue box of tequila

hiding in the back corner of the storage room under a dusty box of Mike's Hard Lemonade.

When I returned, the bar was packed. I held up the bottle in triumph and smiled.

"Why do I always miss stuff?" Shelly asked with a sigh.

I grinned at her. "You have no attention to detail."

"I'd spray you with the water hose...except it's totally true." She laughed. "I'm good at other things."

"Such as?"

She gave me a look like she was thinking something dirty.

"You're such a dude."

The next couple hours flew by as Shelly and I manned the bar, serving customers and vetoing horrid music selections on the jukebox. The tip jar by the register filled up, and it looked like it would be a good night.

When there was a brief lull, Shelly said, "I need to use the bathroom."

I nodded as I reached for a rag, cleaning up a puddle of beer that had spilled across the bar. It was still sticky, so I crouched down to find the spray bottle of surface cleaner. When I stood up, I froze.

"How you doin', sweetheart?"

It took all of my willpower not to flinch. Dev commandeered a stool as his eyes roved over me in appreciation.

"Hi," I greeted in hesitation. "Can I get you a drink?"

He shook his head. "I don't want a drink. Have you seen your boss?"

"Richie? No. He hasn't been at the bar for a few days."

"Really?"

"Really."

"You're not lying to me, are you?" Dev's voice was low and dangerous. "I don't like people who lie to me."

I adamantly shook my head. "I swear I haven't seen him."

His eyes bored into mine. "Give me your phone."

Like an obedient child I reached into the back pocket of my jeans and retrieved my cell. I placed it into Dev's outstretched hand.

He quickly typed something and then handed it back. "There. Now you have my number. And I have yours." He winked. "If you see Richie, you call me. Immediately."

"Okay," I said, feeling faint.

He nodded, rising from his stool. "I'll be back, but there's one more thing." He beckoned me with his finger to come closer. "I don't want anyone to hear…"

Before I realized what he was doing he leaned over and planted his lips on mine. He tasted like stale cigarettes and bourbon. It took everything inside me to keep the bile in my stomach from rising. I was angry with myself for not seeing it coming.

"You're a hot little piece." His eyes dragged over me, like he couldn't wait to see what I looked like naked. "Bet you're fire in the bedroom. It's gonna be fun finding out."

He chucked me under the chin and then sauntered out of the bar. I saw the emblem on the back of his leather cut with *Iron Horsemen* in bold script.

Shelly came back from the bathroom. "What did I miss?"

I somehow managed to plaster a smile on my face and reply, "Nothing."

~

I refused to confide to Shelly about Dev. I hadn't even told her I'd walked in on Richie talking to the Iron Horsemen president a few days ago. If Shelly was warning me away from the Blue Angels, I didn't want to give her more to worry about when I mentioned the Iron Horsemen.

The less she knew the better.

When we closed the bar for the night and I flipped the sign to read *Closed*, Shelly said, "You should go home early. Ditch out."

"Why?" I asked.

"Because you've been working like a maniac and I owe you from when you closed by yourself the other night."

"I don't want to leave you alone here. Richie hasn't made an appearance tonight. I don't know if he will."

"Mark will come."

Mark didn't look like much, but he was proficient in Krav Maga and had his concealed carry permit. It wasn't what I would've expected from a spectacle-wearing computer programmer, but he was an alpha male, through and through.

"Okay, if you're sure," I said, glad that I was leaving Dive Bar for the night.

Shelly called to me, "Hey, I want to go wedding dress shopping this weekend. You in?"

I grinned. "Damn right."

We hugged goodbye. I headed to the back exit and opened the door into the spring evening and smacked right into my missing boss.

"Ow," I mumbled, rubbing my shoulder and glaring at him. "Where the hell have you been? And why are you skulking around? You know Dev is looking for you, don't you?"

He ran a hand through his greasy black hair. "Did Dev come to the bar?"

"Yep. What sort of shit did you get into, Richie?"

He played dumb. "What do you mean?"

"I mean, why is there a biker club president walking in

and out of Dive Bar like he owns the place?"

"I don't have time to explain," he evaded. "Wait here. I need a—just promise me you won't leave right away."

I paused, considering. Then I said, "I'll be in my truck."

"Give me five minutes. I left something in the office."

Before I could reply, he dashed through the doorway and disappeared. I found my keys at the bottom of my purse and unlocked the truck. I got the engine going so as soon as Richie and I parted ways, I could go home.

Richie came out of the bar and ran to the passenger side. He scrambled into the truck, ducking down, keeping out of sight.

"Are you going to tell me what the hell is going on?" I demanded.

He pinched the bridge of his nose. "I got into bad shit with the Iron Horsemen. I'm leaving town. I have to get out of here or they'll kill me."

Fear skated down my spine.

"But—but what about the bar?" I faltered.

"Don't worry about the bar," he growled. "You need to get the hell out of town for a little while. Lay low. Shit's about to go down and you don't want to be anywhere near it."

"What kind of shit?"

He shook his head. "The kind of shit where people die."

"Why are you being so cryptic? Just tell me what's going—"

"For fuck's sake!" he yelled. "Have you heard a word I've said? Listen to me or don't. That shit's on you."

I rubbed my temple, trying to process Richie's words. It was futile. He wasn't going to divulge anything more. "Are you going to get out of my truck?" I asked finally.

"I need a ride to the bus depot."

"I'm not your chauffeur, asshole, and you just got done telling me to leave town. I'm not fucking taking you anywhere," I snapped.

"Please," he begged. "Mia, I need your help…"

I glared at him, but I wasn't immune to his plight. "Fine."

He exhaled. "We have to make a quick stop on the way."

"You've got a lot of nerve—"

"Mia, fuck, come on—"

"Where do you need to go?" I asked with reluctance. The sooner we took care of this errand, the sooner I could be rid of Richie.

He gave me the address of a storage unit a few minutes from the bar and we drove to it. I pulled into the main lot and he guided me around the side of one of the buildings through a gate.

"Keep the engine going."

He was out of the truck before I could respond. He dashed across the pavement to the unit. Richie reached into his back pocket, extracted a key, and then shoved it into the lock. He lifted the rolling door a few feet off the ground and ducked inside.

A few minutes later, the storage unit was locked up again and Richie was back in my truck. We headed for the bus depot and when we arrived, Richie fiddled with the door handle. "Thanks, Mia."

He climbed out. Before shutting the door, he said, "Give it a couple weeks. You'll be fine to come back then."

Richie took off for the bus terminal.

"Fuck you, Richie," I said to his retreating form. "Fuck you."

Chapter 3

I CALLED Shelly the moment I got home, even though it was nearly one a.m. She didn't answer, so I left a voice message telling her to call me back immediately. My adrenaline had run its course and exhaustion was tugging at my eyelids. I looked around my grandmother's house. Nothing had changed when she'd died. Same furniture, same curtains. It was like I was waiting for her to come back, as though she'd only run to the grocery store.

Waco hadn't felt like home for a long time. Ever since Grammie had gotten sick, it hadn't been normal. Not her house, not my job, not my life. When we found out she was terminal, I'd quit school and Shelly had gotten me a job at Dive Bar. Working nights at the bar left my days free to take care of Grammie. After she died, I picked up more shifts, took on more responsibilities at the bar, and generally did anything I could to stay out of the house—a house still filled with Grammie's favorite things.

Boredom and sadness were a strange combination. To say I'd felt itchy in my own skin for a while was an understatement. I wanted to move and do something different, but for some reason I clung to the familiarity of Waco. The house was paid off, so there was no financial burden to contend with. What was really keeping me here aside from Shelly? Was I supposed to live my life for other people? She had Mark. In a few months, they'd be married and then they'd start a family and everything would change.

Where did that leave me? Jumping from one dead end job to another? Seeing Shelly and Mark on weekends when they weren't doing couple things? And what about when they had a baby? Their time wouldn't be their own. I would not see my best friend with any sort of regularity.

I didn't realize until that moment, standing in my grandmother's kitchen in the middle of the night that I was so incredibly lonely. I'd shut down while Grammie was sick—just trying to hold it together and get through the hardest thing life had ever thrown at me. But it was two years later and I was still in that place, just existing from one moment to the next. It had been easier to float through the last few years in numb acceptance. I smiled, I laughed and pretended things were fine, but the feelings of joy and satisfaction never reached my soul.

In truth, my life was utterly desolate.

Maybe the situation with the Iron Horsemen was the push I needed to start over somewhere else, to finish my last semester of college, to decide what I really needed in life to be happy. The status quo was no longer working, and thanks to Richie my present was now riddled with danger.

My phone rang, jarring me out of my cycle of thoughts.

It was Shelly.

"Just saw that you called," she said in way of greeting. "I didn't listen to your voicemail. What's wrong? Are you okay?"

"I saw Richie tonight as I was leaving."

"No shit. What did the scumbag have to say for himself?"

I paused for a moment and then said, "He told me he got into some shit with the Iron Horsemen."

"The Iron Horsemen? Oh my God—"

"I don't know the details, but I just dropped him off at the bus station. He's scared enough to get out of town. But before I left him at the bus depot, he told *me* to get out of town too."

"What the fuck? What aren't you saying, Mia? There is more to this than you're letting on…"

I quickly briefed her about the night I walked in on them and told her about Dev coming back to ask if I'd seen Richie.

"Why didn't you tell me sooner?" she demanded. "Do you know how serious this is?"

"You were already giving me grief about the Blue Angels and I didn't want you to worry." I paused. "I'm scared, Shelly."

She fell silent for a moment. "You need to listen to me. You cannot call the police. Do you understand what I'm saying? These people work with dirty cops all the time. If you call the cops, it could be dangerous. It could make it worse for you."

"I'm definitely not going back to Dive Bar, and neither should you."

"Yeah," she agreed. "Shit. I'll text everyone and tell them to bail. Fuck Richie. He didn't just screw himself, he screwed all of us, too. With the club hanging around Dive Bar, it's dangerous for anyone who works there. You need to get out of Waco. Now."

"Yeah, I'm going to," I said. "I don't want to live my life in fear, but I don't want to be stupid either. You didn't see this guy, Shelly. He's—there's definitely a screw loose. I don't want to be around when he finds out Richie skipped town and bailed on him."

"Where will you go? And for how long? Do you think you'll be able to come back to Waco?"

"I don't know. If I do decide to come back, it won't be for a while. I'm thinking Coeur d'Alene."

"What's in Coeur d'Alene?" she asked.

"Mom lived there. Grammie told me she loved it. It's on the water, but has mountains nearby."

"Can I ask you something?"

"Yeah, of course."

"If this shit with the Iron Horsemen wasn't happening, would you still think about leaving Waco?"

I paused a moment before answering. "I don't know. Maybe. All this feels like a giant wake up call. I can't keep doing this, can I?"

"Doing what, exactly? Eating takeout and working too many nights at the bar? Not dating or even *thinking* about dating? I actually support your decision to leave. I just wish it wasn't happening this way."

"Me too. I'm packing a bag and will leave early tomorrow morning."

"I'll miss the shit out of you, but I want you safe."

Sadness enveloped me—for a different reason this time. "I'll miss our morning coffee and pastry time."

"Me too."

I would be missing so much when I left town, but I knew I couldn't stay. Richie's warning drummed in my bones.

"Love you, girl," she said quietly. "Call me when you've touched down."

"Love you too. Be safe, okay? Be alert."

"I will, but that guy didn't come to me."

"Thank God for that. I'm glad it's me and not you."

Shelly had Mark. She had the promise of a beautiful future. I didn't want this dark cloud to storm over her head. No, I'd weather it alone. Deal with it myself.

We hung up and I tossed my phone onto the bed. I had just enough energy to pack a bag. I needed a few hours of sleep and then I'd hit the road in the morning. I took a shower to wash the bar smell off me and then put on a pair of my most comfortable pajamas.

I pulled back the comforter and turned out the light of my bedroom. Climbing into bed, I breathed a sigh of relief. My neighborhood was old and quiet, and there was no street traffic at this time of night. Even though my mind was active, my body was exhausted and I managed to drift off into a light doze.

It was the roar of a motorcycle that woke me.

I shot up in bed and listened, my head cocked. I heard the sound again, only this time I could tell there were two bikes. They were drawing closer, and like an animal that knew it was prey, I realized without a doubt that they were coming for me. There was no stealth to them—they wanted me to know they were coming.

They wanted me afraid.

An icy finger of fear trailed down my spine and for a moment I froze like I was trapped. But my brain finally kicked my inert body into action. I threw off the covers and scrambled out of bed.

I slipped on the pair of flip-flops and grabbed my cell from the nightstand. I unlocked the phone and started to dial 911, and then remembered what Shelly had told me about crooked cops. I stuffed the cell into the pocket of my pajama bottoms and rushed to the bedroom window in a panic. My purse and truck keys were in the front room and I didn't want to waste precious time getting them. I scrambled through the open window as I heard the engines of the motorcycles shut off somewhere in front of the house. I landed in the brush beneath the window. My flip-flops didn't protect my feet from the bramble and I held in a stream of curses.

I listened for sounds of boots on grass, but there was nothing. Pressing my back to the house, I inched away, heading toward my neighbor's backyard. I heard a knock on my front door. After a moment, there was another knock, and then after a brief pause, someone kicked in the door.

Keeping to the shadows, I continued to edge away, moving farther from my house. Only when I zigzagged down the neighborhood of old homes with neat lawns did I give in to my urge to run. I tripped over an exposed withered tree root and went sprawling, landing hard on my left wrist and knees. I somehow held in a moan.

I forced myself up using adrenaline to fight through my terror and pain.

I kicked off my flip-flops because they were slowing me down, but I grabbed them before taking to the sidewalk, avoiding broken glass and raised cracks in the old cement as I trekked on. I sprinted across the pavement at the end of the block. I kept going, despite scraping the bottoms of my feet bloody. My lungs burned, but I pushed forward. I ran until I was out of the neighborhood.

I knew exactly where I was headed. Charlie's Motorcycle Repair was nestled in between my house and the commercial district of downtown. I hadn't realized that it belonged to the Blue Angels—not until the night Colt kissed me and I saw the Blue Angels logo on his leather vest. When I reached the garage, I looked up at the sign with the now familiar emblem; a skull flanked by open angel wings.

If I was going to turn to anyone, it would be to a man who had already proven he was a protector of women.

My truck and wallet were still at my house. I was in pajamas, alone and injured. I couldn't call the cops and I refused to call Shelly. Better to take my chances with the Blue Angels than get her mixed up in any of this.

I sat down on the steps that led to the shop's office, knowing it was a terrible idea to be a sitting duck, but also knowing that I didn't have much of a choice. So far, the neighborhood was quiet and there had been no street traffic. After sliding on my flip-flops, I tucked myself into the doorway and made myself as small as possible, so that if anyone drove by, they would see nothing but shadows. My heart rate eventually slowed, and I had a hard time staying awake. Cradling my tender wrist in my lap, I leaned my head against the doorjamb and succumbed to sleep.

"I didn't know you could order chicks from Amazon," a voice said, tugging me from unconsciousness.

"Wake her up," another voice commanded.

A hand touched my shoulder, nudging me into consciousness. "Shit," the first voice cursed. "Colt, it's your bartender from the other night."

My eyes opened and I flinched in recognition at the face in front of me. I put my wrist down to move and sit up straight and an involuntary moan escaped my lips.

"Mia, right?" Zip asked.

I nodded.

My gaze wandered from Zip's leaner form to the man standing behind him. Colt wore a ferocious scowl, along with a few days' worth of scruff that did nothing to hide a strong, angular jaw. A bruise lingered at the corner of his eye and his lower lip was split from the fight with the meat-head. He crossed tattooed arms over his leather cut.

Colt clearly remembered me—and didn't look happy about it.

"Can we go inside?" I croaked. "My butt is kinda numb."

"Sure we can," Zip said. He reached down to help me, and I gave him my good hand, keeping my injured one close to my body. "Have you been here all night?"

"Yeah."

"How'd you hurt yourself?" Zip asked as he took out keys from his pocket to unlock the office door.

"I tripped over a tree root and braced my fall with my wrist. Not the brightest idea."

Zip opened the door and gestured for me to go inside. There was a desk in the far corner with a new laptop, two chairs, one in front of the desk and one behind it, and a long brown leather couch up against the wall. My neck had a twinge from resting it against the doorjamb and I wished I had been able to sleep on the couch instead. Bright sunlight filtered through the creases of the blinds, but I didn't know the hour. There were still no sounds of traffic, and I realized it was still early.

"You're wearing pajamas," Colt stated.

It was the first time he'd addressed me since discovering me asleep on the doorstep. And it came out sounding like a surly growl. His voice was just as I remembered it. Gritty, but not smoker gritty. More like Tom Petty, rock n' roll kind of gritty.

"That I am."

I took a seat on the couch and looked at my feet, which were covered in dried blood. My cheek stung. No doubt from falling into the bramble. When I saw my swollen left wrist, I let out a low curse.

While I had been busy taking stock of my body, Zip had pulled up a chair in front of me and Colt perched his burly form on the edge of the desk.

Even from a few feet away, he engulfed the space. I tried not to stare at him, but he drew my gaze like a polarizing magnet.

"You better start explaining," Colt rumbled.

"Easy, Colt," Zip said.

"No, I won't take it easy. When I come to my garage and find a battered woman on my steps wearing pajamas, I won't buy the 'I tripped over a tree root story'."

"Battered woman?" My mouth gaped stupidly. "I really did trip over a tree root. And I'm in my pajamas because I had to go out my bedroom window in the middle of the night."

"Who are you runnin' from, darlin'?" Zip asked.

I sighed. Was there any harm in telling them the truth? It might be easier to enlist their help if I was honest with them. "The Iron Horsemen."

Neither of them said anything for a moment and then Colt demanded, "And you're here why?"

"The Iron Horsemen came to my house early this morning and I escaped through my bedroom window with only my cell phone. I ran, and this garage happens to be in between my house and downtown."

"How did you get involved with the Iron Horsemen? And why didn't you just call the police? Normal people call the cops," Colt said, his voice tight.

When I didn't answer right away, Zip pressed, "Darlin'? Tell us how you got involved with those bastards."

"*I* didn't get involved with them," I finally said. "My boss did. Does any of that even matter? I didn't call the cops because—well—I have a friend who told me I couldn't. Not if bikers are involved." I blew out a puff of air, stirring the matted hair at my temples. "I just want to be able to get out of town without the Iron Horsemen on my ass. Can one of you give me a ride to my house so I can get my truck and leave?"

"You're not going anywhere until someone takes a look at that wrist," Colt commanded. "And if the Iron Horsemen went to your house last night but didn't find you, I'd be willing to bet they're still there, waiting for you."

The men exchanged a glance and Colt nodded once. Zip stood up. "I'll head to your place, take some guys and check it out." He looked back at me. "Where do you live?"

I gave him my address. "The keys to my truck are in my purse by the door. Do you think you can grab them? On second thought, just grab the purse. My wallet and ID are in there, too. And the truck is old so sometimes the carburetor sticks. Be careful not to flood it."

"I'll see what I can do." His lips twitched in humor. "You drive a truck with a carb?"

"We're in Texas, right?"

He grinned. "I like you, babe." Zip left, leaving me alone with Colt.

"You're not fucking one of the Iron Horsemen, are you?" Colt asked as soon as we were alone.

"That's offensive," I snapped. "And disgusting."

"I need to know if I have to worry about some jealous boyfriend shooting me in the back for kissing you."

"No, it's not like that," I said.

"Do you have any idea the shit you're bringing to my door?"

"What am I bringing? I'm asking you to help me get my truck so I can get out of town. And your boy just went to my house, so I'm guessing that means you're going to help me?"

"It's looking that way." He glared. "What kind of shit did your boss get into?"

"I don't know. That's the truth."

He stared at me a long moment, clearly studying me to see if I was lying.

"Come on," Colt finally said, gesturing for me to get up.

"Oh, have you decided I'm no longer public enemy number one?"

He shot me a look that told me he wasn't amused.

"Where are we going?" I asked, even as I followed him out of the office. He locked up and then gestured to a shiny black F-250.

"You need to get cleaned up and have someone look at that wrist." Colt opened the passenger door to the truck. I struggled to get in due to its height. With little patience and no effort on his part, Colt lifted me up and set me inside. "Watch your feet," he grumbled.

"We're not taking your bike?" I asked.

He looked at me. "Why would we take my bike?"

"I don't know. I just assumed... Don't you prefer to ride your bike?"

"Your wrist is probably broken. I'm not gonna make you ride behind me with a broken wrist. I'm not an asshole."

"You're not?" I blurted out. "Well, you're doing a great job imitating one."

"Don't poke the bear, babe. I don't care how hot you are, I don't need your lip."

I grinned, feeling bold. "You think I'm hot."

With a grunt, he shut the door and then walked over to the far edge of the parking lot and pulled out his phone. His face never lost its ferocity as he spoke to someone on the other end. The call was short and he marched back to his truck. He climbed in and got the engine going. When we were finally on our way to an unknown destination, I rested my head against the seat and looked out the window. My stomach rumbled, like an ominous thundercloud in the distance.

I pretended to ignore my hunger pains and Colt said nothing about it. But a few miles later, he pulled into a fast food drive-thru. I looked at him with gratitude.

"What do you want?" He reached into his pocket for his wallet. I asked for a breakfast combo and coffee. Colt handed over a few bills to the woman at the window before grabbing the bag of greasy fast food. As I unwrapped the breakfast sandwich, I mentally assessed him.

"Thanks."

"For?" he asked.

I shrugged. "Food. For starters."

He looked at me for a moment and then commanded, "Eat. Before it gets cold."

When we were fifteen miles outside the city, Colt turned off the main road onto a dirt one. We jostled and bumped our way along for a few minutes until we arrived at a closed gate. Two men in leather cuts were standing guard, but went to open the gate as they saw Colt's truck approach. With a greeting in the form of a wave, Colt drove through and parked in the corner of a gravel lot about twenty feet from a house. A cluster of parked motor-cycles sat out front, right on the lawn.

The brown structure was large and looked new, the grass manicured and tended. It didn't strike me that bikers could keep such a tidy place, and I wondered if the inside was as clean as the outside.

"Where are we?" I asked.

"The clubhouse."

Colt got out of the truck and I fiddled with the door handle. Before I could get the door open, Colt was there, pulling me into his arms.

"What are you doing?" I demanded as he carried me toward the clubhouse.

"Your feet," he said in way of explanation.

"I'm wearing flip-flops."

"You could barely get into the truck."

"That's because it's high off the ground and has nothing to do with me being injured."

"Right," he drawled.

"I'm okay, I can walk these next few feet on my own," I said after he climbed the porch steps.

He looked down at me and I realized how close I was to him. I could see the whiskers on his neck and the deep, dark brown of his eyes. He smelled of woodsmoke, leather, and skin. Colt's scent was distracting, and I instantly tried to breathe through my mouth so I wouldn't do something stupid—like lean my head in the crook of his neck and sniff him.

"I'm not an invalid," I stated.

He didn't reply, and continued to hold me.

Fine. If Colt didn't care that I wore pajamas and looked like a street orphan, then I wouldn't worry about it either.

Lies.

The sooner I got cleaned up the better. I wanted to be ready when Zip returned—hopefully with my truck keys in hand—and then I would leave town.

Colt walked inside. The unmistakable smell of bacon and coffee teased my nose. Though I'd just eaten, my stomach growled. There was a rumble against my back and it took me a moment to realize it was Colt laughing.

I enjoyed the sound far more than I should have.

"Prez." A scruffy blond man with gray eyes greeted Colt before turning his attention to me. "Is it adopt a lady-in-distress day?"

I snorted in amusement and put a hand to my head in fake torment. The blond man winked at me flirtatiously.

"Enough," Colt snapped. "Fix her a plate of food and bring it to my room."

"Your room?" I asked in surprise.

Colt ignored me as he went on, "Tell Joni where we are when she gets here."

"Why does she need to see Joni?" Flirty asked.

"Look at her wrist," Colt stated. Flirty's gaze dropped to my arm, which I held up to show him. Colt wasted no more time and carried me through the clubhouse, past the brown leather couches and the kitchen. The place was clean, but it definitely looked lived-in.

Colt traveled down a long hallway and pushed open the door to a room that was small yet uncluttered. The bed was made, the gray walls were devoid of posters or photos, and the gray carpet was unsullied.

He stalked to the bathroom and deposited me onto the closed toilet so I could use it as a seat. Colt then went to the tub and turned on the water. Without looking at me, he commanded, "Take off your pants."

"In your dreams, dude."

He looked at me over his shoulder and grinned.

Holy. Hell.

I thought the man was dangerous when he was scowling? That smile had enough power to light up a city.

"Your feet need cleaning," he reminded me.

"So I'll roll up my pajama pants."

"It's not just your feet that need cleaning. Have you looked in a mirror?"

"Well, take me, sailor, you know just what to say to a girl." I glowered but stood up and pointed to the door.

Colt rose and came toward me, crowding my space, but not in a way that was intimidating.

Sensual.

I was breathless, air trapped in my lungs.

Humor lurked at the corners of his lips. "Just shout if you need help. I promise to be gentle."

Chapter 4

COLT'S HUMOR had thrown me for yet another loop. I'd seen him stoic, broody, and now teasing and blatantly sexual.

Shaking away thoughts of the surly biker, I looked in the mirror.

Big mistake.

Scratches covered my cheeks and dirt smudged my pale skin. My brown hair was a tangled mess, and I looked less lady-in-distress and more street urchin.

Pulling myself away from my terrifying reflection, I went over to the tub and turned off the water. I sat on the edge and moved to roll up my pajama pants, forgetting about my injured wrist.

"Son of a bitch!" I cursed, closing my eyes in pain as tears formed. When the throbbing in my wrist lessened, I scrunched up my pajama bottoms, using only my good hand, and then eased my feet in the warm bath water. They stung, and I gritted my teeth as I reached for the soap. I tried to brace myself, but my control was precarious. Losing my balance, I fell into the tub, hitting elbows and knees. Before I could even yell for aid, the bathroom door opened and Colt loomed in the doorway.

"Jesus Christ, woman," he muttered, coming toward me.

I was fighting tears, and when I looked up at him, it was through watery eyes and a curtain of drenched hair. "I think I need help."

"No shit," he said in wry amusement and leaned over to help me out of the tub.

"Are there any women here who could help me?"

"Nope. It's me or no help at all. It's nothin' I haven't seen before, darlin'.

"I don't even know you."

"That didn't stop you from approaching me at Dive Bar."

I sighed. "That was out of necessity."

"And this isn't necessity? You nearly drowned yourself trying to save your pride."

"Why does it seem like there are different versions of you? I'm not sure which one I'm getting right now."

"Explain."

"Do you always speak in one word commands?"

"Usually."

I rolled my eyes. "When I asked you to help me get rid of the guy at the bar, you kissed me."

"I remember."

"Then I saw you in the alleyway…"

"Yeah. And? Were you scared of me?"

I thought for a moment. "At first, but then you explained what was going on and…"

"And?" he prodded.

"When I realized why you were fighting I wasn't scared anymore. And when you touched me, you were gentle."

"I don't hurt women."

"Why were you so mad when you saw me this morning on your steps?"

"I thought someone beat you."

Warmth curled through me, but I shoved it aside. "Now you're being kind to me. Why?"

"Seems like you need it. Are you done busting my chops?"

"I guess so."

"Arms up."

"No." I stated. "I'm not wearing a bra."

His smile was slow. "Yeah. I know."

"Bite me."

"Don't tempt me, babe."

"Don't *babe* me. And the pajama tank stays on."

"Fine. Put your hand on my shoulder," he commanded, playing with the drawstring of my pajama pants. I placed my good hand on him to keep my balance. My gaze found a spot on the far wall while he slid my pants down over my legs. I stepped out of them, clad in nothing but black, serviceable underwear.

Granny panties.

I wanted to die of embarrassment.

"Hmmm."

"Don't," I warned. "Just don't."

His smile was full of laughter and teasing as he stood up straight. Colt's hands went to my hips and a spear of heat went through me.

Unexpected.

Unwelcome.

Sort of.

"Sit on the edge of the tub. Stick your feet in the water and try not to fall in this time."

"Where are you going?" I asked him when he moved away, taking his smile and warmth with him.

"Getting a washcloth."

"Oh."

He didn't go far, just to a narrow linen closet to pull out a green washcloth and a big matching towel. After setting the towel on the sink, he came back to the tub. He kneeled and dunked the washcloth into the tepid water.

"Give me your foot."

I awkwardly swung around and set a tender, scraped foot onto his knee. I marveled at his caress. For such a large man, a rough biker, it was completely surprising. He cleaned my foot and then gestured for the other. Just as he was finishing up, there was a knock on the bathroom door and then a female head popped in.

I frowned. Colt had said there were no women here to help me. Had he lied?

"Hi," she greeted with a smile, her eyes darting between Colt and me.

"Hey." Colt's answering grin was easy when he looked at her, and useless jealousy blasted through my stomach.

"Clear out," she commanded. "Let me get a look at the patient."

"Yes, ma'am." Colt gently set my foot down and then stood.

"Thanks for your help," I mumbled, suddenly feeling shy. He nodded and dipped out of the bathroom, leaving me with the unknown woman.

"I'm Joni," she introduced. "Colt got you out of your clothes already, huh?" Her blue eyes were teasing. She wore indigo scrubs with a pink heart pattern all over them and her sorrel brown hair was pulled into a perky ponytail.

"What?" I asked.

"Just giving you a hard time," Joni said. "Let me see your wrist." She examined my swollen appendage, and when she grazed the bones on the outside of my wrist, I saw stars and scrunched my eyes closed in anguish.

"Ah, sugar, I'm sorry. I can wrap it now, but you need an X-ray. I think it's probably just a bad sprain, but it could be broken based on the pain you're feeling."

"Damn," I muttered.

"Have you taken anything for the pain yet?" she asked.

I shook my head.

"Idiot," Joni stated. "Colt—not you. Give me a minute to find some Tylenol. You should ice it immediately."

She left me in the bathroom for a few minutes and then came back with a glass of water, four pills, and a bag of mixed frozen vegetables.

I swallowed the pills and then gave her my wrist. She was gentle as she wrapped it, crooning words of encouragement. When she was finished, she set my hand in my lap, covering it with the frozen veggies.

"Let me take a look at your feet. Jeez, what are you, a size six?"

"Five," I corrected.

She shook her head. "I'm a size nine." She set my right foot down. "You should stay off your feet, but you didn't cut yourself deep. They will heal in a few days. Colt washed them with soap?"

"Yeah."

Joni helped me out of the bathroom and into Colt's room. She made me sit on the bed and then with great authority, opened a drawer of Colt's dresser. Pulling out a pair of his navy boxers, she looked over her shoulder at me.

"Here," she said. "You can wear these for now. I'll throw your pajama bottoms in the wash for you."

"Ah, thanks." I pulled on the boxers, relieved that I

wouldn't have to parade around in my underwear. "You know your way around here…"

"I'm Colt's sister," she explained with a wide smile.

There was no mistaking the curl of relief that settled low in my belly.

Huh.

"Oh, I don't—I didn't think—"

Her grin intensified. "Yeah, you were thinking something about me, but you were too polite to ask. You rest now. I'll go get you a plate of food."

She shut the door behind her and I was alone on a surprisingly comfortable bed that begged me to take a nap.

A few minutes later, Joni returned with a plate of steaming food and a mug of hot coffee. My mouth watered. The fast food sandwich had been nothing more than a gut plug.

"Eat," she commanded.

"You know, you don't look a thing like your brother, but you have the same domineering personality," I said as I dutifully lifted a bite of scrambled eggs toward my mouth.

She smiled. "Noticed that already, did you?"

"Maybe."

"I look like our mom. Colt looks like our dad," she said, explaining away their lack of resemblance.

I ate while Joni kept up a steady stream of chatter about her nursing job at the hospital. I didn't have to contribute to the conversation, which was nice.

"So…you asked him to help you get rid of a jerk giving you a hard time at your work?" Her blue eyes were wide with curiosity.

The fork stopped halfway to my mouth. "How did you know that?"

"Zip told me." She grinned, but then her smile slipped. "Zip said you also saw Colt fighting."

I nodded. "It was—I've never seen anything like it."

"My brother is crazy protective of women."

"I'm glad he and Zip were there and prevented something really bad from happening to that woman."

"Seems like good fortune, doesn't it?"

"Very. They're like leather-wearing guardian angels."

"I wouldn't go *that* far." She laughed. "So tell me something... My brother was smiling when he left the bathroom. That's very unlike Colt. What did you say to him?"

"He wanted to take off my pants; I told him *in his dreams*. Unfortunately, I nearly drowned trying to take care of myself, so I needed his help and he got to take them off anyway. I think he enjoyed the show."

She chuckled. "Keep giving him grief. He needs it."

I didn't want to tell her I wouldn't be around to give her brother grief, but decided to keep it to myself.

I wondered why the thought depressed me.

After I ate, dressed, and had a cup of coffee, Colt drove me to the hospital where Joni worked. Awkwardly explaining to her that I didn't have medical insurance was embarrassing, to say the least. She dismissed my statement with a wave of her hand and told me not to worry about it. I wasn't going to look a gift horse in the mouth, but I did have pride. Charity was charity, right? Still, I needed to know how badly I'd messed up my wrist and there was no amount of pride that would get in the way of that.

The X-ray confirmed I had a hairline fracture. It was an injury that would heal, but it would take close to six weeks and I'd have to wear a cast. I was also advised not to drive.

"Color preference?" Joni asked. "For your cast."

"Oh. Purple, I guess."

Forty-five minutes later, Colt drove me back to the clubhouse. He didn't say a word and I kept my gaze on my injured wrist, feeling trapped, defeated, and generally pathetic.

I took a seat on the couch and rested my head against the back cushion. Zip came down the long hall, shrugging in to his leather vest. Colt sat in one of the recliners and Zip gave him a chin nod in the way of a greeting and then went to pour himself a cup of coffee.

"There's an Iron Horsemen prospect camped out in your house," Zip said as he took a seat in the other recliner across the coffee table, facing Colt.

I looked up at him. "So that means…"

"Couldn't get your stuff. Couldn't get your keys or your truck."

"So then I'm stuck."

Stuck in town. Stuck wearing the same clothes. Stuck without access to my bank account.

What the hell was I going to do? I had no money, no ID. I couldn't drive even if I'd had my truck due to my stupid wrist. I didn't have a safe place to stay—I wasn't going to ask if I could crash with Shelly and Mark.

"Mia? Mia!"

"Huh?" I looked at Zip and then at Colt. "Sorry. I zoned out. What did you say?"

"I was askin' if your wrist is hurting," Colt growled.

He was back to surly—his general MO. I'd realized that at the hospital when he told me to sit my ass down and wait while he went to find us coffee. He grumbled as he took care of me, but he *did* take care of me.

"Yeah, it hurts a bit," I admitted.

"I got it. I'll grab you the Tylenol and a glass of water," Zip said, getting up.

"Thanks."

"You got a prescription for something stronger," Colt reminded me. "I can get one of the boys to fill it."

"No thanks," I said. "Never touch the strong stuff. I like to stay in control."

Colt peered at me with intelligent brown eyes. "I respect that," he said softly. "What are you thinkin'?"

I shrugged.

"That's not an answer. Talk to me."

I bristled at his command and glared at him. "You know the saying *you catch more flies with honey*?"

"You catch more flies with shit."

I blinked. "Was that a joke? Did you just make a joke?"

He sighed like I exhausted him.

"Where am I supposed to stay?" I blurted out. "I can't go home, obviously."

Colt stood, looming over me, his usual scowl in place.

"Don't look at me that way," I seethed. "I have the right to be upset."

His face softened. "Mia—"

"I've got nothing, Colt." The anger vanished from my tone as suddenly as it had come. Fury was exhausting, and I didn't have the energy to waste on it. "I don't have access to my bank account. I don't have my driver's license. Christ, I don't even have my own clothes and there's some strange man in my fucking house."

After a moment, he said, "You'll stay here."

"Here?"

He nodded. "The clubhouse. You can crash in my room."

I frowned. "With you?"

"I don't live at the clubhouse, Mia. I have a house."

"Then why do you have a room here?"

45

"It's a place to crash after the parties. I don't always want to drive home at four in the morning."

I opened my mouth to protest, but Colt shook his head. "Look, you're shit out of luck right now. Even if you had your truck, you can't drive yet. Your only option is to stay here."

"That's not the only option. I can stay with a friend—"

Colt interrupted, "Right now you're a burden, and anyone you stay with is going to be put at risk."

"You're an ass," I snapped even though I'd already gone through the same logic in my head and come to the exact same conclusion.

"No, I just tell it like it is. Besides, why wouldn't you stay here? We've got the space."

"Maybe because I don't feel entirely welcome. What did you call me? A burden?"

"Jesus, woman." Colt ran a hand through his dark hair in obvious frustration. "I'm trying to help you out and—"

"I don't need your *help*, you arrogant—"

"She can't stay here," Zip interrupted as he walked back into the living room holding a glass of water in one hand and a few pills in the other.

I jumped, having completely forgotten he was in the same room and witnessing my argument with Colt. My cheeks heated in embarrassment at my behavior. Colt was turning me into an angry shrew.

"Why not?" Colt demanded with a glare at Zip.

"You said it yourself—the clubhouse is a place to crash after parties. And you know how wild they get. Wild is a tame word for it, actually." Zip grinned. "Nice girls like Mia don't belong at our parties. She can stay with me."

"Like hell she will," Colt boomed.

My gaze bounced back and forth between the two

men. Zip was smiling, relaxed, while Colt looked like he wanted to pummel Zip into the ground.

"Doesn't *she* have a say in things?" I ventured to voice. Neither one of them was paying any attention to me, so my question fell on deaf ears.

"You're right, Prez," Zip drawled. "She should stay with you. It's just for a little while, right?"

Colt's scowl could peel chrome off a trailer hitch, and I was glad it wasn't directed at me.

"You've got a guest room," Zip pushed. "Oh, wait, you have that one little rule, don't you?"

"What rule?" I asked.

"Zip," Colt warned.

Zip's grin widened. "He doesn't bring women back to his house. Not ones he wants to fu—"

"Shut it!" Colt yelled, making me jump. "Mia, let's go."

"Go?"

"My house."

"Yeah, no. I'm good. I'll just stay here."

"I'm not asking, I'm telling. Now get your ass up. You're coming with me. And you can save the smart ass retort."

Apparently I was taking too long to follow his edicts because he reached down and scooped me up into his arms.

Right now, I was dealing with Colt, MC president. But earlier, when he'd washed my feet, I had been dealing with someone else. Perhaps that was the man beneath the leather.

"Bye, darlin'. See you later," Zip said with an irreverent grin and a wave.

"Yeah, if Colt and I don't end up killing each other, I'll see you later."

Zip's laughter followed us out onto the porch and then

faded away. Colt managed to open the passenger side door of the truck with me still in his arms and he set me down on the seat.

"Buckle up," he commanded.

I rolled my eyes but did as he said. I shook my head. "You're such a grumpy old man."

Colt came around to the driver's side and hoisted his large body into the seat. He closed the door and then jammed the key into the ignition. "I may be grumpy, but I'm not old."

"Whatever. You've got to be pushing what—thirty-five?"

"Thirty-eight," he admitted.

"Positively ancient."

"Are you even legal, darlin'?"

"I'm twenty-five."

"Baby."

I hated his mocking tone. "It's okay, Grandpa," I taunted. "You couldn't keep up with me."

"You wanna bet?"

The carnal promise in his voice was so unexpected I couldn't stop the shiver that raced down my spine. I stared out the window and pretended he didn't affect me. That was the last thing I needed. Getting involved with one biker president while trying to run from another.

"I don't like grumpy men," I huffed.

"Maybe not. But you like me."

"I do not."

Colt's gaze dipped down my body and lingered on my breasts. "Then your nipples are liars."

"You're crass. And an asshole."

His smile was slow, heated. "Yeah. And you *definitely* like it."

We drove to Colt's home in silence. After he'd commented on the state of my nipples, I was feeling a bit exposed. My wrist was in a cast and I had a cut along the apple of my cheek. I was feeling needy and he'd called me a burden.

I peered at Colt out of the corner of my eye, trying to discreetly study him. He was attractive, there was no denying it. Coffee colored dark hair, brown eyes, stubble for days. Not to mention his body. Tall and broad. Tatted. Muscled. He smelled like woodsmoke and something else …something entirely uniquely him. I'd tried not to pay attention to his scent, but the man had carried me several times and it was impossible not to notice.

Colt turned his head and caught me staring at him. I couldn't see his eyes behind his aviators, but his grin said enough.

"Almost there," he said.

"Good."

He chuckled but fell silent again.

We were twenty minutes outside of Waco when he turned off the main road onto another path. After a few miles of windy gravel, we arrived at his place. It was a two-story white home that looked like it had been built in the forties. The lawn was well-kept, and the trim was newly painted. There was a swing on the wraparound screened-in porch. It was the perfect spot to curl up with a good book.

"You live here?" I asked in surprise.

"Yup."

I glanced at him. "Don't take this the wrong way, but it seems…out of character."

"And you think you know my character?"

"I think I have a pretty good grasp on it, yeah."

He gave a slight smile. "I like space. Big guy like me can't do an apartment. This house was falling apart when I bought it a few years ago. I wanted to fix something with my own two hands. Something that wasn't a bike or a car." He cut the engine. "I can sit on the porch, watch the sunset, listen to the cicadas."

"I like that you restored it instead of tearing it down."

Colt stared at me for a moment and then said, "Nowadays when things break people don't fix them, they just throw them out."

I nodded. "Disposable."

"Yeah." He looked at the house. "Didn't want it to become just another pile of wood and nails. I wanted it to have a life again, you know? I needed it to have life."

It was the most Colt had ever said in one go. I wasn't sure what to say. It felt like he was talking about one thing but meant something else entirely.

He had given me something honest, and for some reason, I felt compelled to do the same. "My home hasn't felt like a home in a while. Not since my grandmother died. No place like home as they say, but what really makes a home? People, I think."

He looked at me for a long moment and slowly removed his sunglasses. He continued to stare at me. His jaw was clenched and I wanted to know why. What was he holding back? Colt didn't seem like the type to hold *anything* back.

"Come on, let me show you the place," he said.

I was glad he brushed past the moment between us.

The living room was large and open, decorated in taupe and shades of brown. The kitchen was modern with white cabinetry and an island. We headed upstairs, and he led me down the hallway.

He opened a door. "Guest room."

"It's nice," I said as I stepped through the doorway.

Colt leaned against the doorjamb. "Bed's pretty comfortable. Got a new mattress for it a few months ago."

"Yeah?" I turned to him. "Great."

His gaze traveled down my body, his eyes warm and inviting.

"Hey, eyes up here," I stated, snapping at him and then pointing to my face. "Let's get something straight."

"What's that?" Humor radiated off of him and it was nearly my undoing. Surly Colt made me want to keep my distance. Happy, smiley Colt made me want something else entirely.

"I'm leaving town—"

"How do you expect to get out of town without your truck? And don't forget that the doc told you not to drive."

"Zip will get my truck when the coast is clear. And the doctor *advised* me not to drive. He didn't forbid it."

"Is it a stick?"

"What does that matter?"

"Color me curious."

"Yeah, it's a stick."

"That's hot, by the way. The idea of you driving a stick."

"Stop flirting with me," I snapped.

"Why? Does it make you uncomfortable?"

"If I said yes would you stop?"

"Probably not." He grinned. "What are you going to do about money?"

"I have money. I just don't have access to it at the moment because I left my bank card in my wallet which is still in my house."

"So you *don't* have money. Okay, what about clothes?"

"Stop asking me questions!" I groaned. "You're such a pain in the ass."

He barked out a laugh and pushed away from the doorframe to come toward me.

Damn, he was tall. And huge.

"What are you doing? Stop right there." My hand shot out to halt him, but he kept coming and eventually my fingers hit his expansive, muscled pectoral.

"Are you afraid of me?" he asked huskily. He covered my hand on his chest with his, effectively ending the futile struggle.

I swallowed. "No, I'm not afraid of you."

"I think you're a liar." He shifted his stance, bringing himself into my space. He was so close that his leather cut nearly grazed my pajama tank. I wanted to draw him closer. I wanted to touch him, stroke the skin of his neck to see what it felt like against my fingertips.

"If you're not afraid of me," Colt continued, "then look at me."

After a moment, I forced myself to gaze up into his face. His eyes were dark with desire.

"I can't figure you out," I admitted. "One minute you're cold, the next you're laughing at me."

"I can't seem to help it," he said with a wry grin. "You make me smile. What can I say?"

I dropped my eyes from his to stare at his chest when I said, "I don't like having to rely on anyone."

"It doesn't mean you're weak if you need help."

"Who said anything about being weak?"

"You don't have to say it; I've been watching you. You can't stand needing help."

"Most things I can handle on my own," I admitted. "This thing with the Iron Horsemen? I'm way out of my element."

"I rely on my brothers, my club. They're my family. Does that make me weak?"

Colt was anything but weak. He was strong, assured; the man swaggered when he walked. But for him it wasn't a struggle, it came naturally.

"You want me," he stated, changing the conversation entirely and calling me out directly.

I shook my head in negation.

"I want you. I've been thinking about you since I kissed you at Dive Bar," he said huskily, his hands grasping the back of my head as he bent down to kiss me. His lips met mine in a show of sexuality. He plundered my mouth with his tongue as he held me to him. My hand touching his shirt curled into his body to feel his strength. It was a kiss of ownership, and I felt it everywhere. I was buzzing from the electric charge between us.

Colt pulled back but kept his hold on me, his eyes lit with hunger and promise. His hand came up to tease the strap of my tank top.

I swallowed, needing space, needing to get my bearings. "I won't have sex with you as a thank you for letting me stay here. You're not expecting that, right? Because—"

"Woman, you've got all kinds of issues."

"That came out wrong."

Colt released me. "How was it supposed to come out?"

I stepped away from him and shrugged. "I dunno. I didn't mean to insult you but...I have nothing, Colt. And you have everything I need right now." I looked away, hating my vulnerability. "I won't be a pity fuck."

"What makes you think you'd be a pity fuck?"

My gaze snapped back to his. "Look at me."

"I am." His brown eyes stayed on mine.

"You brought me here under duress."

"You think anyone can make me do something I don't want to do?" He shook his head. "You needed a place, I got a place."

"I could've stayed with Zip," I pointed out.

"Like hell you could have," he snapped.

"Why couldn't I have stayed with him? He's your brother, right? You clearly trust him."

"Not when it comes to you."

"You think he would've made a move?"

"No."

"Then I don't understand." I cocked my head to the side. "If you weren't worried about his actions, were you worried about mine? Did you think that if I stayed with him, I'd fall for his charms and throw myself at him?"

"This is why I don't talk to women," he grumbled. "They're nothing but trouble."

"*We're* nothing but trouble?" My eyes widened. "You've got three different personalities and I never know which one I'm talking to."

He sighed. "Fuck, I'm no good at this."

"Good at what? Conversation? Yeah, I realize that." I turned away from him, but his hands were still on my shoulders and he forced me to face him.

"Look, I don't connect with people easily," Colt stated.

"Okay." I stared up at him with a quizzical gaze.

His thumb stroked along my neck, making me shiver.

"You don't owe me anything. This isn't payment."

"Why are you helping me, Colt?"

"I may be an asshole," he smiled slowly, "but I don't turn my back on people who need help."

He pressed a quick kiss to my lips and then left the room, leaving me to stare after him in dumb amazement.

Chapter 5

I TOOK a few minutes to look around the guest room. There was no bathroom suite, but when I left the bedroom, I found the bathroom just across the hall. I headed downstairs, pausing briefly to look at the framed photographs hung up along the wall of the staircase. Following the series of a happy couple were photos of a young Joni and Colt. I didn't know their age difference, but there was one picture of a teenage Colt holding Joni, who must've been ten or so. Both of them wore huge smiles and I wondered where the seemingly easygoing Colt had gone.

I walked into the kitchen. Colt was at the counter, making himself a sandwich.

"Want half?" he asked, slicing it down the center. "It's turkey and Swiss on rye."

It was a thoughtful gesture. One I hadn't been expecting. "I'm good, thanks. Do you have a cell phone charger? My phone is dead."

He took the plate to the kitchen table and sat down. "I'm getting you a new phone," he stated.

"Why? I have a perfectly good phone."

"Did you give your cell phone number to Dev?"

"Yeah…"

"Then you get a new phone."

"You know I can just block his number, right?"

"I want another layer of protection."

"Wow."

"What?"

"When you go into protector mode, you go all in, don't you?"

"Yeah. I do."

This was not a battle I was going to win. "Fine. I'll fold on the new phone thing, but I need to call my best friend first."

"Why?"

"Why? What do you mean why? She's my best friend. She knew I was leaving town and I told her I'd call her when I got settled."

"But you're not settled," he pointed out. "You're in a shit storm and the best idea is to go underground."

"Colt—"

"Mia."

We stared at each other and finally Colt said, "I'll get a message to her, but you shouldn't call her."

"How are you going to get a message to her? If you call her and she doesn't hear my voice, she's going to worry. If you send one of your guys to talk to her, she's going to worry."

He smiled. "I guess I'll have to convince her that you're safe and not being held against your will."

"She doesn't trust bikers," I announced. "She told me I should've chosen someone else to help me get rid of the guy at the bar. That I made a mistake by approaching you."

"Probably," Colt agreed. "But you're in it deep now, darlin'."

"In what, exactly?"

"You kissed me."

"Actually, *you* kissed *me.*"

"Damn right I did. I'd do it again in a heartbeat, too."

"Is this the possessive biker thing Shelly was trying to warn me about?"

Colt let out a laugh. "What did she tell you?"

"I'm not sure I understand exactly what she was trying to tell me. Did you—were you *claiming* me? When you kissed me in public?"

"Sweetheart, if a kiss was all it took to claim a woman, I'd have a damn harem."

I glared at him.

"You're cute when you're riled. Grab a beer and stop thinking so much."

"Just when I think I'm about to like you, you're an ass again."

He took a bite, chewed, and swallowed. "How am I an ass?"

"The next time you're stressed, I'll just tell you to chill out and completely ignore how you feel. See how you like it."

"I didn't tell you to chill out. I told you to stop thinking so much."

"What's the difference?" I demanded in a huff.

"Mia, grab a beer. Then I'll give you my phone to use, but only so you can call your bank. Deal?"

"Deal."

Colt jotted down the clubhouse address and said, "Have your shit sent there."

He left me alone while I sat at the kitchen table to take care of business. A beer later, I had cancelled all my credit cards and requested new ones. Until then, I was at Colt's mercy. If I wanted anything, I'd have to ask him.

My pride prickled at the idea. But I was shit out of luck. I'd keep a running tally in my head of everything I owed and when I had access to my bank account again, I'd pay him back.

I didn't know Colt. And here I was, sitting in his kitchen, my bare feet resting on his wooden floor. It was unsettling, but only because it *wasn't*. I felt comfortable in his home, despite his growly nature.

Colt walked into the kitchen and opened the fridge, pulling out another beer. "How's it going?"

"It's done."

"Great. I've got some good news."

I perked up. "Zip was able to get my truck?"

"No. Joni is coming over with clothes for you."

"Ah, just call me Charity Case Barbie."

Colt's laughter boomed through the kitchen and I found myself laughing along with him. I was so deep into our moment that I didn't hear the front door open and I jumped when Joni appeared in the doorway of the kitchen looking shell-shocked.

"What the hell is going on here?" she demanded. "Are you laughing? Did you actually get my brother to laugh?"

"It's not the first time," I said.

Her gaze went to Colt. "Interesting."

"It's not that interesting," Colt drawled.

Joni rolled her eyes. "I thought you'd forgotten how to smile. I'm immensely glad to find it was just in hiding for the past few years."

"Great. Now I'm saddled with two broads who like to give me shit," Colt muttered.

"Saddled?" I asked. "You've been saddled with me?"

He shrugged, but didn't reply.

"I could stay with Zip. I'm sure his offer is still good," I taunted.

Colt's face tightened and I looked away to speak to Joni. Her face had gone blank and the color in her cheeks had fled.

I frowned in confusion, wondering about her sudden change in mood. She'd obviously come directly from the hospital since she was still in her scrubs. "Do you live here, too?"

She smiled, but I could tell it was strained. "No. There's no feminine touch here to speak of. It's a dude paradise. Have you seen the giant flat screen in the living room?"

"You were the one who told me I had to have it," Colt pointed out. "You're also the one that has reality TV watch-parties at my place."

"The screen is so high def you can see pores," Joni explained.

I laughed, enjoying their banter. Colt was relaxed with her in a way he wasn't with other people. Even with Zip, his vice president, Colt held himself apart.

"Where are the clothes you promised?" Colt asked.

"Laura is bringing them."

Colt looked at his sister and sighed.

I didn't like that sigh. "Who's Laura?"

Joni glanced at Colt and raised her eyebrows. "You going to take this one?"

"Yeah," I drawled in Colt's direction. "You going to take this one?"

Colt glared at his sister who walked over to the fridge and pulled out a beer and popped the top off. She took a sip and then said, "We're waiting."

Understanding registered and I threw a smile with just a little too much teeth at Colt. "Girlfriend?"

Joni snorted into her beer, but Colt's glower only made her laugh harder. "Colt doesn't have girlfriends."

"Fuck buddy, then? You're having your fuck buddy come over to clothe your new charity case?"

"She's not my fuck buddy," Colt barked. "She doesn't belong to me."

"Belong to you?" I repeated. "Joni, translate please."

"Joni, wait on the porch for Laura," Colt countered.

She didn't push her brother, but instead took her beer and walked out of the room. I watched her leave, and when I was sure we were alone, I turned back to Colt who looked unperturbed by my outburst.

"Laura hangs around the club and fucks the bikers. Whoever she wants."

"Well, thanks for not mincing words." I frowned. "So she's what…a Blue Angels groupie?"

"Basically."

"But that's so offensive."

"To you maybe. She's not forced into it. It's a choice, until someone makes her an Old Lady."

"And an Old Lady is what, exactly?"

"A biker's woman. A wife or a steady girlfriend of a brother. They have the protection of the club, but it also means she's off-limits to any other club member. And when there are parties with other clubs, Old Ladies are *not* fair game."

"So, Laura sleeps with whoever she wants in the club and none of you care?"

"Some care more than others," he stated.

"Do you care?"

"Nah, doesn't bother me."

"Are you still sleeping with her?" I demanded.

Colt's smile was slow but hot. "No."

"Do you want to still be sleeping with her?"

"No."

I hated the relief that blasted through me. I had no right to be jealous. Colt could sleep with whoever he wanted.

His eyes dipped and I knew he was staring at my mouth. Joni's return interrupted our moment. A curvy brunette with wide, brown doe eyes followed her. The woman's tank top and mini skirt showed a lot of skin and tattoos, but her smile was wide and friendly when she greeted me.

"Into the living room," Joni commanded.

"Why?" I asked, even as I stood up.

"Because that's where all the bags are," Laura said.

"Bags?" Colt asked as he trailed behind me.

"Bags," Laura reiterated.

"We ran to the store to get you underwear and toiletries."

"Then what's the other stuff?" Colt demanded.

"Laura is helping organize the charity yard sale for the elementary school. I asked if she had any women's clothes in teeny-tiny sizes." Joni grinned. "Someone dropped off a bunch of stuff."

"A lot of the clothes still have the tags on them," Laura said.

"Wow," I said, riffling through one bag and pulling out a pair of dark skinny-leg jeans. "This is great. Thanks, Laura."

"You're welcome."

"Let's separate them out and get the wash going," Joni suggested.

"Oh, you don't have to help me with that," I protested.

"It's okay, I don't mind. Besides, your wrist must be hurting."

"Sit down and let us do this," Laura said.

"Look how cute these are!" Joni held up a pair of adorable red wedges I couldn't wait to wear when my feet healed.

"And that's my cue," Colt said. "You guys got this?"

"Yes," we all chimed together and then laughed.

Colt shook his head and glanced at me. "Do you like steak?" When I nodded he said, "Good. I'm grilling. You guys staying for dinner?"

Joni and Laura both declined and then looked at each other, which made my antenna go up. Colt either didn't notice or pretended not to as he ducked out of the living room, leaving us to gab and examine the clothes.

The girls separated the garments into piles and Joni took the pajama load to the washing machine in the basement.

"So," I began.

"We only slept together once. Long time ago," Laura said as she cut off a tag on a gray V-neck T-shirt.

"Oh, that's not…"

She threw me a smile. "You had that look."

"What look?"

"The look like you were dying to know," she teased. "It meant nothing, okay?"

"Doesn't bother me if it did," I countered.

Damn dirty liar.

Why did Colt let me think he and Laura had been a recent thing?

I wasn't able to give it much more thought because Laura asked, "Why aren't you staying at the clubhouse?"

"He said it had something to do with the parties, I guess," I stated. "And he didn't want me staying with Zip."

"Zip?" Joni repeated her tone flat.

I peered at her closely and understanding finally

dawned. Joni had a thing for Zip, but for some reason she wasn't open about it.

"Zip offered his guest room, but Colt squashed that idea immediately."

"Interesting," Laura murmured.

"Very interesting," Joni agreed.

Laura peered at Joni. "Do you think he—"

"Oh yes, most definitely," Joni interrupted.

"It's a good thing, right?" Laura pressed.

"Absolutely. Totally necessary. Long overdue."

"I so agree."

My gaze lobbied back and forth between the two women who were clearly speaking in code.

Laura glanced back at me and grinned, holding up a black halter dress. "I think you'll look awesome in this."

I was really starting to like her.

I wanted to ask Joni everything there was to know about her brother, but I battled my curiosity and shut it away. After a few more loads of laundry, Laura and Joni left, and I was alone with Colt in his home. Alone with a man I didn't really know. So much had happened since he'd found me curled up on the steps of his garage.

Now I was in his house, feeling like an unwanted intruder that had to be tended to, like a plant you had to water if you didn't want it to die.

Colt popped a beer and handed it to me.

I took it, our fingers touching.

"Come sit outside with me while I grill the steaks," he said.

I nodded and followed him out of the kitchen, past the

table that had been set with plates and a salad bowl, to the sliding back door that led to the patio.

He gestured to one of the chairs with a blue cushion. I took a seat and watched as he lifted the hood, took a pair of tongs, and set two huge ribeyes onto the grill. They sizzled, and my mouth watered in Pavlovian response.

I searched for a topic of conversation, not wanting to sit in silence. "I like your sister."

He grunted.

"I like Laura too," I said, not deterred by his stoicism. "Both are incredibly kind. Generous."

"They bring you some good stuff?" he asked.

"Yeah. They did."

The early evening sun was still fully aloft and I took a moment to gaze at the acreage at the rear of Colt's property. It was green and gold, and I could imagine large family gatherings here. Noisy with laughter and conversation. It was a nice vision.

"What are you thinking about?" Colt asked.

Startled, I realized he'd been staring at me for a few minutes while I'd been lost in thought. "Your house. Seems like it's fit for a family." I paused. "I saw the photos on the staircase wall."

He fell silent again and I was almost sure he wouldn't tell me anything about his life, but he surprised me when he said, "Dad was from Dornoch, a really tiny town in Scotland. Left home at seventeen."

I shook my head. "Wow. Seventeen. He was still a kid."

"Not him. He grew up tough." He shrugged. "Anyway. He bought an old Harley when he got over here and decided to see the country. He was passing through Waco and met my mom."

"Yeah?" I was completely riveted by Colt's story.

Colt smiled. "Dad claimed he accidentally wandered

into a cowboy bar. Mom was with her friend. Mom's friend asked Dad to dance. Dad said yes but couldn't take his eyes off Mom. When he was done dancing with her friend, he came back to where Mom was sitting and asked her if she wanted to get on the back of his Harley. They were together from that moment on." He flipped the steaks. "He started the Blue Angels in Waco. Mom helped, actually. She grew up in Coeur d'Alene in biker culture. My dad liked the idea of living...freer."

"Coeur d'Alene? My mom lived there briefly before moving back home to Waco and having me."

"Small world," he murmured.

"Small indeed."

I thought he was done sharing, but I was wrong when he said, "She died when I was seventeen. Joni was thirteen at the time."

"And your dad?"

"Lung cancer. Two years later, he was gone." He shook his head. "When he got sick, he passed the gavel to his VP. Buddy was a good president, but he didn't really want it. He knew he was just holding the title until I was old enough to lead. But after my dad died, I couldn't stand to be here, so I left Waco and fucked around in Scotland."

"Drinking?"

"Yeah."

"Women?"

Colt sighed. "Yeah."

"Fighting?"

He shrugged. "I've always been big for my age. I was never a bully. Some people need protecting. I like to protect. Sometimes that means using my fists."

"You came back though. Why?" I asked.

"Joni. She needed me more than I needed to drink, fuck, and fight my way through Scotland." He grinned in wry humor. "My head wasn't screwed on straight, but she was just a kid. Fifteen without a mom or a dad. Realized I was being a selfish asshole leaving her with the club while I tried to get my own shit straight."

I remembered when I was fifteen. Hormones, a teenager without a mom. Joni hadn't had either of her parents. I'd at least had Grammie.

Colt pulled the steaks off the grill and set them on a clean cutting board. "Dinner's ready."

I hopped up and went to the sliding door and opened it for him since his hands were full. He brought the cutting board to the table, served us both, and then we sat down to eat. I couldn't remember the last home cooked meal I'd shared with another person.

"How's the steak? Cooked okay?" he asked.

"It's perfect."

"Not too bloody?"

I grinned. "Just bloody enough."

"Your turn." He reached for his beer bottle and took a sip.

"My turn what?"

"I told you about me. Now you tell me about you."

I frowned in confusion. "You actually want to know about that kind of stuff?"

He arched an eyebrow but said nothing.

I blew out a breath of air, stirring the hair around my face. "My grandmother died. About two years ago." I looked down at my plate, suddenly not hungry. "I'm glad she's gone."

"You are?"

I nodded. "I hate to think what would've happened if the Iron Horsemen had come to my home and Grammie was still alive. It probably would've given her a stroke. Better she's not here to worry about me."

We ate a few more bites in silence and then he asked, "What about your mom and dad?"

I shook my head. "Never knew my dad. He just wasn't part of our lives. Mom died when I was five and left me with Grammie."

"We're orphans."

"Yeah. I guess we are."

He lifted his beer bottle and I held up mine.

"To orphans," I said.

"To surviving." He clinked his bottle against mine and then we drank.

When we finished dinner, I stood up, needing to shatter the intimacy we had shared in the kitchen. This was why I didn't eat meals with people. Conversation was exchanged, stories about life, laughter over simple jokes. It was easy to fall into a rhythm, lulled into a sense that I wasn't alone.

That I wasn't desperately lonely.

I attempted to gather the empty plates but had trouble due to my useless wrist.

"Mia," Colt said, his hand going to my good arm, stopping me from moving past him toward the sink and dishwasher. "Stop. You don't have to clean up."

"It's the least I can do."

He looked at me, his brown eyes intense.

I lowered the dishes to the table. "It's been a long day. A really long day. I'd like to shower and go to bed. Will you plastic-wrap my cast?"

He gently let go of my arm. "Plastic wrap is in that far drawer and the rubber bands should be in there, too."

I brought the supplies to the kitchen table, pulled up a chair, and faced Colt. Holding up my arm, I waited for him to tear off a piece of Saran wrap. A few minutes later, I had a plastic coating around my cast.

"I think you missed your calling," I said. "You're good at that."

He grinned. "There's a clean towel in the bathroom for you."

"Thanks." I scampered out of the room and headed upstairs, pausing a moment outside of Colt's bedroom before moving along. I could hear the faint sounds of clanging dishes being loaded into the dishwasher.

The hall bathroom had a spacious tub and shower. Turning on the water, I adjusted the temperature, letting it get hot and steamy. I stripped out of my clothes and looked at myself in the long, rectangular mirror over the sink.

I was a fucking mess.

But I was alive.

I'd lived a lifetime in the span of a few days. I'd dropped my boss off at the bus station, escaped the bikers who'd come to my house, and kissed Colt this afternoon. Even now, my lips were remembering the shape and feeling of his. Between the lust and the heated banter, along with the intimacy of sharing our pasts, it felt like I'd known him a lot longer than I had. I could get used to the idea of relying on him. His house was a home. Though it was masculine, it had personal touches. Touches I hadn't expected from a man like him.

With Colt I felt protected. He wasn't what I expected. Shelly had warned me away from bikers, and under normal circumstances I would've heeded her advice. But these weren't normal circumstances, and Colt wasn't an ordinary biker. As limited as my knowledge was, I knew he was different.

By the time I finished my shower, I was wrung out and ready for bed. I draped a towel around my body and then opened the bathroom door, almost barreling into Colt's broad chest. I jumped back and let out a squeak.

"Sorry," he said, his gaze drifting down before coming back up to meet my eyes. "I figured you'd want these." He held up a pair of pajamas I had forgotten in the dryer.

"Thanks," I said, reaching for them. The towel was slipping, and I grabbed for that too. I couldn't hold both, and I felt the towel was more important.

My clothes tumbled to the wooden floor; both Colt and I didn't notice as we continued to stare at one another. Something was brewing between us, something I would be smart to resist. I was about to open my mouth to warn him off, but Colt turned and stalked away.

Chapter 6

"Mia," someone whispered. "Come on, darlin', wake up."

My gaze fluttered open and I stared into dark brown eyes with tiny lines at the corners. Sunlight winked through the blinds, telling me it was morning.

I sat up and absently ran a hand through my hair, wincing when I encountered a snarl.

"Why are you on the couch?" Colt asked as he stood over me.

His coffee colored hair was damp and he clearly had already showered. His white T-shirt showed off his muscular chest and the golden light of the sun highlighted the gorgeous ink on his skin. Ink I hadn't been able to get a good look at yet.

Lack of caffeine was surely responsible for me reaching out to grasp his right hand. "F-O-R-T. Fort? What's that mean?" I ran my fingers across his knuckles.

Colt made two fists and put them together. On the left hand were the letters U-N-A and then the Blue Angel's skull with wings logo on the fourth digit.

"Fortuna," I said. "Fortune in Latin."

He looked impressed. "You got any ink on you?"

I shook my head. Colt dropped his fists and then asked, "Didn't you go to bed in the guest room?"

"I did."

"Then how did you wind up down here?"

"Woke up in the middle of the night with a throbbing wrist. I got up to take some Tylenol. Sat down to give it a minute to work and fell asleep on the couch." I heard clanking in the kitchen and looked at Colt. "Someone's here?"

"Zip. Coffee's on if you want some."

"I didn't even hear the doorbell ring," I murmured.

Colt smiled. "You were conked out."

I followed Colt into the kitchen, wondering if I should've taken the time to put on real clothes.

"Mornin'," Zip greeted as I poured myself a cup of coffee.

"Good morning."

"This guy treating you right?"

I smirked at a stoic Colt. "He's a gallant host."

Zip chuckled. "Yeah, I bet he is."

"What brings you here so early in the morning?" I asked Zip, blowing on my coffee in hopes that it would cool down faster.

"Business," Colt answered for Zip but didn't elaborate.

"Learn to be more succinct, Colt, really." I set down the coffee cup and went to the refrigerator.

"Succinct?" Zip asked in amusement. "Someone went to college."

With my hand on the fridge door, I peered behind me at the two of them. They were staring at one another, conversing without words like leather-wearing cavemen.

"You certainly seem comfortable here. That didn't take long," Zip commented.

"He fed me steak last night."

Zip grinned. "Did he now?"

"With salad."

Colt made a noise in the back of his throat that sounded very much like a growl.

"Don't mind him," Zip stated. "He's just a grump."

"I noticed," I said with a laugh.

"Is that any way to treat the man that feeds you?" Colt taunted.

Shaking my head, I went back to looking in the fridge. "I rescind all claims that you're grumpy. You're generous and thoughtful, and when I'm in your presence, I have to stop myself from swooning."

I took out an individual yogurt container and closed the fridge with my bottom.

"Wow, she gives you as much shit as your sister," Zip noted. "I like it."

"I don't," Colt huffed.

I saw a humorous twinkle in Colt's eye and bit back a grin. I turned my attention to the yogurt container and struggled with the foil.

"Need some help," Zip asked.

"Please."

"Bring it here. I'll do it," Colt ordered, shooting his second in command a surly look.

It only made Zip smile wider.

Clearly Zip enjoyed goading Colt, and he was using me to do it.

I began opening drawers, looking for a spoon, and then brought the yogurt to Colt who peeled off the foil in one move.

"Thanks," I said, taking the container back. Instead of sitting, I leaned against the counter and spooned in some yogurt.

"What did you major in?" Zip asked. "In college."

"Who said I went to college?"

"Didn't you?" he pressed.

"Yeah."

"I love being right. It happens a lot."

I let out a laugh, but then sobered. "I'm a semester shy of my undergrad degree in accounting."

"Accounting?" Zip asked. "I wouldn't have guessed that."

"What would you have guessed?" I asked in sheer curiosity.

"Dunno. English, maybe."

"Nah. I had no interest in sitting around reading the works of a bunch of dead guys. No appeal whatsoever."

"Makes sense to me. I couldn't sit still in school. Don't know how I made it through high school. Unlike this guy." He gestured to Colt.

I looked at Colt. "You did well in school?"

"I did okay," he replied.

"Yeah, if you call Valedictorian okay. He's got a photographic memory. It's easy for him. Had a free ride to University of Edinburgh and turned it down so he could work with his hands. He can put an engine together faster than anyone. He's just good at everything. One of *those* guys."

Colt's face was passive, but I saw the tick in his jaw. Finally, he seemed to unfreeze and then he shrugged. "Mom wanted me to go to college, but I didn't care that much about a degree." He pinned me with a stare. "You plan on going back and finishing yours? Seems a waste not to finish if you're only a semester away."

"Eventually. When things calm down, I think."

"Why'd you drop out in the first place?" Zip asked. "When you were so close to finishing."

I looked down at my yogurt when I answered, "Because my grandmother got sick and I dropped out to take care of her." I coughed. "I only have some basic requirements left, actually. Shouldn't be that hard."

I chucked my empty yogurt container into the trash and said, "That was a joke of a breakfast. What does a girl have to do to get a real meal around here?"

"I'm gonna run," Zip said, standing up from his chair. "Mia, ask Colt to make you eggs." He slapped Colt on the back in a show of male affection.

"You don't want to stay and eat all my food?" Colt asked with a wry grin.

"Nah. I'll leave that to Mia. Something tells me she's got a healthy appetite." He winked at me.

"Subtle," I muttered, my cheeks flaming.

Zip laughed and then left the kitchen. A moment later, I heard the front door closing. Colt and I were alone.

"How do you want your eggs?" Colt asked as he stood.

"You don't have to make me breakfast. I can have cereal or something."

He sighed. "Babe. Eggs?"

"Poached, please."

"Good choice. I make damn fine poached eggs."

He got out all the breakfast fixings and then filled a pot with a few inches of water. I sat at the kitchen table and sipped my lukewarm coffee. There was something really sexy about a big, tatted, muscled biker making me food. Sure he was cooking because one of my wrists was injured, but the fact that he knew his way around the kitchen made him irresistible.

"Did you learn how to cook from your mom?" I asked quietly.

"Yeah. She was a dynamite cook." He threw me a grin over his shoulder. It was open, natural, and came easily.

"She used to be in charge of all the Blue Angel barbeques and potlucks."

He shook his head and turned back to the stove. "Deviled eggs."

"Huh?"

"Her deviled eggs were fucking delicious." He cracked an egg on the side of the pot and gently eased it into the water, not breaking the yoke. "What about you? Do you cook?"

"I can. I don't usually though. I've been living off of takeout for a while. My best friend is worried I'm not getting my veggies."

He chuckled. "Why haven't you been cooking? Too busy?"

"No busier than anyone else, I guess. It was just something Grammie and I used to do together, you know?"

"And she's not here anymore and you don't want the memories."

I paused and then admitted, "Exactly."

"Bread's by the toaster. You mind putting two slices in?"

"I think I can handle that," I said, getting up. "Then I can pretend I actually helped." I untwisted the tie holding the plastic bread bag closed. "Colt?"

"Yeah?"

"Why didn't you go to college?"

"Because I wanted to work with my hands, just like Zip said."

"You really expect me to buy that explanation?"

"Everyone else does." He fished out an egg from the pot of water and gently slid it onto a plate.

"I don't think everyone else knows the real you. I think you hide it."

"Thought your almost degree was in accounting, not

psych." His tone had hardened and I knew I'd struck a nerve.

I took a deep breath and powered through. "I saw the photos of you on the wall. It doesn't take a genius to see the evolution of your smile. I thought I was closed off, but you—you're something else."

"Why do you care so much?" he demanded. "You don't know me. You're just crashing here until you can get your truck and get out of here, remember?"

I recognized insurmountable walls. I had a fortress of my own. But there was something about Colt…

His curt attitude masked a great pain.

So I waited, not rising to the bait, not taking his tone or accusations personally. It would've been easier to let it go. To walk away and let him suffer in his own silence. But I thought of Joni and Zip; both had said something about Colt acting differently around me. Maybe they'd been trying to open him up for years, and he'd remained steadfastly clammed shut.

The toast popped and he grabbed the two slices and settled them on the plates.

"It was Dad," he finally said.

"His death?"

"No. I mean, yeah, partly. But it's what happened before he died. He found out he had lung cancer, right? Except his was treatable. His case wasn't terminal."

I looked at him.

His brown eyes bored into mine as he waited for me to put the puzzle pieces together.

"Wait," I said slowly. "Are you telling me your dad *refused* treatment? Treatment that would've saved his life?"

He nodded, his jaw clenched.

"Does Joni know?"

"I don't know. Maybe. We've never talked about it. Not directly."

I raised my eyebrows. "Seriously? That's a pretty big thing not to have discussed."

"Thanks for your opinion on the matter. I definitely remembered asking for it."

"Well, why did you tell me, then?" I asked in exasperation.

"Because you are relentless," he replied.

I pointed my fork at him. "No one else challenges you, do they? Mr. Biker President with a fierce scowl and a mean disposition. You've been left alone for too long. You've gotten comfortable in your isolation and you didn't expect anyone to have the wherewithal to get in your shit."

"You wanna talk about getting in someone's shit?" He leaned over so his face was close to mine. "You've been here one day, Mia. And you've got a lot of opinions about how things are. You don't know shit."

I smiled slowly. "I scare the living crap out of you, don't I?"

He scoffed and reared back. "Scared of a woman? Please."

"Then why are you so prickly?"

"I'm not prickly. Men don't do prickly. Eat your eggs before they get cold."

I did as he commanded, thinking I'd provoked him enough for one morning.

"What do you know about Richie?" Colt asked when I was halfway through my plate of food.

"Why are you asking about my boss?"

"Humor me."

"I don't know much about Richie," I admitted. "He wasn't around a lot."

"Really?"

"Yeah. I mean, he would come and pick up each night's receipts and cash and do the bank drop. But mostly, he was an absent owner."

"Were the Iron Horsemen ever at the bar? Lurking around or hanging out?"

I shook my head. "Not until a few days ago. I was shocked to find Dev in the back with Richie. Dive Bar isn't a biker bar—which is why I was confused as hell when you and Zip showed up. Why *did* you show up there?"

"Good brews. Good burgers," Colt said.

I stopped chewing mid-bite to look at him. "You're kidding me, right? You appeared out of the blue and a few days later Dev was in the back with Richie." The more I thought about it, the more I realized there was something going on that I didn't know about.

"You know what Richie was up to, don't you?" I pressed.

"I have an idea."

"Care to share that idea with me?"

"No." He smiled. "Club business."

"Is that the excuse you're going to give every time I ask you a question you don't want to answer?"

"Let's get one thing straight." He leaned toward me again. "You're here because I allow it. You're not family. You're not a Blue Angel. If anything, you're a pain in the ass who walked into trouble—the only reason you're safe is because I took pity on you and let you stay in my house."

The last bite of toast sat in my mouth partly chewed before I swallowed.

He wanted to make me feel small and inconsequential because I'd gotten close to him—close enough to see behind his mask.

I pushed back from the table and took my empty plate to the dishwasher to load it.

"I'm going to go take a shower," I stated, pulling my shoulders back and standing tall, despite the fact that I felt cut off at the knees.

"I'll wrap your cast for you," he said gruffly.

I arched a brow. "I don't need your help." Without another word, I turned and walked out of the kitchen.

~

It turned out I did need Colt's help if I wanted to wrap my cast, but I found a way around the issue; I took a bath instead.

It wasn't relaxing and it didn't help me work through the conversation I'd had with Colt in the kitchen.

How had we gone from swapping very personal history to Colt telling me to mind my own business, and that I was nothing more than a charity case he was stuck with?

I quickly finished my bath and drained the tub. I gripped the edge of the counter and finally let out the tears. I cried silently, wishing Grammie was still alive. Not because misery loved company, but I just wished there was someone on this earth who'd once loved me unconditionally. I had Shelly, but it wasn't the same.

When I finally felt in control of my emotions again, I swiped at my cheeks, making sure all the tears were gone. My eyes were red and the scratch on my face was noticeable, but I was a warrior. I'd survive this too, just like I'd survived Mom dying, just like I'd survived watching Grammie get sick and die, just like I'd survived everything life had thrown at me. I'd get through this mess with the Iron Horsemen and then I'd leave Waco—and Colt—behind, forever.

I opened the door with the intention of walking out

into the hallway. I didn't open the door with the intention of running face first into Colt's chest.

"Ow."

"Shit," Colt muttered, his hands reaching out to steady me.

My nose had crunched and I gently reached up to touch it. "That really hurt. What are you made of? Granite? And why were you loitering outside the bathroom door?" I tilted my head back to glare at him. "Why is this becoming a habit? Do you like to lurk outside bathroom doors? Do you like me running into you?"

He was smiling down at me, his eyes filled with tenderness. It instantly gave me pause.

"I own this bathroom. It's not loitering if you own it," he explained. "I didn't mean to give you another injury to add to your list of bruises."

"My nose is fine."

He clearly didn't believe me because he reached up and gently touched me. His large hands cradled my face as we stared at one another.

I remembered I was wearing nothing but a towel and made a hasty grab for it to ensure it didn't open, but my body hummed at the idea that it might fall.

Colt dropped his hands from my face but made no move to step away. "And I—ah—came up here to apologize."

"Why?"

"Because I was an ass." He ran a hand across his stubbled jaw. "I haven't lived with a woman since Joni. I'm not used to having someone in my space, not used to having someone ask me a bunch of questions."

I looked down at the ground so he wouldn't see the emotion that was still lurking just below the surface. "I'm sorry too."

"What do you have to be sorry about?" he asked, his tone turning gruff.

"It was presumptuous of me. Just because you told me things about your past doesn't make us friends. It doesn't make us—well, anything more than what we are."

"And what are we?" His voice was whisper soft now and I couldn't stop the shiver that raced down my spine.

"Two people who can't stand one another."

His low chuckle caressed my skin. It took all of my courage to look up and meet his gaze.

"I think that would make us both liars, don't you think?" His mouth slammed onto mine, holding me prisoner. His tongue was demanding and needy and it stroked against mine with insistent yearning.

He lifted me up and pushed me against the wall. I tried to open my legs, wanting to cradle his hardness, but the towel got in the way. He tore his mouth from mine, but only so that he could draw in a ragged breath, and then his lips were on my neck, biting and nipping.

My core throbbed and I was ready to lose the towel and beg Colt to take away the ache between my legs, to fill me up so I didn't feel lonely.

I ran my fingers through the hair at his nape, marveling at the silky feel of it.

"Colt," I whispered.

"God damn, Mia." He pulled back. "Shit, did I hurt you? Your wrist."

Shaking my head, I licked my lips, wanting to get his shirt off him so I could trace his ink with my tongue. I'd start at his knuckles and work my way across the entire canvas of his body. I wanted to spend hours drawing the lines and patterns, getting to know what made him tick, what made him lose control.

His eyes were glazed with desire and I was sure mine looked the same.

"I don't pity you. You get that, right?"

"Hard to get that straight when you make me feel like a charity case," I told him.

"Christ, I've wanted you since the moment I walked into Dive Bar and you sauntered your ass up to me, wearing those jeans that left nothing to the imagination." He grinned. "It took all of my willpower not to lift you over my shoulder and cart you out of there."

I could picture Colt doing just that and I found I really enjoyed the fantasy. To be handled by a man like Colt. To be treated like a woman—and to be the one who bore the brunt of his pleasure…

Colt's lips came back to capture mine, but gentler, as if he had all the time in the world to seduce me. But I didn't want slow; I didn't want a chance to think. I wanted a moment to forget about all my worries and enjoy nothing but my time with him.

I knew I was acting desperate, but I didn't care. I hadn't known Colt long at all, but I wanted him anyway. It had been a while since I'd felt my body tighten and release from the pleasure that came from a partner.

Colt made a noise in the back of his throat—I wasn't sure what it meant exactly, but I didn't care because he continued to kiss me with blatant intent.

And then I heard the ringing of his phone.

With obvious reluctance, he released me and I slowly slid down until my feet were on the ground. He reached into his jeans and pulled out his cell. "Yeah?" Colt's hand rested on the curve of my shoulder before pulling me to his side. His fingers dipped down across my shoulder blades, raising goosebumps along my skin.

"Okay," Colt said. "We'll be there in about half an

hour." He hung up and shoved his phone back in his pocket.

"Half an hour?" I asked, looking up at him with amusement. "That doesn't give us a lot of time."

He let out a low chuckle. "You have about five minutes to get dressed and then we've got to get to the clubhouse."

I didn't want to go to the clubhouse. I wanted to finish what Colt and I had started in the hallway.

"What's at the clubhouse?" I asked.

"Your friend."

I frowned. "Shelly?"

He nodded.

"Why is she there?"

"I had Zip talk to her and tell her you were okay, that you were with us. She seems to think we kidnapped you."

"What!"

"She showed up at the clubhouse threatening to call the cops if she didn't get to see you with her own two eyes." His lips curled in amusement. "Time's a tickin', darlin'. Get dressed so you can call off your friend."

Shelly jumped off the bed in one of the clubhouse bedrooms and immediately came to me. She placed a hand on my shoulder and then another on my chin to turn my face so she could see the scratch on my cheek. And then she saw the cast on my wrist. "Oh my God! What the hell happened to you?"

"Long story," I evaded. I waved away her hand, hating the fuss she was making.

Colt hovered in the doorway, refusing to leave.

"Can we have a minute? Alone?"

"No," he said.

"We need a minute." I paused. "Please?"

Colt's dark brown eyes surveyed me and then went to Shelly. Finally, he nodded and then left the room, closing the door behind him.

As soon as he was gone, Shelly dragged me over to the bed and forced me to sit down.

"Whose room is this?" I asked.

"I dunno. Some guy named Boxer. They took my phone," Shelly said with a scowl. "I haven't been able to call Mark. You were supposed to be on your way to Coeur d'Alene. Now you're wearing a cast, your cheek is scratched, and you've taken up with bikers."

"I haven't taken up with bikers," I muttered.

"Liar. I've known you since we were kids. I can tell when you're lying." She glanced at the door. "Don't you remember what I said? This is exactly what *not* to do."

I kept silent, knowing the last thing I needed was Shelly freaking out on me when she found out I was staying with Colt and that I was close to jumping into his bed.

"Mia? What's going on?" she asked. "You have to tell me."

"I don't want you getting mixed up in all of this."

"Mixed up in what? Richie's crap?"

"Yeah, Richie's crap."

"I texted the entire staff and we didn't show up for our shifts. I drove by Dive Bar and it was closed. I start working at a nail salon next week, answering phones and making appointments."

"Good. That's good." I breathed a sigh of relief. "I had plans to leave town. I swear I did." I proceeded to tell her about the motorcycles in my neighborhood and then my middle of the night flight to safety.

"You slept on the steps until they woke you up?" she marveled. "Wow."

I nodded. "They've been really—ah—nice to me."

She peered at me. "You're blushing."

"I don't blush."

"Fine, then you're flushing. You got involved with their president, didn't you?"

"Define involved." I shrugged. "I'm staying at his house for the time being."

"You trust this guy? He's got a black eye. What kind of trouble did he get into?"

"It doesn't matter," I said without hesitation. "I trust him."

Shelly embraced me, hard. "You scared me. I'm glad you're safe."

"They're going to help me get out of town. You don't have to worry about me, okay?"

"I'll always worry about you. You have a knack for finding trouble."

"Trouble finds *me*," I corrected.

"Either way, a shit storm is a shit storm."

"Yeah, no kidding."

I hopped up and went to open the bedroom door and saw Colt leaning against the wall. I knew we hadn't been talking loud enough for him to eavesdrop.

"You guys good?" Colt asked.

I nodded. I heard Shelly come up behind me and rest a hand on my shoulder. "Take care of her, yeah?"

Colt's brown eyes darted to mine. "I will."

Chapter 7

AFTER WE SAW Shelly to her car, Colt and I headed to his truck. Once we were on the road back to his place, he said, "You're worried about her."

"Yeah."

"Don't be. She quit Dive Bar. She's staying out of things."

"How do you know that? Did you actually hear our conversation?"

"Nah. She told Boxer. Or yelled it at him, actually. He relayed it to me."

I fell silent and stared out the window, thinking about Shelly, wondering when I'd get to see her again. Maybe she and Mark would want to come for a week when I was settled in Coeur d'Alene.

Colt reached over and set his hand on my thigh. His thumb stroked my skin, offering me a small measure of comfort. It wasn't the gesture of a man who only wanted to screw me. It was the genuine pull of intimacy.

Everything was happening too fast—my emotions felt

like they were at the end of a yoyo. One moment, Colt and I were adversaries, glaring at one another. The next we were sharing details of our pasts while he cooked me food. Add in the bouts of lust and my desire to feel his skin against mine, and I was in danger of my heart and body falling for a man my mind wasn't sure about.

We pulled into the driveway of Colt's house and a strange sense of relief overwhelmed me. As much as I didn't want Colt's home to feel warm and welcoming, it was.

The house signified comfort. Like a strong embrace. Like shelter from a thunderstorm. It was a place you could plant roots and watch them grow.

Colt looked at me, and whatever he saw on my face made him mutter, "Ah, fuck."

My gaze was solemn and I nodded. "I know."

There was something between us, something stronger than just physical desire.

He got out of the truck and slammed the door shut before stalking up the porch steps. I followed but at a much slower pace. I found him in the kitchen, yanking open the refrigerator. He pulled out a beer and popped it. Tension rolled off him, but for all Colt's scowling intensity, I wasn't afraid of him.

"I don't want this," he gritted out.

"Me. You don't want *me*," I stated. "Say what you mean."

"I do want you, Mia, but I don't want all the bullshit that comes with it."

"Jesus."

"I don't do relationships."

"I've gathered as much." I raised my eyebrows. "You think I want this? You think I want to get to know you? It will complicate my life and I already have enough complications."

"This is a mistake."

"Yeah, I got that memo," I snapped.

"You should get out of Waco and finish your degree. Marry a nice guy. Have a couple of kids. Buy a minivan. That's the only way you escape this shit."

Even though I was angry, his words gave me pause. My hurt and pain went down to a simmer when I realized what Colt was really doing.

He wasn't protecting himself from getting involved with me. He was protecting *me* from getting involved with him and his lifestyle. He was trying to let me go before I got trapped.

"What would've happened between us this morning?" I asked. "If you hadn't gotten a phone call, what would have happened?"

"You know what would've happened. And it would've been a mistake."

I smiled slowly.

A muscle in his jaw ticked. "Why are you grinning?"

"Because you're catching feelings."

Instead of answering, he tilted his head back and guzzled his beer. I watched his powerful throat move, entranced by it.

When Colt emptied the bottle, he set the glass down. He looked away from me and pressed his hands to the counter to push against it.

"I don't have to stay here," I reminded him. "I should stay with someone else. Zip, maybe."

"Like hell you will," Colt stated. It took him two strides to reach me. His hands went to my waist and hoisted me up onto the counter. He moved between my legs, invading my space, taking my air, giving me his anger.

Anger because feelings were unnecessary problems.

Anger because we were both in an explosive push and pull of emotion we couldn't escape.

"You're trouble," he said, voice husky. "I knew it the moment I walked into Dive Bar."

"Pot, meet kettle," I shot back.

His mouth slanted over mine—forceful, like a tempest unleashed, but I was ready for it, ready for him. My hands were sure as they trailed up his strong chest to wrap around his neck.

My fiery skin grew hotter as Colt continued to kiss me, his tongue seductive and masterful. His hands snaked down from my waist to yank my legs around him so he could press against the crevice of my body. The heat and hardness of him was dizzying.

I pulled my mouth away from his, dragging air into my lungs as fast as I could. Colt's own labored breathing was harsh in my ears. Placing a hand on the center of his chest, I urged him back. Colt moved, albeit reluctantly.

I looked into his dark brown eyes. "Feel better?"

His tongue snaked out to drag across his lips. "Fuck no."

"What do you want from me? Because you're sending a bunch of mixed signals. You say you don't want me and then you kiss me. So tell me what you really want, Colt."

"Fuck if I know anymore," he muttered.

After my strange encounter with Colt in the kitchen, I tried avoiding him. But every time I came out of the guest room, he was suddenly there, in my way, wearing his leather cut.

He looked at me with an indiscernible expression.

I couldn't see what was going on behind his eyes. It was irritating and it kept me even more unbalanced than I already was. My lips were still burning from the feel of his mouth on mine and my body hungered for his.

I was a flat-out mess.

Night was no better. I hardly slept, restless, feeling hot and feverish, flinging off the covers only to shiver in cold-ness and drag them over me again. I forced myself out of bed early, just after the sun had risen because there was no point in tossing and turning.

I made coffee and took it out onto the back patio to get some air. Colt found me there. He appeared well rested—and sexy.

So. Damn. Sexy.

He was staring down at me, a mug of coffee to his lips. "Sleep well?"

My glare was my answer.

He didn't smile, but I could see the humor lurking in his eyes. "I gotta run to town. You're gonna stay here," he commanded.

"No." I crossed my arms over my chest. "Absolutely not."

"You don't have much choice in the matter," Colt drawled.

"You really can't expect me to sit here all day waiting for you to get home while you go off and get to do what-ever you want."

"I do expect it," he said mildly.

"Why can't I come with you?"

"I'm not running errands, Mia." He sighed. "I want you to stay out of the limelight, okay? I don't want you in town because I don't want to give Dev and the Iron Horsemen a chance to see you."

I wrinkled my nose, hating to admit that he had a valid point. "What am I supposed to do while you're gone?"

"You need me here to entertain you?" Colt laughed.

"You know that's not what I meant."

"Do whatever you want. Watch TV. Cook. Or bake. Yeah. Why don't you bake a pie?"

"Bite me."

"Tempting." He laughed. "I'm kidding, okay? Joni is off work today so she's gonna swing by."

"Oh. Well, why didn't you lead with that? I like her."

"And she likes you."

The sound of a motorcycle drew my attention, and I got up off the couch and headed to the living room window to peer out. A guy parked his bike and took off his helmet. He looked young. My age.

"Who's that?" I demanded as I took in the lanky, brown-haired guy.

"That's Cheese."

"Cheese? What kind of name is Cheese?"

"It's his road name," Colt explained. "He's a newly patched brother."

"And he's here why?"

"To keep an eye on things."

My gaze narrowed. "You mean to keep an eye on me."

"Well, that too."

"I don't need a guard dog."

"I'm thinking trouble could find you in the dark." He reached into his pocket and tossed me a cell. "Finally got you a phone of your own. I programmed in a few numbers in case you can't get ahold of me."

"Why would I want to get ahold of you?"

"I dunno. Maybe you'll miss me."

"You wish."

"Yeah, I do wish."

"What's gotten into you?" I demanded.

He stared at me for a long moment. "Nothing."

Colt was lying, I was sure of it. Only I couldn't figure out why. We were playing a game. I didn't know what it was, but I knew I wanted to win.

Chapter 8

THIRTY MINUTES AFTER COLT LEFT, I walked out on to the porch and held out the PB&J to Cheese. "Sandwich?"

He looked up from the paper he was reading while sitting out on the screened-in porch. Smiling, he didn't appear at all perturbed to be my babysitter. "Thanks," he said, taking the plate from me.

I sat down in the chair next to him. "I didn't know anyone still read an actual paper."

He chewed for a moment and then swallowed. "I like it. Makes me feel like I'm still connected to something tangible. That's weird, right?"

"No. Not at all. So how did you get suckered into watching me?"

"I didn't get suckered. It was an order, and I'm glad to do it. It's an honor."

"Why?"

He frowned. "Why what?"

"Why is it an honor?"

"Because you're Prez's woman."

"I think you've been misinformed. Colt and I barely

know each other. I'm staying here until Zip can get my truck and I can get out of town."

"You can't drive a truck with your wrist the way it is." He nodded at my arm. "You know that, though."

"Yeah, I do. About that other thing you said? I'm not Colt's woman," I insisted.

He looked at me long and hard. "Prez is not a man who invites women to his home. You could've stayed at the clubhouse. Or with Zip."

"Heard about that, did you?" I asked in amusement.

What the hell had Colt told his brothers? What was I missing?

"Can I ask you a question?" I asked, wanting to change the subject.

"Sure."

"What made you decide to become a Blue Angel? I mean, what was the appeal?"

He paused for a moment and leaned over to rest his elbow on his thigh. "I didn't have a lot growing up. Dad has chronic back pain and he's on disability. He spends it all on booze and pills. Mom does the best she can, but she works at the Winn Dixie—a cashier. There was never enough, but we made do. Shopping at thrift stores, coupons, that sort of stuff.

"Last year, my eleven-year-old brother came home from school with a black eye. He got into a fight because some kid called him trailer trash. We grew up in a trailer, so I know what it's like to be taunted at school, you know? Kids are mean. They hear their parents say shit. They repeat it even if they don't know what it means.

"I asked Silas why the fight started. You know what he told me? The kids were making fun of him because his jeans were too short and they could see his socks. He didn't tell Mom about having outgrown his pants because he knew there wasn't money to get him new ones. Not at the rate he was growing." He shook his head. "As a member of the club I can provide for my brother."

"You could've joined a different club," I said, my heart breaking for the little boy that had been picked on. "Why the Blue Angels?"

"Because of what they do for the community. I knew if I joined the Blue Angels, I wouldn't be earning a living in a normal way that people understand. Not a respectable nine to five. There are risks that come with being in the club, but what's life without a little risk? But this is more than that. The reward is more than just financial security. I've got a family now, one I wasn't born into, one that's been made. And I can take care of Silas."

I pondered his words. "What about your brother? Are you going to let him grow up in this world?"

"As opposed to…"

I blinked. "A world without bikers?"

"So he can learn what, exactly? Listen, it's easy to judge what you don't understand. It's easy to judge what doesn't fit into a conventional box. But here's the thing. Our world isn't normal. It isn't widely accepted. And that's okay. You just have to live your life and follow your gut."

"How old are you, Cheese?" I asked.

"Twenty six."

"How'd you get to be so wise?"

He smiled and looked down, appearing bashful. "Life's too short, Mia, to live it for anyone else. Just remember that."

Nodding, I got up from the chair to head back inside. "You can come in, you know. Hang out, watch TV."

"Thanks." He smiled, looking too boyish to be a biker. "But I've got my orders to stay outside."

"Well, I'll leave you to it, then."

I had plans to leave him alone, but I wanted to take a shower before Joni showed up. And to do that, I needed someone to Saran wrap my cast. That had been Colt's job. A sudden stab of loneliness at his absence caught me by surprise.

With a sigh, I went into the kitchen and grabbed the supplies before heading back out onto the porch. "Will you help me?" I asked Cheese.

"Sure."

While he wrapped my cast I asked, "So, how did you get the nickname Cheese?"

"It's not a nickname," he corrected. "It's a road name."

"Right. How did you get the road name Cheese?"

"On the night of my initiation, the boys dared me to eat an entire block of cheddar cheese."

"That's a weird form of hazing."

"It was all in good fun."

"Did you do it?" I asked in amusement.

"Hell yeah, I did it." He grinned. "The fuckers made fun of me all the next day because I didn't leave the bathroom."

"Charming," I said with a snort.

Placing a final rubber band around my cast he said, "There ya go."

"Thanks. What's your real name?"

"Chester," he said, his tone serious.

Well, at least I understood why he went by Cheese.

I headed back inside and took a fast shower. I was just pulling on a pair of new jeans and a red T-shirt when Joni arrived. With a smile, I offered her a cup of coffee, which she accepted.

"You didn't have to come over and entertain me," I said, placing the half-and-half in front of her.

"I know," she said. "Though I have to say it's not completely altruistic."

"You want to grill me, don't you?"

"Yep."

"Sister's prerogative, I guess," I said with a smile.

"Definitely." She tapped the rim of her coffee mug. "I'm just going to get down to it. Okay?"

I nodded.

"I think Colt wants to keep you."

"What's that now?"

"Keep you. Like, for good."

"You can't keep a person. I'm not a sheep in a petting zoo. You don't just—what are you even saying right now?"

She took a sip of her coffee. "Let me give you a little insight to Colt, okay?"

I nodded, my heart pounding in my ears.

"He hasn't been the same since our dad died. And that was nineteen years ago."

"He told me," I said slowly. "About your dad's death."

"Did he." It sounded like a statement and not a question. "Well, that only confirms my suspicions. You got through his wall. Somehow, you did. In a short time, too. I've already seen him smile more, laugh more in two days than he has in years. And I know that's because of *you*."

Her words made me uncomfortable.

"I've never seen him behave this way around a woman."

"Am I supposed to be flattered by that?" I asked, trying to stem the flow of panic.

"Yeah, you should be flattered. Because Colt has the biggest heart in the world, but he's kept himself shut away."

"It's only been a few days, Joni. You know that, right? I

don't think you can assume I'm responsible for Colt's change."

"He told you about our dad's death. Did he tell you about our parents? And how they met?"

I nodded.

"My dad knew my mother was the one the moment he laid eyes on her. And she had no qualms getting on the back of his bike and riding off into the sunset with him. Westons just *know*."

"Weston," I repeated. "That's your family name?"

"Yes."

"What's Colt's real name?"

"James."

James.

"What about you?" I asked.

"What about me what?"

I smiled. "Who do you want to keep?"

She sighed. "Zip."

"No."

"Yeah."

"Oh man. It all makes sense now. When I said he offered to let me stay in his home, you went all…"

"Yeah, I went all…" She shook her head. "I knew he was doing it to get Colt's goat and to make Colt stand up and say he wanted you to stay with him, but it still hit me hard."

"Why is there no you and Zip?"

"Because he sees me as Colt's younger sister."

"You *are* Colt's younger sister."

She shook her head. "You don't mess around with a club member's family. Like, you don't fuck their sisters or cousins or anything. Plus, Zip's kind of a whore."

"Excuse me?"

"A man whore. A big, fat, man whore. No, not a big fat one. A big, hot, tatted one."

"So he sleeps around," I stated.

"Yup. It should totally be a turn off. I know that. But damn. He's so fucking hot and I want to keep him and make cute little biker babies. But he avoids me and I avoid him and we both pretend we don't want to rip each other's clothes off."

I laughed. "Plus, babies. What man isn't terrified of a woman hungry for seed?"

"Do you really have to put it that way? You make me sound like a desperate woman."

"Sorry." I grinned.

"What about you?"

"What about me?"

"Do you want to make cute little biker babies with my brother?"

If I'd been drinking something I would've spit it out all over her. "You're insane. I barely know him."

"Uh huh."

"I'm leaving town."

"Okay," she said like she didn't believe me.

"I am."

She snorted into her coffee.

"You're cute," she repeated, "but so oblivious."

There had been no word from Colt all afternoon. Not that I expected any word from him.

Okay, that was a lie.

I had hoped he would want to check in with me, see how my afternoon with Joni was going or ask if I was taking good care of Cheese.

Joni cooked dinner and refused my help. She left early because she had a morning shift at the hospital. I waved goodbye from the porch and then turned to go back inside. Cheese was in the same spot. He hadn't moved in hours except for one quick bathroom break.

"Thanks, Cheese," I said.

"For what?"

"For keeping watch. Sorry it's so boring."

He flashed me a cute grin. "I'm glad it's boring. It means you're safe."

"Do you guys really expect trouble?"

"Gotta be prepared for anything. The Iron Horsemen…"

"What?" I demanded.

He scratched his jaw with his thumb. "I shouldn't say anything."

I held my tongue but kept my eyes on him. Cheese caved. "Rawlins scares the shit out of most grown men. And the ones who aren't scared of him are just too stupid to know they should be. It's good you're here and we can look out for you."

A pang of emotion hit my throat. "Thanks."

I went back inside and settled onto the couch, the cell phone Colt had given me by my side. I kept glancing at it, willing it to buzz. Turning on the TV, I listened to some asinine show playing in the background as I picked up the cell. Debating all of five seconds, I scrolled through the three numbers in the phone and shot off a text to Colt.

Hey.

As soon as I sent it, I wanted to take it back.

"Darlin'," a low voice whispered. "Mia, wake up."

"No," I murmured, trying to sink deeper into the couch cushions.

There was a sigh and then I felt arms moving underneath me. I was being lifted and carried, my face pressed against a warm chest and soft cotton. I snuggled into the embrace.

"Ah, fuck."

"Stop saying that," I said, refusing to open my eyes. I pretended it was a dream; in my dream, I could be vulnerable.

When I was awake I'd have to ignore this thing between us.

He set me down on the bed in the guest room and settled the comforter over me. I heard the faint sound of rain against the window.

"Stay," I whispered when I felt Colt begin to move away.

"Mia," he said, his voice dark, pleading.

"Please," I begged. I wiggled over to give him room. I heard the unbuckling of a belt and then the sound of jeans hitting the floor, and something heavy being set down on the nightstand. Colt climbed into bed next to me and pulled me into the wall of his chest. His body curled around mine as his lips brushed my ear.

I let out a sigh. "I'm not catching feelings."

There was a soft rumble against my back as Colt's hand wormed its way under my shirt and rested on my stomach. "Go to sleep, sweetheart."

The next morning I woke up alone and confused; there was no evidence of Colt having slept in bed next to me. I bit my lip when I thought of him pressed against me from behind. I'd never felt safer.

After I got dressed in a pair of cut off shorts and a T-shirt, I headed downstairs, both dreading and hoping to see Colt. He was in the kitchen, dressed for the day and drinking a cup of coffee.

His eyes roved over me, lingering on my legs. "Mornin'," he drawled.

"Morning," I replied, heading to the coffeemaker and pouring myself a cup.

"You're a very…active sleeper."

His sensuous tone had my hand shaking, and I spilled the coffee I was pouring. I set the coffee pot back in its place and then grabbed the dishtowel hanging off the fridge to mop up the mess.

I looked at him over my shoulder. "What does that mean?"

Colt's smile was slow. Hot. A rush of embarrassed desire flamed my cheeks, but I held his gaze. He didn't lose his smile. I wanted to wipe it off his face. I dropped the dishrag and walked over to him. Just when I thought I was in control, Colt reached out to grasp my hips, hauling me toward him. He settled me onto his lap and then his hand was holding the back of my neck. His brown eyes looked liquid.

"Joni gave me some interesting insight about you," I said.

"Oh yeah?"

I nodded. "She said something about you wanting to keep me."

"What if I do?"

"What changed?"

"You get one life. One life to be free, to choose how you live. You want to leave town? I'll make sure you can do that—and not have Dev on your ass. No use leaving town if you have to keep looking over your shoulder and feel like you're on the run. But I've also been doing some thinking," he admitted. "Ever since I walked into Dive Bar and kissed you. It was like I'd been surviving this whole time, but not really living." He stared at me with deep brown eyes. "You get what I mean, yeah?"

I nodded. I knew what it was like to float from one moment to the next. Not really sad, but not happy either. Just...there.

"Each day we're one step closer to the end. Don't want to die and wish I'd really lived."

I was drugged by his words. A spectator weighing in might think we didn't know each other at all, that because of circumstances, I'd turned to him in an hour of need. But maybe Colt needed me too. Maybe we needed each other and it didn't matter what it looked like on the outside.

We were close enough that I could smell the coffee and mint toothpaste on his breath. My tongue darted out to touch my lips and I swore his eyes darkened.

I went in for the kill. Our mouths met in ferocious hunger and our tongues fought each other for dominance. Colt's hand on the back of my neck tightened and I leaned into him, ready for more, ready for it on the kitchen table.

A phone rang. Colt's lips tore from mine, his face wreathed in annoyance at our thwarted lust.

"Fuck, why does this always happen?" He shifted me on his lap so he could get to the cell in his pocket and answered it. "Yeah?"

When I made a move to get up, he stopped me.

"Yeah, okay. Be right there." He hung up and set his phone on the kitchen table. "I gotta go."

"Okay."

We stared at each other and then our lips were meshing. "I really have to go," Colt growled against my mouth even as he kissed me again.

"I heard you," I answered, tugging at his shirt, wanting to get to the skin beneath.

He pulled back and grasped my hands to still their wandering. "Not like this."

"Not like what?" I demanded. "Every time I decide I want to have sex with you, we get interrupted."

He didn't smile from my jest. "If all I wanted was sex, it would've happened by now."

"Well, that's a bit arrogant, don't you think?"

Colt's gaze dropped to my traitorous nipples, but said nothing.

I rolled my eyes. "Fine."

"I want you, but not like this. Not when you're still confused."

"Confused about what exactly?"

"Confused about what it means when I take you to my bed. It's gonna mean something, babe. And I'm not sure you're ready for all that."

"What if I'm never ready?" I ventured to ask. Colt's intensity scared me, but I valued his honesty.

"Then you were never meant to be my woman."

With that pronouncement, Colt stalked from the kitchen, leaving me with a lukewarm cup of coffee.

Chapter 9

THE NEXT THREE days ironed out into a routine. I spent the daytime bored in Colt's home while Cheese hung out on the porch, acting as a guard. At night, I slept alone, feeling restless and achy. Colt hadn't made another move to sleep next to me and he hadn't kissed me again. The man was a sensual battering ram and he'd gotten through my fortress walls. But that was exactly why he kept his distance.

Colt wanted something real with me, something lasting. And he was giving me the opportunity to decide if I wanted to be in it for the long haul. I didn't know if I would've chosen to be with Colt if my circumstances had been different. Even though I hadn't been able to stop thinking about him after we'd kissed at Dive Bar, I'd done nothing to seek him out of my own volition. I'd turned to him only because he'd proven to me that he was a protector of women.

If I chose to be with Colt now, it meant risking an unknown future, my safety, and being pulled deeper into a lifestyle I didn't understand.

Rationally explaining all of that to my overworked libido wasn't doing the trick.

"Will you please, please, please take me to the garage with you?" I asked again, setting down the crust of my toast.

"No," Colt said for what had to be the hundredth time that morning.

"I'm bored out of my skull."

"No, Mia," Colt said, setting down his empty coffee cup. "It's not safe yet."

"It might never be safe. You can't keep me locked up here."

He grinned. "Sure I can."

"Colt, seriously."

"Dev went underground," he said. "That's a bad enough sign already. Men like that don't go underground unless someone very dangerous is after them, and there's still a prospect at your house, so we know Dev hasn't forgotten about you. This is serious shit, Mia."

A chill of fear skated down my spine and I was grateful that I had a safe place. "I'm okay lying low, but can't I hang out at the clubhouse or something? I'm going crazy with the lack of entertainment."

Colt's face morphed into a ferocious scowl. "I don't want you at the clubhouse without me."

"What do you think will happen?" I asked.

"I won't leave you alone at the clubhouse until you tell me you're mine."

"Seriously?"

"My brothers are good guys, but if you're unclaimed, then you're fair game. Rules are rules."

"I'm sorry, did we suddenly time travel back to the eighteenth century?"

"It's just the way of things, Mia. You're not a club whore. But you're not an Old Lady either."

"So yet again, I'm being punished for not making a decision."

"How else are you being punished? I invited you into my home. I promised to get you out of town. Fuck, woman, I've even cooked for you. What else do you want from me?"

"You're using sex as a weapon!" I yelled. "You haven't been here the last three days, and all I do is sit here and stew."

"You've got to be kidding me. Sex as a weapon?" He grabbed my hand and placed it at the fly of his jeans. "You don't think I'm suffering, here?"

"You're the one who put this stupid edict in place," I reminded him.

"You still don't get it." He shook his head. "I'll give you raw and dirty so good that you'll never want to leave and then you'll be stuck in this life you didn't want to live, all because you couldn't keep your legs together. Trust me, darlin'. I'm doing you a massive favor."

"No," I stated, yanking my hand away from him. "All you're doing is treating me like a child who doesn't know her own mind and body. I want to be in your bed. So why won't you let me?"

He stilled and clamped his jaw shut.

"You think I'll still want to leave," I said slowly. "You think if it's only sex, I'll leave. You don't want me to leave you…"

Something dark moved in his eyes and my heart cracked open in understanding.

"You've had enough of people leaving you, haven't you, Colt?"

He didn't answer my rhetorical question.

But he was correct, I wasn't ready to commit to him or to this life—and it had nothing to do with time and how long I'd known him. I was still unsure.

Colt wanted me to choose him and he wanted me to do it without being swayed by him. So he'd stayed away, pulled back from spending time with me because even though I wasn't committed, Colt was.

It all made sense now, what Joni and Zip had told me about him, about how fast Colt declared his intentions despite trying to fight them.

"You have a few more classes you have to take for your college degree, right?" he asked, finally breaking the silence.

My head was still reeling from what I'd just figured out about Colt. His change in conversation threw me for another loop. "What?"

"Your degree. You have some classes you need to finish?"

"Yes."

"Can you take any of them online?"

I blinked. "I don't know."

"Look into it," he said.

"Don't tell me what to do," I said without any real heat, and it caused Colt to give a small smile.

"You like it when I tell you what to do. I think you like it more than you want to admit."

"Don't you have somewhere to be?" I asked pointedly.

Colt was unable to hold in his laugh. He shook his head and then left. I wished I could say I enjoyed the quiet after our heated exchange, but I still felt the current of tension in the air. Tension that wasn't going anywhere anytime soon.

I had two choices: commit to being with Colt and

everything that entailed, or remain his houseguest until he could get me out of Waco safely.

There was no middle ground with him.

I put the dirty breakfast dishes in the dishwasher and then wandered into the den where Colt had a new desktop computer set up. For the next few hours, I researched online classes offered at the local community college. I had a few lined up and ready to go, but I couldn't pay for them until I got my new credit card.

By mid-afternoon, I was going insane. I couldn't do anything about my college courses and I replayed my conversations with Colt over and over in my head.

I needed to talk to someone who might be able to offer me some insight. I scrolled through the three numbers in my phone and shot out a text message to Joni asking if she wanted to come hang out with me. Chances were she was working a shift at the hospital, but I crossed my fingers and hoped.

"I don't understand your brother," I said, half way through my first margarita.

Colt's sister grinned and raised her almost finished cocktail. "Tell me all the things."

"I thought men were scared of commitment."

"They are."

"I thought bikers were unfaithful—according to my friend Shelly."

"Some are," she agreed. "Except my brother isn't wired that way. He's never been wired that way. I mean, he's had his interludes, of course. He is a dude. But he was never a playboy."

"Has he ever been serious about anyone?"

"No."

"Why does he want me?" I asked in confusion. "I'm a mess. I'm trouble. I've got the Iron Horsemen on my back. If he was smart, he'd send me on my way and wish me well."

"Colt never takes the easy road. And you give him something no one else does."

"Lip?"

Joni laughed. "No. He keeps himself separate, you know? He's my older brother, he's the president of the Blue Angels. He runs things, but he hasn't—he doesn't let people in. Not even those he considers family. But you, he's different with you. I don't know how to explain it, but you have to trust me. Colt isn't like this with *anyone*."

"That only adds more pressure. Thanks."

She stared me down, swirling her margarita in her glass. The ice clinked and it was the only sound in the otherwise quiet kitchen. "It would be worth it. All the bullshit, all the ups and downs. Colt has so much inside of him, and if you choose him, the way he's already chosen you, then he'll never let you regret it."

"It's too soon."

"Says who?"

"Says—"

"Society?" She snorted. "Over sixty percent of marriages end in divorce. And how long were those people together before they even got married?"

"Are you a proponent for marriage or against it?" I asked in wry amusement.

"I'm a proponent for happiness. For following your own path. For choosing someone who may not have been the person you thought you were going to wind up with."

I paused and then chugged the rest of my drink.

"What you're saying makes a lot of sense. I blame tequila for that."

She grinned, revealing the dimple in her left cheek.

I was just drunk enough to lean over and place my finger in it. "If you and Zip have babies, there's a good chance they'll get that dimple."

She giggled and swatted my hand away and then reached for her buzzing cell phone on the kitchen table.

"Hospital?" I asked.

She shook her head, her sorrel brown ponytail still high on her head after her shift. Joni hadn't gone home to change out of her puppy dog patterned scrubs before coming over. Pediatric nurse. She definitely looked the part.

"Darcy—she's married to Gray. Have you met Gray?" When I shook my head, she went on, "Anyway. She was wondering if she could come over and hang out."

"Oh, sure."

"She's bringing Rachel and Allison. Two other Old Ladies," she explained. "They're dying to get a look at you."

"Why?"

"Woman, please," Joni said with a laugh.

"I guess that means we should make another pitcher of margaritas."

Twenty minutes later, the three of them showed up. They greeted Cheese and then tromped inside, boisterous, big-haired, heavily made-up, and tattooed. They were a lively, warm bunch and filled the silent house with their laughter and jokes.

When we were three margaritas in and everyone's cheeks were flushed, Darcy asked, "You mean to tell me you have no tattoos? Not one?" Though she was in her forties, she had the body of a thirty-year-old.

"Nope, no tattoos," I said. "How many do you have?"

"Five," she answered.

"Wow."

"They're addictive," Rachel added. The pretty brunette pulled up the short sleeve of her T-shirt to show me a scrawled tattoo of her man's name, Reap.

I reached out and touched the ink. "You don't feel…branded?"

"It's not a one-way street, ya know," Darcy said. "Gray has my name on his chest."

"Yep, and Reap has my name on his…" Rachel trailed off as her face went a shade of poinsettia red.

We all laughed, but the ladies kept their attention on me.

"I think Colt would enjoy seeing his name on your butt," Joni said.

"You do know that's your brother you're talking about right? And no man's name is ever going on my butt," I said lightly.

Joni and Darcy exchanged a look. "You should tell her how you and Gray got together. She's a bit of a non-believer." Joni winked.

"I'm not a non-believer," I protested. "I just don't understand how it's all or nothing."

"That's kind of the way of the Blue Angels," Rachel said. "They live by different rules."

"Because they're criminals?" I blurted out.

The four women sitting in Colt's living room all glanced at one another. Allison appeared uncomfortable, Rachel clearly was deferring to Darcy, as did Joni with an arch of her eyebrow.

"There are things as Old Ladies that even we don't know," Darcy began slowly. "But what I can tell you is this; our men are strong, loyal, and fiercely protective. They provide for their families and give back to the community."

Darcy hadn't answered my question outright. She neither confirmed nor denied the Blue Angels were involved in criminal activity. Maybe she wouldn't disclose any of it unless I became one of them. Maybe she genuinely didn't know. Though I was curious, it wasn't enough of a reason to dive all in.

"I'm sorry," I said softly. "I didn't mean to—I don't know. I didn't know how to ask that question without coming out and asking it."

"I didn't grow up knowing anything about bikers," Darcy began. "Wasn't in my sphere of knowledge, you know? I grew up sheltered. Really sheltered—and not in the good way. My friend from college took me to a party—I thought we were going to a frat thing. She surprised the hell out of me when she pulled up outside the Blue Angels clubhouse. I almost didn't go inside, but she talked me into it. The bitch disappeared almost immediately with one of the brothers, leaving me to fend for myself."

She smiled in fond remembrance. "A guy came up to me and offered me a beer. It was Gray and he didn't leave my side all night. He knew I was uncomfortable. We spent the evening hanging out in his clubhouse room talking about music and our childhoods. The next morning, my friend stumbled out of a clubhouse room and we left. I never expected to see Gray again, but the next weekend he drove to Austin to see me. Stood outside my dorm building. Took me to lunch at this diner on the side of the highway that still has the best hash browns I've ever tasted. By the end of that year—my junior year—I became his Old Lady. My parents shit a brick when I brought him home. They threatened to cut me off if I didn't break up with him. I knew he was the man for me, so I told them to go ahead.

Gray helped pay my final year of college so I could get my degree. He not only took care of me financially, but emotionally, too. See, my parents' love was conditional. Be the daughter they wanted and they'd continue to pay for my life. It was no life at all, really."

"Everything in our world moves fast," Rachel added. "It was the same with me and Reap. I chose to be with him after three weeks of dating."

The idea of committing to Colt so soon after we'd met was still a foreign concept. And no stories from the other Old Ladies would sway me about it. I hadn't had a lot of control in my short life. Mom died when I was young. Grammie died when I was in my early twenties. I'd been too numb to live and now I was tangled up with MC business thanks to my asshole of a boss.

I wasn't going to settle down with some biker. The idea was ludicrous. It didn't matter how much I liked Colt or felt like he saw a piece of me that no one else did. I would have to be crazy to choose this life…to choose danger.

It was too intense. It was too much. Colt was too much.

"We need more margaritas," I muttered, jumping up from my seat, attempting to escape the eyes resting on me.

"I'll make them," Allison volunteered. The bottle blonde had been quiet, but when she took the pitcher from me, she gave me a small smile. Leaning a bit closer, she whispered, "Do what's right for you. Whatever that looks like."

I smiled at her in gratitude, but before Allison could leave the room, Joni stopped her.

"We can have more margs later," Joni said, getting up from her spot on the carpeted floor. "Colt has a kick-ass sound system. Let's dance. Your feet okay?"

"They don't hurt at all." I nodded. "Dancing sounds like fun."

"That's tequila for you," Darcy said.

Joni turned on music and before I knew it, the five of us were bouncing around Colt's living room, laughing like loons and enjoying the hell out of ourselves. I liked them; they were straight shooters, which I greatly appreciated. Their offers of friendship felt genuine and even though I had no idea how long I'd be stuck in Waco, it was nice that there was a group of women who were willing to accept me into their fold. Despite my blunders, despite my reservations, despite the fact that I'd been judgmental about the Blue Angels and what I thought I knew of them.

"What the hell is going on?" Colt demanded, taking in the scene of dancing women.

I hadn't even heard him come in, but the look of astonishment on his face had me giggling.

Joni cut the music and said, "You've been acting like a prison guard. So we came to entertain her."

"We approve. Just so you know," Rachel stated.

"I don't need your approval," Colt grumbled.

No one looked uncomfortable or afraid of him. I found that oddly fascinating. While I was studying his expression, I wobbled and had to reach out to steady myself using the back of the couch.

Colt looked at his sister. "I blame you for this."

"Me?" Joni raised her eyebrows. "Are you referring to the mess or Mia's inebriated state?"

"I'm not that inebriated." I hiccoughed which only caused the girls to snigger. "Okay, maybe I'm slightly toasted. But I can still walk a straight line. Want me to prove it?"

"Please, don't," Colt said. "The last thing I need is for you to trip over your own two feet and hurt yourself. You're a walking liability, you know that, right?"

I wrinkled my nose and stuck out my tongue.

"I think that's our cue to leave," Joni said to the others. "This feels like some weird version of foreplay."

"None of you are sober enough to drive," Colt muttered, pulling out his phone. He pressed a button and then, "Get over here. Bring reinforcements."

Colt hung up and then stepped further into the room until he was close enough for me to touch him.

"Are you mad they're here? Are you really upset I'm kind of inebriated?"

His gaze softened. "No, I'm not mad they're here. I'm glad they like you."

It's what I read between the lines that fascinated me— that he was happy they liked me because it meant I could fit in with his life, long term.

It was there for the taking. All I had to do was reach out and press my lips to Colt's and nestle myself in the crook of his body. I kept shooting him sidewise glances as the girls trickled out of the house when their men came for them. Joni hitched a ride with Darcy and Gray. The front door closed and Colt and I were alone.

"My house is a mess," he stated.

I looked around the living room, noting the empty margarita glasses, the crust-filled plates, and empty pizza boxes.

"You *are* mad."

"Yeah, I'm mad." He grinned. "Mad that you didn't save me any pizza."

I laughed. "Who says I didn't save you any pizza?"

"Did you?"

"No."

He peered at me for a long moment. "You had fun? With the girls?"

I nodded. "Yeah. It was…enlightening."

"Enlightening. Did it change anything for you?" When

I didn't reply, Colt said, "Leave it. It can be cleaned up tomorrow."

He walked past me up the stairs to disappear into his bedroom. I looked after him, wondering why there was an ache in my chest, wondering why I felt like I'd made a mistake by not being honest with him.

I headed up to my bedroom, lonelier than I'd felt before.

Chapter 10

By the time I woke up late the next morning with a slight hangover, Colt was gone. Cheese sat on the porch in his customary chair and I waved at him through the front window. The remains of my impromptu party littered the living room. While I sipped on a cup of coffee, I cleaned up. As I threw the last of the empty pizza boxes into the garbage, my cell phone vibrated. I followed the sound of it, wondering where I'd left it the previous evening. It wasn't like I had tons of people trying to get in touch with me. Finding it between the couch cushions, I fished it out and answered it.

"Hello?"

"Get dressed," Joni commanded.

"Um…"

"We're going to the clubhouse for a barbecue. So nothing fancy. Jeans will work."

"But I—Colt—"

"You're getting sprung, chicken. Everyone wants to meet you."

"Everyone? Everyone who?"

"The club."

"Oh, boy."

"Yeah, so we're having a potluck, grilling out. The kids will be there, so it's just family. Nothing crazy. Promise."

I laughed, though part of me was curious about the Blue Angels I was hearing so much about. I'd only interacted with Zip and Cheese. "Okay, well, what can I bring?"

"Nothing."

"I have to bring something. What will these people think of me?"

"They know you're a bit of an invalid and cooking and or stirring things is difficult."

"I'm not showing up to a potluck without beer or chips. I'm not a moocher."

"Fine, we'll stop by the grocery store on the way."

"Promise?"

"Promise. Can you be ready in an hour?"

"Yes."

"Okay, see you soon."

She hung up, and I shook my head. Before I could dial Colt to confirm the potluck, my phone buzzed again.

Colt.

"Are you calling to tell me about the barbecue at the clubhouse?" I asked.

"Yeah. How'd you know?"

"Your sister. She's coming to pick me up. I need to hit the store and get some stuff."

"No," Colt commanded. "Zip will drive you."

"But Cheese—"

"As soon as Zip gets to you, Cheese is on party duty."

"Do I even want to know what that means?" I asked.

"No." I heard the smile in his voice.

"Why can't you drive me?" I demanded.

"Do you miss me?"

"No," I lied. "You're just a control freak, so I'm surprised you're letting Zip drive me."

"I'm in town. I'll be at the clubhouse later."

"Okay," I said, giving in.

"And no grocery store."

"But I want to bring things.

"I'll swing by and get some stuff."

"Get beer, chips, and a premade salad. Or a fruit tray."

"Yes, dear," Colt chimed like a chastised husband. "There's a spare set of house keys in the drawer next to the fridge. Use those to lock up the house."

"Yes, dear," I parroted.

He laughed, the sound easy on my ears. I liked knowing I was responsible for it.

I didn't call Joni back to tell her not to bother coming over because I had a plan. A plan to get Joni and Zip in the same place and see what happened. It was pure evil, but maybe they needed a push in each other's direction. My new friend wanted him, and I wanted to see his reaction to her.

Thanks to Laura—the club groupie who had brought over bags of used clothes—I had a wealth of new cute outfits to choose from. I settled on a comfortable spaghetti-strap, blue cotton dress that hit just above the knee. It showed off the freckled skin of my shoulders. I was just putting the finishing touches on my lashes when the doorbell rang. I went downstairs to answer it, glad to see it was Joni looking hot and tall in a pair of dark, skinny-leg jeans, a black, flowy tank top, and long, silver, dangle earrings.

"You look amazing!" I stated, waving her inside.

Her high heels clacked on the wood floor as she entered. Smiling, she said, "Thanks. You look pretty, too. You ready to go? Cheese can follow us."

"Uh, yeah, about that. Colt wanted Zip to drive me."

"Oh." She frowned. "Then why am I here?"

There was a knock on the door and I shot her a look. "Just go with it, okay?" She nodded, and when I opened the door Zip stood on the porch. Leather cut, wavy blond hair, sharp blue eyes—focused on Joni.

"Hi," he greeted.

"Hey," she answered.

"I'm such an idiot," I chirped. "Joni offered to give me a ride, and I forgot to call her and tell her you were driving me."

"No sweat," Zip said.

"Why don't we carpool?" I suggested.

"Isn't it easier if Joni takes her car?" Zip asked.

"She wants to drink," I blurted out. "And I don't want her to drive."

Zip's eyes slid to Joni.

"Uh, yeah. I want to drink," Joni stated. "A lot."

"Okay," Zip sighed in feigned annoyance, though it appeared to be all for show. "You guys ready to go?"

"Yeah," I said. I grabbed my cell phone off the coffee table and a spare key, realizing that I didn't have a purse.

"I can hold those for you," Zip said after I locked up. Cheese was on his bike. Revving the engine, he waved and then pulled away.

"Thanks," I said, handing Zip my two items of importance. I was excited to get out of Colt's house. As comfortable as his home was, I was about to scale the walls just to have something to do.

I climbed into the back of Zip's black SUV before Joni could. I wanted to give her the front seat. It was unbelievable watching them. They repelled like magnets, except for their gazes. They couldn't stop looking at one another. I wondered if Colt had any idea about the attraction between his VP and his sister.

The drive to the clubhouse was quiet. I stared out of the window, watching the flat land swish past. The entire ride was filled with tension and silence. When we arrived at the clubhouse, I immediately hopped out of the car, wanting to escape Joni and Zip's weird bubble of avoidance and sexual tension.

I waited for Joni to get out of the car and then followed her inside. We moved through the expansive living room to the open-designed kitchen. Darcy stood at the granite island, cling-wrapping a plate of raw hamburger patties.

"Hey, sugar!" Darcy greeted, leaning over to give me a cheek brush. "How did you feel this morning?"

"Slow to start," I admitted. "But after my second cup of coffee, I felt okay."

She nodded. "Girls' nights can get rowdy. That one was pretty tame. Wait until we go out dancing."

I paused, surprised that she was already inviting me to another girls' night out.

"I'm so glad I didn't have to work at the hospital today," Joni said with a laugh. "I was fairly useless until about ten this morning."

"Didn't we drink the same amount?" I looked at her. "Did I drink you under the table?"

"It would appear that way, yes," Joni said with amusement.

I gestured with my chin to the counter. "What can I do?"

"Take that plate of hotdogs outside and hand them to Gray. He's at the grill."

"Put me to work," Joni commanded.

"Condiments need to go on the tables," Darcy dictated.

"Got it." Joni went to the fridge and rooted around the shelves, pulling out bottles of mustard and ketchup. Her butt was on display in her amazing jeans and I caught Zip staring at it.

"Zip, find me a prospect and send him in," Darcy said. "I need another case of beer brought up from the basement."

Zip grinned. "These parties would be a shit show without you here."

Darcy rolled her eyes. "They turn into a shit show after a few bottles of bourbon."

He kissed her cheek on his way toward the hallway. He gestured for me to follow and when we got to the back door, he opened it, allowing me to go out first.

Before I could continue to the grill, Zip put his hand on my arm and stopped me.

"What are you doing?" he asked.

I frowned in confusion and lifted the plate of hotdogs. "I thought it was obvious."

"Not that. The shit you pulled with me and Joni?"

"You and Joni?" I asked, feigning innocence. "There is no you and Joni."

Zip's jaw clenched and his blue eyes went frosty. "Stay out of it."

"Stay out of what?"

"For fuck's sake," he muttered. He reached into his pocket to retrieve my phone and keys before stalking away to join a few Blue Angels sitting around in folding chairs, coolers of beer nearby.

Smiling to myself, I approached the guy at the grill who was at least ten years older than Darcy. His salt-and-pepper hair was pulled back into a ponytail, his muscled arms heavily inked. He shut the lid of the gas barbecue grill and glanced at me.

"Those for me, darlin'?" he asked, gesturing to the plate of hotdogs.

"I think they are." I handed the plate over and said, "I'm Mia."

He grinned, white teeth appearing through a salt-and-pepper beard. "I know who you are."

"Oh, okay."

"Welcome. Grab a beer and get to know the boys."

"I'll do that," I murmured.

I had plans to introduce myself to everyone, but Joni was a step ahead of me and took it upon herself to lead me around after she set out the condiments. I sipped on a beer while conversing with Boxer—the blond flirt I'd met the first day. He was charming and carefree, but I didn't think for a second he couldn't be strong and forceful. He was a Blue Angel.

Kids ran around, yelling and laughing. Adults conversed near the salsa and chips while Gray manned the grill. When Boxer left me alone to grab another beer, I escaped. Everyone was nice, but curious, so the questions had been steady for the better part of an hour.

Colt still hadn't shown up yet.

I wandered away from people, ambling toward a group of kids that were hanging out under a tree. I didn't know who belonged to whom, but there were eight of them, with more girls than boys, age range varied.

Two of the older girls glanced at me with shy smiles. A young boy, maybe ten years old, was bolder. He got up off the ground and ran toward me, a mop of dark brown hair falling into his eyes. Brushing his hair away from his face, he peered up at me with a huge grin. He was missing his two front teeth, and it only made him cuter.

"Hi!" he said.

"Hi, there."

"Who are you?"

"Mia. Who are you?"

"Cameron. You can call me Cam. Did you know asparagus makes your pee smell funny?"

I bit my lip to keep from laughing. As solemnly as I could, I answered, "I did know that."

"He's been telling everyone that fun little fact," one of the older girls said, calling out from her spot under the tree.

"What happened to your arm?" Cam asked, gesturing to my cast.

"Oh, I tripped over a tree root."

Cam's brown eyes widened. "Really?"

I nodded. "I'm clumsy."

The boy latched onto my uninjured hand and pulled me toward his friends. "Want to sit with us?"

"Sure," I said, parking it on the grass and sitting on my haunches so my sundress hit my knees.

Because they were kids and naturally inquisitive, they asked me tons of questions without worrying if they were inappropriate. But they were adorable and full of energy, and before I knew it, we were all engaged in a game of tag and I was *It*.

Pretending to be out of breath and slow, I sank down to my knees. The youngest girl of the group—a little blond moppet named Lily who happened to be Cam's sister—approached me.

"Help!" I panted. "I'm tired!"

The girl took another step toward me, coming within my reach. I attacked her with tickles, her shrieks of laughter loud and infectious.

"You're *It!*" I teased, standing up, brushing the grass off my knees. My dress was dirty, but I didn't care.

"I don't want to be *It*," she said. "I want a hotdog."

"Me too," I said. I held out my hand to her, and she clasped it. "Let's go." I looked at the other kids. "You guys hungry?"

There was a chorus of 'yesses' and then we were off for food. The gaggle of kids surrounded me. The older girls, who I learned were thirteen—Allison's sister and her friend—were at that age where they thought adults weren't cool. But they were excited to talk to me. Guess I didn't scream adult to them. They asked me questions about clothes and makeup, and they brought me into their inner circle.

"Will you fix my hotdog for me?" Lily asked, scrambling up to take a seat on a picnic table bench.

Before I could answer, Darcy jumped in, "You don't have to make her a hotdog. I can do that."

"Ah, so Lily and Cam belong to you," I said with a smile. Lily had Darcy's nose, and their resemblance was easy to see once they were together.

"I claim them," Darcy said, picking up a paper plate and filling it with a little bit of everything and a hotdog.

"Plain," Lily reminded her.

Darcy set the plate down in front of Lily and then before the little girl could protest, Darcy had a paper napkin tucked into the front of Lily's dress so she wouldn't get food on herself. "I'm not a baby," Lily muttered as Darcy moved on, fixing a plate for Cam.

I made my own paper bib and stuck it in the front of my dress. I winked at Lily who giggled. I procured myself a plate of food and was munching away, purposefully getting mustard all over my face to make Lily feel better.

"You're messy!"

"Yes, I am," I agreed, wiping the mustard off my cheeks.

She lost all interest in me when she looked across the lawn and bellowed, "Uncle Colt!" She climbed down from her seat and ran toward him.

I watched in amazement as the broody biker lifted the little girl high in the air above his head. His face was soft and open as he carried Lily back to her seat and plopped her down. She began eating again, a wide smile across her face as she chewed.

"What happened to your eye?" she asked Colt.

"I walked into a tree branch," Colt said, not missing a stride.

"Really?" Cam piped up. "Mia tripped on a tree root. You guys are clumsy."

"Yes, we really are," I agreed. I bit my lip to stem a smile.

Colt grinned at me and reached up to wipe something off my cheek.

"Mustard?" I guessed.

"Yeah."

"Did you stop off and get beer and chips?" I asked him, spearing a piece of watermelon and putting it in my mouth.

"Nope." Colt piled his plate high with potato salad, a hotdog, and a cheeseburger.

"What? Oh man, now everyone will think I'm a bad party guest."

Colt looked at me in amusement. "This party is for you, you know."

"Really?"

"Yeah," he said, taking a bite of the cheeseburger. "The guys wanted to meet you."

"Why?"

He grinned. "Why do you think?"

"Because I'm a novelty."

Looking up from his food, he stared at me. "One of a kind."

Happiness curled through me and I couldn't stop the grin from spreading across my face.

Chapter 11

AFTERNOON SANK INTO EVENING. Gray lit the bonfire and Darcy brought out the ingredients for S'mores. Lily and Cam sat on either side of me on a log, asking me to make them dessert. I looked to Darcy who told them they could have one each. They grumbled, but when I promised I'd only eat one too and then smeared melted chocolate on all of our faces, they giggled and didn't care.

I caught Colt's gaze, flickering and dark in the firelight. Looking relaxed, he sipped his beer, nodding every few beats to something Zip was saying. Throughout the barbecue, I'd sought him out. Even when I was talking to Joni or Rachel, and some of the other Old Ladies, my mind and gaze wandered to Colt. There were a few times that I'd caught him looking at me, too.

Studying him in his element with his club showed me a different side of him. Though he was always in control, this was Colt around his tribe. I gave myself the luxury of a fantasy of what my life would look like if I chose to stay.

Acceptance. Family. Home.

Was I knowingly going to walk away from that?

The more time I spent with Colt, the more I was beginning to think he was right. We did fit together, we did understand one another, we were both looking for something more out of life than to just get by after the deaths of loved ones.

My thoughts were heavy as the night wore on. Those with children were gearing up to leave. Cam and Lily hugged me goodnight and then Darcy took them home. The kids who were siblings of members or girlfriends had their mothers come get them and then it was just the adults. Conversations turned low, and people split off into couples. I watched Joni and Zip sit next to each other but not touch or talk.

Wanting to be just a little bit closer to the fire, I got up off the log to sit on the ground. I felt someone at my back, and then the sweep of my hair off my shoulder. Colt's large, warm hand rested on my neck, his thumb stroking the curve. I leaned back against his knees and closed my eyes, the heat of the fire warm at my front. A slight spring breeze tickled my ear and I let out a sigh.

He leaned down and inquired, "Meant to ask…did you sign up for online classes?"

I shook my head. "No, I need my credit card to seal the deal and it hasn't arrived yet."

Colt paused. "I've got a credit card."

"You're not suggesting what I think you're suggesting."

"Use my credit card," he stated.

"You trust me not to do an online shopping spree?"

"Yeah, I trust you."

My insides felt like mush. "I'll pay you back."

"Fine," he answered brusquely.

I smiled even though he couldn't see me. I would never be someone who would take handouts and give nothing in return. I wasn't wired that way. I liked to contribute on my own and bring something real to the table. Colt seemed inclined to want to take care of me. He was president of the Blue Angels and an older brother. It was in his DNA to be in control and to protect. I could appreciate that about him, but I had no trouble pushing back and letting him know I could take care of myself. I was glad he'd take my money when the time came.

The atmosphere of the party changed with the departure of children and the arrival of young women in tight clothing. I watched as some of the married men groped and made out with the women who had come to the club gathering. Darcy and the other Old Ladies hadn't talked about this part of club life. It was one thing to sleep around when you were single, but these were married men and it felt like a different deal all together.

Zip got off the log next to Joni, took his beer bottle and went to a skimpy-clad woman with fake breasts. She screeched in excitement and then jumped into his arms. He caught her and then they started making out.

"Ew," I muttered and then discreetly glanced at Joni. Her gaze had dropped to her lap, and I knew she was battling her hurt.

With a squeeze to Colt's leg, I stood up from the ground, my tailbone numb. "Bathroom," I said to Colt. He nodded. I walked over to Joni and without a word, grabbed her hand, pulling her away from the party and the man she couldn't have.

"I think I'll ask Cheese for a ride," Joni said when we were far enough away from the bonfire not to be overheard. Defeat weighed heavily in her voice. "He's sober and I've got to get out of here."

We entered the hallway of the clubhouse, passing more women on their way out to the bonfire. They looked ready to party, some of them already swaying on their high heels.

"Don't go," I pled. "Hang out with me."

Darcy had left. Rachel had disappeared with Reap into his clubhouse room, and Allison was too quiet and I felt like when we spoke, I was speaking *at* her.

"I can't do this," Joni said. "I've watched him do this for years, and I'm done. I need to be done."

"Stay and fight for him."

"He doesn't even see me—and if he wants to play around, then fine, but I won't wait for him anymore."

"I'll walk with you to find Cheese."

"Most of them are like that," Joni said. "Fuck anything that walks—a lot of the married guys are the same way."

"Gray plays around on Darcy? I find that hard to believe."

"I said 'most'. Gray's a solid, faithful guy."

"I guess not all men are cheaters."

We exited the clubhouse and stood on the porch. I looked around for Cheese and found him standing guard with a prospect named Acid.

"Colt's not like that," Joni said.

"He's not?"

She shook her head. "Dad never played around on Mom and Colt is cut from the same cloth as our father."

"Is that why you all keep pushing me to be with Colt? Even though it's so sudden? I'm not sure I'm ready for that kind of intensity…"

"He's my brother, and I love him," she began, "but I'm telling you, even if I wasn't his sister, I'd still push you toward him. He's one of the best men I've ever met. Loyal. As loyal as they come."

"It's not enough of a reason. I want to want him because I can't breathe without him, you know?"

"That's how I feel about Zip."

"Then how are you supposed to let him go?"

She shook her head. "I don't know. I just know I have to."

I squeezed her hand, my heart beating in sympathy for my new friend. But there was nothing more to say, so I stood with her on the front porch of the clubhouse while we waited for Cheese to grab his bike and take her home.

～

"I'm gonna fuck Colt tonight," a girl slurred.

The words stopped me cold and I immediately tucked myself into a nook where I could eavesdrop in privacy. I couldn't see the two women's faces, but I could hear them clearly—not that they were attempting to be quiet.

"Good luck," her friend replied. "He hasn't been able to take his eyes off that girl all night."

"That girl," the drunk woman spat. "What the hell does he see in her? She's not even that hot. And she's so fucking short. If he fucks her he's gonna break her in half."

"You would know," her friend teased. "The last time you slept with him you were hurting the next day."

"Oh, but I hurt so good!"

The sound of their heels and laughter disappeared down the hallway, their words echoing in my ears. I sank down onto the floor, pulled my legs up to my chest, and rested my head on my knees. I hadn't been prepared for their gossip. Not that I was ever going to be prepared to hear another woman talk about Colt in any sort of intimate way. A way I had yet to experience, but wanted to.

Desperately.

I admitted my desire for him. But I knew by the churning in my belly it wasn't just about sex. Because Colt hadn't taken me to his bed, I'd had time to live in his house, in his presence and had begun to feel things for him.

I'd catch him staring at me, his dark brown eyes warm and soft. There were lines around the corners of his eyes —but not from smiling. He hadn't grown up smiling. He'd grown up fast because he'd lost his parents young. Parents who were in love, who meant everything to one another.

"Babe?"

I flinched, not having heard Colt approach. He stood above me, a frown on his face. "What are you doing?"

"I needed a minute away from the party. Joni left," I added.

"I know. Cheese texted that he was taking her home."

"I'm tired," I said, not at all lying. "I want to go home." I didn't want to go back to the party and watch loose women crawl all over married men. I didn't want to watch them make a play for Colt—I didn't want to feel like he was mine when I was too much of a chicken shit to take what he was offering me.

Colt held out his hand and I grasped it. He hauled me up and brought me to him. If I leaned forward, I would be able to press my forehead to his muscled chest and enjoy the soft fabric of his cotton T-shirt and the firmness of his body. I wanted to breathe in the scent of him, know him the way I knew myself.

All I had to do was say yes. Jump into the unknown with Colt by my side.

He laced his fingers through mine and led me through the clubhouse, but not to the exit. Instead, he took me down the hallway toward his bedroom. "We'll crash here tonight," he explained.

I swallowed. "We?"

With his free hand, he reached up and tucked a strand

of hair behind my ear, his thumb lingering on my jaw. "Yeah. We."

"I don't know if I'm ready, Colt. For all this. For you."

His thumb moved to the center of my chin. "You've got the tiniest cleft." He smiled slightly. "It was the first thing I noticed when you came to me at Dive Bar. Not your eyes, not your mouth. Not your gorgeous legs in those tight as fuck jeans. No. I noticed the cleft. And then you saw me in the alleyway, and instead of calling the cops, you let it be. I knew you were special."

I tilted my head back to stare into his languid brown eyes.

"I thought *this woman isn't afraid of me and can handle my life.* Even when I saw you on the steps of my garage, with your injured wrist and scratches on your face, you didn't look beaten down. Is that woman truly scared of what a man can make her feel?"

"I'm not ready to be owned by feelings."

"Mia." He sighed. "You don't think it's a one-way street, do you?"

He dropped my hand and placed it on my waist as he pushed me against the door of his room. His lips came down on mine, hungry and dangerous. I no longer cared about anything except Colt.

Colt lifted his head. "You own me. I'm yours for the taking."

My tongue darted out to sweep across my lips. I could taste him and it only made me greedy for all of him.

We had so much in common and it made us understand one another. When you were marred by grief and loss, touched by darkness, only another person who'd gone through the same thing could understand.

"I'm not gonna force you into anything. Just know that I want you."

135

He stared at me and waited. I bit my lip, letting him see my indecision. Was I really going to turn away a man who made me feel alive? Who reminded me that I hadn't died with Grammie? That life was more than just a shitty job at a bar and forgotten dreams?

I brushed past him and turned the knob of his bedroom door. We stepped into his room and Colt flipped on the light.

A naked woman rested in the middle of Colt's bed, legs spread, all on display, her hand trailing down her body. I wondered if it was the same woman I'd overheard in the hallway.

"Colt," she purred. "I've been waiting for you." Her glassy eyes darted to me. "Wanna join us?"

I was about to bolt, but Colt's grip on my arm stopped me. "Get out," he snapped at her.

She closed her legs and managed to sit up, shiny brown locks trailing over a breast. She stood, not caring that she was nude. The woman bent over and shimmied into her tight skirt and low-cut tank. Sauntering past us in a wave of perfume, she gave Colt a lingering look before leaving. But the ghost of her presence remained.

"Let go of my arm," I breathed.

He paused a moment and then released me.

"So that's what you meant when you said these parties get wild?" I asked.

"Yeah."

"Were you planning to—with her, I mean?"

"Seriously," he barked. "I just got done telling you you're all I want. You really think I had a backup plan in mind if you told me no?"

Colt took a step toward me so he could reach out and haul my body to his. I felt how much he wanted me, and all my fears of inadequacy faded.

"I'm not going to be one of those women," I said slowly.

"What are you talking about?"

"I won't turn a blind eye when her man fucks around. I won't have it, Colt."

His smile was slow. "All right, babe. No fucking around. Promise."

"And I'm not sleeping on those sheets."

Colt leaned down to kiss me. "There's a clean set in the bottom dresser drawer." His hands dropped, and he took a step toward the door.

"Where are you going?"

He looked back at me, his eyes glittering. "To have words."

I somehow managed to change the sheets even with my bum wrist and then went into Colt's private bathroom to freshen up. I finger brushed my teeth and gargled with mouthwash. An hour passed and Colt still hadn't returned. I got up off the bed and went to a dresser drawer to find one of his T-shirts to sleep in. I flipped on a bedside lamp and then turned out the main light. The sounds of the party were muted, but every now and then I could hear someone laugh.

I fell asleep, my face pressed into Colt's pillow. Sometime in the middle of the night, I felt him slide into bed next to me. He wrapped his arm around me and pulled me against him. I turned my head and his lips captured mine. His tongue swept inside my mouth. I sighed, loving the hard feel of him at my back.

He brushed the hair off my neck and pressed a kiss to my nape before hugging me tighter.

Morning light filtered through the small window of the clubhouse bedroom. I was nestled against Colt, his large hand cupping my breast.

Warm lips grazed my collarbone that peeked out from Colt's T-shirt. "Mornin'," he whispered. His brown eyes were dark and clear, his stubble thick.

I rolled over so I could face him. There was something intimate about this morning. Maybe because we cleared the air last night and some of my concerns had been addressed. I didn't know how any of this was going to go, but Colt had promised me fidelity.

"I don't remember you coming to bed."

"I was only gone an hour and a half," he said in amusement. "You couldn't even stay awake long enough to wait for me."

"Adrenaline dump. I was wiped. What were you doing?" I asked.

"I was getting Bianca out of the clubhouse. And then I made an announcement that my room is now off limits. And I got pulled into club shit and had a few beers with the guys."

My arms enveloped his neck and I slipped my leg between his, feeling his erection against me.

His hands wormed their way into the front of my underwear so he could stroke bare skin. "I like you in my shirt."

Colt's fingers splayed across my flesh, igniting my desire. I rolled into him, forcing him onto his back. He hauled me on top of him so I could straddle his waist. His chest was uncovered, and my eyes greedily drank in the artwork on him.

"You're beautiful," I said softly. I leaned down to press my lips against his left pectoral, my mouth covering the two sets of numbers over his heart.

I had a guess for what they meant—the dates of his parents' deaths.

"I need to see you," he whispered, his hands grabbing the bottom of the T-shirt and slowly pulling it up over my head.

I sat astride him, topless, in the morning sunlight. His brown eyes were hooded with desire and his hands reached out to caress my aching breasts.

"Christ," he muttered, his fingers twisting my nipples into hard points. "I knew once I saw these I'd be done for."

I laughed softly. "Are you a breast man? Or an ass man?"

One hand slid away from my breast to press against the small of my back while the other gently grabbed my hair to tug me toward his mouth.

"I'm a *you* man." His lips took mine in a ravenous kiss. Our tongues fought, inflaming my desire. I took a deep breath and grew dizzy from the scent of him. Warm skin, sensual eyes, his body primed and ready to take mine.

God, I wanted him.

I cradled him between the juncture of my thighs as I gently ground against him.

He tore his mouth from mine, his teeth sinking into the skin of my neck.

"Closer. Lean over me."

I scooted up his body so that my breasts were level with his mouth. His velvet tongue stroked my nipple before taking it with his lips. Liquid heat singed my core. The throbbing between my thighs made me spread my legs, wanting more friction, wanting more of Colt.

"Bet you're like hot, wet silk." His eyes were on me. "Should I find out?"

I nodded eagerly.

His hand pushed aside my panties to cup the heat of

me. He teased my folds and then slid one huge finger inside my body.

I couldn't stop the shudder.

"Hot as fuck," he growled.

"Give me another finger," I commanded.

He grinned. Colt slipped in another finger and curled them both ever so slightly, hitting that spot inside me that was so elusive, it had me clenching him hard.

"Damn, woman," he muttered. "I can't wait to feel you come."

His free hand settled on my hip and urged me to use him for my pleasure. I rode his fingers, tightening around him, mindless of anything but the feel of him between my legs.

It was good, but it wasn't what I wanted.

"Colt," I begged. "I need more."

"Not yet. Come for me this way, darlin'. I know you're close."

"Kiss me," I moaned.

"No. I want your eyes on me when you come. I want to see you."

My skin was glazed with pleasure and it felt like it was the only thing holding me together.

"Feel me, Mia," he whispered.

His fingers, combined with the use of my given name, sent me over the edge. I tightened around him and let out a strangled cry.

I shivered and shook, feeling him deep inside me, gripping him. Colt waited to slide his fingers out until my aftershocks faded.

I rolled off him and collapsed onto my side of the bed and closed my eyes.

"Babe?"

"Just, give me a minute," I muttered.

He let out a low chuckle. "You wanna get out of here? Get breakfast?"

My eyes flipped open. "How can you think about food at a time like this?"

His smile was infectious and light-hearted. "Believe me, this is all I'll be thinking about through breakfast."

"Don't you want—well, are we really done?"

Colt maneuvered his arm underneath my body and cradled me into his side. "There's no rush."

"Rush? Who's talking about rushing? I'm just ready for more of you."

"Are you now?" he murmured, his head turning so his lips could graze my ear.

I slithered my hand beneath the covers, brushing his thigh before snaking up the side of his boxers to grasp him.

"Jesus," Colt murmured when I squeezed and stroked my finger across his tip.

"I want to see you."

"God, I'm begging you to wait."

I looked at him in confusion. "Why?"

"Because when you touch me, I'm gonna want to touch you back, and then we'll never leave this room."

My grin was wide and full of arrogance. "I fail to see that as a problem."

"I want you in my bed. My bed at *my* house. I wanna walk to the kitchen naked. I wanna shower with you and take you against the wall. I don't need my brothers hearing me screaming your name."

Colt's fingers plowed through my tangled hair as he brought his mouth to mine. It was over far too soon and he released me. He sat up to swing his legs over the side of the bed.

"Spare toothbrush in the drawer," he said.

I shot him a grin as I rose and went to the bathroom.

After washing up, I slipped on my dress. I took one last look in the mirror, pulled back my hair into a ponytail, and went into the bedroom. Colt was already dressed, and I watched him reach for his Glock on the nightstand and put it in his vest.

"Ready?" he asked.

I nodded. He opened the bedroom door, took my hand, and we walked through the clubhouse. The party had clearly moved indoors some time during the night. Empty beer bottles littered the floors and tables. Not to mention the naked bodies, including Boxer who had two busty, bare women in his arms. I lifted a hand to my eyes to shield my view and heard Colt chuckle.

"I have to open the gate," he said when we got out onto the porch. "Prospects usually do it, but they were allowed in to the party last night, so they're all still passed out." He reached into his pocket to grab his truck keys and tossed them to me. "Get the engine going, yeah?"

I nodded and headed for his truck while he went to the gate. I unlocked the vehicle and was about to climb into the driver's side, but I stopped to watch Colt. He was crouched over something I couldn't see.

Out of sheer curiosity, I walked through the open gate toward him. When he heard my steps on the gravel, he turned and looked at me over his shoulder. "Babe, stop." He stood up quickly, but he wasn't able to conceal a pair of legs twisted at an odd angle.

"You don't want to see this," he stated, coming to stand in front of me.

"Yes, I do," I said softly. "Please?"

He paused in obvious hesitation and then Colt moved aside to reveal a naked body sprawled on the ground. The swollen and bruised face was covered in blood, matting the dark hair and scalp. Grotesque burns covered the chest.

A sound of disbelief escaped my mouth and I dropped the truck keys that were in my hand. I shook my head in denial. A faint breeze stirred, carrying the smell of blood and charred flesh toward me.

My stomach revolted, and I turned my head and retched.

Chapter 12

Richie was dead.

All that was left of him was a scorched, beaten corpse. I heaved until there was nothing left.

"Mia," I heard Colt call as I shuddered and wiped my mouth. A hand went to my back, and I jerked away.

"Don't," I said.

"Look at me," Colt commanded.

His face was stoic and unyielding. Something inside of me broke; I threw myself at him and he caught me, hauling me to him, his strong arms wrapping around me.

"I got you," he whispered against my hair. Shaking, I refused to cry. I wouldn't break down, despite the sight of my former boss's body.

"We were looking for him, babe," Colt murmured.

"You were? Why?" I asked into his chest.

"To get some answers. We wanted to know what he had gotten himself into and why Dev sent his boys to grab you in the middle of the night."

"Colt," Zip called.

I turned my head to see the Blue Angels had roused

themselves from sleep and were now standing on the porch of the clubhouse. There was no evidence in any of their postures that there had been a raging party the night before. They all looked fierce and ready for battle. I thought of the women who had spent the night. They would see Richie if they came outside.

Colt gestured with his chin. Reap and Boxer came down off the porch and went to Richie's body. "Go back inside, darlin'," Colt said, still holding onto me. "I'll be there in a bit." To Reap and Boxer he said, "This could be a trap. Get this body out of here now before the cops show up."

He let me down and I bolted for the clubhouse, wanting to forget what I'd just seen.

Women from the party had finally begun to stir. They were too hungover to peer at me with much interest as they began slithering into their microscopic clothes. There was no chatter or greetings. They grabbed their belongings and stumbled toward the exit. When the clubhouse was finally quiet, I looked around at the mess, hating the disorder. I sprung into action immediately and began to clean up.

When the living room was spotless, I tackled the kitchen. After an hour, Colt and his brothers walked into the clubhouse. They looked around the living room and into the open kitchen, their faces shifting from subdued to confused.

"It's clean in here," Reap said. "It wasn't clean when we left."

"I needed something to do," I said with a shrug.

"And now you're cooking?" Boxer asked, his face slack in amazement.

"Bacon and fried eggs. Is that okay with everyone? It's all I can really manage with my wrist."

There was a round of nods and murmurs.

Boxer looked at Colt. "If you don't officially make her your Old Lady, I call dibs."

Colt glared at him.

Boxer held up his hands. "Never mind. I don't want to get my ass pistol whipped."

The oven timer dinged and I removed the bacon. Before long, everyone had a plate and they were devouring their food.

"Have you eaten yet?" Colt asked me, his hand reaching out to push a strand of hair behind my ear.

"Just coffee. I'm not hungry."

His hand slid down my body to rest on my hip. "You're too thin as it is."

I raised an eyebrow. "Too thin? I thought men liked thin."

Colt leaned in and said, "Men like tits and ass."

"You wouldn't be trying to distract me from the Richie thing, would you?"

"Is it working?"

I picked up my cup of coffee and didn't answer. I didn't want to know what they'd done with him or how they were handling it.

His brown gaze was steady. "Let's go for a drive."

Thanks were called out as Colt and I left. I stepped out into the sunshine. I looked around, expecting to find danger at my back, but there was nothing except the club-house on a stretch of wide-open land.

Colt opened the passenger door of his truck for me and I scrambled inside. He shut the door and then went around to the driver's side. He started the engine and then we were driving through the open gate, past the guarding prospects who were now awake and on duty.

"Give it to me straight, Colt," I said, looking out the window.

"Sure you can handle it?"

"No."

He was quiet and then, "You saw the burns on Richie's chest, yeah? It was the Iron Horsemen logo."

A surge of bile swam in my belly. "He was tortured—before they killed him?"

"Yes," he said with a sigh. "And they dumped him on Blue Angel territory. It's a message for us...and for you."

"So they know, then? Dev knows I came to you?"

"He knows," he said. "Your truck has been parked at the Blue Angels garage for the past week."

"You lied to me this whole time? You told me it was still at my house..."

"Yes."

"Why?"

"Because I knew you'd want to leave town the moment you got your truck back."

"Damn right."

Colt's face was grim. "Why is Dev after you even though you know nothing about what Richie was up to? Any way you cut it, Dev thinks you're involved."

I cleared my throat. "It might be more than that..."

When I paused, Colt said, "Go on."

"He made no secret about wanting me in his bed."

His jaw clenched. "Not shocked by that at all, but I don't think Dev would do this for that reason. There's more to it. I'm telling you, he thinks Richie clued you in."

"I overheard them talking," I said slowly, remembering the night I'd first met Dev. "Dev asked Richie if I knew anything about their arrangement, and Richie said no. They were talking business, something about a shipment. Richie disappeared for a few nights and then resurfaced and asked me to take him to the bus depot."

"Ah, fuck. You definitely can't leave town now. Not until all this shit is sorted. He'll just come after you."

"You had my truck this whole time," I murmured. "I could've gotten out. I could've started a new life."

"Tell yourself that if you want," he rumbled. "But you don't know Dev like I know Dev."

"You *know* Dev?"

"Yeah." He paused, like he wanted to say more.

"Go on. You can tell me."

He shot me a look of dark amusement. "You're already mad at me. Like I want to give you more ammo?"

"I'm not mad," I said slowly.

"Liar."

"Fine. I'm mad. You could've helped me get out of town as soon as you got my truck. Why didn't you?"

"Dev would've found you. Just like he found Richie, but this is deeper than you running from Dev. The Iron Horsemen came for you in the middle of the night. When you told me that, I realized something's been going on in my own backyard. I'm gonna find out what it is."

I looked out the window to get away from his intense stare. "You still didn't tell me about you knowing Dev."

"We've had sit downs in the past. Hashing out territory disputes, that sort of thing. But we avoid each other. Our clubs don't get involved in each other's shit. Until you."

"Until me? Why?"

He was silent for a long moment, long enough for us to drive into a restaurant parking lot.

Colt looked at me, his hands resting on the steering wheel. "Because you made it personal."

"Am I supposed to be flattered?"

"Take it however you want. The Blue Angels and the Iron Horsemen weren't enemies. Not until now. But if Richie's ass isn't enough and they come after you…then they'll start a war. I told you I'd keep you safe, and I meant it."

"Even if that means never letting me go?"

His gaze softened. "Yeah, darlin'. Even if that means never letting you go."

When I turned away from him, his hand gently reached out to grasp my chin and forced my gaze to his.

"If you really wanted to leave Waco, you would've demanded it. You would've kicked and screamed, you would've begged. You would've offered to trade in your piece of shit truck for a fucking Honda—something you can drive with a busted wrist. But you didn't, did you? You put up the bare minimum fight. You know why?"

Mutely, I shook my head.

He leaned forward and brushed his lips against mine. "Because you don't really want to run. And I make you feel something. Just like you make me feel something. So blame me if you want, but I know the truth. I know you want to stay. I know you want a home."

His eyes bored into mine, daring me to dispute his statement. But the truth was, Colt saw past my words, past my weak arguments, and deep down he knew what I really needed.

He was giving me a way out. He'd shoulder the burden and say he'd made the choice for me.

But I was done hiding from life.

I was done living inside a box that constrained me and held nothing but misery. I reached out to stroke his cheek. He needed a shave. Colt always needed a shave.

"Why are we stopping here?" I asked.

He smiled as he turned his head to kiss my palm. "Best Mexican food in the city."

"I'm not hungry."

"Best margaritas in the city too. Trust me, you'll need tequila for this conversation."

It was just past noon and all I'd had was coffee.

Coffee and fear.

The adrenaline dump and stress had drained me, and it took all of my willpower to climb out of Colt's truck. It felt safe there, and I knew the moment we sat down at the restaurant Colt wasn't going to hold anything back.

He took my hand and led me inside. I salivated immediately at the smell of tortillas and sizzling meat. A wave of hunger hit me hard and I wondered how I could possibly want to eat after what I'd just seen.

We followed the hostess to a booth and Colt took the seat across from me. "I'll have a Dos Equis," he said with a smile, refusing the menu from the waitress. "She'll have a margarita on the rocks with salt and the cheese enchiladas."

I glared at him, but didn't protest.

The cute, curvy waitress eyed Colt one last time before disappearing. Maybe at another time I would've felt a spark of jealousy, but I'd had his fingers inside of me not even two hours ago. Not to mention Colt didn't even spare her a glance.

It was the little things, I realized, that proved someone wasn't full of shit. Colt told me I didn't need to worry about him and other women, and I believed him. Not just because he'd told me to trust him, but because of that small action. It was like he didn't even see her.

A few minutes later, the waitress returned with our drinks and a bowl of chips and salsa. I took a sip of the margarita. It was the perfect blend of tart and sweet and I couldn't taste the tequila.

"Wow, yeah, this is dangerous," I said to him.

"Yup."

I set it aside and took a chip but didn't eat it.

A glimpse of Richie's burned corpse flashed before my eyes. "I don't understand something," I began.

He took a sip from his beer and waited for me to continue.

"Why did you come to Dive Bar with Zip that night? I've never seen bikers at Dive Bar. Did you have a hunch that Richie was into shady shit? Were you there to see if Dev showed up?"

"No. Like I said before: it was coincidence. You think I'd be beating the fuck out of some guy in the alley if I was there for Dev?"

"What do you think Richie got involved in?" I asked.

"Meth."

"Why do you think it's meth?"

"Look, biker clubs don't get donations from church ladies and PTA moms. But they have to make money. That's how their members take care of their families and the clubs keep operating. It's complicated, but meth can be made in a homemade lab. You don't need land in Columbia to grow crops or the cartels in Mexico to traffic shit from other countries through South America for you, and meth is highly addictive, so it's an obvious thing for clubs to get involved in. You cook enough of that shit up in a lab with the muscle to protect it, and once it hits the street it's an almost immediate return of pallets of cold, hard cash."

I quickly downed the rest of my margarita, feeling my head grow buzzy. But it also gave me courage to ask him point blank, "What do the Blue Angels do for money?"

He stared at me long and hard. "I can't tell you that. It's for your own protection."

"From the law, you mean?" I asked.

He nodded. "We don't involve our women in our business. If cops get wind of something and question our women, they don't know shit. None of them, and I mean that. Not one. It's as much for their protection as it is ours. But make no mistake, the Blue Angels don't live within the confines of the law."

My breath hitched. I knew they were criminals—I knew I was falling for a criminal, but for Colt to admit it outright had me spinning.

The waitress sailed by with my steaming plate of enchiladas. Despite what we were discussing, my stomach rumbled in anticipation. She set the plate down in front of me.

"Another marg?" she asked me.

I shook my head.

"Another beer, sugar?" she asked Colt.

His eyes remained on me when he replied, "I'm fine, thanks."

She wasn't able to hold in her remorseful sigh. "Enjoy." She left again, leaving us alone.

I picked up my fork and cut into the blue corn enchiladas. They were too hot to eat, so I waited.

"What's going on in your head," Colt asked.

"I'm trying to process what you just told me."

He looked down at his hands. They were big, scarred, tatted. They'd gently cleaned my feet and brought my body to the heights of pleasure. But they were the hands of a delinquent.

"I'm president of the club, right?"

I nodded.

"I've got responsibilities. I shoulder the burdens. The choices I make—some of them are gonna weigh me down. There will be times I come to you. Times in the middle of the night when I gotta sink inside you, to get some of that light in a world of dark. I'm gonna need to turn to you in a way that a hard as fuck man turns to a woman. You won't always understand and you won't get answers. But I gotta know if it's something you think you can handle. For the long haul. Because I'm in this. And I want to be in this with you. Not just because Dev is on your ass and your boss showed up dead. I've wanted you since that first night at Dive Bar and if shit had been different, I would've come back and let you know."

"Why didn't you?" I asked, feeling the tequila buzz through my blood, making me heated.

"Was on a run out of town," he explained. "I got back a few hours before you showed up on my garage steps. Didn't like what I saw. Thought someone had put their hands on you."

A slight smile appeared on my lips. "I wouldn't stand for that, Colt."

"Yeah." He grinned. "I know that now. You're feisty."

"Does it ever get any easier?" I asked him.

"Does what ever get easier?"

"Knowing the people you love are in constant danger because of who you are and the life you've chosen to live?"

"I grew up this way. Grew up knowing what the Blue Angels were all about. It's different for you."

The blue corn enchiladas were finally cool enough to eat and my fork fell on them with purpose.

"Women and children are off limits," he said when I'd put away half the plate and finally had to stop for breath.

"What do you mean?"

"There's an honor code of sorts. Clubs don't go after Old Ladies or kids. The innocents stay innocent. That's how we avoid total war between clubs. Shit can get settled between men, but no one fucks with family."

"So theoretically, if I became your Old Lady, I'd be off limits?"

"Yup. Becoming an Old Lady is serious shit, Mia. To the brothers, it's more binding than marriage. Marriage is a piece of paper. Marriage is an institution created by society that can be dissolved. Becoming an Old Lady is a way of life, so you gotta make sure you're ready for it before you commit."

I couldn't eat another bite. I'd left a quarter of the enchiladas on the plate, which I pushed away. The moment I signaled I was done, Colt took my fork and ate the rest of my food.

The waitress came by and dropped off the check before flouncing back to the bar where she not so secretly watched Colt. He reached for his wallet and took out a few crisp bills.

It made me wonder if the money had come from his garage or from his criminal enterprises.

Shelly had warned me to stay away from motorcycle clubs. Colt might've been a criminal, but what did that say about me—the woman who was deciding whether or not to be with him?

I'd directly benefit from Colt's business. I'd be taken care of financially, I wouldn't have to worry about little luxuries, and I knew he wanted to pay for my last semester of college.

Colt could protect me, take care of me.

"Shoulda ordered you another margarita," he muttered. "I can hear you thinking."

"You can't hear a person think," I said with a dry laugh.

"All your thoughts are flashing across your face like a movie reel. I know what you're thinking."

"What am I thinking right this moment?" I taunted.

"You're thinking about how much you want me inside you."

My eyes widened.

He grinned wickedly. "Have you ever been on a motor-cycle?" he asked, changing the subject.

"No."

"When your wrist is healed, I'm gonna get you on the back of my bike. There's nothing like it, feels like you're flying. Feels like freedom. I'll take you to one of my favorite places. A tiny little town off the Oregon coast. We'll rent side-by-sides and drive down to the beach and then watch the sunset."

He took my hand that rested on the table and traced my ring finger. "I'll take you back to a bed and breakfast I know. It's a place that if you leave the windows open, you can smell the mist from the ocean. I'll slide into you, Mia, and stay there until dawn."

I swallowed at the shot of desire between my thighs.

"You're not fighting fair," I murmured.

"Who said anything about fair? You want me, yeah?"

"Yeah. I want you," I admitted. "What about marriage?"

"What about marriage?"

"You called it an institution. A piece of paper."

"It is," he insisted. "But I'd still marry you. If you become my Old Lady you get the protection of my club. Then you become my wife and you've got the protection of my last name and the fact that you can't legally be forced to testify against your husband in court if it ever comes to that."

Practical as well as decisive. That was Colt. When he knew what he wanted, he went after it. But he thought things through. Wasn't going to get caught up in emotion and let it rule him.

I was suddenly exhausted. It was like I'd been constantly swimming upstream, trying to get away from

Colt and all that he made me feel. Trying to get away from Dev and the blanket of terror he'd thrown over my life.

I hadn't even slept with Colt yet. Only this morning had things escalated to a physical level—and the man had been right. Not arrogant, just right. When I was in his bed, I wanted to stay there and I hadn't even had him the way I wanted him.

"Let's get out of here," he rasped.

We got back to Colt's house and it felt like I'd come home. Pairs of my shoes were by the door, haphazardly strewn like I'd kicked them off in haste.

My brain went into overdrive. There was a problem with overthinking just like there was a problem with following emotions. Unfortunately that meant I lived in a weird state of limbo.

Colt talked about marriage like it was nothing. He wasn't gun shy. We hadn't even slept together yet and he was tossing the word around like it was just a formality, which I guess for men in his world, it was.

He'd never said he loved me. But he was ready to make me his Old Lady.

"I have to make some calls," Colt said, setting down his keys on the table in the front hallway. I placed my keys and phone next to his.

"Will you Saran-wrap my cast? I want to shower."

We went into the kitchen and Colt pulled out the plastic wrap and a rubber band. He leaned down to peck me on the lips. "Shower in my bathroom."

"Why?"

"Because it's the good bathroom. Trust me."

After he wrapped my cast, I left him to his phone calls

and headed upstairs. I gathered my toiletries and a clean towel and took them into Colt's bedroom. The furniture was solid oak, the walls a soft dove gray. The bed was huge, big enough for Colt—and me. I shivered in anticipation. I knew what would happen when we finally got together. It would be explosive and dynamic. It would make me feel everything that I'd been missing from my life.

It would bind me to him in a way I'd never been bound to another person. It would make me emotionally vulnerable, something I hadn't allowed myself since Grammie's death.

The bathroom had a long white counter with a sink, and there was a separate glass shower from a Jacuzzi tub. I envisioned us in that tub, surrounded by candles and bubbles.

I turned on the water in the shower, waiting for it to heat. It steamed up quickly and the water pressure was strong. I let it rain down on me, closing my eyes and turning my face into it. Halfway through washing my hair, I heard a quick knock on the door, followed by the sound of it opening.

"How's it going in there?" he asked.

"Going," I replied.

"Was I right? About my bathroom being better than the guest one?"

"Maybe. I thought you had calls to make," I replied.

"I finished them."

He waited.

I knew what he was waiting for.

"You're killing me here."

I inhaled a shaky breath. "You're welcome to join me."

I heard the thump of his boots and didn't bother holding back a smile. A moment later, there was a cold draft of air as Colt stepped inside behind me. I turned around so I could look at him. Ink covered his tan arms, but I hardly noticed the work as my eyes drifted lower, taking in his size and breadth. Though we'd been in bed just this morning and things had happened between us, seeing him in all his nude glory was different.

He could see me, too.

All the teasing and flirting was absent. The desire that had been on a simmer was now cranked up to a rolling boil.

But before I could say anything, Colt said, "Turn around."

I did as he commanded. His hand skated up my side and the curve of my waist until he got to my neck. He brushed my wet hair off my back and trailed a finger across my shoulder blades and down my spine.

I shivered.

A few moments later, I felt him spread bubbles along my skin, working slowly and gently as he cleaned me. I wanted to moan, but I bit my lip to stifle it.

"Selfish," he muttered.

"Who? Me?"

"Me. Shoulda let you go. Shoulda gotten you out."

"Richie tried to disappear," I reminded him. "Look what happened to him."

"Might've been different if he'd had the club to help him out."

"None of that matters now."

His hands moved from my back down, down, down. He rubbed circles on my thighs, his touch soothing.

"You don't owe me anything, darlin'. You know that, right?"

I looked at him over my shoulder. His gaze was dark, but I caught the tiniest measure of vulnerability. It made my lip wobble with emotion as I thought of all that Colt had gone through alone.

"I needed you," I said softly. "I just didn't know I needed you."

He sighed, taking a step closer to me and wrapping me in his arms. "Babe," was all he said.

One day, Colt would need me too. He'd come to me, needing my touch, needing the embrace of a woman to wash away the heaviness that came with being president of a motorcycle club.

"She told me," I admitted. "Joni."

"What did she tell you?" he asked, brushing his lips across my shoulder.

"She told me you were worth it. That if I wanted to be with you, you'd never make me regret it."

"When you need a rock, I can be that for you. You won't believe me until something happens and you're forced to lean on me. Richie's death doesn't count. He wasn't someone you loved."

"I don't think I'd survive losing someone else I loved," I murmured. "I've lost enough."

"Yeah, darlin'. We both have." He paused. "But life happens. And you get through it with family."

I turned in his arms and pressed my lips to his left pectoral with the dates of his parents' deaths. He'd never told me that's what they were for, to honor and remember them, but he didn't have to say it.

We understood each other without words and that was something that couldn't be replicated or replaced.

I ran my hands up his wet, naked body, enjoying the droplets of water on his honey colored skin.

"You're so beautiful," I whispered, reaching for the soap to lather him with bubbles.

"I've got scars. You're the one who's beautiful."

My fingers traced one long, thin mark that marred his shoulder. "We've all got scars, Colt. It's just…some of them aren't visible."

"You're killing me. You know that, right?" His hands went to my hair and gently tugged my head back so I was forced to look at him. His lips took mine in a hot and hungry kiss that left me breathless. "I need you. I need to be inside of you. I can't wait any longer."

I gently pushed him back under the spray so that he could rinse off while I stepped out of the shower and quickly dried off.

Colt shut off the water and snatched a towel from the hanging rod.

My skin prickled with goosebumps of anticipation.

It was all happening so fast with Colt, and yet it seemed inevitable.

I strode into the bedroom with Colt not far behind me. His damp skin glistened as his hungry gaze raked over me.

"Gonna lose the towel?"

Arching an eyebrow, a grin spread across my face. "You first."

He dropped his towel and my gaze dropped with it. Colt was perfectly made, like a marble statue carved by Michelangelo himself.

And he was mine.

My hands went to my towel and I unfastened it, letting it fall to the floor.

Colt's stare was hot as he sauntered toward me. He placed his hands on my arms, taking us down onto the bed. My back fell against the comforter with Colt looming over me. His mouth descended to take my lips in a ravenous kiss and his hands wove their way through my wet hair.

He kissed my mouth and then my neck before moving

down to my breasts. His hands caressed and teased my nipples, making them ache, making me want him to lavish me with his mouth.

But he didn't stop to worship them; he dotted kisses down my flat stomach and belly button. And then he looked up with an arrogant smile, and continued to kiss his way downward.

He spread my legs and just stared for a moment. It made me uncomfortable and I tried to close my thighs, but Colt's hands prevented me.

"Stop," he said softly. His eyes lifted to meet mine. "Why are you embarrassed?"

"You're hanging out down there. It's…weird."

He chuckled. "This is the prettiest thing I've ever seen. I gotta take a minute to enjoy it."

I smiled at him. "You're not at all how I thought you'd be."

He arched a brow. "How'd you think I'd be?"

"I don't know. Rougher. Unable to wait."

His fingers inched across my skin to tease my folds. "Told you when I had you in my bed, I'd take my time. And that's what I'm doing."

Colt's tongue slid across my aching flesh making me shudder and spread my legs wider.

He chuckled against the juncture of my thighs and continued his ministrations. He held nothing back, licking and sucking with abandon. Like a starving animal that had been lying in wait to feast.

Colt was relentless, unyielding. He gripped my hips to keep me stationary while his tongue devoured my essence.

"I knew you'd be sweet," he murmured. "I know you're close. I wanna hear you moan."

He gently sucked me into his mouth and when my back bowed toward the ceiling, I came with a cry.

As I shuddered and shivered, Colt slid up my body, taking my lips with his. I tasted myself as he kissed me, and it only made me want him more.

He reached over to the bedside table and fiddled with the drawer. In a few quick motions, Colt was sheathed and his hand was on my knee, bending it so that it rested against the bed.

Colt poised at my entrance, looming over me. Eyes on mine, he slid into my body.

Even though I was slick with want, it still took a moment for me to adjust to him. And then I felt him everywhere. My nerves were on fire.

Colt's gaze was bright and resolute. "Wrap your legs around me," he commanded.

He skated his hand underneath me, bringing me closer to him.

"Oh God," I moaned as another spark danced between my legs.

Colt's thrusts were gentle at first, but then it was nothing but heat and chaos. I felt him in places I didn't know I had. The pressure and intensity was so overwhelming that my eyes rolled back into my head.

He buried his face in the crook of my neck, increasing his pace. Thoughtful desire gave way to mindless thrusting and our bodies intertwined like we were animals in heat. He growled low in my ear and when I looked down to see where our bodies connected, I saw him sliding in and out of me.

"I'm close," he muttered.

I bucked against him and with his pelvis perfectly angled I detonated again, clenching around him hard.

With one final thrust, Colt shouted. He shuddered, his release pumping out of him.

He collapsed on top of me, our breathing ragged, our hearts ready to gallop out of our chests.

I felt like I'd been broken apart, and was only now beginning to piece myself back together.

Colt lifted his head to stare down at me. His eyes were glazed and his skin was flushed. He pressed his lips to mine and didn't say anything as he gently pulled out.

I noticed the loss of him immediately, wincing at the tenderness between my legs.

I'd been ridden hard and fast, but damn if I didn't feel like a woman.

He went into the bathroom. I heard the sound of him washing his hands and then he came back to bed. Colt lay down, his gaze languid and drowsy, his hand gently tracing the contour of my hip.

"Did I hurt you?" he asked.

I shook my head, my tangled hair brushing across my shoulders. I leaned over and skimmed my lips over his and then cuddled against his chest.

We were content to stay there for a moment, but then I finally rolled over to get out of bed.

"Where do you think you're going?" he asked with a grin.

"To clean up. And then I plan on making some food."

"You're ready to eat again? After those enchiladas?"

"I didn't eat them all," I reminded him.

"Yeah, good point. What are you making?"

"I wanted to make pancakes, but I don't know if I can whisk with my left hand."

"I'll whisk them for you."

"Yeah?"

He nodded.

I went to one of his dresser drawers, rooting around for

a T-shirt. I found one and slid it on before heading to the bathroom.

"I like you in my shirt, darlin'," he said gently.

I smiled as I closed the door.

~

"You've been holding out on me," Colt said as he pushed away his empty plate.

I grinned. "I'm a decent cook, but I have two specialties: guacamole and pancakes."

I finished off the last bite of my own short stack and then got up from the kitchen table to take the plates to the sink.

"Why are those your specialties?" Colt asked.

"When Grammie got sick, she lost her appetite. Pancakes and guacamole were the only things she could stomach. So I got really good at making them."

While I loaded the dishwasher, Colt put away the maple syrup and then wiped down the kitchen table. I'd noticed he was someone who preferred his space tidy. He didn't have clutter or a stack of mail by the door or magazines on the coffee table.

If I hadn't seen the photos on the wall, I would've thought he was renting the house.

"You any good at laundry? Or cleaning the house?" Colt asked, reaching into the refrigerator and pulling out two beers. He popped the tops with a bottle opener from the silverware drawer and handed me one.

"What are you really asking me, Colt?" I demanded.

"Nothin'. Just trying to figure out if I should give my housekeeper a raise." He winked. "Since there are two of us living here now."

"You have a housekeeper?"

"Damn right I do."

"My, my, aren't we spoiled?"

"I hate all that shit. Better off paying someone to handle it for me—and now you. I like cooking, but that's because I grill mostly. But it's nice coming home to a stocked refrigerator and clean sheets."

"Yeah, I could see how you'd get used to that," I agreed with a grin. "But I'd like to address something you just said."

"Can you do it on the porch?"

I waved at him to lead the way. He opened the back door to the patio and we sat out in the spring afternoon. It wasn't even close to sunset yet, but I doubted I'd be awake for it. I was exhausted; having run the gauntlet of emotions, not to mention the intimacy we'd shared earlier had my eyes drooping.

"What is it you wanna talk about?" He sat down on one of the patio furniture chairs and patted his leg.

I perched on his thigh, feeling like we were a couple that had known each other a lot longer than ten days.

Ten days? How had it only been ten days?

"You said *now that we both live here*."

"Yeah? So?"

"Colt, I don't live with you."

"You do right now, don't you?"

"Well, yeah, because of what's going on. But what happens when all that's over."

"You still planning on getting out of dodge? Leaving town?" He took a sip from his beer, his brown eyes on me.

My gaze fell to the column of his throat and then lower to his bare chest. He was wearing a pair of jeans and no shirt, so his ink was on full display. I was riveted by his artwork. The massive Blue Angels logo on the underside of his left forearm, the modest Scottish flag underneath the dates of his parents' deaths.

"No, I'm not leaving town," I said slowly. "But I do plan on moving back into my house when the Iron Horsemen are no longer on my ass."

His hand stole underneath the shirt I was wearing to rest on the small of my back. "You scared of tattoos?"

"Why are you changing the subject?"

"Don't like the idea of you moving out of my place, that's all. So, tattoos?"

"Never really thought they were for me." I shook my head. "Does anyone call you James?"

"Never," he said. "How'd you know my given name anyway?"

I grinned. "Joni told me. What about Jamie? Anyone call you that?"

He snorted. "Fuck no."

"What's wrong with the nickname Jamie? I think it's cute."

"Cute enough to get it inked on you?" His smile was devilish and just a tad hopeful.

It was my turn to snort. "Yeah, right. Like I'd let you brand me."

"I'd get your name on me."

"But that's permanent!"

"Kinda the whole point."

I shook my head. "You're insane."

He laughed.

"I wonder if I'll ever get used to your way of life."

Colt leaned over and set his bottle of beer down before standing, lifting me in his arms and carrying me inside.

"What are you doing?" I asked as he made his way to the stairs.

"Distracting you from thinking so much," he said with a rueful grin.

We entered his bedroom, and he placed me in the center of his bed. The next thing I knew, I had a large biker's body covering mine, and for the next few hours he found a way to pleasurably distract me from all my thoughts.

Chapter 13

A scream tore through my throat as the hazy nightmare held me hostage. Hands gripped my arms and I instantly tried to fight them off, but my limbs felt like they'd been filled with sand.

"No," I whispered. "Please."

"Mia!" the voice called through the mist. "Mia, darlin', wake up."

I forced my eyes open. Warm lamplight spilled across Colt's clover-honey colored skin.

It took my body a moment to realize I was safe. I collapsed against the pillows as my surroundings came into focus.

His eyes rested on me, searching my face for answers. "What did you dream about?"

"I don't know," I admitted slowly. "It was one of those dreams where I couldn't see, but knew I was terrified."

"Yeah, I know you were terrified," he rumbled. "You screamed in your sleep."

"I did?"

He nodded. Colt settled back down and pulled me into

his side. I lay my head against his chest and breathed him in, enjoying the comfort of him.

"Think you can go back to sleep?"

"I don't know, I'm still pretty shaken." My fingers swirled across his chest and then began to inch lower underneath the covers to find Colt hard.

I loved that he slept in the nude.

He groaned. Turning his head, his lips sought mine. His kiss melted my body until I was nothing but want. Colt rolled me onto my back, his hands easing down my underwear. His fingers found me wet and ready.

Colt reached for the condom on the bedside table. Soon, his large hands were back on me, driving me wild. His lips seized mine in a voracious kiss.

I moaned against him when his fingers delved between my legs.

"Christ, woman," he murmured. His hand skimmed along my leg to gently push it open. And then he was inside me in one swift motion.

I arched against him, clawing his back with my nails, scoring his skin, branding him on the outside, knowing he was branding me on the inside.

He tilted his hips and hit the spot that made me shake. Colt thrust and thrust, relentless, demanding of my pleasure. I came with a hoarse cry, clutching him to me, not caring that my injured wrist twinged.

Burying his face in the side of my neck, Colt continued to piston his body into mine, and a few strokes later he came with his own guttural shout.

Our bodies stilled. The AC kicked on, cooling our heated skin. Colt shifted to slide out of me and I shivered and tightened around him, going up in flames all over again.

With a light chuckle, he pressed a kiss to my forehead

and then my mouth. He went into the bathroom to take care of the condom and when he came back to bed, I crawled out.

"Where do you think you're going?" he asked, his voice amused, sleepy.

"To clean up," I said, leaning over and pecking his lips. "Be just a few minutes."

After tending to the tender spot between my legs, I washed my hands and then went back to the bedroom.

Colt's heavy breathing told me he'd conked out. Smiling, I climbed in bed next to him and fell into a dreamless sleep.

I tried to roll over, but there was a heavy arm thrown across my waist and a warm, hard chest at my back. Sleepily, I wiggled up against him. Colt pulled me closer, his lips grazing the back of my neck.

I heard the crinkle of a foil wrapper and then Colt's hand slid between my thighs, stroking me into a fevered pitch of desire. He moved my leg and then he was sliding into me from behind.

"Oh God," I whispered.

Colt rocked his hips against me while his hand continued to play and tease the bundle of nerves just waiting to explode. It didn't take long—when he kissed the sensitive spot below my ear and pressed the heel of his hand against my cleft, I broke apart around him.

He gripped my hip and rode out his own storm. Instead of pulling out immediately, he dragged me even closer so that my shoulders were against his chest.

"Well," I murmured. "I've never been woken up that way before."

His hand cupped my breast, gently teasing my nipple. "You approve, yeah?"

"Yeah," I said with a laugh.

"I'm gonna get the coffee going." His hand slid up from my breast to catch my chin and gently turn it toward him. He gave me a quick kiss. "Come down when you're ready."

When I was finally alone I took a moment to stretch and luxuriate in the soft bed, wallowing in the smell of us on the sheets. Smiling, I threw back the covers and padded to the bathroom to brush my teeth.

In search of coffee and Colt, I headed downstairs to the kitchen. Without a word, he poured me a cup of coffee and doctored it the way I liked.

As he handed it to me, he said, "We're leaving in an hour."

"We are? Where are we going?"

"The garage."

"Why are you dragging me to the garage?" I demanded.

"You don't want to be locked up in the house, and you have this odd need to pull your own weight," he teased. "You can work for me."

"Doing what, exactly? I'm not really mechanical."

"You can work in the office. Answer phones. Computer shit. We both know it's a short term gig and its only so if anyone asks, you have a legit job. Take it for what it is."

"Really?"

"Really."

I set my cup of coffee down so I could launch myself at him. He caught me easily. I pecked his lips a few times in rapid succession. "Thank you."

His response was to squeeze my ass. "Go take a shower. I'm ready when you are."

I slid down his body and then headed up to Colt's bathroom. While I was lathering my hair, I heard the door open and the sound of his heavy boots across the tile.

"Please, God tell me you're almost done in there," he muttered.

"Nearly."

"Christ. You're wet and naked and I'm about to climb in there with you."

"I wouldn't object."

We made it out of the house two hours later.

My body felt like it was made of butter and my mind was muddled from the attention Colt had given me in the shower. He certainly kept me on my toes. One moment he was driving into me fast and hard, making me scream in pleasure. Another moment and he was sinking into me slow, making me beg for more.

I stole a glance at him. His eyes were shielded behind a pair of aviators. The strong breadth of him in his leather cut made me sigh.

He turned his head ever so slightly and grinned. "Like what you see?"

"Kinda, yeah." I smiled back. I reached over and stroked his jaw. "Do you ever shave?"

"Rarely."

"Good."

His laugh was easy and full. I was getting addicted to the sound. I liked to think I had something to do with it—after all I'd noticed a change in myself after a short time with Colt. Somehow he'd battled through my walls, dismantling them stone by stone.

I'd had relationships before—I knew the early stages were spent in bed. But it felt different with Colt. Maybe it was because of how we met. Maybe it was because of who

Colt was—a man who lived by his own rules and had grown up with two parents who'd had love at first sight.

Colt finally pulled into the bike garage parking lot. He cut the engine and engaged the parking brake.

"Ah, sweet freedom," I said with a grin. "Oh my God."

"What?"

I pointed to the green truck in the corner of the lot. "That's mine!" I got out of and ran to my truck and all but flung myself across the hood. "I've missed you!"

Colt chuckled from somewhere behind me, but I didn't care.

"Give me the keys," I demanded, looking at him, my cheek still pressed to the faded paint.

"One condition," he said, reaching into his jeans pocket. "You don't go for a joy ride and then decide to leave town."

I held up my cast wrist. "Have you forgotten how hard it will be to drive stick?"

His smile was slow. "I dunno, babe. You handled my stick well the other night."

"Oh good, I see we've entered the teasing, juvenile sexual innuendo phase of our relationship."

Colt's brown eyes rested on me, warm with amusement.

"What?"

"You admitted we're in a relationship."

I rolled my gaze heavenward as I pulled myself off the truck hood. "You gonna show me the ropes or what?"

Colt came to me and in a possessive gesture, slid his arm around my shoulder and guided me inside the office that was already open, the smell of fresh coffee permeating the air. Boxer was at the desk, his gaze glued to the screen. He typed something and then rubbed his eyes. Looking up at Colt, he grimaced. "Damn spreadsheets." He looked at me. "Morning, darlin'. How ya doin'?"

I shrugged. "Okay. I guess."

"We're here for you. Don't forget that."

"Thank you," I said, feeling my throat close up at his sincerity.

Colt walked me to the chair next to Boxer and gestured for me to take a seat. "You're going to learn the programs."

"Programs?"

"Our bookkeeping programs for the shop. Boxer will show you how to order parts, schedule appointments, stuff like that."

"Phone girl?" I asked with a smile.

"Phone girl," he repeated with a nod. "Spend a few hours learning the ropes. After you finish up, we'll head home."

Home.

With Colt.

Colt left me alone with Boxer who was looking at me with a wide, knowing grin. "Stop that," I commanded and gestured to the computer. "Show me your stuff."

"You want to see my stuff?" he asked, all flirty and scruffy and hot.

"Show me your spreadsheets," I demanded in a husky tone.

Boxer laughed. "A woman who saves me from looking at numbers all day. My kind of woman."

The programs were intuitive. Before I knew it, Boxer and I had switched chairs and I was taking the reins. Customers called and after listening to Boxer field them, he let me take the next few.

A few hours later, he stood up and stretched. "You think you can man the phones alone? I have to run out and take care of something."

"Uh, sure," I said.

"Reap is in the garage, so if you run into trouble or have questions, you can ask him."

"Okay."

Boxer left the office, the door clicking shut. I got up to stretch my legs and make myself a cup of coffee. I was just stirring in some cream when the phone rang. I retook my seat and reached for the receiver.

"Good afternoon, Charlie's Motorcycle Repair."

"Darlin'," the voice on the other end greeted.

A shiver of fear worked its way down my spine.

"Dev," I replied, my voice sounding rusty.

"You've been bad, Mia," Dev chastised.

I swallowed a gulp of scalding coffee to coat my suddenly dry throat.

"Why'd you run to the Blue Angels? Are you scared of me? Is that it?"

My heart thundered in my chest and my palms grew slick with sweat as I gripped the phone. I forced out a fake laugh. "No, you don't scare me."

"You don't want to end up like Richie, do you?"

"No." I felt faint, sick. "But I'm not involved in what-ever Richie was involved in. I swear it. I know nothing."

The other end of the phone line was silent for a moment. "If you're not involved in Richie's shit, then why did you run from me?"

"I—"

"You took him to the bus depot," he interrupted. "Tried to help him get out of town. Yeah, I know about that, babe. Which means you know more than you're letting on. You better tell me where the shipment is or I'll do to your new friends what I did to Richie. And you—you don't even want to know what I'm going to do to you."

The phone clicked off. I set the receiver down in a daze and stared at it like I expected Dev to crawl through it and attack me.

"Babe? Mia?"

I turned my head, surprised to see Boxer. He'd returned, and I hadn't even heard him.

He frowned. "You okay?"

I attempted to smile, but my lips barely moved. "Yeah." My shaky hand tipped over the cup of coffee, spilling it all over a stack of papers.

"Sorry," I muttered as I looked around for a rag to clean up.

"It's okay," Boxer said. There was a stack of napkins by the coffeemaker. He grabbed them and blotted the papers. "You sure you're okay?"

I nodded. "Did Colt say when he was coming back?" I asked, dragging my fingernail across the material of my jean shorts.

"Now," Colt said from the doorway.

Chapter 14

"I'm just gonna wait outside," Boxer said, leaving the small office. The door shut and a rush of air whooshed out of my lungs.

I found a way to stand up, but my legs gave out and if Colt hadn't been near, I would've fallen to the floor. "Mia?" Colt asked, brown eyes surveying me, his hands on my arms. "You're pale. Are you sick?"

"Dev called me just now. On the garage line. He's been keeping tabs on me."

"What did he say to you?" he asked, voice devoid of emotion.

"He knows I dropped Richie off at the bus depot." My gaze dropped to the ground. "He threatened me, Colt. Threatened you. Threatened the club. He told me…"

Colt's fingers reached out for my chin and gently pulled my gaze to his. "Told you what?"

I swallowed. "He made it sound like he was going to kill me."

He stared at me but didn't move.

"I—I'm scared, Colt,"

Before I knew it, Colt pressed me to his chest. "I've got you. Do you trust me?"

I nodded into his shirt.

"Let's go."

"Where are we going?" I asked.

"Sending a message."

"What kind of message…"

He didn't reply as he took my hand and led me out to his truck. I didn't want to be led around by him, so I dug my heels in, literally, and made Colt stop. He looked over his shoulder at me and frowned.

"Where are we going?" I asked again.

"To a tattoo parlor."

"Why?"

"You're getting inked."

"Uh, no, I'm not."

"You are," he insisted. "With my name and the Blue Angels logo on your skin, no one will fuck with you."

"You're kidding, right? You think a tattoo is going to stop Dev?"

"Mia—"

"You are out of your fucking mind! He knows we're together, Colt. He threatened you specifically. I don't care what you think—he's not going to abide by the no-women-no-children code of honor."

"Babe," he said quietly. "If Dev makes a move against you in any way, I can call up brothers in other chapters in other cities. I can't do that, I can't ask them to make this shit personal, get involved in a war that has nothing to do with their city, unless *you* become my Old Lady. Unless you get my name and my club inked on you. They gotta know that if shit gets real, they're not fighting for random club ass. Trying to protect you the only way I can, darlin'. And right now that's by getting my name on you."

Somehow I'd wound up in his arms. He lifted me up until we were nose to nose. I heard nothing except the thump of my heartbeat, the blood rushing to my ears. I wanted to cover his lips with mine, wrap my legs around him, and drown in sensation. Forget the cold terror that had taken up residence in my body since I'd heard Dev's voice on the phone. His threats had pummeled me, gotten through the layer of safety I thought I had surrounded myself with.

"I'm askin' ya," Colt said softly. "Get my name on you. I can take care of the rest."

"Prez," Zip called, shattering the moment.

I turned my head, my nose grazing Colt's cheek. Four scary bikers had stopped working and were watching our exchange. My face heated when I thought of them hearing us yell out our dirty laundry.

Colt released me and my feet touched the ground. "Truck, babe."

I climbed into the truck and shut the door. Colt and Zip had an exchange. Zip got in Colt's face and I swore Colt was about to punch Zip. Colt said something and then they both looked at me. I shrank down into the seat, wishing I was invisible.

Colt stalked toward the truck and nearly ripped the door off its hinges. He got in, slammed the door, and ground the key into the ignition. We sat for a moment in silence; he unrolled the windows to let in some of the Texas spring air.

"Getting your name on me means this is for real," I said softly.

"Yeah, I know that," he bit out.

I shook my head. "No, I mean—if I do it, it means I'm one of you. It means," I swallowed, "I'm asking for people who don't know me to put their lives on the line for a shit storm *I* triggered. I couldn't bear it if…"

"If what?"

"Seeing you get hurt. Seeing any of you get hurt."

"Hey. Look at me." When I refused, he said gruffly, "Eyes. I need to see your eyes."

I looked at him reluctantly, feeling emotion sting my throat. "You haven't had family in a long time. Families lean on each other when shit gets bad. That's what we are, honey. Family. I'm giving you my family by bringing you into the fold. This shit with Dev? It's only gonna get worse. I want to make you a legit member of my family so everyone knows they can't fuck with you. And babe? If anyone actually is stupid enough to fuck with you, I'll rain down hell."

"You've never said you loved me, Colt, and now you want me to get something permanent on my body. You don't think that's a little insane?"

"I just told you I'd rain down hell if anyone fucked with you. What the hell do you think I was talking about?" he demanded.

"This is a high functioning level of insanity," I stated. "You know that, right?"

His smile was slow. "Does that mean you love me too?"

"I was actually referring to the tattoo."

"It's still throbbing," I whined. "You totally downplayed how much it was going to hurt."

"Not gonna lie, babe," he began. "Can't wait to fuck you from behind and see my name staring back at me."

I glared at him in the bathroom mirror. His grin was

cheeky. "I'm glad *you're* feeling better about the entire situation with Dev."

"You're not feeling better?" he asked.

I shook my head.

"I think I can make you feel better."

"I don't want to have sex with you right now," I snapped.

He threw his head back and laughed. "No, I wasn't talking about sex—though I'm sure I could change your mind. I was gonna tell you that with my name on you, I feel better about you going out with Joni tonight."

"I'm surprised you're even letting me out of the house. What with all this Dev shit going on."

"You're going to a Blue Angels bar and both Acid and Cheese are going to be standing guard. Can't keep you locked up and out of sight anymore. Sends the wrong kind of message, yeah?"

He leaned down and plopped a kiss onto the top of my head. "Got something else to show you." Colt took my hand and led me out of the bathroom into the bedroom.

"It'll be a little while yet before you can show off your tattoo. So I got you something else to wear."

He went into his closet and came out a moment later holding up a leather cut—small, feminine, with a patch that read Blue Angels on the right breast pocket. Property of Colt was on the back.

"Not really my style," I said, touching the leather. It was soft and new and made my head spin with gravitas.

"Thought you might say that," he said with a chuckle and then placed it on the bed. "There's a box in the closet. Why don't you open it yourself?"

I frowned. "Box? What box?"

He gestured with his chin and I immediately scampered to the walk-in closet. In the center of the floor was a pink wrapped box with curled silver ribbons. I reached for it and brought it back into the bedroom.

"What did you do?" I asked.

"Just open it." He leaned against the doorway of the room and waited.

I tore into the box and brushed aside the tissue paper to reveal the sexiest, most bad ass ankle boots I'd ever seen. Black leather with metallic silver spikes and studs all over. Including the heel.

"Holy shit," I breathed when I felt inside the lining.

"Like 'em?" he asked with a knowing grin.

"I *love* them," I corrected.

"What about me?"

"What about you?" I couldn't take my gaze off the boots. They were a shoe fetishist's dream. I'd worked at a bar, on my feet. I had always chosen comfort over fashion, but now…

"Waitin' on you to give me the words. Want to hear them."

"You haven't said them either," I reminded him with a reproachful look.

His gaze was hot as it raked over me before coming back to rest on my face. "Love you, darlin'."

My smile was slow. "I love you, too."

His mouth quirked up on one side. "So you'll wear the boots tonight when you go out?"

"Hell yeah!"

"You'll wear the leather cut, too. You get one thing. I get one thing."

"Technically you got two things. The cut and the tattoo of your name on me." I arched an eyebrow daring him to argue. "Besides, the cut will rub against my bandage. Guess you didn't think about that, did you?"

"My woman's got a smart mouth."

"You like it."

"I'd like it better wrapped around my—"

"Do you have a Blue Angels T-shirt?" I interrupted. "With the logo and everything?"

"Yeah, I got one." He pushed away from the doorway and went to his dresser. He pulled open the bottom drawer and dug out a red T-shirt with the logo. It had Blue Angels written across the back. It was perfect for what I needed.

"And a pair of scissors?"

"Nightstand drawer. What are you going to do?" he asked.

"I'm going to surprise you," I said with a grin.

He didn't smile back. Instead, his gaze felt heavy with intensity.

The doorbell rang.

"Joni," he said.

I nodded. "Will you get that? And tell her to come up. I need her help getting ready."

"You're bossy." He marched toward me and kissed me, slow and deep. "Let's just see how bossy you're going to be tonight when you get home and I strip everything off you except those boots."

"Promises, promises," I muttered.

We were engaged in a breathless kiss when the doorbell rang again.

"Really should get that," he said, pulling away.

The door clicked shut and then I grabbed the T-shirt and scissors. Joni walked in when I was standing in front of the mirror, holding the top in front of me.

"What did you do?" she asked. "That's so cool!"

"The art of T-shirt cutting," I told her. The back and sides were sliced and it would reveal skin.

"You are going to have to show me how to do that," she said.

"I will." I looked her up and down, taking in her leather dress that crisscrossed down her back with the front looking like a corset. Her rich brown locks had been curled and sprayed, her makeup dramatic and heavy. She wore red vixen pumps to complete the outfit.

"You look amazing," I said.

She brushed aside my compliment with a wave of her hand and then pointed to the boots. "Oh my God. Those are gorgeous."

"I know," I said with a laugh. "I was going to wear them with a pair of skinny black jeans and this shirt I just doctored. I won't be under dressed next to you, will I?"

She shook her head. "We'll just make sure the makeup and the hair go along with it."

"I don't have any of the heavy duty stuff."

"Shoot, I should've brought my arsenal of makeup and hair products over."

"That's okay."

"I can have Colt send one of the prospects to the drugstore."

I shook my head. "I don't want to wait to go out. I want to leave the house before Colt changes his mind."

"Changes his mind? Or yours?" She grinned. "I heard he was quite persuasive about the tattoo when you guys were yelling at each other in Charlie's parking lot." She gestured to the bandage peeking out from my tank top. "He got his way, didn't he?"

"How did you know about all of that?" I asked in surprise. I slid out of my denim shorts and then got into the jeans that were on the bed.

"Reap told Rachel, Rachel called me. So can I see your tattoo?"

I gave her my back and tacit permission to move the bandage. "Wow. You really did it."

"Yeah, I did."

She concealed the tattoo, ensuring the dressing stuck to my skin. "Why?"

I took a step away to slide the cut T-shirt over my head. "Why? What do you mean why?"

"I mean you seemed pretty adamant about not getting involved with my brother and now you're not just involved, you're like, his woman. His Old Lady."

I smirked at her in amusement and then went to the bathroom to do my hair. "Weren't you the one who told me Colt was worth it? Loyal, strong, brave. All that stuff?"

"Yeah."

"Not to mention, he's wicked good in bed."

She covered her ears. "And that's my cue. Meet me downstairs. Hurry up, I gotta drink away what you just said."

An hour later, Joni and I were sitting in a booth at Shortie's, a bar in Blue Angel territory. We'd gotten more than a few looks as we entered, much to Joni's delight. There was no way I was under the radar now. Not with Colt's T-shirt and his name on my body. Even though the tattoo wasn't on display, the two burly bikers who'd followed us in and then taken a seat in the corner to watch over us alerted anyone who was paying attention that we were with the Blue Angels.

Colt had been gone by the time I'd gotten downstairs. Zip had stopped by and they had both hopped on their bikes to drive away. I didn't like that he'd left the house without telling me goodbye.

I wasn't sure I knew how to do any of what was being asked of me.

"You look so pathetic," Joni commented, her gaze drifting from me to her pint of beer.

"Me? You look just as pathetic as I do," I stated. "In fact, why *do* you look so pathetic?"

She sighed. "Trying to tell myself to move on and actually moving on are two different things. I'm bummed Zip didn't even spare me a glance."

"Then he's an idiot. You're amazing."

"Thanks." She shot me a wobbly smile. "I'm going out on a date with a doctor I work with."

"No way. Really?"

"Really."

"When?"

"Next week when I get my next night off. He's cute and funny, but he's not Zip."

"Then why even bother if all you're gonna do is fake it?" I asked.

"Because maybe if I fake it and let some other guy distract me, it'll take." She took another sip of her beer. "I still can't believe you got Colt's name on you."

"Yeah, I can hardly believe that myself. It's been a crazy past few weeks."

"What made you decide to get the tattoo?" she asked. "When the girls came over, you made it seem like you'd never do something like that. And now you've gone and changed your tune."

"I got your brother's name on my body because I love him."

Her eyes widened. "No."

"Yup."

"Seriously?"

"Seriously."

"But, how? How did that happen so fast?"

"I don't know." I shrugged. "But it did."

"What does this mean for you guys?"

"It means whatever it means."

"That's so stupidly vague."

"You've been in love with Zip for years, right?"

"Don't remind me," she grumbled.

"Sorry. I just mean, you've had years to think about what a life with Zip would look like. You've explored every avenue, you've grown up in this world, you understand what you're getting into."

"Yeah, so?"

"I love Colt," I said slowly, finding it a miracle I didn't trip over the words. "But that doesn't mean I have it all figured out. You know?"

"I get it. Sorry if I've put any pressure on you to decide anything. I'm just glad he found you—and you found him."

"You're kind of amazing, you know that? I think you'd get along really well with my best friend."

"I'd love to meet her. Why don't you invite her out to join us?"

"Another time. I don't want to have to explain the tattoo. She tried to warn me away from biker guys…"

Joni laughed. "Then she's going to be in for quite a shock."

A terrible new country song came on the jukebox. I jumped up from my seat and said, "I have to change it or I'll go crazy."

Joni pulled out her phone. "Okay, but you're not allowed to play *Journey*. That's my only stipulation."

I wandered past the tables. Most were occupied by people laughing and having a good time. It wasn't too crowded yet, and I was contemplating ordering a burger. I stood in front of the jukebox, sorting through the albums.

"Hi," a guy said from behind me.

I jumped, startled out of my music perusal.

"Sorry. Didn't mean to scare you." He held up his hands in an obvious show of apology.

I noted his sterile, clean-cut good looks.

"It's okay. I just didn't hear you approach." I turned back to the jukebox and kept sorting through songs.

"Not a fan of country?"

"Nope."

"Me neither. I like punk."

Despite myself, I laughed. Mr. Clean Cut did not look like the type who listened to punk.

"Just kidding. I hate punk, too," he said, a wide smile spreading across his face. "Allow me."

He fed a buck into the slot and then gestured for me to press a button.

Moments later, "Paint it Black" by *The Rolling Stones* played.

"Well done," Mr. Clean Cut said.

"Thanks. Can't go wrong with The Stones."

"Can I buy you a drink?"

Before I could answer, I felt a large, warm body behind me. "She doesn't need a drink."

To make matters worse, Colt hauled me to his side and curled his large hand around my neck in a possessive show.

"This is Colt," I introduced. "Sorry, I didn't get your name?"

The man almost squeaked as he turned and scurried away. I looked up at Colt whose eyes were still following the retreating form of Mr. Clean Cut. Colt finally dropped his gaze and his lips curved into a seductive smile.

I frowned. "I'm confused."

"About?"

"Why you're here."

He tilted his head down and smiled at me. "I missed you."

"You…missed me?" I asked in surprised delight.

"Yeah, babe." His hand tightened ever so slightly. "Are you gonna kiss me hello, or what?"

I pressed my palms to his chest, my lids fluttering closed. His mouth met mine, warm, eager, demanding.

"You left the house without saying goodbye," I admonished.

He grinned. "Had something to take care of."

"What could you have possibly needed to take care of?"

Colt let me go and took a step away from me. He reached up to his white T-shirt collar and pulled it down, showing off his right pectoral that was covered in a bandage.

Exactly the same type of bandage that was on my shoulder.

"No," I murmured, my hand touching the edge of the tape.

"Yeah." His tone was gruff. "You didn't really think I'd ask you to get my name on you and not do the same in return?"

"You never said anything. Why didn't you do it after I was in the tattoo chair?"

He lifted my chin to meet his gaze. "I wanted to surprise you."

"Well, I'm surprised."

Colt took my lips in a gentle kiss before pulling back. "Figure we got years before you know all my habits and I know yours. But I know all the things I need to know about you right now." He leaned down and whispered in my ear, "I know how you bite your lip and your forehead wrinkles when you're trying to work something out. I know you like to be independent, but I also know you were dying for a family. I know you love your friends enough to protect them. I know what I need to know about you, Mia. I'm honored to have your name on me."

"Colt," I breathed, feeling tears coat my lashes.

The Stones song came to an end, and for a moment there was a lull in the music, just long enough for me to hear the motorcycles.

I didn't think anything of it since we were on Blue Angel territory and was about to ask Colt if I could buy him a beer when he suddenly pushed me to the ground.

I fell to the floor and Colt's body draped over mine. Air whooshed from my lungs and my shoulder throbbed in dull pain.

"What the hell?" I groused, but the words lodged in my throat when I heard the sound of gunshots. Bullets began to spray the room. Windows exploded and the walls burst with clouds of dust. Shards of metallic-backed razor sharp mirror flew everywhere as bullets struck the glass behind the bar. People screamed and a cacophony of mayhem and destruction made my ears ring. Tables and chairs scraped along the scarred wooden floors as customers dove for safety. People scurried to find protection, spilling beer and liquor and knocking each other to the ground in a panic.

I was numb with terror, but I got out a strangled, "Joni!"

"Acid's got her," Colt said, voice hard.

When the noise ceased and the room had gone eerily quiet, I attempted to peer around. My breathing was shallow and spots danced before my eyes. "Colt," I wheezed. "I can't breathe."

He lifted himself off me and stood. Reaching down, he took my hand and helped me up. The bar was wrecked. Bottles behind the bar were nothing more than shattered remains; tables and chairs were kicked over, the walls riddled with holes. There was a long crack down the front of the jukebox's glass. It made a noise, trying to turn back on, but after a pathetic warble it fell silent.

People slowly emerged from their stunned confusion. They looked at the bar, taking stock of each other and themselves.

Someone whimpered in pain.

"Colt!" Cheese called out. "Over here!"

We ran to Cheese who was helping a struggling Joni sit up. "Don't worry him for nothing," she groused, pressing a hand to her upper arm. "I'm fine. It's just a cut from glass."

"Let me see," Colt barked.

"I'm a nurse," she reminded him, even as she removed her hand so Colt could inspect her injury. Blood oozed a bit from the wound before Joni pressed her palm to it. "It's superficial."

"Prez, we got trouble," Acid said with a glance at the doorway.

"Iron Horsemen?" Colt asked, not taking his eyes from Joni who was sitting in a chair, looking far too pale.

"Cops."

"Fuck," he muttered. "Guys, get Joni and Mia out of here. I'll deal with the cops." He squeezed my hand and then let me go.

Acid hoisted Joni up and all but carted her to the back of the bar. Cheese and I followed at a quick pace. The four of us piled into Joni's car and left the parking lot as quickly as we could without attracting any more attention. I sat in the back with Joni and kept up a steady stream of chatter in hopes of distracting her from the discomfort.

We got her checked in and registered at the hospital.

She was taken back immediately, and the three of us moved to the waiting room.

"Coffee?" Cheese asked.

Acid shook his head.

"I'd love a cup. Thanks," I said.

Cheese went off in search of caffeine and Acid pulled out his phone and shot off a text. Twenty minutes later, the elevator doors opened and Zip burst out.

"Where is she?" he demanded.

"Doctor is stitching her up, she's going to be fine," I said, my gaze resting on him.

Zip nodded and then reluctantly took a seat. His leg bounced with nervousness and then he got up from his chair and began to pace.

"Who told you we were here? Colt?" I asked, pitching my voice low so Cheese and Acid didn't overhear me.

"Acid texted," Zip answered.

Another ten minutes passed in silence and then I saw Joni walking down the hallway toward the reception desk.

When she noticed Zip, her mouth gaped. "What are you doing here?"

"I'm going to drive you home in my truck," Zip replied.

"Mkay. They gave me painkillers. The good shit," Joni stage-whispered and then grinned. "I'm feeling pretty light and airy. So let's go, pretty boy…"

A slight smile tugged at Zip's lips and he couldn't take his eyes off Joni as he led her toward the elevator. Cheese and I followed behind them and Acid brought up the rear. Joni babbled incoherently, but the rest of us were subdued.

When we got to the parking lot, Joni threw her uninjured arm around me. I winced when she pressed her hand against the bandage on my shoulder, but I managed to hold it in.

"You're a great friend," she yelled.

"And now I'm your partially deaf friend, thanks," I said with a laugh and a pat to her back. "I'm really glad you're okay."

"Hey! Look! We're both injured."

"That we are," I agreed in amusement.

She nearly fell over into Zip's side. "I'm tired," she muttered.

Zip pushed a curl of hair behind Joni's ear and let his hand linger. "I know, babe. Let's go." He looked at Cheese. "You still have her car keys? Good. Take Mia to the clubhouse."

"The clubhouse?" I asked. "Why can't I go home?"

Zip's gaze was dark. "Home isn't safe anymore."

Chapter 15

I SAT in the passenger side of Joni's car. Cheese drove and Acid sat in the back. When we arrived, the prospects opened the gate. I was glad to see that there was no party raging.

Cheese parked in the gravel lot. Before I could get a word out, Acid exited the car and sauntered toward the clubhouse. The stoic young biker made Colt seem downright chatty.

"Can I get you something to drink? Water? Bourbon?" Cheese asked as he locked Joni's car and pocketed the keys in his cut.

"No, I'm okay," I said quietly.

The lights were on and Boxer and Reap were sitting on the couches watching TV. When we came in, Boxer muted the television and they both stared at us.

"Where's Acid?" I asked.

"Hit the sack," Reap stated. "He's got patrol in a few hours and needs to be alert."

I nodded thoughtfully.

"You okay, darlin'?" Boxer asked. "We heard about what went down."

"I'm okay. It was Joni that got hurt in the crossfire." The mood in the room was somber, heavy with emotion. "It was the Iron Horsemen, wasn't it?"

The three of them exchanged a look but none of them said anything. They clearly kept information on lockdown and I wasn't happy about being in the dark.

This was Colt's way of life, and I'd need to find a way to get used to it. From the moment I showed up on the Blue Angels' doorstep, Colt hadn't been entirely truthful.

"Fine. Don't tell me," I said suddenly exhausted. "I'm sorry, guys."

"Sorry? Sorry for what?" Reap asked.

"Sorry for bringing you into all of this. If it weren't for me—"

"Hey, none of that now," Boxer interrupted. "The Iron Horsemen have been causing trouble for a long time. Now they're fucking with you. They've crossed a line."

Well, that confirmed it.

"Hey," Reap said with a smile. "I almost forgot. Welcome to the family."

"Oh, shit, yeah!" Boxer said, a huge grin across his face. "Though, I gotta say, babe, kinda wish you'd given me a chance."

I chuckled. "Something tells me you aren't quite ready to settle down."

His hands went to his chest like I'd wounded him and then he flashed a devilish grin. "Too many great ladies, not enough time."

Despite the gravity of the situation, I felt my heart lift. I didn't know if Boxer was trying to cheer me up by being utterly ridiculous, but it was working.

"Should we drink some bourbon and toast Colt's good fortune in locking my ass down?"

The guys roared with laughter. Boxer waved to the empty recliner, gesturing for me to take a seat while he and Reap grabbed the bottle of bourbon on the kitchen counter and four shot glasses.

Reap poured out the shots. "To Mia—the only one willing to put up with Colt's grumpy ass."

"Here, here," Boxer shouted.

We threw back the liquor like champs. Reap served another round and we downed those too.

"Let's cool it for a second," Cheese said. "She can't drink like we can drink."

"Says who?" I demanded. "I used to be a bartender, you know. I can *drink*."

"I'm sure," Cheese said. "But we're twice your size. I don't think Prez will appreciate having to hold your hair back for you when he gets home. Especially not after the shit that just went down."

"Hmm. You make a good point." The two shots of bourbon were already doing the trick. A pleasant numbness was settling into my bones and somehow, my worries about the Iron Horsemen were melting away. That was the danger of booze. It lulled you into a false sense of security and in the morning you woke up hungover, miserable, and all your problems were still there.

"Am I allowed to ask? How you guys got into the Blue Angels?" I looked at Reap and Boxer who were lazing back against the couch.

"My old man and Colt's old man were friends," Reap said with a shrug.

"From Scotland?" I asked.

He raised his eyebrows in obvious surprise. "No. They met when Jimmy came to Waco. My dad loved old bikes.

They met at a trade show. Charlie's Motorcycle Repair? That belonged to my old man. Colt bought it when Pops retired."

"Why didn't you buy it?" I asked in surprise.

"Didn't want the responsibility. Love the work, but also love not having to deal with all the shit that comes from owning the shop, you know?"

"Sure," I said, my head reeling. Why didn't Colt tell me he owned the garage?

Well, that's what I got for jumping into a relationship with a man I hardly knew.

"And you, Boxer?"

He rubbed a thumb across his chin and looked abashed.

"Tell her," Reap said, his grin wide with amusement.

"Joni. We were in the same class in high school. I was a little shit back then."

"Now you're just a big shit," Cheese voiced.

"Damn right," Boxer agreed. "Anyway. She was a major bookworm. Quiet. I liked to tease her. Not like harassment or anything. One day, we were in the hallway and I was ragging on her. She dropped her books and then took me down. I was flat on my back and this girl was on top of me, whispering in my ear that her brother could do more damage.

"After we both got out of detention," he smiled, "I walked out of school with her. Colt was waiting with his bike, looking like a bad ass. I asked to become a prospect. He said no. I bugged the ever-loving shit out of him for a year. The day we graduated high school, Colt finally said if I was still interested to come to the clubhouse."

"And you never left." I laughed.

"Never left," he agreed with a nod.

I loved hearing their stories, learning their history, but

the conversation turned decisively to me after that. Even though I'd spent time with them at the clubhouse party the other night, this was different. This felt like we were all getting to know each other, and not as brother versus a brother's woman, but as real people. There was no divide between us now. They saw me as family, which I greatly appreciated, but I also wanted them to like me.

Cheese decided to hit the sack and said a quick good-night before escaping to his clubhouse room. I reached into my back pocket for my phone. I lit up the screen. No word from Colt. I wondered how long it took to talk to the sheriff.

"You guys have been really wonderful to me," I said quietly. "I just want you to know that even though I didn't grow up in this world and I don't always understand the way things are handled, I respect Colt. I respect all that he's done to earn your loyalty and I just—I don't want you to think I'm going to piss all over it or lead him around by the balls. Not that I think I even could."

"You're not like I thought you'd be," Reap said.

"No? How'd you think I'd be?" I asked, setting my phone aside.

"You're one of the guys," Reap said with a wry grin. "I thought, maybe, you needed to be taken care of, you know? Since that's how he rolls. Takes care of shit. Takes care of people."

"Prez has always been methodical," Boxer said, looking into my eyes. "He never does anything without thinking through every scenario."

"Are you saying he did that with me? Went off the rails and did something completely out of character?"

Reap shook his head. "You know what he did the night he met you?"

I shook my head.

"We had church."

"Church? What's church?" I asked.

"It's when all the brothers meet to discuss club business," Boxer explained.

"I was club business?"

Reap grinned. "Yeah, babe. He wanted to bring you into the fold. Wanted to let us know that's how it was gonna be."

"Wait a second. Are you saying if a brother wants to make a woman his Old Lady, he has to run it by the club?"

"Yeah, that's what we're saying," Boxer said, "But not because he needs approval or anything. It's a courtesy. Just letting us know he's ready to make that step."

My eyes widened. "Seriously?"

"Yup," Boxer said. "When Colt said you didn't call the cops after seeing him beat the shit out of that rapist, he knew for sure what you were made of. We were shocked as hell."

"But Zip totally vouched for it. Now look, we're trying to be gentlemen here, so we're not gonna repeat some of what was said." Reap's brown eyes seemed to twinkle with devilish enjoyment. "But some of your assets might've been mentioned."

Boxer made an obvious show of checking out my body.

"Up here, dude," I growled, causing him to laugh.

"Colt is the best judge of character I've ever seen," Reap went on. "He's got an instinct about people, you know? He just knew you were the one for him. Never seen him like this around another broad, either."

His words made my heart expand. "Never?"

He shook his head. "Never. And point blank, I didn't think he'd meet a chick who'd put up with his moody ass."

"Moody?" Boxer shook his head and looked at me. "Not lately."

"Well, a steady supply of pussy will do that," Reap pointed out.

"Yeah, as much fun as this is," I said, my tone snarky, causing them to grin, "I think it's time I said goodnight."

"Goodnight, darlin'," Boxer said.

I got up and he pulled me in a side hug very much like a big brother.

"He needed you and I'm glad he saw that. We're keepin' ya, babe."

"Then I get to keep you too, right?" I asked with a wide smile.

"That's usually the way it works, yeah," Reap said.

I waved and headed off to Colt's room, my heart full and light despite the horror of the evening. Either I was becoming desensitized really quickly to this way of life, or I'd been right for it all along.

I washed the makeup off my face in Colt's clubhouse bathroom and then went to his dresser to find a shirt to sleep in. It was only when I slid beneath the clean sheets that smelled faintly of Colt that I realized I no longer cared what people might think about the choice I had made.

A biker babe.

That's what I'd become.

The Blue Angels had taken me in, no questions asked. My fight had become their fight. If that was the way they treated family, then I could've done a lot worse. I'd just have to find a way to explain to Shelly that this was truly what I wanted. To be with Colt. To have his protection. To learn how to weather the storm with another person by my side. Someone strong and loyal, someone who didn't shy away from the grit and loss of life.

Colt may have been a rugged, tatted, biker, but his heart beat in synchronicity with mine. He understood me in a way no one else ever had. He understood the losses I'd endured, having faced similar losses himself. He knew what it meant to make a family with people that were good and true, and damn what they looked like on the outside.

I fell asleep with a smile on my face, warm and happy.

A low curse woke me up.

"Colt?"

"Sorry, babe, did I wake you?"

"It's okay. What time is it?" I asked through a yawn.

"Late. Or early, depending on who you ask. I'm gonna flip on a lamp. I just busted my knee on the bed."

I slowly opened my eyes. "Okay."

A low glow washed over the room.

"How'd your talk with the sheriff go?"

"Valenti isn't gonna be a concern." Colt reached into his pockets and took out his cell phone and keys.

And then he reached under his T-shirt and pulled out a pistol.

He kept his eyes on me when he did it. "Does this bother you?"

"It's a little late if it does, don't you think?" I asked, smiling into the pillow.

"Guess it doesn't bother you, then."

"If you'd had your boy sweep my glove box, you'd have found out I carry too."

"Do you now?" His smile was slow. "Well, well, Ms. O'Banion. Aren't you full of surprises."

He removed his cut and laid it gently across the back of the chair in the corner and then removed his shirt.

"I've yet to see this tattoo of yours," I said, finally sitting up.

"Go for it." Colt came over and took a seat on the bed next to me. I could smell the faint traces of sweat on his skin, mingling with his own unique scent. Something that made me want to trace his body with my tongue. Instead, I locked down my hormones and gently touched the edge of the bandage.

My name was written in a curly script on the right side of his chest.

Tears pricked my eyes. "It's beautiful."

His hands came up to caress my cheeks. "Yeah."

"Why did you get it on the right side? Your heart is on the left."

"The left side is for those I've lost. The right is for the living."

Colt pressed his lips to mine. He tasted like whiskey and smelled like perfume. I wrenched my mouth from his.

He frowned. "What's wrong?"

"You smell like perfume."

His brow unwrinkled and he smiled slightly. "It belongs to my sister. I went to see her after talking to the sheriff. Which is why I just got home now."

"Oh."

His humor fled and his mouth softened. "I'm a man of my word, Mia. I promised you fidelity and I meant it."

I drove my fingers through his coffee-colored hair. "But it was so fast. Us. Our...togetherness."

"I wasn't a saint before you."

I arched an eyebrow in silent admonishment, causing him to chuckle.

"What about you?"

"What about me?" I demanded.

"Were you a saint before me?"

"Of course not."

"I've got thirteen years on you. I've had more time to sow my oats. I don't regret my past, but I don't miss that shit anymore either."

"You're not saying that just to get brownie points, are you?"

He let out a laugh. "You're in my bed and my name is on you. I don't need brownie points." His hands tightened on my hips. "I don't have any regrets about us. Do you?"

"It's too soon to tell," I said with a grin, letting him know I was teasing.

"Kiss me, babe."

I leaned down and conquered his lips. I needed him. Needed to feel him, to treasure him and let him know that I was all in; through the good and bad, through whatever life was going to throw at us.

He fell back against the bed with me on top of him. Colt lifted the shirt off me, mindful of my tender skin and the new ink I sported.

His hands and mouth were everywhere, trailing up and down my body, playing with my sensitive nipples, stroking the heat between us into an out-of-control inferno.

I wiggled out of my underwear and gave him time to remove his. Then I was back on top of him, feeling the heat of him at the juncture of my thighs.

"Hold on, babe," he whispered, his hand seeking the nightstand drawer. He grabbed a wrapper and tore it with his teeth. Colt slid on the condom and then his hands grasped my hips.

Aching and wet, I was more than ready for him. I desired to be filled, and slid down his body.

"Look at me," he stated. Our gazes locked and it felt like something had clicked into place, something I'd been waiting my entire life to feel.

Overwhelmed, I dipped my head forward, letting my hair fall over my eyes. I pressed my hands to Colt's chest, mindful of his new tattoo, and began to move.

"That's it, darlin'." His voice was raspy and thick and it only inflamed my desire.

I gave him all my worry and concern, branding him with my body the way he'd branded me.

It was hard, slick and fast, but it wasn't enough.

"More," I commanded. "I need more."

He gave it to me as he bucked beneath me. And then his hand snaked between our bodies where we were joined and teased me until I came.

I dug my nails into his shoulders as I shuddered around him. He thrust up into me, grabbing my hips and slamming me down. A few deep strokes later and he shouted, "Fuck!"

He fell back against the pillows, breathing hard. The lamplight highlighted his skin, making it seem gilded in gold. I leaned over and dotted his chest with kisses.

I slid off of him and my feet hit the floor. I went into the bathroom to clean up, and when I was in the middle of washing my hands, Colt knocked on the door and then came in.

He removed the condom and dropped it in the trashcan. My eyes gazed downward, admiring that he was still engorged. My gaze traveled back up to his chest where there were half-moon red gouges on his skin.

"Did I do that?" I rushed forward and touched his chest. "Jesus, I'm sorry. Do they hurt?"

His mouth turned up at the corners. "I'll be okay, darlin'. It was worth the pain." Colt's hand reached out to touch my cheek. "Let's get back in bed. I'm fucking wiped."

I nodded and went back into his room. I looked around for his discarded T-shirt and threw it on before climbing into bed and settling on my belly. Sleeping on my back would only irritate my new tattoo.

"What happened with the sheriff?" I asked.

Colt got in next to me and then turned off the lamp. "I

paid him off. Told him this was club shit he didn't want to get involved in."

We breathed in the darkness for a few moments before I said, "Your sister was injured tonight because of me. The Iron Horsemen came to the bar and shot out the windows because of me. Someone could have died."

"How do you know it was the Iron Horsemen?" he asked, voice carefully blank.

"Who the hell else would it be? Why else would I be staying at the clubhouse instead of your house if it wasn't the Iron Horsemen? I've noticed there's a little bit more protection here."

"Our house."

"What?"

"My house is your house, babe."

"Thank you," I whispered.

"Joni really is fine. Flesh wound. I wanted to bring her here to look after her, but Zip said it was no trouble to stay with her for tonight."

I wisely bit my tongue. That was a hornet's nest I was not going to stir.

"She could've been really hurt, Colt."

"But she wasn't."

"This time."

He fell silent for a moment and then he said, "It's the life. No getting around it."

I woke up when a streak of sunlight peered through the blinds. I looked at the clock—it was late morning and Colt was still asleep. I watched him for a moment and then got up to brush my teeth and wash my face. When I stared in the mirror I saw tired, red-rimmed eyes. The scratch on my cheek was nearly gone, but I had stubble burn on my jawline and neck. My lips felt raw, the kind of raw that came from hours of kissing.

My brain was tired and hadn't had a chance to process the events of the previous night. Sheriff Valenti could've been a problem, but the protection of Colt's name and wallet had taken care of it. Too bad it hadn't taken care of the Iron Horsemen issue. If anything, it seemed only to add a match to gasoline.

I came back into the bedroom just as Colt was stirring. His sleepy eyes opened and he turned his head, his gaze finding me watching him. He smiled.

"Mornin'."

"Hmmm."

"Is that anyway to greet your man?"

I pushed away from the doorway and sauntered over to him. When I got to his side of the bed, I leaned down, intending to brush my lips across his, but he clearly had other ideas. He wrapped his arms around me and pulled me toward him.

"How's your shoulder?" he asked, nuzzling my neck.

"It's okay. How's your chest?"

"From the tattoo, or from the claws of a foxy vixen I was in bed with last night?"

I laughed, feeling warm and secure. "Either. Both."

"Yeah, I'm okay."

My fingers traced the swirls of artwork along his upper arm and bicep. "None of this seems real." I rested my head against his chest, his light hair tickling my ear.

His hands skimmed underneath my shirt to rest against the small of my back as he listened to me talk.

"Three weeks ago, I was a bartender. I was getting harassed by my newly engaged best friend about my lack of living life to its fullest and I'd never even thought once about motorcycle clubs."

I closed my eyes, enjoying the sound of his heartbeat in my ear, the steady rhythm of it solid and sure.

"Never know what life is gonna throw at you, ya know?" he said.

"That's the truth. Sometimes I feel like…"

When I didn't go on, Colt gently prodded me to continue.

"I feel like I react to life. Like, things happen *to* me and I'm just along for the ride."

"You do remember that you walked up to a stranger in a bar and asked him to pretend to be your boyfriend, don't you? If you ask me, that sounds like someone who takes control. That sounds like someone who doesn't let life come at them."

"I only did that out of a reaction," I explained.

"Want to know what I think?" he asked quietly.

I nodded.

"I think you changed your entire life that night at Dive Bar when you walked up to me. I think even if you hadn't gotten wrapped up in this Richie shit, you'd still be here with me, right now."

"Do you really believe that?" I smiled and lifted my head to look at him

"Yeah, I do." His dark eyes softened. "You'd be here in my bed." He brushed the hair away from my cheek. "You're still worried about what people think, aren't you?"

"I guess I am, yeah." I bit my lip. "I feel like—never mind."

"Nah, you can't do that. You gotta say it now."

"I feel like people will think I'm trading sex for protection."

"People? Or your best friend? Or you?"

He didn't sound angry; I'd expected him to sound angry.

"You think I'd brand just any girl?" he continued.

I glared at him. "Maybe you shouldn't call it branding…"

Colt laughed. "You know what I mean. You might love me, and I believe you do, but it's like you don't trust your gut. But in life, you have to trust your gut. We're in this together now, yeah?"

"Yeah.

"You got inked for me," he said with an arrogant smirk. "That's no small thing."

"Yeah, I suffered through pain for you." I teased, finally moving away from him, ready to get up to face the day.

"I'll never let you live to regret it," he said, his tone suddenly sober.

My hand reached out to stroke his stubbly cheek. "I know."

After Colt brushed his teeth, he threw on a pair of jeans and a clean T-shirt from his dresser drawer. I had nothing to wear except the clothes from last night, and I wasn't in the mood to slither into skinny jeans.

"Wear a pair of my boxers," he said. "And your T-shirt from last night. We should bring a bag with some shit for you here. Didn't really think about it, though."

"Well, it's not like you knew I'd be staying here last night."

He went over to his dresser and pulled out a pair of his boxer shorts and tossed them in my direction. "Got some other stuff for you though in my nightstand drawer."

I opened the drawer and pulled out a few envelopes addressed to me. "My bank cards! Yes!" I danced around in my underwear as Colt looked on with amusement.

I placed the new bankcards in my wallet. Joni had generously bought our drinks the night before. Colt hadn't said anything about money; and I'd never been out of his sight long enough to require money of my own. Though, come to think of it, he'd never made me feel weird about it. I'd only felt trapped those first few days, but then my fears and worries had melted away when I realized Colt really had wanted to protect and take care of me. Nothing more. With Colt there was no power play to keep me tied to him. No control over me because he didn't care about control in that way.

He just wanted me.

"Oh," I said softly, meeting his eyes.

He was smiling at me, leaning against the door. He knew what I'd just put together.

"Thank you, Colt."

"You're welcome, Mia."

Chapter 16

REAP AND BOXER WERE AWAKE, alert and smiley as they lounged on the couches. Gray waved to me from a recliner and then turned his attention back to the TV. A local news station was on and I could distinctly make out the Shortie's sign in the background behind the cute reporter on screen.

"What's she saying?" I asked with a chin nod at the TV.

"She's talking about a spike in crime in Waco." Gray darted his gaze to Colt. I looked at Colt over my shoulder and his face betrayed nothing of his feelings.

"The clubhouse is full this morning," I commented.

"We're having church in an hour," Colt explained. "So everyone is coming here."

"I need coffee," I muttered, heading to the kitchen where Darcy was directing Rachel and Allison with a spatula.

"Good morning," Darcy chirped. "How are you? We heard about the drive by at Shortie's."

"I'm okay. It was Joni who was hurt," I said, going to a

cabinet and grabbing a mug. I emptied the pot. "Where's the bag of coffee? I need to make more."

"I've got it," Allison said.

Cream and sugar were on the counter and I doctored my coffee heavily before sitting on a stool. Colt had taken a seat with the guys near the TV and was currently talking to Gray in a low voice.

"She's going to be okay," Darcy said. "Flesh wound, right?"

I nodded. I needed to text Joni to see how she was doing. My phone was still in Colt's room and just as I was about to hop off the stool to go and grab it, Joni walked into the clubhouse with Zip behind her.

Her sorrel hair was pulled into a low side ponytail and she was wearing black yoga pants, flip-flops, and a pink tank top that revealed her bandaged arm.

I jumped off my stool and went to her immediately and gently embraced her. "How are you feeling?"

"Dopey," she said with a smile. Her blue eyes looked a little glassy, but she wasn't swaying. "I took some painkillers before we came over."

Zip came to stand by her and I noticed he was carrying a duffel bag.

I pointed to it. "What's that?"

"Joni's shit," he said. "She'll be staying in a spare room at the clubhouse for a few days."

"Why?" I asked in confusion.

"Colt will explain," Zip said. He looked at Joni for a long moment and then took her bag out of the room and headed for the stairs.

"What was that?" I whispered.

"Nothing." She grabbed my coffee and took a sip. Nodding, she added, "Just the way I like it."

I took her hand and led her to the kitchen counter. "Sit," I commanded, gesturing to one of the stools.

Joni plopped her butt down and then Darcy set a plate of food in front of her. "Eat every bite," she commanded.

"Do I need to feed you?" Rachel asked. "I will, you know. I'll even play the airplane game to make it more fun if that's what you need me to do."

"Why are you guys treating me like an invalid?" she demanded. "I'm a nurse. I know how minor this is."

As if to prove her point, she picked up her fork with her dominant hand, which was also the arm that was bandaged, and scooped up a bite of scrambled eggs.

She ate a few bites and then set her fork down. "See? I'm fine."

Zip came back down the stairs and walked over to stand behind Joni. "Your stuff is in last room on the right. Third floor."

"Thanks," she said.

He stared at her for one long moment and then nodded before joining the guys.

"Dear Lord," Allison muttered.

"Right? Is it too early for cocktail hour? I need to know everything that look just meant," Darcy said.

"Nothing. It meant nothing," Joni said before going back to eating her food.

I leaned closer to peer at her and said aloud so the girls could hear, "Her cheeks aren't even red. She's literally got *no* tells. Forget cocktail hour. Let's drive to Vegas and make Joni play poker."

"I don't know how to play poker," Joni said.

"I'll teach you."

"I don't know how to play either," Rachel said with a pout.

"Girls' poker night," I said. "Our next hang out. I'm gonna turn you guys into hustlers."

"You mean you know how to cheat?" Darcy asked in amusement.

"Damn right I know how to cheat," I said with a laugh.

"I'm so in," Allison said with a grin.

Acid and Cheese came in the back, sweaty and out of breath.

"What happened to you guys?" Rachel asked.

"The kids," Acid wheezed. "They have no chill."

"Kids?" I asked and then looked at Darcy. "Your kids?"

She nodded. "Cam and Lily are in the backyard. Along with Silas—Cheese's brother."

The two young bikers grabbed some bottles of water from the refrigerator and then Colt yelled, "Church!"

All the Blue Angels trailed after their president and they disappeared down the hallway. A moment later, the back door opened and then shut.

"And then the women folk were stuck in the kitchen," Rachel muttered, causing Darcy to laugh. "I can't believe three kids tuckered out two huge bikers."

"Children have a special type of energy," Darcy explained. "It's endless. And forget giving them sugar. That's the kiss of death for parents."

"Reap is dying for a baby," Rachel said. "I have no idea why, considering he's never spent more than two seconds in the same room with one."

"I think it has to do with wanting a kid with *you*," Allison pointed out. Her face went pink and she bit her lip like she was hiding something.

"Oh my God," I said, staring at her. "You're totally pregnant."

The girls looked at her in different phases of shock and disbelief.

"No," Darcy said. "Really?"

Allison nodded, happiness shining from her eyes. "I told Torque last night and he was really excited."

I'd never officially met Torque. He was once a nomad, meaning he called himself a Blue Angel, but he hadn't belonged to a specific chapter. When he'd met Allison in Waco, he'd settled down, but he still had the urge to wander. He was constantly on the road, traveling.

I hadn't even seen him in the clubhouse this morning. No doubt he'd been waiting out back when Colt called for church.

"Are the boys really gone?" Darcy asked.

I hopped off my stool and went to the hallway and listened for a moment. There was no sound of voices or footsteps.

"They're gone," I said. "Why?"

Darcy grinned and then she went to one of the cabinets and moved aside boxes of pasta and corn muffin mix to pull out a bottle of Kahlua.

"Seriously?" Joni asked with a laugh.

"Seriously," Darcy said. "I think we need it. After the night you and Mia had, and now to celebrate Allison's good news."

Darcy filled our coffee cups, skipped Allison, and then raised her mug.

"To the Blue Angels women," Darcy said.

My throat tightened.

I was one of them now.

I wasn't sure what it all entailed, but I knew that even with the danger, it was worth it because of the protective fold I'd been brought into.

"To the next generation," I said with a grin at Allison as she beamed with joy.

"Who's next, do you think?" Darcy asked after taking a sip from her mug, her eyes skimming over us.

"Don't look at me," Rachel said. "I could go a few more years without a baby. No offense."

Allison shrugged. "None taken."

"I'm not even dating a Blue Angel," Joni said. "Ah, shit."

"What?" I asked. "Is it your arm? Does it hurt?"

She shook her head. "I'm supposed to go on that date with the doctor I work with. How the hell am I supposed to explain this?" She pointed to her bandage.

"Tell him you're a klutz," Rachel suggested.

"And that you were holding a vase of flowers, tripped over your own two feet, and the vase went flying and you went down and cut yourself on the broken glass," Darcy said.

"You came up with that story really fast," I remarked with a laugh.

"It's a good story," Darcy said.

"Not if you're a nurse and you hold people's lives in your hands," Joni stated. "If I tell that story, he won't think I'm a klutz, he'll think I'm an idiot who can't be trusted. He likes me because I'm competent, not some goof."

Rachel frowned. "I'm pretty sure he likes you because you've got a great rack."

"I've got a great rack?" Joni asked with a smile, puffing out her chest.

"Dynamite," Rachel said. "I'd kill for your rack."

"You guys are kind of amazing, you know that, right?" I smiled. Their banter reminded me a lot of Shelly. I thought about how much she'd like these women and I couldn't wait to introduce her to them. She'd quickly get over her biker aversion when she saw how they all treated me.

Like it didn't matter that I was in a world of shit, or that I brought it to their front door or that Joni had gotten injured because she'd been with me at Shortie's.

"What's wrong?" Joni asked quietly. The other three women were smiling and talking and hadn't noticed I'd fallen into a somber state.

"Just thinking." I shook off my mood. "I'm glad you're okay."

"Stop it."

"Stop what?"

"Stop feeling guilty," she said. "It's not necessary. I'm okay, Mia." She squeezed my hand to take the sting out of her reprimand.

I heard the slam of the back door and then voices. The kitchen was suddenly overrun by Darcy's two children and Cheese's brother, Silas. He was a skinny kid with skinned knees, but his smile was big and goofy. His ears stuck out just a bit, but I knew in a few years, after braces and a growth spurt, he'd be a good-looking teenager. With a biker as an older brother, I was sure he'd learn how to swagger and break a few hearts.

"Mom, I'm hungry!" Cam said.

"Me too!" Lily yelled. "Hi, Mia!"

I smiled at the adorable girl. "Hey, Lil."

The kitchen was suddenly filled with people—church had ended and the bikers were now back, grabbing plates of food and sitting at any available spot.

Colt came up behind me, reached over my shoulder and took a half-eaten piece of bacon off my plate, and popped it into his mouth.

"Hey," I said. "I was going to eat that."

He grinned after he swallowed. "No you weren't."

"Yeah, I wasn't," I admitted with a laugh.

Joni climbed off her stool and waved Colt to it. "Those

pain killers are throwing me for a loop. I think I'll go lie down."

Colt took her seat but not before whispering something in her ear. She nodded and then headed upstairs.

"You ready to go?" he asked me.

Out of the corner of my eye, I saw Zip set his plate of food on the coffee table and stand up. He made his way upstairs, so discreetly that even Colt didn't notice what was going on beneath his nose.

"Mia?" Colt pressed.

"Sorry. Yeah, I'm ready." I looked at him in confusion. "Where are we going?"

"Home so we can grab your clothes and whatever else you need. We're staying in the clubhouse for the next few days."

My gaze narrowed. "Next few days, huh? So that's Colt-speak for 'until the threat has passed'."

He smirked. "You already speak my language. You must be some kind of savant."

I rolled my eyes and pressed my hand to his chest, forgetting about his tattoo. He winced and I immediately pulled away. "I'm sorry."

"It's fine."

"Wait a minute, you two," Darcy said. "Hush, every-one!" The room quieted and all eyes looked to Gray's wife. "We've got a situation here that no one has addressed."

I shrank back into the wall of Colt's chest, afraid that Darcy was going to call out Joni's injury and what had had happened last night. She surprised me when she announced, "Mia and Colt got tattoos. We need to cele-brate that!"

There was a resounding cheer that was deafening and made my eardrums vibrate.

"Tonight we rage!" Boxer yelled.

I looked at Colt and whispered, "Is this a good idea?"

"Is what a good idea?" Colt looked down at me, the smile lines at his eyes crinkling. "Living life?"

"But what about all the other stuff?"

"It'll still be there tomorrow," he said. He wrapped his hand around my waist and pulled me to him. "You never know how long you've got, Mia." His eyes darkened and his mouth clamped shut even though he looked like he wanted to say more.

He'd lost his parents young. I'd lost my family too. By all accounts, Colt and I finding each other, finding some measure of happiness in a chaotic world, was a miracle.

"Okay," I said with a slight smile. "Let's celebrate. One condition, though."

"Name it."

"I want Shelly and Mark to come."

"Mia…"

"She was there for me, Colt. When Grammie died. She was there for me when no one else in the whole world was. She has to be here to celebrate this new life with me. Celebrate *us*. I know it will be weird, and she has thoughts about you and the entire MC thing. She won't get to know you in a night, but it's a start. Please?"

Finally, he nodded. "Boxer is right, though. Tonight we rage. You think she can handle that?"

I grinned. "Guess we're going to find out."

We headed home, leaving the party planning in Darcy and Rachel's capable hands. While Colt showered, I packed a bag full of clothes. I went into the bathroom to gather some of my toiletries, but lost all sense of concentration when Colt stepped out of the shower, naked and wet.

Utterly gorgeous.

He reached for a towel and quickly ran it across his head and then swaddled it around his body. He grabbed his toothbrush and slathered toothpaste across the bristles.

"What did you do with Richie's corpse?" I asked.

Colt looked at me. "Do you really think I'm going to answer that?"

I sighed. "You're not going to tell me."

"Do you even really want to know?"

"I guess not."

"As far as anyone is concerned, Richie is still missing. I'll leave it at that. Okay?"

"Okay." I blew out a breath of air. "Does it bother you when I ask questions?"

He rinsed out his mouth. "No. Does it bother you that I handle shit and might not always be able to tell you what goes down?"

"I thought it might. I don't know. Maybe it will at some point in the future. But not now."

"Speaking of future," he began.

"We were speaking of the future?"

He shot me a look. "We are now."

"Okay, I'm listening." I followed him out of the bathroom, carting my toiletries and setting them down on the bed.

Colt flung off his towel and strode nude to his dresser. "Do you want kids?"

"What?" I asked, startled. "Kids?"

"Yeah. You know. Children."

"Yes, I'm aware of what a child is, Colt," I snipped.

"Do you want one? Or more than one?" He pulled on his boxers but kept his gaze trained on me.

"I don't know if I want them," I admitted.

He stared at me for a long moment and then asked,

"Did you want kids before you got tied up with me and the Blue Angels?"

I swallowed but didn't answer.

"If you want kids, we'll have kids. If you don't want them…then we can fuck on the kitchen floor whenever we want and not have to worry about scarring a kid for life."

A bubble of laughter escaped my lips. "That's your vision? We're on the kitchen floor and our kid comes in?"

"Well," he grinned wickedly, "the real vision is you on top of me while *I'm* on the kitchen floor and you're screaming my name. Never really factored a kid walking in on that, though knowing us, it would be bound to happen."

The carefree way he described the situation made me smile.

"Tell you what," I said. "Let's get through all this crap with the Iron Horsemen and we can reevaluate the kid thing."

"So you're not saying no," he said. "Just so we're clear."

"Not no," I agreed. I cocked my head to the side. "But I think you want kids. Don't you? You're just trying to be accommodating?"

"You think I'm the accommodating sort? You clearly don't know me well enough yet."

I refused to let him sidetrack the conversation. "I think you want kids," I said softly. "I think you want a family like the one you were raised in."

He stilled, the amusement fading from his features. "Truth?"

I nodded.

Colt sat on the edge of the bed in nothing but his boxers, his hands clasped in his lap as he stared at the floor, mulling over his words before speaking.

"My parents loved us. They really did. But they loved each other more. Dad didn't die of cancer. Not really. He let the cancer take him because it was less painful than living without my mom. He died of a broken heart, but you don't say shit like that in our world. You know?"

He shook his head and went on.

"Joni and I...we had each other. Still have each other. I don't know what I would've done without her. Sure, I left her like an ass and tried to figure out my own shit—living in a world that my dad wasn't in anymore, but I came back. And it's been the two of us ever since." He looked at me and smiled. "Until you came along, I didn't think much about having kids. Why have kids if you don't have the love of a good woman to raise them alongside you?

"I don't know, darlin'. One day we'll be old. One of us will go first. Whoever is left behind...well, I like the idea of having the comfort of family when that time comes. A family you and I made together. A part of me, a part of you, will always be left in the world, even when we're gone. And if we have more than one kid, they'll be there for each other when we're both gone."

His words wrecked me and I felt tears coat my eyelashes, but they didn't fall. Somehow, I held it all back. Not because I was embarrassed or afraid of being vulnerable. The walls that I'd erected around my heart after Grammie died were long gone, obliterated by Colt.

But there was something I had to say before I broke apart completely. "I watched Grammie die. Slowly, at first. She suffered for a long time, and then she was gone. Even though I was by her side, she died alone. You're born alone and you die alone, no matter what anyone tells you." I frowned. "I don't know if what you said is a good enough reason for me, Colt. Do I hate the idea of you being old without me? Yeah, I do. But will having children really ease the burden of loss? I can't say. I don't know. But I think, we're supposed to want better for our children than we had. It's one thing for me to choose this life. Choose you and all the shit that comes with it. It's quite another to have kids and bring them into a world where a skewed moral compass is the norm, with mentors and protectors that break laws and teach them it's okay to do it. I just don't know, Colt."

He was silent for a long moment, his dark eyes murky without giving away any emotion.

Was he upset about what I'd said? He was good enough for me. But was he good enough to be the father of the children I didn't even know I wanted?

"Call Shelly," he said finally. "Invite her and her fiancé to our party."

I wrapped my arms around myself, feeling cold down to my bones.

"Okay." I bit my lip. "Are you mad at me? For what I said?"

"No."

"Then why are you—"

"I'm mad because your words have merit." He got off the bed and went to the dresser to grab a pair of jeans and a T-shirt. "I just need a bit, all right?"

Nodding, I left the bedroom, closing the door behind me. We were both strong people. Strong-willed, strong emotionally.

But were we strong enough as a couple to weather the truth?

Chapter 17

I DIDN'T CALL SHELLY. Not after the discussion Colt and I'd had about children. It was one thing to say *I love you*. It was another to decide whether or not you were going to create a new life together. Just because you loved someone didn't mean it was forever. Maybe it had been that way for Colt's parents. Maybe they'd chosen each other above all else and it didn't matter if they agreed or disagreed about the big things.

I'd never witnessed a long marriage. Gramps hadn't even been alive when I was born. I hadn't grown up with a father, and I'd never seen my mother interact with another man. Even though she'd passed when I was really young, there was no hazy vision of me spending time with any father figure.

"This is why I don't do relationships," I muttered, loading the few dishes that rested in the sink into the dishwasher.

"Why don't you do relationships?"

I jumped and yelped, not having heard Colt approach.

A coffee mug slammed against the faucet and broke into a few large pieces. "Damn."

"Let me clean it up. With your luck, you're liable to cut the shit out of yourself," Colt said, his tone gruff. He came all the way into the kitchen and sauntered over to me.

He grasped the pieces of the broken mug and walked to the trash. He wiped his hands on his jeans and then returned to stand directly behind me, caging me in with his hands on the counter. "Why don't you do relationships?" His breath was warm and teased my skin.

I shivered. "Because I'm not good at them. I say the wrong things because I'm emotional first, rational later."

"When are you ever rational?" he teased.

I gently elbowed him in the gut, causing him to grunt. "First of all," Colt began, "every relationship is a failure except the one that works. You and I work."

"You don't know that. Our relationship is barely longer than a mayfly's gestational period. It was stupid. This whole thing was stupid."

I attempted to duck under his arm to get away, but he wouldn't let me. His hands went to my arms to gently turn me around to face him.

"Look at me," he said quietly.

"No." I pinched my eyes shut.

"Mia," he said, laughter in his tone. "Will you please look at me? I want to say something to you."

"So say it. I don't need to look at you to hear you. You don't listen with your eyes."

"But you'll see the truth in my expression. Please, babe, open your eyes."

Finally, I lifted my eyelids and tilted my head back to stare at him. His hands came up from my hips to cradle my cheeks.

"You should always speak your mind. There will be

times that I don't want to hear it. Times that I disagree with you. Times that I agree with you. There will be times that I know you're right, but wish you were wrong. Or I'll know you're wrong but wish you were right." One of his hands left my face to brush against the bandage peeking out from my tank top.

"This? This wasn't a whim. It wasn't bullshit. If you don't buy that this is real or for the long haul, then I don't know what I can do to prove that it is. Time is my only proof, I guess. I know the only thing that will make you realize it's legit is by showing you. So you can do whatever the fuck you want to and try to push me away." He pressed his forehead to mine. "I won't go. You want to call me a criminal. Fine. I am. You want to tell me you don't want babies with me because you don't want them to grow up to be criminals? Well, I get it. But I don't see myself that way even though it's true. It's all true. You don't know shit about this way of life yet because all you've been exposed to is Dev and you've seen Richie's burned, tortured body. Give me some time and I promise you you'll see it all differently."

"Colt," I whispered.

"My name is James," he said, his tone raspy. "James Stewart Weston, and when I marry you, you'll be a Weston. And when we have kids—because damn it, there needs to be tiny yous running around in this world, they'll be Westons too. There needs to be more light in this shit-as-fuck world. And the only way I know how to leave it a better place is to give it a piece of you. Because you're all fucking heart and I know that. I know it in my soul, Mia. I swore I'd protect you and keep you safe. That goes for our family too. I'll protect you," he repeated. "All of you."

The tears that had been hovering finally came with an

intensity I couldn't hold back. Nothing could contain them, and I let out a heaving sob.

From that moment I knew that whatever Colt was, whatever life path he was on, I would be there for him.

I would ride beside him as his woman, forever.

"I've been alone so long," I whispered. "I didn't even know what a family is supposed to look like."

"It can look however you want, honey. But don't say no because you're scared. Don't say no because you think you'll fail. You can't fail, not with me. I choose you and I will not leave you."

"Everyone leaves," I said, my tears blurring my vision. "They don't mean to, but they do."

"Not me. I'm not gonna die and leave you alone. Whoever has the rights to my soul will have to drag me kicking and screaming. You give me too much to live for. So whatever shit we have to get through now, we will. We'll endure. Together."

His words left me breathless, like a powerful aphrodisiac. This strong, brave man—I knew he couldn't protect me from everything. He couldn't shield me from all that life would throw at us. That wasn't the point. The point was he'd be with me through it all.

"I need to feel you," I whispered.

His hands dropped from my body so he could step away. His eyes were dark.

I leaned against the edge of the counter, widening my legs ever so slightly.

He swallowed. "I don't—I can't—be gentle."

"I'm not asking for gentle."

He took me into his arms and our lips crashed together. We tore at each other's clothes in a mindless frenzy. I was still in Colt's boxers and my tank top so it took no effort to slither out of them. His hands went to my hair and his lips found mine again as he started walking backward.

I pulled my mouth from his. "Where are you going?"

"Trying to get you upstairs. You're walking naked through my house, you know."

"I thought it was our house?" I asked with a grin.

"Damn right, it's *our* house."

"They why aren't we having sex on our kitchen floor?"

"I'm out of condoms," he said with a chuckle. "I have more in my dresser drawer upstairs."

I inhaled a shaky breath as I forced myself to meet his gaze. "We don't need them."

"We don't?" he asked, his tone equally as flat as mine.

"I get the shot. I'm—protected."

"You sure?"

I nodded.

"What if something happens?"

"Then something happens."

His mouth swooped in to take mine. For all his dominance, this kiss was sensual, tender. Full of emotion that wasn't just about lust, but about something so much deeper.

Love.

It was about love.

It was about promise. A promise of the life we'd share together until death parted us.

I kissed him back just as eagerly, wrapping my arms around him. We sank to the floor. True to Colt's fantasy, I was on top, straddling him, completely naked. Only he still had all his clothes on.

I helped remove them as fast as possible. Our eyes met, our fingers grazed skin. I took him into my body with no barriers between us. All our walls were down.

"Christ." He swallowed. His brown eyes looked bright against his skin.

I'd never felt anything like it. I'd never been with a man without a condom. It was the ultimate bond of trust between us.

This beautiful, inked, criminal wanted to protect and shield me. He wanted a family with me. He wanted a life with me, and I wanted one with him.

Emotion that I had beaten back suddenly trailed down my cheeks. Colt's hands reached up to cradle my face, his thumbs brushing my tears away. When we came, we came together, and my heart was no longer mine, but had been given fully to the man beneath me.

I rested my cheek against his skin and closed my eyes. I breathed him in, savoring the moment, knowing that when we put our clothes back on we'd go back to being Colt and Mia. For now, we were just two hearts beating as one; bare, naked, unprotected.

"Was it everything you hoped it would be?" I asked, finally lifting my face and setting my chin on his breastbone.

He tilted his chin to peer down at me, a slight grin on his lips. "It was better. I should've known it would've been that way. It was a damn good fantasy come to life."

I smiled and slowly raised myself off him.

"Ah, I need a towel," I said, feeling my cheeks flush. "I'm kinda…"

"Kinda what?"

"You're all—ah…"

He laughed, a large booming sound that I swore shook the walls of the house.

"Dish towel hanging from the oven."

He got up and looked around for his boxers. Colt was just sliding into them when the front door opened, causing Colt and I to look at each other in confusion. Just in the nick of time, I managed to dive behind Colt's huge, brawny form before Zip strolled in.

"What the fuck," Colt barked. "You can't just walk in unannounced."

"Then why did you give me a key?"

I reached for the red and white checkered tablecloth on the kitchen table, one ear listening to Colt lay into Zip. The bowl of fruit rested in the center, but I managed to grab the edge of the cloth and pull it toward me. Unfortunately, the fruit spilled onto the floor, an orange rolling past Colt.

"Fruit suicide," I said and then let out a laugh as I dragged the tablecloth around me.

"Is she drunk?" Zip asked.

"Nope," I voiced. "Just trying to ease the tension before Colt levels you to the ground."

Zip suddenly smiled. "I don't think it's working. He still looks like he wants to smash my face in."

"My woman is naked," Colt stated. "Good thing she's small and can hide behind me out of sight. Now get the fuck out onto the porch. I'll be with you in a minute."

Zip laughed but left. A moment later the front door slammed shut.

Colt looked over his shoulder at me and I gave him a cheeky grin, but he wasn't amused. "No one else gets to see you like this. Do you hear me?"

I hugged him from behind. "I don't want anyone else to see me like this. Okay? Go talk to Zip about whatever it is he needs."

"What makes you think he needs anything except

destroying my post orgasm serenity?" he asked, though he sounded mollified.

"Intuition." I stood up on my tiptoes. "I'll head upstairs. Shower. Finish packing. I need to call Shelly anyway."

Colt's arms enclosed my waist. "Holler if you need help."

"Help? Help with what?"

He grinned. "Cleaning those hard to reach dirty places." Colt lightly smacked me on the butt and I left the kitchen before he had a chance to get me naked again.

"You. Did. What?" Shelly screeched.

I held the phone away from my ear and winced, letting her get out all her emotion.

"Are you done?" I asked.

"Well, I don't know," she admitted. "I can't believe you —well—you got a tattoo? And you're like, Colt's woman? His Old Lady?"

"You've got Mark's ring on your finger. What's the difference?" I demanded, suddenly losing my patience.

She fell silent and I instantly felt terrible. "Listen," I said. "You're my best friend in the entire world. You're my soul sister. I want you to be happy for me and celebrate this."

Shelly paused on the other end of the line. "I am happy for you. I really am. But I can't help but worry about you. You're not the girl that makes these kind of decisions at the drop of a hat."

"Richie's dead," I blurted out. "The Iron Horsemen dumped his mutilated body in front of the Blue Angels' clubhouse."

"He's dead?"

"Yep. I saw his body, Shelly. I saw what they did to him."

"Jesus, Mia. Seriously?" She exhaled slowly. "Is this why you jumped into a relationship with Colt? Because you're scared of the Iron Horsemen?"

"I jumped into a relationship with Colt because I love him."

"You admit that you jumped. And how the hell can you be in love with him? You barely know him."

"I know him."

"You don't."

I pinched the bridge of my nose. "I really don't want to argue with you."

"All right."

Her tone was frosty and I understood why. She felt like she was being shut down, unable to give her opinion on my relationship and love life. She'd wanted me to meet someone; she just hadn't wanted it to be a biker.

"There's a party tonight at the Blue Angels' clubhouse," I said, offering her the olive branch. "I hope you come."

"I'll think about it," she said.

"You're breaking my heart, you know?" I said softly.

"Okay." She sighed. "I'll be there. Even though I don't understand."

"But you love me anyway?"

"Always and forever, soul sister. I just want you to be happy."

"I am."

"Good."

I smiled. "Will Mark be able to come?"

"He's got a work thing. But I promise we'll have you over soon. You and Colt."

Something unfurled inside of me. I'd have Shelly and the Blue Angels. I didn't want them at odds. I wanted Shelly comfortable, and if she saw how the Blue Angels treated me, then she might change her mind about what I had gotten myself into.

"Can't wait to see you," I said. "It's been too long."

"Way too long."

"See you soon," I said, hanging up.

I took a quick shower and changed into a black halter dress that didn't conceal my bandage. I pulled my hair into a loose side braid and just as I was putting the finishing touches on my makeup, Colt walked into the bathroom.

His gaze raked over me. "You're gorgeous."

"Thank you," I said with a smile, my eyes still on my reflection so I didn't poke my eye out with the mascara wand. "What did Zip want?"

"Wanted to talk about Joni," he said.

"What about Joni?"

"About when she goes back to work. He wants a brother to drive her to and from her shift. Stay at the hospital while she's there."

"That's overkill, don't you think?" I asked. I shoved the wand back in its tube and screwed it shut.

"She lives alone, which I hate. She's staying at the clubhouse for the next little while, which she'll completely balk at, knowing her. I know she won't like having a brother dogging her heels, but I'll be damned if I give Dev a chance to pull some shit while she's at work."

I didn't ask if he was capable of that—if I could conceive it, then it was possible. After all, he'd dropped Richie's tortured body at the Blue Angels' clubhouse and done a drive by on Blue Angels' territory. I didn't think there was much he wouldn't do to get his point across.

"I'm gonna call another one of our chapters," he said,

looking thoughtful. "I need more men at our backs. We've got a lot of older brothers—men from my dad's time, but they're not up for this kind of shit."

"I didn't know there were more members," I said. "Will I get to meet them?"

"Eventually." He leaned against the bathroom counter. "Zip volunteered to be the one to drive Joni and sit at the hospital."

"You're gonna make your VP a watchdog?"

His eyes narrowed. "No one I trust more than him to protect my sister. And it was his idea."

"Right. Zip's idea…"

I wondered how Joni would feel when she found out this had all been orchestrated by Zip. Zip, who'd pretended they meant nothing to each other. Zip, who'd stayed over at her house the night she got injured because he couldn't bear to leave her side. Zip, the manwhore of a biker who wasn't supposed to have any feelings toward her.

Something was cooking there, I was sure of it. But for some reason Colt didn't see it, or didn't want to see it. I wasn't going to be the one to let him in on the situation.

"You almost ready?" he asked.

"Yeah, almost. Just need to pack up the last of my stuff and we can go."

"I got something for you." He left the bathroom and after gathering up my makeup and placing it in a floral makeup bag Joni had gotten me from the mall, I followed after him.

Colt was standing by his nightstand drawer, holding a black velvet jewelry box. My eyes flew to his and he chuckled when he saw my panicked expression. "It's not a ring. It belonged to my mother. Open it."

I flipped open the box, completely charmed and delighted by the necklace. It was a dainty skull with wings on a thin silver chain. The pendant was no bigger than a dime.

"Dad gave it to Mom when she became his Old Lady. I thought you'd like to have it."

I held out the box to him. "Put it on me."

He grinned and took the delicate necklace in his large hands. I turned around and presented my neck and a moment later, I felt the slide of cool metal against my skin.

Colt clasped the necklace and then his fingers lingered on the curves of my shoulders and he pressed his mouth to the spot right above the bandage that protected my new tattoo.

I waited for that feeling of impending doom, expecting a tightness in my chest at another emotional tie that bound me to Colt. But it didn't come, and the rightness of the moment settled in my bones like an anchor steadying a ship in a storm.

We finally got out of the house, hours after Colt wanted to leave, but we were on our way back to the clubhouse when his phone rang.

"Yeah?" He listened for a few moments and then said, "All right. Thanks. Get some brothers and we'll meet you there. Bring the van."

He hung up and then turned down a street that would not take us to the clubhouse. "That was Torque. He said the Iron Horsemen prospect hasn't been at your place in six hours. We're gonna go to your house and get your shit—whatever you want—clothes, furniture, and we'll move it to my house. Our house." He shot me an amused smile.

I grinned back in excitement. I would finally be able to grab the things that mattered to me, along with my entire wardrobe.

"What do you want to do with it?" he asked.

"Do with what?" I was distracted thinking about where to hang my family photos.

"Your house. You own it, right?"

"Yeah. I haven't really thought about it, to be honest. I'm not ready to sell it, but I'm not sure I want to become a landlord and rent it out."

I did like the idea of residual income without having to do anything. The house had been paid off for as long as I could remember and the roof had been replaced only a few years ago. It needed to be painted, but everything worked. The appliances, the fridge. It had all been taken care of.

We turned down the street and immediately had to pull over. Traffic was blocked off by cones and a fire engine. Before Colt could even put the truck into park, I was unlatching my seatbelt.

I ran down the block, sprinting into a group of people who were watching and pointing, rubbernecking but not doing anything except witnessing a house go up in flames.

"Get back!" A fireman in his uniform yelled at me when I'd dashed through the crowd, using my elbows.

I watched in numb horror as flames licked along the roof and poured out of the windows. Firemen with hoses attempted to put out the inferno.

"What the hell, Mia? You can't just take off like that."

I felt him at my back, but didn't turn around to address him. "That's my home," I whispered, still unable to comprehend what I'd just seen.

"I know," Colt said, his tone somber. He reached for my hand and gently pulled me toward the fireman in charge.

"Sir, please step back," the fire chief said. He was in his mid-fifties and clearly had been doing this a long time, long enough to have a sense of authority on the scene.

"My girlfriend's house," Colt explained.

The man's brown eyes shot to me. "Your home?"

I nodded. "How did this happen?"

"We won't know for a bit yet," he answered vaguely. "You were lucky you weren't inside."

"Yeah. Lucky."

"Excuse me. I need to talk to my crew." The fire chief dipped his head and then turned and walked away.

I heard the sound of motorcycles and immediately pressed myself against Colt.

"Relax," he said. "They're ours."

A few moments later, I saw, Boxer, Reap, and Cheese striding toward us.

"Acid parked the van on the other side of the intersection," Boxer said. "We couldn't get through. What the hell happened?" His gaze took in the smoking remains of the house.

"My home caught fire," I said, suddenly exhausted, bone-weary.

"Fuck," Cheese murmured.

I started to shake. Every keepsake, every photograph, my entire family history was in that house.

"This is bad shit," Reap said.

The men began to talk in low voices but it sounded like I was underwater and I couldn't make out what they were saying. I somehow found it within me to detach from Colt's side and walk to the fire chief.

"Sorry to bother you," I said, gaining his attention. "I just wanted to give you my number so you can reach me when you have more of an idea about what happened."

As he took my information, he asked me a ton of questions to make sure I wasn't committing insurance fraud.

"If I had to guess the cause, I'd say it was faulty electrical," he said after finishing his questions and realizing I'd had nothing to do with the fire.

"Faulty electrical. Sure." I nodded even though I was screaming inside. Dev and the Iron Horsemen had done this. They were toying with me, instilling fear, trying to manipulate me into giving them what Richie had taken from them.

My phone rang and it said UNKNOWN.

"Excuse me?"

The fire chief nodded in dismissal.

I moved away from the mayhem and walked down the block to get some distance and privacy. "Hello?"

"How's your house?" Dev asked, his tone light. Comical.

"I think you know."

Dev laughed. "Yeah, I do."

"Why did you do it?" I heard my voice. It sounded cool, detached.

"Simple. You take something from me, I take something from you."

"I didn't take anything from you."

"No, but Richie did, and you know where it is."

"Well, you already got him back, didn't you?" I snapped.

"Babe?"

I whirled, phone to my ear to see that Colt had come up behind me, his face downright scary.

"Who you talkin' to?" he asked.

I swallowed.

"Is that your man?" Dev asked. "Put him on. I want to speak to him."

I held out the phone to Colt and he took it. His eyes never left mine as Dev spoke to him. Colt's jaw clenched so tight it looked like his teeth would shatter.

Colt ended the call without saying a word and handed my phone back to me. I didn't want to ask what Dev had said to him. No doubt it would only heighten my fear.

"Party's canceled," he said finally.

I nodded. I wasn't in a festive, celebratory mood anyway.

We headed back to the Blue Angels that were standing on the sidewalk, looking very out of place in the quaint neighborhood. Colt spoke to them and then they disbanded, leaving Colt and I alone.

As we drove away, I looked out the window. I could see smoke in the sky, disappearing into the clouds. I closed my eyes and leaned my head back against the leather seat, scraping my nails against the hard fiberglass of my cast.

"Talk to me," he said.

"About what?"

"About what's going through your head."

"Why?"

"You just watched your grandmother's house go up in flames. You don't have feelings about that?"

"I have feelings," I said. "I know I should be angry. I know I should be ranting and screaming, cursing Dev's name. But right now, all I can feel is sad. My entire life was in that house. Photo albums, my grandmother's favorite teacup with a painted pink rose pattern on the delicate china, the shoebox of my mother's favorite costume jewelry. I have no idea what survived and I can't handle another loss, Colt."

"I fucking hate him for this." His tone was full of anger. "I hate that he's playing this sick game of cat and mouse and he took this from you."

"What did he—" my voice cracked. I cleared my throat before speaking again. "What did he say to you on the phone?"

He took a long time to answer, and when he did, he met my gaze. I nearly shivered from the cold savagery peering back at me.

"Something that's gonna make him beg for mercy before I'm through with him."

Chapter 18

WHEN WE GOT BACK to the clubhouse, he disappeared into the office. While I was trying to process the loss of my childhood safe haven, Colt was sitting alone, dealing with whatever Dev had told him.

And if I'd had the energy, I'd have been spitting mad at him. Our relationship was intense, and I was still new at it. But, I wasn't such a novice to know that when a woman needed a shoulder to lean on, it was her man's duty to be there.

But the Blue Angels were watching me, and I refused to look like a coward. So I left Colt to his own devices and then went to find his sister.

Joni would know what to say to me. She'd grown up with him; she must've had some directives about how to handle Colt's complete emotional shut down.

My heart trembled with pain and confusion. Usually, when he didn't want to tell me something, he blamed it on club business. But this wasn't club business. Whatever Dev said to him had gotten through Colt's tough exterior and turned him into a different man.

The violent man from the first night I'd met him was back.

I was nearly to the third floor when Joni said, "I don't want to talk about this."

"Well, I do," Zip rasped.

I paused mid-step, knowing the right thing to do would be to turn around and go downstairs to give them privacy. Or interrupt them by continuing my ascent.

I didn't do either.

Instead, I decided to stop where I was and eavesdrop like a reality TV drama addict.

"You can't go on a date with that doctor," Zip stated.

Joni snorted in dry amusement. "You can't tell me what to do. You can't tell me who to date."

"I'm not telling you who to date. I'm telling you who *not* to date."

"Why do you even care?" she demanded.

Apparently Zip didn't appreciate her sass because he said, "Last night in your apartment you threw yourself at me."

She gasped.

"You not only threw yourself at me, you took off your shirt and pressed your tits against me." His voice was a low, sexy growl.

Joni didn't reply.

"You pressed your tits against me and then you ground your body against mine."

"Yeah," she said, suddenly sounding tired. "And being the gentleman that you are, you didn't even touch me."

"Babe—"

"Which is why I'm going on a date with that doctor. You don't see me, Zip. You've never seen me. And every time I put myself out there, you reject me. There's only so much of that I can take, you know?"

"It's complicated. Colt's my president. My best friend. You're his little sister."

"It's not complicated. Actually it's really simple. You don't want me enough to risk Colt's wrath. To risk what it will do to your friendship."

"Darlin'—Joni—please."

She sighed. "Leave me alone, Zip. I'm begging you to leave me alone. Give me a chance to be happy with someone else. All right?"

For a moment I wasn't sure he'd answer her and then he said softly—so softly I almost didn't hear him, "All right."

The disappointment in the air was palpable. I heard Zip's heavy booted footsteps coming toward the staircase and I immediately began hiking up the stairs again, hoping that when I ran into Zip I could play off that I was just coming up now.

He turned the corner and came down two steps before stopping. "Mia," he said, surprise coloring his voice. "What are you doing up here?"

Blazes of color trailed up his neck.

Anger? Embarrassment?

I forced a small smile. "Hey. We just got back. Colt's in the office."

He nodded. We moved past each other on the stairs and when he was on the second floor landing, said, "I'm sorry about your house."

My throat tightened with emotion. "Thank you."

I went to Joni's room and knocked. She opened the door, swiping at her cheeks and attempting to hide her head.

"Hey," she said, her tone morose and miserable.

"You look how I feel," I told her, not even able to summon up a smile.

A cry escaped her lips and her eyes filled with tears. "Zip came to tell me about your grandmother's house. I'm so sorry."

"Is that all he came to tell you?" I asked, pinning her with a stare.

Her gaze widened and then she stood back to let me inside the guest room. It was clean and tidy with a double bed. It had its own small bathroom, but didn't have a tub.

She shut the door and leaned back to rest her head against it. "You heard, didn't you?"

"I might've been listening."

Joni let out a strangled laugh. "Here I am, worried about something inconsequential when you're dealing with the loss of your home."

I swallowed. "Got any booze?"

"Not up here," she said. "I can go down to the kitchen and swipe a bottle, but if I do that, Rachel, Allison, and Darcy will know something is up and demand entry into the sanctuary."

I thought about it for a moment. "I'm okay with that if you are. I just—I wanted to talk to you about Colt first."

"What about him?"

I described what had happened after he spoke to Dev on the phone and how Colt had gone cold. No emotion had crossed his face, and I worried he was ready to hurt someone.

Joni nodded. "He was like that the first few years after Dad died. It's Colt's version of survival mode. I couldn't get through—most of the time he couldn't be reached. Like, no matter what I said to him, he wouldn't hear me."

"Years?" I asked. "He was like this for years?"

"Yeah. He's older now. Weathered a few more storms. But this is a part of Colt and whatever Dev said to him— he didn't tell you, did he?" When I shook my head she went on, "Yeah, whatever Dev said to Colt shut him down."

"It's like he turned into someone else. Focused, callous."

"Ruthless," Joni added.

"Colt disappeared into the office the moment we got back here. I have no idea what's going on. I just know the party's been canceled considering neither of us are in a celebratory mood."

"I'm not in a celebratory mood either, if it makes any difference."

"Should I try talking to Colt?"

"No. Let him come to you."

"My grandmother's house was set on fire today," I said softly. "And all I can think about is what Dev said to Colt to make him retreat."

She reached out and squeezed my hand. Unfortunately, she hadn't given me any tools in how to break through Colt's coldness. I shook my head and changed the subject. "What happened between you and Zip?"

"Exactly how much did you hear?" she asked instead of answering.

"Something about pressing your tits against him…"

Her cheeks flamed with sudden chagrin and then she straightened her shoulders. "I could blame the pain meds for my behavior, and maybe they did have something to do with it. It made me bold and I did exactly as he said. But he just…he pushed me off him. Something inside of me broke when he did it, Mia. That was my last straw, you know? I thought nothing could hurt worse than seeing him with tramps climbing all over him. But it turns out, when you offer yourself, body and soul to a man, and he brushes you aside, that hurts far worse than anything else."

I sighed. "We really should've gotten a bottle of booze before diving into this."

She nodded. "No shit."

"I'll go downstairs and grab it," I said. "That way there's no chance of you seeing Zip."

Joni looked relieved. "Thank you."

I left her room and took the stairs quickly, worried that I'd run into Zip and have to lie to his face again. But my feelings were all for naught. The only Blue Angel in the clubhouse was Gray, and he was sitting on a couch with Darcy nestled in his arms. Rachel and Allison were standing in the kitchen, drinking out of red solo cups.

"Where is everyone?" I asked.

Darcy looked over her shoulder at me. "You didn't hear the bikes peel out of here?"

I shook my head.

"They left," Darcy said. "Cheese, Gray, and two prospects stayed back to stand guard. The kids are watching a movie in the theater room in the basement."

They left? And Colt hadn't even had the courtesy to say goodbye?

Fuck. That.

He didn't get to shut down on me and then leave without saying a word. Not after what I'd been through.

"Where's Joni?" Gray asked. "She feeling okay? She hasn't come out of her room all afternoon."

"She's fine. I actually came down to get a bottle of liquor. We're having a girls' pow-wow in her room."

"Great!" Rachel said. "Now you can teach us how to play poker." She opened a kitchen drawer and pulled out a deck of cards.

Darcy kissed Gray's cheek and whispered something to him. He nodded and patted her leg. She hopped up and said, "What are we drinking?"

"Tequila," Rachel and I said at the same time.

"I need a lemonade refill," Allison said, lifting her cup.

"I'll cut the limes," Darcy stated. "Rach, grab the salt."

"On it."

Five minutes later, we were ready to head upstairs when Cheese came inside. "Mia," he said, "a woman is here for you. Says she was invited to the party."

"Crap. Blonde? Tall? Won't take no for an answer?"

He nodded, a slight smile on his face.

"That's Shelly. I forgot to tell her the party was canceled." I looked at the three women who were waiting by the stairs to get our girls' night started.

"Do you guys mind one more?" I asked.

"No, bring her!" Rachel said. "We'll meet you up there."

"Sounds good." The three of them disappeared and I turned back to Cheese. "Is it okay to let her in?"

"Sure thing. I'm gonna call Prez and give him the heads up about the situation."

"You do that," I murmured to his retreating back.

"How are you doing?" Gray asked, startling me. He was so quiet I'd forgotten he was even there.

"Okay. I guess." I sighed. "How did you get roped in to staying back with all the women and children?"

He looked at me. "Why? You think I can't handle shit?"

"No, I didn't mean anything by it." I tried to backtrack.

"Hey, I was just trying to get your goat." He smiled. "Relax. I know how it looks."

He was soft around the middle, like a lot of men in middle age. "One thousand yards," he said.

"Excuse me?"

"All I need is one shot, and if you're anywhere within a

thousand yards it's bye-bye. I was a scout sniper in the Army. I can handle things here, don't you worry."

My eyes widened. "Darcy never mentioned…"

He shrugged.

"This is the saddest party I've ever seen," Shelly said, causing me to turn.

She was dressed from head to toe in all black. Her blond hair was curled and sprayed and she looked ready for a night on the town. Cheese stood behind her, gazing at her with obvious adoration.

"There's been a change of plans," I said, walking to her.

Shelly embraced me in a vanilla perfumed hug and I closed my eyes. She was familiar. She was family.

"What happened?" she asked. "Where is everyone? Where's this man of yours?"

"I'll tell you upstairs."

Shelly pulled back and raised her eyebrows but said nothing.

Gray introduced himself to Shelly with a quick handshake. While Gray and Shelly talked for a few minutes, I went over to Cheese who still looked awe-struck.

"She's engaged," I told him.

"Engagements end."

I burst out laughing, enjoying Cheese's arrogance. I didn't have the heart to tell him that Mark and Shelly were the real deal, and even if they weren't and Shelly was single, she wasn't going to go for a biker.

My phone buzzed in my back pocket and I took it out. Colt's name flashed across the screen. I thought about being incredibly juvenile and ignoring him, but I knew he'd only call back. Or call Cheese to check in on everything.

"Yes?" I asked, answering the phone and going into the kitchen nook for a measure of privacy.

He paused. "You're pissed."

"Damn right, I'm pissed. You didn't even say goodbye to me."

Colt let out a weathered sigh. "I'll be back late. Don't wait up."

He hung up on me and I stared at the phone for a second.

Pissed had just morphed into rage.

"Uh oh," Shelly said.

"Uh oh, what?" Cheese asked.

"Mia's about to go O'Banion on someone's ass."

Cheese frowned. "I don't know what that means."

"It means," Shelly explained, "that she's half Irish and it's about to show."

"I can hear you," I snarled.

"Guess I better get back out there," Cheese said, stepping toward the exit. "Prospects don't know their asses from their elbows."

"You were a prospect not even six months ago," Gray said with a laugh.

I grasped Shelly's hand and pulled her to the stairs. We got up to the third floor and I could hear the sound of laughter and conversation coming from Joni's room. Colt's sister was perched on the bed, leaning against the wall, a cup in her hands. Darcy, Rachel, and Allison had taken pillows and set them on the floor and were sitting in a circle, the bottle of tequila and the bowl of lime wedges in the center.

"There you are!" Darcy said with a grin. "Hi!" She looked at Shelly. "I'm Darcy." The other women chirped their names.

"Would you like a drink?" Rachel asked Shelly.

"Sure." She set her purse in the corner. "What are we drinking?"

"Tequila shots," Joni announced.

"Oh, then I definitely want a drink." Shelly winked.

Those who could drink alcohol did a round of shots. When Shelly spit out her lime, she looked at me and said, "You never did tell me why the party got cancelled."

"The party got cancelled because my house caught on fire. I wasn't feeling very celebratory after that."

"Holy fuck. How did that happen?"

I met Joni's gaze and then my head swiveled to Darcy's. Both of them had blank expressions and I knew what I had to say.

"The fire chief thinks it was something with faulty electric. I won't know until he calls. And I don't know the extent of the damage yet."

"You weren't home, right?"

"No. I was at Colt's."

"Thank God. I'm so sorry about your house. That's like—I can't—why does shit keep happening to you?"

"I told you I'm a beacon for trouble," I quipped, but my lip wobbled.

She squeezed my arm. "Okay, let me finally get a good look at your tattoo."

I gave her my back and pulled my braid to the side so she could uncover the bandage.

My best friend whistled. "This is gorgeous."

"Yeah?"

"Yeah. Whoever did your tattoo did a stellar job." She covered it back up.

"Roman over at Three Kings did it," I said.

"I'm trying to convince Mark that we should get matching ink. He's not having it."

"Who's Mark?" Rachel asked.

"My fiancé."

"You're engaged!" Allison squealed. "Show us the ring!"

Shelly whipped her hand out to present her classy, elegant diamond.

"When's the wedding?" Joni asked.

"I'm not sure," she said slowly, looking at me. "I kind of wanted to wait until Mia can be part of the festivities." She shook her head. "You were leaving town and now you're shacked up with a…Blue Angel. Jesus, things change fast."

"Yeah. They do."

Darcy tossed me the deck of cards. "You promised to teach us how to play poker."

"No, I promised I'd teach you how to cheat at poker." I laughed.

Joni slid off the bed and squeezed into the circle.

"Did you get a tattoo too?" Shelly asked, gesturing to Joni's arm.

"Take another shot," I told her. "I have some shit to tell you." I wasn't able to divulge everything that was going on, but it was for her own protection.

Three hours later, we were all hammered. Gray had come upstairs to check in on us, but aside from him, there had been no word from the outside world. My phone didn't buzz with a message from Colt.

"I need my bed," Allison said finally.

"Why? You haven't even been drinking," Shelly pointed out.

"I'm pregnant."

Shelly's eyes were glassy. "Oh. Why didn't you say so earlier? This whole time I thought you were just a straight-laced weirdo."

They all cackled. Shelly fit right in with my new friends

and it warmed my heart.

"I need a smoke," Rachel said.

"I need air," Shelly muttered. "I shouldn't have had that last shot. I'm not safe to drive."

"Last shot?" Joni repeated with a teasing smile. "More like the last three."

Shelly rolled her eyes.

"The sofa in the basement theater room has a pull out couch. You should crash there," Darcy said.

"Really?" Shelly asked.

"Or, if you're feeling dangerous, I'm sure Cheese would let you sleep in his bed," I teased.

"Stop," she said with a laugh.

Darcy stood up off the floor and shook out her leg. "Ooh, it fell asleep."

I put the cards back into their box and also rose and held a hand to Joni to help her stand.

We went downstairs, drunkenly jabbering like magpies. Even though I'd had enough alcohol to fell an elephant, it didn't fill the aching sadness in my chest. I drank to temper the feelings of watching my grandmother's house go up in flames. I drank to forget the feelings of loneliness inspired by Colt's sudden emotional withdrawal.

Despite being in the company of my friends and watching them all get along and joke around, I felt alone.

"I'm going to go check on Gray and the kids," Darcy said. "I'll meet you guys at the picnic tables."

She waved us toward the back door and then turned the opposite direction down the hallway to the living room.

"I'm going to bed," Allison announced. "Seriously, I can barely keep my eyes open."

"You're no fun now that you're knocked up," Rachel said with a playful grin.

"Just you wait. Your time will come." Allison leaned

over and gave me a quick hug and then did the same to Shelly. "It was great meeting you. I hope we see more of you."

With a final wave, she went into Torque's room and closed the door.

"And then there were four," Joni said.

The night air was warm but not sweltering and I breathed in a deep breath.

"Will it bother you if I smoke?" Rachel asked. We shook our heads and Rachel pulled out a pack of cigarettes. "I really do need to quit."

"Yeah, you do," Joni said.

"Now, now, Nurse Joni. None of that." She lit the cigarette and then took a drag. "Jesus. Nothing else relaxes me quite like a cigarette."

"Not even an orgasm?" Shelly asked with wicked amusement.

"Well, not the same ballpark." Rachel winked.

"Whoa, I think I need to sit down," Joni said. "I had more to drink than I realized." She plopped down on a picnic table bench and leaned back, resting her elbows on the table before looking up at the night sky.

I took advantage of the moment while Rachel and Shelly were in conversation to pull Joni's attention away from the group. I took a step closer to her and blurted out, "Zip's going to go with you to your shifts at the hospital."

Her head snapped up. "What do you mean?"

"Colt doesn't want you unprotected. Zip volunteered to be the one to drive you to and from work and sit at the hospital during your shifts."

"That fucker," she seethed. "So when he told me he'd leave me alone, he was full of shit."

I nodded. "Full of shit *and* I'm pretty sure he's on the

edge. Don't give up on him just yet. I think he's close to breaking."

"*I'm* close to breaking."

"Yeah, but what if you could finally get everything you want? What if you could really be with him?"

"I've tried throwing myself at him. He still balked."

I nodded. "I know, but if Zip is going to be at your place of work, he's bound to see you and the doctor who asked you out. Together. Make him jealous, Joni. Make him think he's really lost you and the only way to have you is to take you from someone else."

"That's like my biggest fantasy come to life." She grinned.

"He can't take his eyes off you," I said. "He stares at you when he thinks you're not looking. Bring this shit to a boil and I guarantee he'll be taking whatever Colt gives him. Just make sure when you get him into bed, he has no reason to leave."

"Oh, I'm on it. There are years of sexual tension between us. We might burn the house down." She winced. "Shit. Sorry."

The humor on my lips died and I suddenly felt way too sober. "I think I better call it a night."

She nodded. "It's late. You need to be alert when you give Colt hell."

Rachel finished her cigarette and Joni got up from the table. We walked inside the clubhouse and I paused. "You notice that Darcy never came back to join us?"

"She's probably on top of Gray right about now," Rachel said with a grin. "Come on, Shelly. I'll show you the couch in the theater room. Darcy's kids are probably asleep on the floor in sleeping bags, so don't be alarmed if you see tiny people first thing in the morning."

Shelly laughed. "Thanks for the heads up." She

hugged me hard. "I work tomorrow at nine, so you might still be asleep by the time I get out of here. I have to go home and shower and stuff before then. Can't show up at the salon with mascara around my eyes and smelling like a tequila emporium."

I laughed. "Yeah. That wouldn't be a vote of confidence."

"You're okay though?" she whispered in my ear. "I mean, he treats you well? We never really did get to talk about him. Not in depth, and not in the way that we normally do."

"He's great."

That was the truth.

Right now there was something between us—a cold wall—and I knew Dev was the one who'd put it there. But when Colt got home tonight, I'd claw my way through the bricks and mortar, I'd scale his fortress, I'd dig a tunnel underneath if I had to. I'd find a way back in, because we were stronger together than apart. And even if Colt couldn't tell me everything about the Blue Angels, this thing with Dev was about me specifically and I deserved to know.

Shelly pulled back and her hands went to my shoulders. She took a moment to stare into my eyes. "The house? It's just stuff."

"Photographs, Grammie's favorite tea cup, Mom's jewelry? That's all just stuff? There is sentiment attached to those things."

"What did my father do when I moved out of the trailer? He set all my shit on the lawn and torched it. Things I'd bought with my own money. Tapestries that hid the dirty, water stained walls, the collage posters I spent hours making from recycled magazines I'd found outside the bowling alley. I cried. I did. Because at that moment I only had one suitcase full of shitty old clothes that were falling apart. But I made it through, and you will too." She squeezed my shoulders. "It's just stuff. The fire didn't take your memories. Okay?"

I sighed. "This is why I need you. Always."

"Soul sister."

"Soul sister."

With one last hug, she turned and followed Rachel down the basement steps.

Joni placed a hand on my shoulder, reminding me that she was still there and had heard my entire exchange with Shelly. "She really is amazing. It's too bad she already has a man. She'd be a great Old Lady."

Chapter 19

Cool air kissed my skin and then I felt stubble on the inside of my thighs. A tongue stroked me, making me shiver.

"Colt," I whispered.

My hands reached out to grasp his hair. I saw him in the moonlight, big and brawny, a dark shadow giving me more pleasure than I could take.

He wouldn't let up, not even when I was coming on his tongue, shaking and moaning, crying out with need.

Colt lifted his head. "I need you."

I nodded.

"All fours."

He flipped me over, his hands angling my hips. I felt him at my entrance and then he was inside me. I gasped at the invasion, feeling him everywhere. His thrusts were ruthless, determined to fill me up so that there was nothing but Colt.

My fingers gripped the sheets and he continued to assault my every nerve. I was liquid fire, and with each stroke it became an inferno. One hand pinned my hip, the other reached around to play with me.

Heat blazed between my legs as Colt continued to drill into me from behind. I couldn't see his eyes. I didn't need to, knowing they'd be full of lust.

He slammed into me and I went up in flames. My limbs gave out and I would've collapsed onto the bed if Colt's hands hadn't been there to hold me up, his fingers digging into my skin as he rammed me like an animal.

Brutal and savage.

And I loved it.

"Mia," he growled and then he came.

He wrapped an arm around me and brought us down onto our sides, mindful of my injured wrist. We were silent as our breathing and heartbeats returned to their natural cadence—and with it came the return of my anger.

I pushed away from him and scrambled from the bed, looking for my underwear, which he'd somehow pulled off of me without me knowing. Sure, I'd been woken up in a pleasurable way, but it felt like he'd done it to lull me into a state of acceptance for his behavior.

Sex was not a bandage for the wound of his emotional withdrawal.

I hit my knee on the corner of the bed and cursed, hobbling my way to the nightstand table and turning on the lamp. Colt was on his side, head propped up on his elbow, looking devastatingly gorgeous in nothing but skin and ink. His eyes followed me as I found my clothes and quickly covered myself.

"Words, babe," he said after a moment.

"Words? What words?" I snapped.

"I'm asking you to talk to me instead of cursing and running from the bed."

"You're kidding, right?"

He sat up, looking like a jungle cat stretching before it pounced. "I want to know what's going on inside your head."

"Right now? A whole mess of shit." I stared at him. "You shut down on me today. After you talked to Dev."

"Yeah. I did." He nodded. "But you shut down on me too."

"My grandmother's house was on fire. And what the hell, Colt? We're not talking about me. We're talking about you."

"So—talk."

I was so angry I felt like my nerves were going to burst into flames, causing a raging wildfire within me. "You can't come in here and wake me up the way you did, not after how you treated me this afternoon. You didn't tell me you were leaving; you were just gone. And then you called me to tell me not to wait up."

He didn't reply for a long moment, studying me with a thoughtful expression.

"Where were you tonight?" I demanded.

"Giving Dev a dose of his own medicine."

"I don't know what that means." We stared at each other for a long moment and Colt didn't volunteer what *a dose of his own medicine* meant. "What did Dev say to you?"

"Why do you want to know?"

"Because I need to know what makes you go all dark and cold. I need to know things like that so I can," I sighed, "handle you."

His frigid gaze matched his tone when he explained, "He said that when he got his hands on you he'd fuck you in every one of your holes until you bled, and only when you begged for death from the pain of him, he'd slit your throat. He promised to send a treasure map with your body parts marked on it so I could collect the pieces of you."

No. Words.

I had no words.

Colt reached out and placed his hands on my hips and hauled me forward. "You're shaking. You're terrified like I knew you would be. I didn't want to put that on you. I didn't want to ever tell you what he'd said, and I shut down because I knew it was inevitable. That I would *have* to tell you. I gotta know you're strong enough to hear shit like that."

Nausea rose in my belly. I forced it down. I would not let Dev's words haunt me. I would not give them any power.

I wasn't sure what I was supposed to say to Colt so I just pulled him to my chest and buried my face in his hair.

He tilted his head back so he could look me in the eyes. "Are we okay?"

I swept a thumb across his lips. "Yeah. We're okay."

"I want to see you handle a pistol."

"You think the pistol in my glove box is for show? I can shoot."

"I want to see it with my own two eyes."

"Fine."

"And then you start carrying it on you. Everywhere you go."

"I don't have a concealed carry permit," I said.

His jaw hardened. "You let me worry about that."

The next morning, I rolled over and stared at the ceiling, trying to quell the subtle nausea that came with just a bit too much tequila.

Colt's arm was thrown across my waist, his face pressed into the pillow. I knew by the sound of his breathing that he was awake, but we didn't say anything to each other.

Somehow I managed to prop myself up in bed. I reached for my cell on the nightstand. Shelly had texted a few hours ago, saying that she'd left. I shot back a reply and asked if she was hungover too.

I set my phone aside and tried to get out of bed, but Colt's fingers gripped my thigh. "Where are you going?"

His voice was gravelly and deep, and it made me think of when he'd come to me last night, needing to slake his pleasure. He'd used me in a way that hadn't made me feel used at all.

Need erupted between my thighs, but I knew I couldn't stay in bed and let him make me forget everything I had to face.

"I need coffee and Aspirin. And a shower," I added as an afterthought. "Preferably in that order."

"Yeah. Definitely a shower. I can smell the tequila coming out of your pores."

I pulled a pillow from behind my back and swatted him with it. He tried to roll over to protect himself, laughing when I caught him in the stomach. He retaliated and easily got the pillow away from me. Before I knew it, we'd changed positions and I was on the bottom, breathing hard.

"I know a good cure for a hangover," he said, his smile wicked, his eyes languid.

"Do you?" I murmured.

His fingers sought the place between my thighs and I winced.

"I hurt you last night." Colt's expression was contrite. "I'm sorry."

I let my legs fall open. "Don't be."

"You sure?"

"It's a good kind of hurt."

"I'll be gentle this time," he promised.

Twenty minutes later, after a very satisfying wake-up call, we both managed to get moving. I stumbled to the shower as Colt reached for his toothbrush.

By the time I was done, I was feeling marginally better. I dressed in a pair of denim shorts and a black tank. I threw my hair up into a messy bun and paraded barefoot out of Colt's clubhouse room.

"You look like hell, darlin'," Boxer said in way of greeting. He was lounging on a couch, his feet propped up on the coffee table.

"I showered. Don't tell me you can smell the booze coming off me?" I asked. With a sense of familiarity, I grasped his mug of coffee and took it for my own.

"Nah, I was referring more to the fact that you're pale and your eyes are bloodshot."

"You know, you're like the older brother I never wanted."

He grinned.

Colt poured himself a cup of coffee and then took a seat in the recliner. He patted his leg and I perched on his lap, happily sucking down Boxer's coffee.

"Is no one else awake?" I asked.

"No. I mean, the kids are. They're downstairs in the theater basement watching movies and eating cold pizza for breakfast."

"You've got to be kidding. Where are Darcy and Gray?"

"Still conked out."

"I want to take Mia out back to the range. I want to see her shoot. You in?"

"Hell yeah I'm in. Just as long as she doesn't use me as target practice."

"I'm an excellent shot," I said with a wide grin.

"That's what worries me," Boxer joked.

I looked at Colt. "You have a range out back?"

"Yeah, we use it as a place to blow off steam. It's nice owning property."

My cell buzzed in my back pocket, and I pulled it out, hoping it was a text from Shelly.

No dice.

It was an unknown number, but I refused to answer it. It was probably Dev. I silenced the call and stuck my phone into my back pocket. A moment later, I felt a buzz, knowing I had a voicemail.

Colt and Boxer were talking so I got up off Colt's lap to get some distance. I pressed the voicemail button and listened to it, releasing a slow breath when I realized it wasn't Dev.

When the message ended, I stood for a moment in the kitchen, feeling dazed.

"Babe?" Colt called. "You okay?"

"Yeah. I'm okay," I murmured.

Colt and Boxer exchanged a look and then Boxer got up. "I'm gonna grab a shower. Then I want to see her shoot."

He saluted me before he left the room.

"You look like you've seen a ghost," Colt said, getting up from the recliner and coming to me.

"Richie's lawyer just called me." I met Colt's dark brown gaze. "And he wants to meet with me."

"Name?"

"Santoro. Leo Santoro."

"I'll check him out. See if he's who he says he is. Then we'll go together, okay?"

Leo Santoro was a short man with very little black hair left on his balding head. He was somewhere in the age bracket of forty-five to sixty-five. His brown suit did nothing for his appearance, and made him look like every other two-bit hack-job of an attorney. He was just the sort of lawyer I'd expect to represent Richie.

"Miss O'Banion," he greeted, standing up from behind his cluttered desk. "Thank you for coming." He held out his hand, and I shook it. It was clammy, and it took all of my willpower not to wipe my palm on my jeans right in front of him.

The room he called an office was musty and smelled of mildew. A shaft of sunlight crept through a dirty glass window and dust floated in the air, backlit so that it was much too obvious.

"Would you and your...companion like something to drink?" Leo's eyes flicked over Colt, who stood in front of the closed door, looking menacing and ferocious.

"This is my boyfriend," I said quickly, noting the look of displeasure on Colt's face. He clearly didn't like the lawyer any more than I did. "And we're fine. Thank you."

I took a seat in an old, wooden chair. It wasn't very comfortable and looked like it was about to collapse.

"Perhaps your boyfriend would like to wait outside?" Leo asked. "This is a private legal matter."

"That's okay. It's fine if he stays," I stated.

Leo shrugged. "Your prerogative. Let's get down to it then. You're here because Richie DeMarco ordered the transfer of the deed to Dive Bar directly to you."

I blinked. "Excuse me?"

Leo opened his desk drawer and pulled out an envelope. He flipped it open and took out the top paper and handed it to me. "This is the deed to Dive Bar. Richie set things up weeks ago so that you would get the bar—which is fully paid off, by the way. So long as you remain in good standing with yearly property taxes, business licenses, and insurance, the bar is yours."

"He *gave* me Dive Bar?" I asked, taking the deed but not reading it. "I didn't even know he owe it."

"He bought it in cash years ago, and all the insurance policies and forms are up-to-date, complete with your name as beneficiary should anything happen to the bar." Leo cleared his throat. "Richie is a stickler for paperwork."

What an oddity, considering he had no problems getting into bed with the Iron Horsemen and stealing from them.

"I don't understand. Why did he do this?"

"Why, I can't say. I don't get paid for why. I just do as my clients ask. And this client made it very clear that you now own Dive Bar. Just sign here, and this copy too please."

I took the pen from his outstretched hand and signed my name next to a sticky arrow on the deed and a copy of the paperwork for the attorney to keep.

"Thank you for reaching out to me, and for your time today." I stood, making sure I had all my belongings, including the paperwork, needing to get out into the sunshine and breathe air that didn't reek of mold and dust mites.

When we escaped the lawyer's office, I inhaled deeply. And did it a few more times. The street smelled of grease and urine and I instantly wished I hadn't bothered taking such a deep breath.

My head spun with everything Leo had told me; none of it made any sense at all. It only made me more confused.

"Let's get back to the clubhouse," Colt said. "We can talk there. Yeah?"

I nodded.

We climbed into his truck. "I can't wait to get you on the back of my bike. I hate having to take the truck everywhere."

I held up my cast.

"Your safety is my top concern," he said, pulling his aviators out of his vest pocket and sliding them onto his nose.

"When did you get on a motorcycle for the first time?" I asked.

"Twelve."

"That seems young."

"I was big for my age."

I laughed. "Yeah, I bet you were."

He grinned. "Why do you think my road name is Colt?"

"Then you really are nicknamed after a young male horse?"

"No, it's not a nickname, but a road name. Road names are given by your brothers."

"So how did you get your name?" I queried.

He scratched the stubble on his jaw. "When I was fourteen, I went with my dad to visit another club. The meeting place was a strip joint." He shot me an amused look. "While my dad was taking care of business, I was told to sit at the bar, enjoy a cherry coke, and wait. Well, I heard a noise coming from one of the dressing rooms, so I went to investigate."

His jaw clenched at the memory. "One of the bouncers had a stripper on her knees and he was forcing her to give him a blow job. She was choking on his dick and not enjoying it. Her eyes shot to mine, tears streaming mascara down her face, and before I could even think, I had my dad's old Samuel Colt revolver out from my back pocket, and I was pistol whipping the shit out of him. I put that fucker in the hospital."

"Holy shit, are you serious?" I asked, my mouth agape.

"Completely. Told you I'm protector of women."

"Yeah." I nodded. "You really are."

"Does that story change how you view me?"

"I saw what you did to that shithead the night we met, remember? I—the world needs more men like you, Colt."

He grinned. "So… do you have any nicknames?"

"No. None that I'd like to remember, anyway."

"Guess I'll have to come up with a nickname for you then."

"I guess so."

He started the ignition and then we drove away. Colt turned on the radio to a classic rock station, almost like he knew I didn't want to talk and needed time to think. The papers on my lap drew my attention, but I made no move to study them.

Acid and the other prospects let us through the gate. Colt took the papers from me as we walked into the clubhouse. Cam, Lily, and Silas were eating grilled cheese sandwiches at the breakfast bar. Lily jumped off her stool and ran to me and embraced my legs. I swept her up into a hug, closing my eyes and breathing in the smell of little girl and sunshine. She was exactly what I needed after the morning I'd had.

Darcy was sitting with Gray in the living room and Rachel was drinking a bottle of Pepto Bismol.

"Still hungover?" I asked after setting Lily down. She ran to her mother and crawled up next to her.

Rachel nodded. "It's awful. I've only been able to suck down coffee and eat a piece of toast."

"I haven't even eaten today," I said.

"You can have half my sandwich," Cam said, offering the mangled shred to me, complete with sticky child's handprints in the bread.

"Thanks, but you should finish it." I smiled and then looked at Darcy. "Where is everyone?

"Joni had a shift at the hospital," Darcy said. "Zip went with her, much to her consternation. They got into a big argument in front of everyone."

"I didn't want her out there on her own," Colt said. "Not with all this sh—"

"Colt," I interrupted, widening my eyes and gesturing with my chin to the kids.

He grinned suddenly. "Stuff. All this stuff going on."

"I agree with you," Darcy said. "But clearly Joni had some other ideas about how it was supposed to go down. Allison—last I knew—was suffering from a bout of morning sickness and Torque has been looking after her. Cheese is conked out after being on watch last night. Reap and Boxer are at the garage and Acid and the prospects are out front—which you saw when you came in."

She pinned me with her eyes. "You guys get done what you needed to get done?"

I shrugged. Colt had told Boxer where we were headed and apparently Boxer had relayed it to everyone. It was difficult to keep a secret from any of them. They were a close-knit family, all up in each other's business. It was still a foreign concept to me, but I was slowly coming around to the new dynamic.

"Let's go to the office," he said.

I followed him down the hall. He closed the door once we were both in private. It was a small room with a desk and laptop, a file cabinet in the corner, and two chairs in front of the desk. It wasn't a place for all the Blue Angels to congregate, but Zip and Colt often disappeared into the room to discuss things privately between them before taking it to their brothers.

Colt set down the stack of papers on his desk and waved me toward them. "Have a seat."

I took the swivel leather chair and started pawing my way through the papers. "Why?" I asked, my hands stilling.

"Why did Richie give you the bar?"

I nodded. "It doesn't make any sense. I was his employee. I mean, he knew me. He knew I had no one except Shelly. Besides, he told me to leave town for a while. Why would he tell me that and then give me his bar?"

"Maybe he was giving you a new chance at life if you decided to come back to Waco," Colt said.

"But you don't just give someone a profitable business. Richie owed nothing on the building. You know?"

"Wait a minute. Think about what you just said. Richie left you the bar, with no clear reason, right? And Dev is looking for a shipment, yes?"

"Yeah, so?"

"So Richie gets in bed with the Iron Horsemen, but it proves to be too much. So how do you wipe out your enemy? *The Art of War*. The enemy of my enemy is my friend.

"Richie stole a shipment from Dev thinking someone else was going to get rid of Dev for him. He left you the bar because he didn't expect Dev to be around to cause you problems. And he certainly didn't expect Dev to catch up with him. If Dev was gone and Richie had gotten away with the shipment, he wouldn't give a fuck about the bar; he'd be loaded."

It was a sobering pronouncement and I nodded. Neither of us mentioned that my fate would be similar to Richie's if Dev had his way.

We both fell silent for a moment and then he asked, "The night you dropped Richie at the bus depot, did he tell you anything? Say anything that stuck out?"

"He told me to get out of town for a few weeks. That's all."

I stood up and began to pace across the office and then suddenly ground to a halt. "We made a stop. Before I dropped him off at the bus depot." I looked at Colt. "I took him to a storage unit in town. He was only in it for a few minutes and then he was back in the truck. I didn't see what he did when he was in there, though. And he came back empty handed. I thought maybe he was dropping something off for safe keeping, but come to think of it I don't remember him bringing anything into the unit either."

"Do you remember which storage unit?" Colt asked.

I thought for a moment and shook my head. "No. I was too caught up in my own thoughts and wasn't paying attention."

"But you didn't leave Waco to get to the unit…"

"No, we didn't leave Waco."

"Come on," he said, heading for the door of the office.

"Where are we going?" I demanded, as I trailed after him.

"We're looking in your truck to see if Richie left you any information or clues."

We walked through the clubhouse and out the front door. My truck had been moved from Charlie's to the club-house parking lot.

I dug through my purse for my keys and went to the driver's side door to unlock it. Grasping the handle, I dragged it open and then leaned across the flat bench seat to unlatch the passenger door.

I roved my hands over the floor of the truck, encountering loose change, but nothing of true value. I lifted myself up, trying to stem the feeling of disappointment. "Did you find anything?"

Colt didn't reply; he merely arched an eyebrow and held up a silver key—a silver key that no doubt fit into the lock on Richie's storage unit.

"Colt Weston, you might be my good luck charm."

We met Reap at a roadside diner on the outskirts of Waco. Reap and Colt sipped watered-down coffee while I consumed a hamburger and fries. I hadn't eaten anything all day and my stomach had been gnawing itself.

"You want me to do what?" Reap demanded.

"Distract the Iron Horsemen so Mia and I can move through Waco without anyone following us," Colt repeated.

"A diversion," I piped up between bites, feeling like a mix between the Hamburglar and a criminal mastermind.

He glared at me but said to Colt, "You don't want me to go with you?"

"We need to stay under the radar."

Reap ran a hand through his hair in frustration. "You think whatever Richie stole from the Iron Horsemen is in that storage unit."

"Yup," Colt said. "But we don't know which unit."

"I don't like you doing this without having someone covering your back," Reap said.

"I'm covering his back," I piped up. "I've got a pistol."

"Yeah, so I've heard." A slow smile spread across his face.

"Brother," Colt said softly. "I know you have my back. I

need you to handle protecting the clubhouse right now, and to arrange for a diversion."

Reap's eyes glittered with intention and the heaviness of the situation. Finally, he nodded. "I'll protect them— and I'll get Boxer on the diversion. He's good at starting shit."

"Yeah," Colt said with a dry chuckle. "He is."

Reap turned to me. "Darlin', even though you know how to shoot, I hope like hell you don't have to."

Wiping a glob of ketchup from the side of my mouth, I replied, "That makes two of us, dude."

Chapter 20

It was eleven p.m. I was exhausted, discouraged, and pissed-the-hell-off. I wanted to curse Richie, but he was dead and that seemed like bad juju.

"Who the hell would've thought Waco had so many storage companies?" I grumbled.

Colt pulled me into his side as we walked across the parking lot. "Eighth time's a charm."

"Let's hope."

We rounded the corner and headed down the long walkway to the second to last unit in the row. I pulled out the key from my back pocket and slid it into the lock.

"Well, this is a good sign." I looked at Colt in excitement as I turned the key. The lock snapped open. Colt reached down to the gate handle and lifted it just enough so we could duck under. He slid the gate shut, bathing us in darkness.

"Where's the light?" I asked as I felt along one wall.

"I think I found it. Hold on."

The room brightened. In the center of the storage unit

was a mound covered in a blue tarp. Colt moved toward it, picked up the edge, and pulled it back.

"Shit. Mother fucking fuck shit," he cursed.

"What is it?" I demanded, inching closer in curiosity and trepidation. "Meth? Like you thought?"

Instead of answering, Colt swept back the rest of the tarp revealing stacks and stacks of white powder in plastic bags. He picked one up, ripped open the edge, and sniffed.

"Not meth. Coke. Millions of dollars' worth of coke."

"Richie stole coke from Dev?"

"No," he said, his tone bleak. "Richie stole coke from a cartel by way of Dev. This just went from bad to holy fuck. Dev we can deal with, but nobody fucks with the cartels. *Nobody*."

I started. "How do you know this is cartel coke?"

"You remember what I told you before? You can't make this shit in a lab. Stuff like this has a country of origin, sweetheart, and it isn't the USA. Besides, I talked to the Jackals a while back. They said they'd been seeing an uptick in coke on the streets. It's like the nineteen eighties are back."

"Well, that's new information." I wrinkled my nose. "So Richie got into bed with the Iron Horsemen, who got into bed with a cartel?"

"Yup."

"And Dev will do anything to get this shipment back."

"Yup."

"This is awful. This is really awful."

He sighed. "You have no idea. The cartels make ISIS look like amateurs."

I closed my eyes and something clicked and I said, "That's why you haven't launched a full on attack on the Iron Horsemen. You were worried this was bigger than

Dev and you're trying to find out who's involved, aren't you?"

He nodded and sighed, suddenly looking like the weight of the world was resting on his impressive shoulders.

"What do we do with this?" I asked, gesturing to the packages of coke.

"For the time being, we leave it. I'm not moving this shit to the club. Somehow Richie managed to get it here and Dev still isn't the wiser. Last thing I wanna do is bring it back right under Dev's nose. We're going to leave it here. We're going to make a plan, and then we go from there."

Before pulling the tarp back over the stack, Colt took a small package and stuck it in his vest pocket, close to his chest.

"What are you doing?" I demanded.

"I gotta friend who can trace this shit. Country of origin, remember?"

I knew he wouldn't tell me anything more. He covered the product, and when he was sure it was concealed, we went to the gate and I turned off the light. Colt lifted the gate and went out first. He kept watch while I closed up. We kept our pace steady and calm, not wanting to appear like we were rushing. The storage lot was deserted this time of night, but we made sure to stay to the shadows and away from cameras. No one was getting our faces on security feeds.

I didn't breathe a sigh of relief until the doors of the truck were locked and the engine was running. There was something sinister about the storage unit. Who knew how many others were slinking around the dark, just like us.

"Are we going to go visit your friend?" I asked in exhaustion.

"*We* aren't headed anywhere," he said. "I'm dropping you off at the clubhouse and then Zip and I will—"

"Nope. Not happening."

He took his eyes off the road to glance at me. "You're not going, Mia."

"Why? Is your friend dangerous?"

"She's not my friend."

"Ugh. Fine. Your *colleague*."

"She's not that either."

"Colt," I warned.

"Mia," he said in the same tone.

"Why don't you want me to go? This involves me and Richie left this in my lap. I'm not going to let you clean it up without me."

"It's dangerous."

"I came with you tonight," I said in exasperation. "I can't just sit at home like a good little woman and wait for her man. Unless that's what you're expecting of me?"

Colt's lips twitched in humor. "How do I answer that so I don't get smacked?"

I smacked him.

"Guess that answers that."

I looked out the window. "You don't think I have the right to be there? I'm in this as much as you. Maybe more."

"What is it you want?"

"Control. Over what I learn. Over my involvement. I'm the one Dev is harassing."

"Hate to break it to you, darlin', but if it's control you're after, you're not going to get it."

"Don't patronize me.

"I'm not," he said, still rational, still calm. "But this shit is bad. We are talking ultra-dangerous—and I'd never forgive myself if something happened to you because of the life I dragged you into. I'm trying to protect you, darlin'. Don't you see that?"

I was quiet a moment and then, "You didn't drag me. I came running to you."

"Yeah, I guess you did."

We drove in silence for a few exits before he said, "You can come. But you will stay in the motel with Boxer. I'll take Zip as backup."

"Zip? But he's guarding Joni."

"I need my VP for this. I'll get Cheese to take over Joni's watch."

"But he's so young. Is he...experienced?"

"Yup. I trusted him enough to let him guard you, didn't I?"

I thought for a moment. "Okay. I'll stay with Boxer."

"No fight?"

I settled down in the seat, feeling sleepy, my eyes closing. "Nope. You were completely reasonable. Thank you. Where are we headed? Back to the clubhouse?"

He didn't answer as he fished his phone out of his vest pocket, flipped it open, and pressed a button. A moment later he said, "I need you and Boxer in Odessa by tomorrow at ten a.m. Get Cheese to cover you. It's worse than we thought. Come ready for a fight. I'll explain later." He hung up and set his phone in the center console.

"You didn't ask them about the distraction they caused."

"Didn't need to," Colt said. "Mia?"

"Yeah, Colt?"

"I'm sorry."

I opened one eye and looked at him as a pit of worry dropped into my belly. "For what?"

He glanced at me with a devilish grin. "For having the boys torch Dive Bar."

My mouth dropped open. "What is it with you guys and arson? First Dev sets fire to my home. And now the bar, *my bar*, had an arson problem?"

"It's not really your bar. Deed only. Dive Bar has been crawling with Iron Horsemen," he pointed out. "None of that matters at the moment anyway. We needed a distraction, right? That was perfect. It'll keep everyone busy for a while. And besides, you heard the lawyer, it's insured and the paperwork is up to date."

"I—you—seriously?" I glared at him.

He had the audacity to smile. "You should get some sleep."

"How the hell am I supposed to sleep now? Arson. Coke. A *cartel*. This is freakin' nuts."

"That's putting it mildly."

I swallowed. "I'm terrified, Colt. I mean, it was one thing to worry when I thought it was just the Iron Horsemen, you know? But a cartel? They take violence to an entirely new level and they don't give a *shit* about your moral code of not touching families or Old Ladies."

His hand clenched the steering wheel. "I know. Christ, I know."

"What did Richie think he was doing?" I asked, trying to figure out the thought process of my deceased boss. "Do you think Dev was screwing Richie over in some way and Richie wanted Dev to get into shit with the cartel?"

"He's not here to ask, sweetheart. All we can do is speculate."

Had it just been about money? Had it been all about greed?

Richie had never been terrible to me or to any of his employees, he'd just been an absent boss. He certainly didn't deserve the death he'd gotten.

No one deserved to die like that.

Somehow I was able to doze for a bit and woke up as we pulled into a shitty motel parking lot—one that looked like it could be rented by the hour. It was early morning and there wasn't any foot traffic. Colt knocked on door number 6 and Boxer answered. Zip was sitting on one of the two double beds smoking a cigarette.

"Let's get this shit done, yeah?" Zip asked in surly impatience. He sucked on the cigarette as he dashed from the room.

I looked at Boxer. "What's wrong with him?"

"No fucking clue. He's been like that for hours. Little ray of sunshine."

"We shouldn't be gone long," Colt said, gathering me into his arms. He kissed me, bringing me flush against his body.

The horn blared, causing me to jump and Colt to turn around and shoot a scowl in Zip's direction. "Bastard," he growled. "I'll see you soon."

I closed the door, making sure to lock and dead bolt it. Not that it mattered. If someone was determined enough to get through the door, then a thin chain wouldn't stop him. Boxer lounged on one of the double beds, his booted feet crossed at the ankles, smiling in reassurance.

"Take a load off, Mia. It's gonna be a while."

I removed my shoes and slid underneath the taupe bedspread. It was old and faded, but it was clean enough.

"Why are these motels so…"

Boxer looked around at the decor. "Brown? Tacky? Trapped in the seventies?"

"All of the above."

I closed my eyes, but instead of relief, the strain was worse.

"He'll be fine," he assured me.

"I know," I said, eyes still shut. "You guys rode your bikes?"

"Yeah."

"Where'd you stash them?"

"Cluster of trees behind this shit hole." Boxer was quiet for a moment and then in an effort to distract me, he asked, "So you got any single friends?"

"No," I retorted.

"How about a single cousin?"

"None of those either."

"Leave Colt for me."

"Never gonna happen. Besides, I already got his name on my back. You don't think that would be a pain in the ass to remove?"

"I'll scratch it out with a Sharpie. See? I don't even want to cause you pain."

"You're not really looking for a lady, are you?" I opened one eye and peered at him. "If I recall correctly, I saw you with two naked women one morning. In broad daylight. On the clubhouse's living room floor."

He suggestively dragged a finger across his lip. "Thinking about me, are ya?"

"You couldn't handle me." I closed my eyes.

"Yeah," he said with a laugh. "Probably not. Fucking handful that's for sure."

A few hours later, something woke me from a sound sleep. I shot up from the bed, scrambled to get my hair off my face, and looked to Boxer.

He was awake, alert, boots on, a pistol in his hand. He put a signal to his lips to be quiet and I nodded. On silent feet, he padded toward the door.

"Dude, it's us," came Zip's agitated voice.

Boxer stuck his pistol in his vest pocket as he peeked

through the peephole. A moment later, he slid off the chain, turned the lock, and opened the door.

Colt and his VP entered the motel room. I looked Colt over. He wasn't bleeding, he had no injuries, and I breathed a sigh of relief.

"Miss me?" he asked with a knowing grin.

Before I could reply, a cell rang and all the guys searched for their phones. It was Zip's. "I gotta take this," he said, striding to the front door, his eyes glued to the screen.

I briefly wondered if it was Joni, but then I turned my attention back to the man whose name was tattooed on my skin.

We stared at one another, but didn't move. I was sure that once I was in his arms I'd never want to leave.

"And that's my cue. We'll be at the diner for a while," Boxer said. "Happy humping."

The door shut and Colt secured the room. Then he was turning to me, his eyes dark, his steps predatory.

A while later, I rolled off of him and collapsed onto the bed. I closed my eyes and took a few deep breaths.

"What do you want now?" I asked him. "Food or sleep?"

"Food." His stomach rumbled in obvious agreement. "Let's have a quick shower and then you can buy me a burger. I can sleep later."

I grinned. "Get the shower going. I'll be right there. I just want to check my phone for messages first."

When I tried to get out of bed, he grabbed my arm and brought my lips to his for another long, drugging kiss.

"Don't take too long." His voice was husky and his eyes glittered with promise.

I shivered. How could I want him again after I'd just

been with him? "I thought sex was supposed to dwindle when a couple settled down."

He let out a chuckle and rose from the bed like a hulking bear. "For most people, I'm sure it does. Not us. I won't let it. Now check your messages and then get your sweet ass in the shower."

"Sweet ass? God, you're a regular Roman poet."

"You don't like me for my poetry. You like me because you know where you stand with me. Don't you?"

"I do."

His gaze softened. "I'm glad you were able to change my mind."

"About what? About coming to Odessa with you?"

Colt shook his head. "About thinking there wasn't a woman in the world who'd put up with my shit."

It wasn't poetry. But it was honest, and heartfelt, and vulnerable.

"I love you," I said quietly. "Did I tell you that today?"

"No. Say it again."

"I love you."

He smiled. "Good."

"You're supposed to say it back. You can say it in biker language if it makes you feel less like a sap."

Colt laughed, and the somberness banished from his eyes. "Love you, Mia. No one else for me. I want you in my bed, on the back of my bike, and one day, a ring on your finger."

"One day, I'd like that too."

"Yeah?"

I shook my head. "I don't get it."

"Get what?"

"Get how you seem so—I don't know. Looking to the future when our present is a pile of shit."

He scrubbed his hand across his jaw, suddenly looking

more exhausted than he'd been letting on. He hadn't slept. He'd driven us from Waco to Odessa, and while I'd cat-napped in the motel room, he'd gone to see his colleague. How was he even still awake?

"It's always a pile of shit. Life, I mean," he said. "Sure, there are times of calm. But the thing is, it's always a mess to clean up. One fire after the next. Do you think it would be any different if you were just a normal civilian with no idea about the MC feud and a cartel in our city? No, it wouldn't be any different, you just wouldn't know about it. It wouldn't be in your face."

"I stopped being a regular civilian the moment I met Dev."

Colt nodded. "On his radar."

I sighed.

"You're not regretting sticking around are you?" he asked. Naked vulnerability was etched across his face.

I went to him and pressed my head to his chest. "No regrets," I admitted. "But what would you do if I told you I did have them?"

He cupped the back of my neck and gave it a light squeeze, silently demanding that I look at him. "I'd let you go. I'd get you somewhere safe with a new identity."

"You'd let me go? Really?"

He chuckled. "You sound disappointed."

"I thought you'd be all possessive and demanding and tell me under no circumstances you'd let me go."

"Love is about doing what's best for the other person, yeah?"

"Yeah." I stood on my tiptoes and brushed my lips against his. "I don't want to go. I want to stand next to you when we come out on the other side of this."

"You will. I know you will."

He turned away, giving me a perfect view of his

muscular, inked back and his tight ass before slipping into the bathroom.

Jesus. Where had he come from?

And how did I get so lucky to call him mine?

An hour later, we met the boys at the diner down the road. They were sitting across from one another, drinking sodas and Boxer was eating a plate of chili cheese fries while Zip went for a more traditional breakfast of a short stack with fried eggs.

Boxer looked up at Colt and grinned. "You're in a good mood."

"Yeah," Colt said lightly. "Don't ruin it."

Boxer shoved his plate across the table next to Zip and then got up so Colt and I could sit together on the same side of the booth. After the perky young waitress took our order and left, I asked, "So, when do we find out what we find out?"

"Few days," Colt replied vaguely.

The boys exchanged a look and then Zip altered the direction of the conversation when he said, "Gotta call from Knight. They're on their way."

Colt nodded. "I hate calling them in for back up."

Boxer shrugged. "They've called us before for back up. It's why we have brothers."

"Who's Knight?" I asked.

"Knight is president of the Blue Angels in Coeur d'Alene."

The waitress brought our food and check. With bedroom eyes sent in Boxer's direction, she told us to have a nice day. Boxer watched her depart. "If y'all will excuse me, I need to see the waitress about something." He scooted out of the booth and went in search of the woman about to be on the receiving end of Boxer's charm.

I watched him lean over the counter and say something to her. She laughed and nodded. Before I knew it, they disappeared down the hallway, no doubt seeking the back exit and the alleyway.

"You've got to be kidding," I said. "She's going to have a quick romp with him?"

"Looks like it," Zip said with a chuckle. His phone buzzed in his pocket and he took it out to look at it. "Gonna take this outside." He slid out of the booth and headed to the front door. The doorbell jingled as Zip walked out, cell to his ear.

"And then there were two," I muttered, picking up my fork and diving into my cheese omelet.

"Talked to the fire chief," Colt said, his tone conversational. He was already halfway done with his huevos rancheros and I'd barely touched my food.

"You got a call? I gave him *my* number."

"But I'm me."

I rolled my eyes. "Okay, anointed one. What did the fire chief have to say? How bad is the house?" I held my breath.

"Kitchen and living room took the brunt of it. Bedrooms are mostly untouched, but he says to give it about a week before going in there because of the smoke."

"Okay." I nodded, taking a deep breath. "Okay. That I can deal with."

"He also mentioned your bar."

"My bar? Oh, Dive Bar. Wow. I forgot for a moment that Richie gave me his bar. Isn't the fire chief suspicious about all these buildings belonging to me going up in flames?"

"Naturally," he said with a wry grin. "But considering

you weren't on the premises when either of the fires started, there's speculation but no outright accusations."

"All he has to do is look into who I've been associating with for him to put the puzzle pieces together."

"His job is to put out fires and tell the cops if arson is suspected, not start a criminal investigation."

I stared at him. "How much did you pay him?"

"Pay him what?" Colt asked.

"Colt," I warned.

"Mia."

"Did you bribe him to look the other way?"

"Nah, of course not."

I let out a breath.

He looked at me and grinned. "I bribed him so he'll lie to the insurance companies."

Boxer eventually wandered back and slid into the booth across from us, looking relaxed and flushed.

"You're disgusting," I said with a laugh.

He flashed a grin. "Lady, you have no idea."

I looked at the waitress as she stepped onto the dining room floor, tying the strings of her apron around her waist. She looked at Boxer and wasn't at all discreet about checking him out. Boxer lifted his half-empty glass of soda and silently toasted her.

Her chuckle was throaty, her eyes sparkled, and her dimples winked from her cheeks as she beamed. She got back to work to serve the few customers that were at the counter who hadn't noticed her absence.

"Magic dick," Boxer stated.

"Dick is right," I teased.

Colt lifted his arm to rest on the booth, his fingers

running up and down the skin of my arm. I scooted closer into the crook of his body and enjoyed the solid warmth of him despite the humid air circulating through the diner.

He didn't say anything or remark on the fact that Boxer and I were ribbing each other. But I knew he was enjoying our exchange.

"You gonna eat the rest of that?" Boxer asked, gesturing to my plate.

I pushed it to him.

"Where's Zip?" he asked, dousing the omelet in hot sauce.

"On the phone," Colt replied. "Don't know with who."

"Probably Cheese," Boxer stated. "He's been checking in with Cheese about Joni."

"Really," Colt drawled. "Why?"

I had to force myself to remain lax even though the insides of me were tense and coiling with the truth.

"He feels like a shit that he said he'd watch her and then had to give Cheese the duty while he was out of town."

Boxer's announcement did nothing to ease the tension I felt in Colt's body. "Those two can't stand each other," Colt remarked.

"Yeah, I dunno. But Zip takes his duties seriously," Boxer said. "You know that."

"Hmmm." Colt looked out the window and Boxer took a moment to glance at me. We had an entire conversation with our eyes—both of us knew what was really going on between Joni and Zip and yet neither us wanted to be the one to let Colt in on the secret.

What would happen when it all exploded?

There would be hell to pay for sure.

The waitress appeared at our table and gently set the

check down, addressing Boxer. "Thank you so much for joining us. You can pay at the cash register."

Boxer grinned. "Thank you for the excellent service, darlin'."

She giggled and then fluttered away like a love-struck blonde butterfly.

"Yup, exactly as I said. Magic dick," Boxer crowed.

"If your dick is so magical why did we have to pay for breakfast?" Colt asked, finally joining the teasing train.

Boxer's face fell.

I let out a deep belly laugh. "That totally just made my morning."

Zip was on his bike, helmet and sunglasses on, ready to depart. He glowered when he saw the three of us come out of the diner. "Bout damn time."

"Why so happy, sunshine?" Boxer needled.

"I just want to get the fuck out of here."

I didn't blame him. Even though I'd had more sleep than Colt, my eyes were gritty. I'd added a Red Bull to our check and held the cold can in my hand. I popped it open and took a long sip. I needed the energy and caffeine if I was going to keep Colt awake while he drove. I certainly couldn't drive his truck—not with my wrist the way it was. A truck that big needed serious power and both hands to control.

"See you guys," Colt said, heading around to the driver's side. We waved and Boxer and Zip pealed out of the parking lot.

"Are you sure you're going to be okay to drive home?" I asked.

"Yeah, I'll be okay," he said.

"You've been awake for hours—"

Without a word, he filched the Red Bull from my hand and guzzled it. "This'll keep me going for a while. I swear. If I get tired, we can pull over and I'll crash for a bit."

"Why didn't you want Zip or Boxer to drive the truck back?"

"It would've been more trouble than it was worth to get one of the bikes stored properly in the truck bed—besides, three of us sitting in this truck would've been cramped.

"If only my wrist wasn't in a cast," I muttered. "Then I could've driven your truck. I've got experience driving a truck, you know."

"Your truck is an accident waiting to happen. When was the last time someone took a look at the engine? It's gotta be at least twenty-five-years old."

"It belonged to my grandfather," I told him. "And it does just fine."

He made a noise in the back of his throat. "We gotta get you a new truck."

"You could just give me this one." I slid my hands over the hood. "It's a beautiful, purring beast."

"Maybe for an anniversary gift," he said with a grin.

"How about an I'm-sorry-I-torched-your-bar gift."

"We'll see."

We got into the truck and then drove away from the diner. "Who taught you to shoot?" he asked. "Been meaning to ask you that."

I briefly looked over at him. Even with exhaustion tugging at the lines around his mouth, I thought he looked formidable and in control.

"Grammie," I said. "She and Gramps are both from Chicago. Gramps was from the North side. Grammie was from the South side. A regular West Side Story, you know?

They weren't supposed to be together. They both came from—ah—less than stellar families."

"O'Banion," Colt murmured. "That name sounds really familiar, but I can't place it."

I sighed. "My grandfather's side of the family were Chicago bootleggers in the nineteen twenties. Big feud with the Italians, aka Al Capone's crew...who just so happens to be one of Grammie's relatives."

There was a moment of stunned silence and then Colt started to laugh. He chuckled for a good few minutes before he was able to calm himself.

"All this time, I was worried about how you were gonna adjust to my life and running around with a bunch of criminals. Turns out, you've got notorious criminals on both your sides of the family." He looked at me. "You really are the perfect woman for me."

Chapter 21

WE MADE it back to the clubhouse in record time.

"Has he slept at all?" Boxer asked after a hug in greeting.

I shook my head. "I think he's running on pure adrenaline. He's going to crash soon though, right? I mean it's been over twenty four hours since he's slept."

"Church!" Colt barked.

I looked at Boxer. "Finish your meeting quickly and then he needs to go to bed."

"You know," Boxer said, stroking his jaw, "he wouldn't take kindly to knowing you're calling the shots."

"Trust me, we'd all be better off if he got some rest. You can't be clear-headed when you're exhausted."

"He's just gonna fill everyone in. Should be a quick meeting." Boxer squeezed my shoulder and then followed his brothers out to the shed.

I went into Colt's bedroom to change and there was a knock on the door when I was drawing the string tight on my pajamas.

"Come in," I said.

The door opened and Joni's face appeared. "Hey, welcome back."

"Thanks." I waved her inside. "You can enter the room, you know."

"Well, you looked like you were about to crash. I wasn't sure."

I shook my head. "I'm trying to stay awake until at least nine p.m., but I'm dragging hard."

"You hungry? I was about to order Chinese food."

"I'm starving. All I've had today is a cheese omelet and a couple of Red Bulls."

"I gotcha. Please tell me you're a beef and broccoli fan."

"You know it," I said with a laugh. "How have things been here?"

"Cheese has been keeping Zip in the loop about me. I made sure to flirt extra hard with Doctor Patterson in front of Cheese. Made him extremely uncomfortable. It was awesome."

"So that's why Zip was in such a shit mood," I said with a laugh. "He was grumpy as hell."

"I know I should feel bad about what I'm doing, but I really don't."

We wandered out of Colt's room and I sat down on the couch. Joni took it upon herself to order half the menu. "The guys will be hungry, no doubt." She hung up the phone and sat down next to me. "I don't know about you, but I'm going crazy here."

I nodded. "I feel like a prisoner, which is weird because I know it's for our own safety, but I can't help feeling like—well, fuck it. You know?"

"Yup. I'm ready to demand my freedom."

"I missed karaoke night with Shelly. We usually go once a month."

"Dude. You sing karaoke?"

"I do."

"Are you any good?"

"After three tequila shots, who cares?"

She laughed in a way that showed me she had seen a night or two of karaoke in her time. We kept up a steady stream of chatter and the two prospects on duty brought in several bags of Chinese takeout. Joni and I didn't bother waiting for the guys to finish church—we dug into the food straight from the boxes.

"Why are wontons so freakin' good?" Joni demanded as she shoved an entire dumpling into her mouth.

"No clue, but I'm inclined to say MSG."

Joni moaned. "Don't tell me that. Let's pretend we're getting all our vegetables in this one fried food dish."

"Deal."

The backdoor opened and the brothers strode inside, looking tense. Not even the sight of Chinese food brought a smile to their faces. Well, except for Boxer, who plopped down next to me and opened his mouth.

"What are you, a baby bird?" I demanded.

"Feed me, Mama," he pleaded.

I slid a piece of beef between his lips.

"You *actually* fed him." Joni grinned.

"I'm afraid he'll die if I don't," I said. "Boxer is the human equivalent of a lab puppy."

Reap and Gray chuckled, but Colt didn't show any signs of humor. Instead, he walked over to the refrigerator and grabbed himself a beer. He held it up and I shook my head. Colt closed the fridge and then leaned against the kitchen counter.

"There's something we need to discuss," Joni said. "Mia and I are tired of being caged in. We want to go out."

"You already go out," Zip stated from the recliner, his eyes on Joni.

Joni glared at him. "Going to work is not the same as going out. We want a night on the town."

"Not so much a night on the town, just karaoke," I interjected. "We can make that happen. Right?"

"What happened the last time you and Joni went out?" Zip asked pointedly. "On Blue Angels' territory."

Joni opened her mouth to reply, but Colt jumped in and said, "The brothers from Coeur d'Alene arrive tomorrow afternoon. We should show them a good time."

"Safety in numbers," Reap said with a slow nod.

"We should just have a massive bonfire here," Zip groused. "No reason to flaunt shit in town."

Colt rubbed his thumb across his jaw. "I was thinking we could meet the boys at The Rex."

Reap's eyes gleamed. Zip's gaze hardened. Even Boxer's humorous expression sobered.

"So it's going to be like that, huh?" Zip asked finally.

Colt looked at each Blue Angel in the eye. One by one they nodded.

"You'll call Bishop," Colt told Zip. "Tell him about the new meet up spot."

Colt was speaking in riddles, but I knew better than to ask him to explain. He'd explain when we were alone.

Hopefully.

"Are we done for the night?" Torque asked. He'd been standing in the corner of the room, tatted arms crossed over his shoulders. "I got a pregnant Old Lady at home who's demanding ice cream."

Gray grinned. "It just gets worse. Trust me."

"She's carrying my kid." Torque shrugged. "She wants ice cream. She gets ice cream. And any other thing she wants."

The group broke up almost immediately. Torque and Reap headed out at the same time while Zip went out back to make a call, no doubt to Bishop, whoever he was. Colt was talking to Gray and Cheese in hushed tones and Boxer continued to lounge on the couch, his eyes half closed.

"What's The Rex?" I asked Joni as we cleaned up the takeout containers.

"The Rex Hotel. In Dallas."

"Why are they telling the other Blue Angel chapter to meet there?"

"I have an idea, but I'm not one hundred percent sure…"

"Joni. Tell me."

"Ask Colt."

"Ask me what?" Colt said from behind me, causing me to jump and drop fried rice all over the floor.

"Really?" I asked in exasperation. "How do you do that?"

"Do what?" he asked with raised eyebrows.

"Walk silently in heavy boots." I gestured to the broom next to the fridge. Joni handed it to me. I quickly swept up the mess and dumped it into the trash.

Colt settled his hand on the curve of my neck and gently brought me into the side of his body. "Are you ready?"

"For?" I looked up into his eyes and got lost for a moment.

"Yeah, that's my cue," Joni muttered. "I'll be in my room reading a book, trying not to pass out from boredom."

"You're coming to Dallas with us, right?" Colt asked.

She nodded. "Try and stop me. I gotta get out of this place."

Colt grinned. "See you in the morning." He dragged me to our room and shut the door.

I flopped down onto the bed and buried my face in the pillows. "I'm pretty sure I could sleep for days."

He laughed. A moment later, I heard his boots hit the floor. He came over to the bedside table and set his wallet and pistol on it before removing his jeans, cut, and T-shirt.

"Why are we going to Dallas?" I asked. "Are you going to tell me?

"Yeah, I'll tell you." He sat down on the bed. "Take your shirt off first."

"You're not going to distract me with sex."

"Wasn't planning on distracting you with sex."

"Then why—"

"I just want to feel your skin, okay?"

I wormed my shirt off and then lay back down. His fingers began stroking down my spine as he talked. "There are two reasons we're going to Dallas. One, you and Joni want a night out. I don't want you out in Waco because of Dev, but I don't have a good enough reason to keep you both locked up."

"Hmm," I hummed, my eyes drifting shut.

"Two, Flynn Campbell is the owner of The Rex Hotel empire. Our fathers knew each other when they were younger. The Rex is a safe place, so to speak."

My head whirled. I'd heard of The Rex Hotel empire, but I'd never been to one of the hotels. I knew they were decadent, expensive, and catered to the elite. More surprising was that my biker boyfriend was a friend of sorts with the owner.

"I still don't understand why we're going there, though. I'm sure there are dozens of places we could go to in Dallas. Some shitty dive if all we're doing is welcoming the

Blue Angels from Coeur d'Alene and giving Joni and I a chance at temporary freedom."

Colt felt silent but his hands continued to caress my tight, sore muscles. He was the one who needed to be rubbed down—he'd been awake longer than me and no doubt his crash was imminent.

"Roll over," I told him.

"Hmm?"

"Roll over onto your stomach. You deserve a massage."

Colt heaved his mass away from me and collapsed onto his belly. I straddled his lower back and then got to work on his tight muscles.

"Damn, that feels good." He didn't speak for a while and I thought he'd fallen asleep. He surprised me when he said, "Campbell has resources that we could use right now."

"Your brothers from another chapter aren't enough?"

"Correct. The guys from Coeur d'Alene are mostly former military and they can handle their own, but that's just defense. We require something bigger than that."

"What about other MCs in Waco? Can't you ask some other clubs to help you push the Iron Horsemen back?"

"It's not just the Iron Horsemen," he said. "A cartel too, remember? That's a different level of shit entirely. You know?"

"It's their city too. If the cartel has their way and takes over through the Iron Horsemen, that doesn't just affect the Blue Angels. It affects all of the clubs." I leaned over so I could look him in the eye. "What aren't you telling me?"

He ground his jaw tight before answering. "When this is all said and done, we want to be the only shop in town."

I frowned. "You want—oh. You don't want to involve the other clubs because you want to be able to go to them and tell them you cleaned it all up, so you and the Blue Angels will have all the power."

"This is why you don't tell smart women shit like this—they figure out your motives within minutes. What do you think about that, darlin'? You wanna be married to the king of Waco?"

"You're not the king. And we're not married."

"Not yet. On either account."

"I still can't believe you're the type of man that wants to be settled."

"You get tired, you know?"

"Yeah, it must've been really exhausting to have all the club groupies throw themselves at you. Mindless, string-free fucking. Sounds rotten. Why did you trade all of that for me?"

"Who says I traded?" he joked.

I reached out and pinched his thigh.

"Woman, you took a lot of work to get into bed."

"Yeah, like two weeks—if that. God, do I feel bad for you."

He laughed mischievously. "You know what I mean. You were worth it. You *are* worth it. I knew what I was getting when I went for you, Mia."

"What's that, Colt?"

"Fishing for compliments isn't your style."

He fell asleep with my hands stroking his back, a smile on his face.

Chapter 22

"Bishop told Knight about the change in our meeting point. They'll meet us in Dallas," Zip said early the next morning over breakfast at the clubhouse.

"Who's Bishop?" I asked as I put two pieces of bread into the toaster.

"VP of the Coeur d'Alene brothers," Colt said.

"So, Zip's equal of the Idaho boys."

"No one is my equal," Zip said, leaning back in his chair and flashing an arrogant grin.

"Saints preserve us," I muttered.

Colt chuckled. After a good night's sleep, he looked rested and alert.

"Want me to rouse the brothers and get them ready to ride?" Zip asked.

"I want them here."

Zip frowned. "I don't get it."

"I'm taking Mia to meet with Campbell. You'll greet Knight in my stead. Everyone else stays."

"Wait a second. You're asking boys from another chapter to come and have our backs, told them to meet us in Dallas instead of here where we can welcome them with a bonfire and party, and now you want me to be the one to greet the president? Respectfully, it needs to be you, Colt. Prez to prez."

"I've talked to Knight on the phone. Explained to him why I need to speak with Campbell first. He trusts me. And he's not gonna care. Not with Rex pussy waiting for him."

I choked on my coffee.

Colt shot me an amused look. "Problem there?"

"I wasn't ready for that word first thing in the morning."

Colt raised an eyebrow and slowly lowered his gaze down my body. My cheeks flushed and my skin buzzed with warmth. He'd woken me up not that long ago with his head buried between my legs and the bastard wanted to remind me of it.

"Why am I not sitting in with you and Campbell?" Zip asked.

"Three reasons. One, I trust you to greet Knight and the rest of his boys. Two, my sister will be with you, and you're responsible for seeing to her protection. And three, Campbell is bringing his wife."

Zip's eyes darted to me and then back to Colt. "They do things differently than we do. We never have women sitting in on club business."

I made a move to leave, toast all but forgotten. But when I passed by him, Colt's arm shot out to wrap around me. Boxer wandered into the kitchen wearing nothing but a pair of black basketball shorts, half asleep, and not at all aware of the sudden tension that had sprung up between Colt and Zip.

"Something's burning," Boxer said, sniffing the air.

"Shit," I muttered. Colt's arm dropped from around

me and I rushed to the toaster, but the bread couldn't be saved.

"Smoke alarm is gonna go off," Boxer mused.

"So why don't you do something about it?" Zip snapped, grabbing the dishtowel from the refrigerator door handle and tossing it at Boxer.

"Why the fuck are you so grumpy?" Boxer demanded as he began to fan the smoke alarm.

"I want you driving Joni," Colt commanded, looking at Zip. "Reap will follow on his bike. Boxer and the boys will get everyone else to the clubhouse. Darcy, Rach, all the kids."

Boxer wiped a hand across his exhausted face. "Lemme guess. Official lockdown?"

"Yup."

"This is bullshit," Zip growled. "I'm still on babysitting duty. Fucking great."

"You're an asshole," Joni said from the living room.

I hadn't even heard her footsteps on the stairs. She was dressed in a pair of jeans and an old gray T-shirt. Her luxurious brown hair was pulled into a high ponytail and the apples of her cheeks were flushed with anger. "Do you think I like having you as my shadow? I can't even go on a date with a hot doctor."

A muscle ticked in his jaw. "Make the date."

"Why? So you can sit at the table between us?" She rolled her eyes. "You're crazy." She stalked from the room, but Zip was hot on her heels. A moment later, the back door opened and then slammed shut.

Colt stared after them, his gaze lingering. I shot Boxer a look, but his face was purposefully blank.

"Those two are like oil and water," Colt said softly with a shake of his head. "I was thinking we could head out later this morning. Does that work for you?"

"Yup. As long as I get to wear my new boots." I grinned. Who's cooking breakfast?"

"Don't look at me," Boxer said. "If it doesn't come from a microwavable box, I'm out. And why aren't you cooking? I want pancakes. I'm a lab puppy, remember? I can't take care of myself."

"I feel bad for the woman you trick into falling in love with you," I said, even as I moved to the fridge to grab the eggs.

"I feel bad for her too," Boxer stated. "Whoever she is."

The Rex Hotel was a stunning experience of architecture and fashionable beauty. The ceilings were high; the chandeliers were golden and twinkling; the patrons wealthy and gorgeous.

Colt and I garnered more than a few stares when we entered the lobby. We were leather and ink in a sea of Armani and Chanel. Though Colt's natural swagger showed the people watching us that he didn't give a shit about how he looked, I didn't have the same level of confidence. Sure, I put on a front because I was with Colt, but I was walking across a marble floor in leather biker boots, not Jimmy Choos.

Colt would never be a suit or tuxedo wearing guy. Not even at black tie events. Not that I thought he'd ever be the type to attend a black tie event, but what about weddings? What did bikers even wear to weddings?

I firmly thrust that line of thought from my mind as we strode to the hostess of the restaurant. She looked us up and down, and yet her expression didn't change.

"Mr. Weston?" she said finally with a smile.

Colt's grin was arrogant. "Yes, ma'am. That's me."

"Mr. Campbell is expecting you. Please, follow me." She ushered us through the busy restaurant to the back. Opening a door, she gestured for us to enter a private dining room.

An attractive man, with dark hair and cobalt blue eyes, rose from his chair and buttoned the middle suit button of his gray jacket. An auburn haired woman sat in the seat next to him but didn't move to stand.

"Thank ye, Janet," he said, his voice thick and husky with a Scottish brogue.

"Will that be all, Mr. Campbell?"

"Aye."

Janet left and shut the door.

My eyes darted between Mr. Campbell and the woman who had taken her time rising from her chair. She was stunning and regal, and though we were the same height, it was only because my boots put us at eye-level. Her auburn hair hung in loose waves about her shoulders, her white, asymmetrical gown more suited for a gala than a sit-down dinner.

As if noticing my hesitation, her smile widened in a show of genuine welcome. She came toward me, hand held out. "Hi, I'm Barrett."

Her lack of formality surprised me. Taking her palm, I gripped it. "Nice to meet you. I'm Mia."

"I love your boots," she said, eyeing the studded footwear Colt had bought me. "They look like they're made for stomping on hearts."

I laughed. "I feel very under dressed."

She dismissed my statement with a nod of her queenly head. "Knowing Colt, he wouldn't be caught dead wearing a suit."

"Your wife knows me well, Campbell," Colt drawled.

Campbell grinned and looked at me. "It's good to meet you, Mia. Call me Flynn."

"How are the boys?" Colt asked Barrett.

"Driving us both to drink," she said with a wink. She turned to me and explained, "We have three boys under the age of five."

"That sounds like a handful," I said. I tried to hide my astonishment. The woman standing in front of me had *three* children? I never would've guessed it judging by her trim, elegant figure.

Flynn pulled Barrett to his side and draped an arm around her. She placed her left hand on his chest, and I immediately noticed that her wedding band was demure and elegant. These people, despite the hotel empire they ran, were not gaudy and I began to relax.

"What, you don't say hello to me anymore?" Colt asked as he raised an eyebrow at Flynn.

Flynn rubbed his jaw, pretending not to smile. "If I jumped into your arms, could you catch me?"

"Let's find out," Colt shot back.

"Let's not," Barrett interrupted.

Flynn let go of his wife and then approached Colt. The two men stared at each other for a moment before they engaged in a manly bro hug.

"You look well," Flynn said, peering at Colt a moment before shifting his gaze to me. "Are you keeping this one in order?"

"As much as Barrett keeps you in order, I'm sure," I quipped, causing laughter to ring out.

Flynn waved us all to the set table. White china, white tablecloth, goblets trimmed with gold.

Colt surprised me by helping me with my chair. I gazed up at him in astonishment.

Leaning down, he whispered, "I can be a gentleman if I need to be."

"Please, don't ever be a gentleman," I replied, reaching up to touch his cheek. Turning my attention back to the other occupants, I froze. Barrett and Flynn were both staring at us.

Colt took his seat next to me and then placed the black linen napkin across his lap.

"Your boys arrived," Flynn said. "They're currently drinking some of my best scotch in the club."

"Club? What club?" I asked.

"There's a burlesque club attached to the hotel," Flynn explained. "There's also a rooftop Whiskey Room—but I think that's better suited for later this evening when you want discuss business."

"You brought your sister to Dallas for a night out and now she's stuck with a bunch of rowdy bikers in a burlesque club?" I glanced at Colt. "How is that a good idea?"

"She'll be fine."

"You didn't tell me he was bringing his sister," Barrett said, looking to her husband.

His gaze swiveled to her. "I didn't know I was supposed to."

"Joni's fine," Colt stated.

"I'm checking on her after dinner," I said. "Besides, I want to see this burlesque club."

"I'll be glad to show it to you," Barrett said.

"What rare delicacy are you going to force me to eat?" Colt demanded.

"Duck," Barrett announced.

"Did Duncan shoot it?"

"No," Flynn replied, amused.

"Duncan is Flynn's best friend—and surrogate brother," Barrett said. "Who happens to also be married to my best friend."

"Tight knit family, huh?" I asked.

"Very," Barrett said with a wink.

"How is Duncan? And Ash," Colt added.

"Good. Got their hands full with the bairns."

"And Ramsey? How's he doin'?"

"Ramsey is Ramsey." Flynn shrugged.

"Ramsey is?" I pressed.

"Duncan's younger brother," Flynn said to me.

"Is it too late to ask for a diagram of the family tree?"

Barrett laughed. "It's hard when you don't have faces to go with the names."

There was a knock on the door and Flynn called out, "Come in."

The door opened and two servers in formal clothing pushed in a cart.

"Butternut ginger soup with a crème fraîche garnish," one server said as his companion poured a light, almost clear white wine.

"Enjoy."

They took the cart and left, closing the door after them. I took a moment to savor the soup, noting that Flynn wasn't eating. Neither was Colt.

Barrett caught my eye and winked. I smiled at her.

"So," Flynn began. "Should we get down to it?"

"Yeah," Colt agreed.

Flynn's eyes slid to mine and then back to Colt. "Do you want to have this conversation in front of her?"

"Mia's got my ink," Colt explained. He gestured with his chin to Barrett. "You have your wife sit in on meetings."

"I've come to appreciate her council," Flynn said, his brogue thick.

Barrett rolled her eyes but said nothing.

"This shit involves Mia. I told you some of it on the phone."

"Aye." Flynn nodded. "Go on."

"I've got a big fucking problem."

"Big, like you need an influx of illegal arms to fight someone, or big like you need someone to disappear?" Flynn asked.

"Big, like there's a cartel in Waco's backyard big."

"Which cartel?" Flynn asked, his tone blasé like he was discussing the weather.

"Garcia."

I shot a look to Colt but held my tongue.

"Why is the Garcia cartel a problem for you?" Flynn asked.

"Mia's former boss stole a shitload of coke from the Iron Horsemen. Their president cut a deal with the Garcia cartel to act as drug mules and move the product through Waco. The best we can figure right now is that Richie wanted Dev gone so he stole from the cartel, hoping they'd kill Dev and his problems would be over. That didn't pan out, and Richie wound up dead. Now we've got a shitload of coke to deal with that belongs to the Garcia cartel and one very pissed off club president who knows if he doesn't get it back he's going to die. Dev we can deal with, but the cartel? That's why we're here."

"And how did Mia get involved if it was her boss who did the stealing?" Flynn asked.

"The last time Mia saw Richie, she was taking him to the bus depot to get out of town. They stopped at a storage unit. Richie dropped the key in her truck to the storage unit, which is full of the product he stole. We found it a few days ago. I don't want my boys moving it."

"You want me to move it." It wasn't a question but a statement.

"Yes."

"I don't get involved in cartel business," Flynn said.

"Right," Colt drawled. "You don't." His gaze shot to Barrett.

They were speaking in riddles and I wasn't privy to the code.

Colt leaned back in his chair, feigning ease I knew he didn't feel. His body was taut and lined with tension.

Barrett looked at her husband. "What do you think?"

"I think he'll want something."

Barrett smirked. "No doubt." She sobered. "Are you okay with this?"

"No." Flynn's jaw clenched. "But I don't see another option. It's only a matter of time before the Garcias expand. That could be bad for our business."

What business was Flynn talking about? Clearly not the hotel business. And why was Colt asking Flynn to deal with the storage unit full of coke?

Who was Flynn Campbell?

Because he sure as shit wasn't just a hotel mogul.

Our conversation was cut off by another knock on the door, this time for the servers to clear our dishes and deliver the duck entrée. I noticed that neither Flynn nor Colt had touched the soup. Barrett's bowl was empty. Clearly this sort of talk didn't affect her appetite.

Once we were in private again, Flynn spoke, "Barrett will reach out to Mateo Sanchez."

"I promise nothing," she voiced. "But I can get you a meeting."

No longer able to hold back my curiosity, I asked, "Who's Mateo Sanchez?"

Barrett looked at me and smiled wryly. "The most powerful man in Argentina."

"You're friends with the most powerful man in Argentina?" I gaped at Barrett.

"'Friends' is a strong word," she answered. "I prefer business associate."

"Business associate, my arse," Flynn muttered.

"How did that happen?" I asked. "Sorry, I'm just—I have to know."

"Mia, I don't think—"

"No, it's fine," Flynn interrupted. "You trust her, aye?"

"Yeah, I do," Colt said.

"Then we can let her in."

"Wow," Barrett said in amusement. "This is certainly a change from the Flynn Campbell I met years ago."

Flynn smiled, showing a dazzling row of white teeth. "I've mellowed with age."

Barrett laughed. "Yeah, sure." She glanced at me. "When Flynn was in trouble, I went to Mateo for help. You'll never hear his name on the news, but no one else has the kind of power Mateo has."

Flynn pulled his wife's chair closer to him and then reached out and touched one of her auburn locks.

"We've been in business with Mateo ever since. Much to Flynn's consternation—it's been lucrative."

"They're friends even though she says they're not," Flynn stated. "He sends her a Christmas card every year for God's sake."

"He sends it to *both* of us," she countered.

"He addresses the envelope to *you*."

Barrett shrugged, but didn't reply. She picked up her glass of wine and took a drink.

I wanted to ask more questions, but Flynn shifted the conversation to other matters. They talked about their family and the antics their young boys got into constantly. Barrett pulled out her phone and showed me pictures.

It was surreal, sitting and talking with the Campbells, having dinner with them. Like we all weren't just discussing illegal activities that would send us to prison for life if we were caught. Every so often, I noticed Barrett watching me with a small smile. It was a smile of understanding, I realized.

After we finished our meal, Colt said, "I think I'd like to bring the boys up for a chat in your Whiskey Room."

Flynn nodded. "I'll clear it out."

"That's perfect. You men can talk all you want while I take Mia down to see the burlesque club," Barrett said.

"Go easy on her, Barrett," Colt said dryly.

Barrett laughed. "She'll be fine. No doubt she can handle herself."

We all left the private dining room to walk through the restaurant to the lobby. Zip stood with a group of men who wore leather cuts denoting them as the Blue Angels Coeur d'Alene chapter.

"Where's Joni?" I asked, approaching Zip.

"Still in the club. She saved you a table," Zip said. He turned to Barrett and grinned. "Look at you."

"Look at me." She smiled back.

Zip embraced her and then pulled away. Despite Barrett's expensive clothes and wealth, she was clearly at ease with the rough and tough biker crowd.

I felt Colt's arm drape over my shoulder. "Come here, I wanna introduce you to Knight." He dragged me away from Zip and Barrett and we headed to the other side of the throng. A tall man with a mostly brown beard sprinkled with gray and weathered skin from the years on a bike was talking softly to a younger biker with a strong, angular jawline.

"Knight," Colt greeted.

He turned toward Colt, his hand outstretched, a smile blooming across his face. But just as he was about to greet Colt, his gaze turned to me and he visibly blanched. Even though his beard hid most of his face, I could see the swatches of his cheeks pale.

"Knight?" Colt pressed, obviously seeing the man's reaction to me. "You okay?"

Knight swallowed and then nodded. He forced a smile and clasped his hand to Colt's. "Good to see you, boy."

"Thanks for coming. The Rex is treating you right, yeah?"

"Just had a glass of the best bourbon money can buy." Knight grinned, shooting me another quick glance.

"Knight, I'd like you to meet my Old Lady, Mia. Mia, this is Knight, president of the Coeur d'Alene Blue Angels."

"Mia," he said, his voice raspy. "Glad to meet you."

"You too." I shook his hand, noting how he held onto mine a little longer than was socially acceptable. I forced a smile and tried to shove my unease aside.

"We're headed up to the Whiskey Room," Colt said to me. "We should be there for a while."

I nodded, understanding what he was telling me without saying it. It was club business and so I was not going to be part of it.

"Barrett and Flynn have given us suites," Colt said. "We won't be driving back to Waco when we're finished."

Which was Colt speak for, *drink and be merry*, and I planned on doing just that.

Out of the corner of my eye, I could feel Knight's penetrating stare. I didn't care for it, so I made my goodbye with Colt brief. I kissed his lips and then slipped from his side, determined to find Barrett.

She was still conversing with Zip but when she saw me, she linked her arm through mine and said, "Gentlemen, enjoy your evening. We will definitely enjoy ours!"

Barrett waved to her husband and threw him a sassy smile, which he pretended not to enjoy, but even I could see the twinkle in his eye. We went into the burlesque club and I took a moment to stop and marvel at the decor. Old school gas lanterns graced the walls and the stage was lit with vaudevillian type bulbs. The female servers were dressed like cigar girls. An eight-piece brass band was in the orchestra pit and the velvet brocade curtains of the stage were currently shut.

"Wow," I said.

Barrett tossed out a laugh. "I know, right?"

"It's unbelievable. I feel like I've stepped back in time."

"Precisely the point. Oh look, there's Joni." Barrett nodded with her chin in the direction of one of the booths where Joni sat with a drink.

Barrett and I came over and Joni was out of her seat before we even reached her. She hugged Barrett. "I didn't know you'd be here! I thought you'd be with the men."

"I think it's nice for husbands to be able to let loose from time to time without their wives looking over their shoulders. Besides, I'd much rather catch up with you— and get to know Mia."

We sat down and immediately a server came by to take our drink orders.

"I'll have another gimlet, please," Joni said.

The server nodded and then looked to Barrett who replied, "The usual."

"I'll have whatever she's having," I said, looking at Barrett.

"Very good. I'll be back in a moment with your drinks," the server said and then left.

Barrett leaned back against the leather booth and crossed her legs. "You don't even know what my usual is. You may hate it."

"Doubt it. You clearly have good taste."

"Yes, she does," Joni teased. "Have you seen her husband?"

Laughing in delight, Barrett joked, "He's okay."

"How'd you meet Flynn?" I asked.

"Yeah, I'm not sure I even know the history between you two." Joni's gaze was curious.

"Long story," Barrett evaded. "Too long, but in a roundabout way, I guess you could say I worked for Flynn at The Rex in New York. Seems like just yesterday, and now we have three children. Time flies, you know?"

I nodded in agreement. "I know. Believe me."

"Oooh, color me intrigued." She leaned forward like I was about to tell her a secret. "What's your story with Colt?"

"Only that they were like, instantly together," Joni said.

I cracked out a laugh. "You were pushing us together. You were *all* pushing us together."

Joni looked at Barrett. "She got inked."

"Oh, that's right! Let me see," Barrett demanded.

I dutifully removed my leather jacket and gave her my back. The tattoo poked out the side of my black tank, but Barrett still had to move the strap aside to get a really good look at it in all its glory.

"It's gorgeous," she breathed.

"Thanks." She dropped my strap and I turned back around to face them. "You don't have any tattoos?"

Barrett shook her head. "Nope."

The server returned with our drinks. I lifted my rocks glass and sniffed cautiously. "Bourbon?"

Barrett turned up her nose at me. "Single malt scotch. Balvenie DoubleWood 17 year."

I snorted. "Snob."

"Excuse me?" she asked, huge grin on her face. "You are one ballsy lady."

I held up my glass. "To ballsy ladies."

"Hell yes," she said. We clinked glasses and then she took a drink. "So. Joni, have you finally managed to seduce Zip?"

At ten o'clock the performances began. Burlesque dancers took the stage, singing and teasing their clothes off much to the enjoyment of the audience.

I was on my third drink—trying to keep up with Barrett and failing. Joni was still upright, yet her eyes were glassy.

"That looks like fun," Joni said, wistfully glancing at the stage.

"It's very fun," Barrett said. "I used to perform, back in the day."

"Did you?" I grinned.

Barrett winked. "Nothing gets a man to admit he wants you faster than when you entice other males to stare at you."

Joni and I exchanged a look.

"We were planning on doing karaoke," Joni said.

"Yes, we were. I forgot to ask if you were any good?"

She smiled. "I'm decent. I can belt 'Proud Mary' with the best of them."

Barrett shook her head. "You need something else, something that goes with the theme of the club."

"I know 'La Vie En Rose'," Joni said after a moment.

"And I think I've had just enough vodka not to be embarrassed if I screw it up."

"Perfect," Barrett said, shooing Joni out of the booth. "Come on, let's get you a costume and tell the Emcee you're going to perform."

"How are we getting the boys to come down here since they're dealing with business?" I asked.

Barrett grinned. "Easy. I text Flynn and tell him I'm thinking about performing. He'll rush down here to try and stop me."

"Stop you?" I laughed. "Why?"

"Because I promised him I wouldn't perform anymore."

An hour later, Joni was outfitted in a gorgeous gold sequined costume with fringe and a feather headband that wrapped across her forehead, her face was done up in the true flapper style, and her hair was wavy and pinned back. She waited back stage, not at all showing any signs of nerves.

"Show time," Barrett said as we retook our booth, which had remained empty the entire time we'd been getting Joni in costume.

Barrett took out her phone and shot off a quick text to Flynn. Not ten minutes later, Flynn Campbell entered the club, followed by the entirety of the Blue Angels.

Colt's eyes met mine and he immediately came to me while his brothers took seats at empty tables and swarmed the bar. Patrons glanced curiously at the intrusion, but quickly turned their attention back to the stage and pretended they didn't see the leather-wearing bikers in the upscale lounge.

"Hen," Flynn growled as he stood at our table, peering down at his wife. "You promised."

She lifted her glass of scotch to her lips and smiled. "Do I look like I'm performing tonight?"

His eyes raked over her. "You lied."

"Had to get you and the boys down here."

"Why?" Flynn demanded.

With a chin nod at the stage, both Colt and Flynn turned their attention. The tuxedo wearing Emcee announced Joni and a moment later she took the stage, her hand going for the microphone.

"How much has my sister had to drink?" Colt demanded. "And she better not be performing burlesque."

"Relax," I said. "She's just singing."

Colt growled and slid into the booth next to me, crowding my space. Flynn sat down close to Barrett and I saw his hand glide under the table to rest on her thigh, but his curiosity won out and he turned his attention to the stage.

I nestled into the crook of Colt's body, having missed his solid presence and warmth for the past few hours. Though it had been nice to be out of the house, out of Waco, I'd missed him.

As Joni began to croon into the microphone, my gaze wandered around the room. I looked at Zip who was sitting with Bishop and Knight, but his eyes were riveted on Joni's body.

I couldn't help the smile that curved my lips.

Knight's gaze caught mine. He looked at me like he was trying to figure something out, shrewd, calculating.

I didn't like it.

Turning my head so I wouldn't have to see Knight, I grazed my lips along Colt's jaw. "Want to get out of here?"

He looked down at me, smile lines crinkling at the corners of his eyes. "Fuck yeah."

Colt got out of the booth first and then helped me up. Flynn stood and shook Colt's hand.

"Thanks, brother," Colt said. I could barely hear him over the sound of Joni's singing, but I was still privy to their conversation.

"Sanchez will be in touch." Flynn then looked to me. "It was good to meet you, Mia."

"Same."

Barrett, a lot less formal than her husband, climbed out of the booth and embraced me. "One day, you'll come to Scotland and I'll tell you the story of how Flynn and I met."

"I can't wait."

She squeezed my fingers affectionately.

Colt all but dragged me from the club, but I forced him to stop so I could watch Joni as she finished her performance.

The applause and whistles were deafening and the audience was begging for an encore. Colt was finally able to get me out of the club, but not before I caught Knight's eyes on me again.

A shiver of foreboding slithered down my spine.

There was something about him, something I didn't trust.

I bit my lip in thought as Colt led me across the marble floor lobby to the elevators. A carriage came almost immediately. "Did you have a good night?" he asked me once we were in the privacy of the elevator.

"I did. I missed you though."

His grin was arrogant. "Did you now?"

I rolled my eyes. "Did you get to discuss everything you needed to discuss?"

He paused for a moment and then nodded. "We won't decide on anything until I talk to Sanchez. Won't touch the product, won't move the product. Everything stays where it is until I know what Sanchez wants."

"Barrett says he's the most powerful man in Argentina. Does that mean he's—is he head of another cartel?"

Colt sighed. "Yeah, babe, he is. I don't like the idea of getting another cartel involved to get rid of the one in our backyard, but what choice do I have?"

"What about the Coeur d'Alene Blue Angels?" I fished. "What about Knight?"

"What about him?"

"You trust him, don't you?"

He frowned at me. The elevator doors opened and then he was dragging me down the hallway to our room. He pulled out a key from his back pocket and then he was ushering me through the open door.

I didn't have a moment to look around at the gorgeous decadence because Colt was marching me toward a wall, not stopping until my back hit it.

He caged me in. "What aren't you saying to me, Mia?"

"I'm not saying anything—"

"Bullshit. You don't think I know how to read you?" He got closer to my face, his brown eyes peering into my soul and knowing things without me having to say anything.

"I don't like how he looks at me," I admitted quietly.

"How did he look at you?" His voice was a dangerous purr.

"He was staring at me like he couldn't figure me out. Not sexual," I hastened to explain. "Just—I don't know. There was something in his eyes, Colt. Something I couldn't decipher."

Chapter 23

I woke up early the next morning. My mouth tasted like peat and I briefly thought about Barrett's choice of drink. It lingered on the tongue. I was giving my teeth a vigorous brushing when Colt pushed open the bathroom door. He came in to stand behind me, dropping a morning kiss on my bare shoulder.

We didn't say anything as we brushed our teeth in companionable silence. Colt was just rinsing his mouth when his cell phone rang. He grabbed a hand towel and wiped his face as he strode from the bathroom.

I heard him answer the call and speak to someone on the other end. When he hung up, he came back, leaned against the bathroom doorjamb, and watched me.

"Yes?" I taunted. "Like something you see?"

"Whole lotta something," he admitted with a sensual grin.

I was wearing a white lace camisole and a pair of clean underwear Colt had thoughtfully packed in a small bag, as if he'd known all along we'd be staying overnight. It was odd to be with a man who planned, had it all figured out, even a spare change of clothes.

I'd gone to bed with last night's makeup on my face and I tended to the destruction now. I threw my hair into a messy bun and turned on the faucet.

"Who was on the phone?"

"Boxer. Everyone is already at the clubhouse for the lockdown."

"Good. I guess."

Colt raised an eyebrow. "What's that supposed to mean?"

"Freedom restricted, everyone on top of one another, barely any privacy. It will get old fast. Joni and I were already going nuts, staying at the clubhouse." I sighed and reached for a bottle of high-end facial cleanser. "I miss our home."

"Our home, huh?"

"Our home," I repeated.

"I need you to be patient, just a bit longer, okay?"

"I know," I muttered. I splashed warm water onto my face and then grabbed a clean hand towel and patted my skin dry. "It's just—well, I feel like I'm just along for the ride, you know? I don't *do* anything. I just sit and wait and let you protect me. I need to do something, Colt."

He ran his hands through his disheveled hair, making the muscles of my chest dance. The ink of my name across his pectoral rippled and my heart felt heavy with emotion.

"I'm talking to Sanchez today. That will dictate every-thing that happens from here on out."

"Sanchez might not come through, you know."

He smiled. "He will."

"How can you be so sure?"

"You've met Barrett."

"Uh, yeah."

"If Sanchez isn't convinced, I'll get Barrett to intervene. She'll step up to bat for us."

"Why would she?" I asked. "I mean, I know you and Flynn are friends, of a sort. But why would they help us unless they will benefit directly?"

"That's just it," he said with a dry smile. "They would benefit."

"I don't get it. Maybe it's the scotch I had last night, but I don't understand."

He rubbed a thumb across his jaw, the noise of stubble against skin sounding like sandpaper against wood. "Barrett talked about her business partnership with Sanchez, yeah?"

I nodded.

"Flynn and Barrett own a scotch distillery in Dornoch, where they live. They make bottles of scotch, pack Sanchez's product in the boxes, and have them distributed."

I blinked. "They're drug mules?"

Colt shrugged. "Among other things."

"But, why?"

Colt mulled his words over for a moment before saying, "They have certain political affiliations they'd prefer to keep close to the vest. But let's just say they belong to the Scottish version of the IRA."

I inhaled a shaky breath. "Okay, I wasn't expecting that. Damn, now I *really* want to know how Barrett and Flynn met."

"It's a damn good story," Colt admitted. He finally pushed away from the doorjamb. "You ready to get out of here? Head back to Waco? I've got more shit to handle than just Sanchez."

I nodded, swallowing. "Are you—what are you going to do about Knight?"

Colt cracked his knuckles. "Have a talk with him. Man to man."

I didn't like the sound of that. On top of Sanchez, the Iron Horsemen, and a hell of a lot of cocaine, Colt was going to have to go face-to-face with another Blue Angel president, a man we needed to show our strength in Waco. A man whose club we needed for back up.

I prayed like hell it didn't turn into a blood bath of Blue Angel against Blue Angel. Colt couldn't afford this to get personal, but Knight was hiding something.

Colt pulled on a pair of jeans and reached for his cell, reading the screen. "Zip just texted. He's gonna get Joni moving. They'll meet us back in Waco, along with everyone else. You almost ready to get out of here?"

"What about saying goodbye to Barrett and Flynn?"

He grinned. "Darlin', they're already on their private jet bound for Scotland."

A few hours later, Colt and I walked into madness.

"Thank God you're here!" Darcy said, throwing her arms around me.

I removed my leather jacket. "Let me change and then put me to work."

Darcy nodded and let out a sigh. She looked at Colt and glared. "Next time, a little more warning would be nice. I'm trying to get the guest rooms cleaned and ready for all the new faces around here. Right now Knight and the boys are out back. I told them to get out of my hair and let me work."

Colt grinned and kissed her cheek. "You're the best."

Someone barreled into my legs and wrapped small,

thin arms around them. Lily looked up at me and grinned, showing the loss of one of her front teeth.

"Hi!" she exclaimed.

"You lost something," I said, poking the hole with my pointer finger and making her giggle.

"Mama says the Tooth Fairy is gonna come visit me tonight," Lily stated in excitement. "Do you think I'll get to meet her?"

"Er," I began, "I don't think it works that way. The Tooth Fairy is all about mystery."

Thank you, Darcy mouthed.

After I changed clothes, I went back to the kitchen to help Darcy. Rachel and Allison were already there.

"The kids keep interrupting," Darcy said in a harassed voice. "Do you mind going to entertain them while we finish getting the meal together?"

"Sure thing."

I waved to the men having beers and sitting at the picnic tables while the kids ran in circles around the yard. After spending a few minutes with them, I realized I was no match for their zeal and energy. How the hell did Darcy do it?

Knight sat on one of the picnic tabletops, drinking from his bottle of beer, watching me. I saw Colt out of the corner of my eye, his face darkening when he realized that Knight was studying me.

I swallowed, wondering when it would come to a head. Colt had enough on his plate. He didn't need the Knight thing weighing on him, and in my state of inebriation the night before, I'd blurted out my thoughts to Colt. If I had it to do over, I would've waited.

Not that I would've handled Knight myself. I didn't know him. I didn't know his personality. I was comfortable with my Blue Angels, but that did not extend to other brothers outside the Waco chapter.

I frowned when I realized how I was thinking about my new family.

Chosen, not born.

Strong. Loyal. Fierce.

What would they do if Knight was a threat to me?

Darcy came out the back to announce that dinner was ready. We were eating relatively early, but there would be leftovers to munch on through the rest of the night. Everyone flocked to the food and formed a line leading into the house and kitchen—the kids went first.

Colt joined me at the back fence as I waited for the line to clear out. "You okay, babe?" he asked, sliding his arm around my waist. "Is it Knight? I promise I'll talk to him."

"It's not Knight," I lied. And then because I wanted to distract him, I blurted out, "Can we please not have kids for a while?"

He looked down at me and smiled. "Sure, darlin'. Whatever you want."

I held up my finger and pointed it at him. "Don't do that."

"Don't do what?" he asked with sham innocence.

"Don't pretend to give in to what I'm asking and then make plans behind my back."

He laughed. "I promise I won't knock you up until you give me the green light. Happy?"

"Happy."

"But I gotta tell ya." His mouth drew closer. "It's all I can think about."

"You're insane." I teasingly pushed against his chest. I looked around the backyard and frowned. "Where's Joni?" I hadn't seen her since we'd gotten back from Dallas.

"Probably in her room sleeping off her hangover," Colt said dryly.

"I'll tell her dinner's ready and ask if she wants me to bring her a plate." I kissed him quickly and then eased away from him.

I wormed my way around the bodies waiting in line for food so I could take the backstairs up to the third floor. As I turned the corner, I saw Zip had Joni pressed against the closed door of her bedroom. There was no space between their bodies and his fingers were in her hair, his lips on hers. Her hands gripped his leather cut like she was afraid if she didn't hold onto him, she'd fall down.

I cleared my throat.

Zip tore his mouth from Joni's and whipped his head toward me. His pupils were dilated with lust and his face morphed into a mask of shock at being caught.

"Dinner's ready," I said lamely.

Zip pushed away from the wall and sauntered toward me. "Don't say anything to Colt."

"Zip." Joni's tone was a warning but it sounded tired.

"I won't say anything," I said. It was Joni who I addressed yet I didn't take my eyes off Zip. His gaze searched my face and finally he whispered, "Thank you."

Zip didn't look at Joni as he headed down the stairs.

When I was sure he was gone, I said to Joni, "You're certainly playing a dangerous game. Out in the open like that."

"Do you want to come in?" she asked, turning the knob on her door.

"Hell yeah I want to come in," I said, still trying to wrap my brain around what I'd just seen. "When did he— how did you—and he—"

"Last night. Well, actually, early this morning." She

smiled slightly. "He saw me on stage and came to my hotel room. And then he—ah—"

"I didn't interrupt you guys just now, did I?"

She shook her head. "We were saying goodbye."

I arched an eyebrow. "Didn't look like goodbye from where I was standing. You guys are playing with fire. Sneaking around in the clubhouse? Just be glad it was me who saw you guys and not someone else. Like Boxer."

Joni sobered.

I nodded. "Yeah. Boxer is totally aware that there's *something* between you and Zip. It's obvious to anyone with two eyes. You have to tell Colt."

"I can't," she pleaded. "Not yet."

"Is this Zip talking, or you? Is this because he doesn't want a relationship?"

She shook her head. "Listen to what you just said. You're already calling it a relationship. I need time—we need time—to figure out what all this is without the pressure of telling my brother."

"I'm in the middle now," I said softly.

Her eyes were contrite. "I'm sorry. I really am."

"No. Don't be. We're friends, and I'll keep your secret. Even if—when—all this blows up."

"I just have to make sure this is real, you know? Before I go messing with everyone's lives."

"What does Zip want?"

"To tell Colt."

"That's surprising. If he wanted you only for a one night stand, would he even bother wanting to tell Colt?"

"I don't know." Her brow furrowed. "They have weird rules about getting involved with sisters. Like a code of honor or something. So Zip might want to tell Colt for the sake of brotherhood and respect, regardless if he has real feelings for me or not."

"This is a clusterfuck," I muttered.

"And I hate that I even have to say this, but please don't tell Darcy or the others."

"I won't. If you divulge one thing."

"What?"

I grinned. "How hot was the sex?"

Joni and I came down the stairs and grabbed ourselves plates of food to take outside. The boys had lit a bonfire and torches to keep the bugs away. The cool beer went down far too easily.

After the sun set, Darcy ushered the kids inside and plopped them in front of the TV in the entertainment room down in the basement. Little ears had a tendency to hear things they weren't supposed to hear, so it was club policy to keep them on another floor entirely.

Colt spent most of the night with his arm around my shoulder and every time I tried to leave, he'd ask where I was going. Clearly he didn't feel comfortable leaving me alone because of what I'd said about Knight.

But Knight wasn't even paying attention to me, or if he was, I was somehow not seeing it.

"Sorry we couldn't offer you a rowdier party," Boxer said to Bishop, Knight's VP.

"Plenty of time for pussy later," Bishop said. "Anyone need another beer? I'm headed to the cooler."

We shook our heads and then Bishop wandered off in search of another brew.

I let out a laugh. "You guys sure are fond of that word."

"It might be my favorite word," Boxer said with a wry

grin. "I wouldn't mind seeing your friend Shelly's pretty pink—"

"That's enough. You're done. She's engaged, dude."

"I can take her fiancé."

"He's trained in Krav Maga and carries a pistol."

"No shit!"

I nodded.

"Then I guess I need to woo her with the promise of my huge—"

I flicked his forehead, lightly, but just enough to get him to stop talking.

"Ow."

"That didn't hurt." I rolled my eyes.

"It could've hurt," Boxer protested.

"You're a weenie."

"You just called me a—Prez, your woman just called me a weenie."

"She's not wrong." An easy smile slid across Colt's lips. It transformed the planes and angles of his face. If it weren't for the bonfire's flames, he would've looked downright boyish, which wasn't a word I'd ever thought to call Colt. But all men had the ability to look young and carefree, impish and up to no good when they were happy.

It was one of those moments where my breath caught and I thought about a time when Colt would have a son of his own and the same expression would be stamped across his face.

Colt stared down at me and I could see the flames from the fire flickering in his eyes. I wanted to tell him what I'd just felt, about the emotions tearing through me with such promise I could almost taste the sweetness of joy on my tongue. But we weren't alone and now wasn't the time.

"Prez," Zip said, sliding out from the shadows and

coming to stand next to Colt, pulling his attention. "It's time."

Colt nodded to his VP. He leaned down to my ear. "I'm about to talk to Sanchez. I'd feel better if you went to our room."

"I'll be okay," I assured him. "I'll hang with the girls. Safety in numbers."

He kissed me quickly and then with a nod at Zip, the two of them left the bonfire, heading for the shed that was built just off the clubhouse where the boys held church.

"Another beer?" Boxer asked me.

"Hmm?" I was only listening with half an ear; my gaze caught Knight's, who was still sitting on a picnic table top, not appearing as though he'd moved. Not even to get another beer. He looked lost in thought. Looked lost in general.

His eyes pinged to mine.

I suddenly didn't want to talk to the girls.

"What's Knight drinking?" I asked Boxer.

He shot me a look. "Why?"

"Because he needs a refill."

"You gonna take it to him?"

"Yeah."

"Why?"

"Stop asking me why," I snapped. "But if you want to know, I think I owe it to Colt to get to know Knight. I'm the president's Old Lady, right? It's my job to make outsiders feel welcome."

"Knight's not an outsider. He's a Blue Angel."

"Semantics. And you know what I meant."

"Look at you, fitting in with your new family." Boxer wrapped an arm around my neck and pulled me to his chest so he could plop a kiss on top of my head. "Proud of ya, Mia."

His words weren't condescending and they felt like a warm breeze on my skin. I smiled up at him. "You're okay, you know that?"

"Just okay?" He puffed out his chest. "Tell everyone I'm amazing."

I pushed against him and he released me. With a laugh I headed toward a picnic table that was covered in full booze bottles, plastic red cups, and a tin bucket full of ice that was rapidly melting in the heat from the nearby fire. I swiped a bottle of Jack and headed toward Knight. He watched me approach with an unwavering, intense gaze.

"Hey," I said.

"Hey." His tone was wary, like he didn't trust or understand why I was standing in front of him.

"Thought you could use another drink." I held out the bottle of bourbon to him.

His eyes dropped from me to stare at the bottle. His fingers gripped the neck and he took it from me. "Why'd you bring this to me?"

I shrugged. "You look lonely over here. Thought I'd come say hi. We didn't really get a chance to talk at The Rex."

"I was busy with other shit." He nodded and unscrewed the lid. "Thanks." He took a swig and then limply let his hand drop so the bottle almost touched the bench.

"So you're from Coeur d'Alene," I said.

"Yeah."

Knight clearly hadn't perfected the art of conversation. I thought about leaving him to his own devices, but then he lifted the bottle of Jack to me.

A silent offering of friendship.

"Thanks." I took the bottle and drank.

A ghost of a grin flittered across Knight's mouth. Half

his face was concealed in shadow, but what I could see was covered in a beard. But he had a nice smile.

"Have a seat," he said, gesturing to the spot next to him.

"Okay." I scrambled up to the table's top and plunked down next to him, far enough away that should our knees fall to the sides, we wouldn't touch.

I stared at the fire when I asked my question. "What was that? Back at The Rex?"

"What are you talking about?"

"When you saw me. You looked—I don't even know how to describe it."

"Are you always like this?" he asked.

"Like what?'

"Blunt."

"What do I have to lose by being blunt?" I asked.

"You didn't answer the question."

"Neither did you."

He took the bottle of Jack back and downed a few swallows.

"How old are you," he asked suddenly.

I frowned. "Why does it matter?"

"Please?" His tone was low, but I heard the plea just the same.

"Twenty-five."

"Twenty-five," he murmured.

Icy fear slithered down my spine. I didn't know why Knight was asking about my age. His expression gave nothing away. He just continued to drink and I sat there next to him, feeling like an idiot.

I made a move to get up off the table.

His hand shot out to grip my knee.

I froze.

Before I knew what was happening, a blur sailed

through the air and tackled Knight. The bottle of Jack dropped from Knight's hand and his back hit the table.

"What the hell!" I yelled, clambering to get out of the way of the fight.

"I saw you touch her, fucker," Boxer growled. "You touched Colt's woman."

Boxer didn't give Knight time to defend himself because he punched the older man right in the face. Knight was no slouch, though. He let Boxer get in one good hit, but then he quickly rebounded, using his legs to launch Boxer off him.

Boxer hit the ground with a thud, but before he made a move to get back up, Knight was climbing off the table. The corner of his lip was bloody, but otherwise didn't look like he'd taken a punch or been winded at all.

"It's not what you think," Knight began.

"Fuck you and fuck your shit," Boxer said, rising. "You don't fucking touch another brother's woman. You're a brother! You know this!"

Sounds of conversation had ceased. Old Ladies and Blue Angels had crowded closer, trying to piece together what had just gone down.

Knight didn't look at Boxer—instead he stared at me. "Your mother…her name was Scarlett O'Banion."

My eyes widened. "How did you—"

"Because," Knight's eyes were grim. "I'm your father."

Chapter 24

Father.

Father?

I looked at Knight; everyone and everything around me disappeared as I gaped at the face of the man claiming my paternity.

"That isn't possible," I blurted out.

His expression was tight. "It's possible. You look just like her."

The air in my lungs whooshed out and I felt myself falling. Boxer was suddenly lifting me into his arms.

"What the fuck is going on out here?" came Colt's angry voice.

I hadn't even heard the shed door open, but then Colt was there. I closed my eyes, not wanting to see anyone, not wanting them to see me.

No one answered Colt.

"I'm not gonna ask the fucking question again. Why are you carrying my woman?"

"It was either catch her when she fainted," Boxer drawled. "Or let her hit the ground."

"Faint? She fainted? Why the fuck——"

"Brother," Knight began.

I moaned. "I didn't faint."

"Here," Boxer said, all but dumping me into Colt's arms. "You need to go inside with her. Knight too. The rest of us are gonna stay out here and get wasted."

"Why does Knight need to come inside?" Colt demanded.

"Ask her," Boxer said and then strutted away.

Colt began to move, his strides long and sure. He was able to get the back screen door open with one hand and then he was walking to the living room. He set me down on the couch and then took a seat on the coffee table, facing me.

"You okay?" His callused hands reached out to touch my face.

My gaze darted to Knight who was standing over us.

My father was watching me with the man I shared a bed with.

I swallowed and nodded, batting Colt's hands away.

"What is all this?" Colt demanded, looking at Knight.

"Your boy tackled me when he thought I put a move on Mia."

"Move?" Colt's voice was deadly.

"It's not like that, Colt," I said before Knight could defend himself. "I don't know how to tell him——"

"Tell me what?"

"Knight says—he's claiming——"

"I'm Mia's father."

Colt slowly stood up from the coffee table, his face dark with anger. "You've got to be fucking kidding me."

Knight shook his head. "It's the truth."

"Why should I believe you?" I asked.

"Your eyes…they turn down at the corners. Just like hers."

My mother was beautiful, but she had looked sad even when she was smiling. Even in old photos of when she was very young.

"So you knew what my mother looked like," I said. "That doesn't mean anything. That doesn't mean you're my father."

"You're right. That's not enough proof." Knight wiped at the corner of his mouth, smearing the almost dried blood. He reached into his back pocket and pulled out his wallet. He flipped it open and drew out a photograph.

I stared at his outstretched hand and with a labored sigh, grasped the photo. It was a picture of Knight with his arm around my mother. She couldn't have been more than nineteen. Twenty at the oldest. She'd died young, in her twenties. Frozen in youth. I was older now than she was when she'd died.

In the picture, Mom was looking up at Knight like he hung the moon. He was staring at the camera, full of swagger and youthful arrogance. He was nearly clean-shaven, but he had stubble.

My mind was spinning out of control. How was this possible? What were the chances of this happening? That I was meeting the man who'd sired me. I remember asking my mother about my father but she had given me evasive answers when I was a child, never fully explaining something that perhaps at the time I wouldn't have been able to grasp anyway. Maybe she'd been waiting to tell me everything until I was older.

But she died before she got the chance.

Grammie had been just as cryptic about my paternity. I wondered if it was because she never knew.

I looked at Colt, whose face was expressionless. He

wasn't going to intervene or stop this conversation from happening. And if it derailed like a train on the tracks, then so be it.

"Did you know about me?" I blurted out.

Knight's eyes went from grim acceptance that I was going to reject him to flaring with hope. "No. God, know. I had no idea. I swear."

I got up from the couch, setting aside the photo on the cushion.

"Where are you going?" Colt asked.

"I need a drink. If we're going to talk about my mother, then I need a drink."

"Why don't you guys take the office," Colt said. "You'll have more privacy in there."

Knight nodded. "Thanks, brother."

Colt rubbed the back of his neck. "I'm sorry for what Boxer did. He's taken to Mia like an older brother. He was just looking out for her."

Knight smiled. "No apologies needed. I'm glad she found you. Found the Angels." He held out his hand to Colt who took it immediately.

They shook hands but said no more. Colt led us to the office. "Bottle of bourbon in the file cabinet. Under Z."

I raised an eyebrow. "That's what you do in your office? Drink?"

He smiled.

I smiled.

Even Knight smiled.

And then I remembered that I'd just found out my absent father was the president of the Coeur d'Alene Blue Angels.

Before Colt headed for the door, he pulled me into his arms and brought his lips close to my ear. "You need me, you call for me. Otherwise, I'm letting you handle this."

I nodded. "How'd it go with Sanchez?"

"Tell you about it later. You've got other things to worry about." He kissed my lips, sent Knight a look, and then he was gone.

Knight waited to see what I'd do. I wanted distance from him, yet I also wanted him to spill everything he knew about my mother. The mother I hadn't gotten nearly enough time with.

I took a seat in one of the office chairs, keeping my posture stiff, my body alert. Knight tapped his fingers against his jeans, clearly nervous. Though why he was nervous, I couldn't imagine. He'd already dropped the bomb that he was my father.

"I always thought my father was older," I said, breaking the tension. "I mean, when I allowed myself to think about him, I always thought of a man in his sixties. Gray hair, you know? A guy who wore khakis and a polo."

"Must be a surprise to find that I don't match your vision." He looked out the window and stared for a moment. What could he see through the blinds? Was he wishing for an escape?

I got up from my chair and headed to the file cabinet. I opened the drawer all the way and pulled out the bottle of bourbon under the Z file.

I shook my head. "It's not even a bourbon that begins with Z. Why not have it under the B file?" I threw him a smile, but his own lips didn't waver in humor, though he was watching my every move. Almost like he was drinking in the years he'd missed, as if studying me would make up for lost time.

"Maybe we don't talk about her just yet," I voiced. "Maybe it's too soon and we should just—I don't know—try and talk like two normal people."

"We aren't normal though, are we? Thrown into this fuckery."

I unscrewed the cap on the bourbon and took a sip before handing it to him. The liquor burned, but then warmed my insides, melting the ball of ice that had lodged itself in my throat since the moment Knight had shown me the photo of him and my mother.

He took a long drink and then sauntered over to the couch and sat down. He leaned back, stretching his long legs out in front of him.

"I don't know what to do here," Knight said suddenly. "I want to hear it all. I want you to tell me all about you and how you grew up and if you were happy. I can't believe this shit—that you somehow wound up in this life when all your mother wanted was to keep you out of it." He frowned. "It's why she left me. It's why she didn't tell me she got pregnant. It's why she left Coeur d'Alene."

"Did you know she went back to Waco?"

"Yeah."

Thoughts swirled through my head. "How did you two meet?"

"She was waiting tables at a diner just outside town. I was newly patched in, looking to throw some swagger around." He smiled in fond remembrance. "Your mother wasn't impressed, but I wore her down enough and after a time she gave me a shot."

"How?"

"I found out she liked boats. My buddy had a small speed boat and let me borrow it. I took her to a picnic on the other side of the lake and she started to fall for me. I was exciting to her. Something more than just waitressing and making ends meet. We were inseparable that summer. Except when I had club business. It was fine at first, but after a while, and a few times I came home with black eyes and blood on my shirt, she started to lose her cool. Said she wanted more out of life and a relationship than what I was giving her. We were both really young. Your mom had dreams, and that didn't include being a biker's woman. Her being left in the dark, wondering, waiting if shit was gonna go down, or if a brother would come to the door with bad news about me was too much for her."

My breath hitched. I'd had the same thoughts when I realized what it meant to be with Colt.

"The night she left," Knight said, his voice soft in the still air, "we had the worst fight of our entire relationship. She was pissed and hurt that I chose my brothers over her and what she considered a respectable life. She'd talked about her parents, not a lot, but a bit. I knew their background, the families they were a part of. But I didn't *really* understand where Scarlett was coming from. This life—the club life—was all I'd ever known. Scarlett's parents left Chicago, right? Neither one of them wanted to be involved with either of their families' legacies. It was easy for Scarlett to choose something better because she'd had that example, you know? Her parents wanted her out of a life of crime. Me?" He shook his head. "My dad was club president. Mom was a club whore who didn't care that my dad dicked around on her. I was twenty years old when I was patched in. Your mother was nineteen. We had no idea what life was gonna look like."

He shrugged, like he was trying to shrug off the past and his regrets.

"So I let her go. That night, she asked me if I really loved her. Asked me if I loved her enough to let her go and be happy with someone who could give her what she wanted." He dropped his head in sudden exhaustion. "I let her go. She took my heart with her—I never got it back. Made the two women after your mother miserable for it. Made the mistake of marrying one."

"Are you married now?" I asked.

He shook his head. "Nah. Divorced. Your mother was the love of my life."

"Any," I licked my suddenly dry lips, "any kids?"

"No. Just...you."

Just me.

Knight talked of legacies. Was this mine? Born from criminals? My mother's family on both sides belonged to notorious gangster families. And my father—Knight—was president of a biker club.

And now I'd taken up with Colt.

Mom had wanted something different for me. Something different for herself. So she'd left Knight and I'd grown up without a father. I'd grown up without a mother, too, and in some strange twist of fate that upbringing led me right back to a life with Colt.

"I came to Waco once," he said quietly. "A few years after she left. Walked right into your grandparent's store and there she was behind the counter. She looked the same as the last time I had seen her." He shook his head. "No, that's not really true. She looked...settled into her body. Lived in, you know? Like the few years apart from me had made her an adult or some shit. Though now I realize it might have been because she had become a mother. I don't know."

I nodded in understanding. "There's something that happens in your twenties. Like you become sure of yourself in your body. I know what you mean."

He smiled slightly. "Yeah, exactly."

"What did she do? When she saw you?"

"Nothing. She just watched and waited." He rubbed the back of his neck. "I wasn't sure what I was supposed to say to her. I knew begging her to come back wouldn't do anything. I'd ridden over eighteen hundred miles on my bike just so I could see her and then turn around and leave again."

I swallowed the emotion brewing in my throat. "Do you think—do you think it would've been different for all of us if you'd said something? Do you think she would've told you about me?"

"I don't know, Mia. I've spent twenty-five years trying not to think about the past. All my fuck ups and great regrets, you know? Shit like that can kill a man."

We fell silent and took a few minutes passing the bottle of bourbon back and forth.

"Did she ever get married? Do you have any siblings?" he asked suddenly.

"You didn't keep tabs on her? Well, I guess that makes sense since you knew nothing about me." My tone wasn't bitter, just honest. "No, she never married and I don't have any siblings. She died when I was five."

"Scarlett died," he stated.

I could hear the tension in his voice, the shock of learning that the woman he'd loved most of his life had passed.

"She drowned. Off the coast of Catalina. She was swimming, and a riptide…" I didn't need to finish.

He made a slight noise, almost like a stifled wail, but it caught in the back of his throat.

I forced myself to finish the rest of the story. Only Shelly and Grammie knew it. I hadn't even been able to bring myself to tell Colt. We had enough horrors to contend with. But I owed this to Knight.

"I saw it," I murmured.

Knight's eyes snapped to mine.

"I didn't speak for two years."

He leaned forward, his face earnest. "Tell me about your life. Tell me everything."

I talked to my father long into the night. Not once was there a knock on the door interrupting us. Questions turned into stories. Stories that made my childhood vivid.

He winced when I recounted when I was eight and fell out of a tree, breaking my arm. He laughed when I told him when I was ten I tackled a schoolyard bully.

"What about you?" I asked finally sometime around two in the morning. "I've told you about me. What about you?"

"Not much to tell," he said quietly. "I have a small house on the lake. Spend my time working on my bike when I'm not dealing with club business."

It sounded like a lonely existence to me, but who was I to judge? I couldn't tell his age since his face was hiding behind his beard and the sun had weathered his skin.

"How old are you?" I asked suddenly.

"Forty-six."

"Forty-six," I repeated. "You were twenty-one when I was born. That's so young."

Mom had been twenty. I couldn't imagine having a baby that young. I couldn't imagine having to scrape it all together. Thank God for Grammie who'd been there through it all.

Still, I couldn't help but wonder what my life would've looked like if Knight had been in it. Would we have lived on the lake? Would we have spent Saturday mornings on a boat? Would my mother still be alive?

The questions were exhausting and the bourbon was causing my eyelids to droop.

"You should hit the sack," Knight said. "You look exhausted."

"It's been a long day."

"Yeah." He nodded but made no move to stand up.

I forced myself to rise and then I went for the door.

"Does he make you happy?" he asked suddenly. "I know I've got no right to ask. I'm your father, but I'm not your dad. But I still want to know…"

I smiled and turned my head to look at him over my shoulder. "Yeah. He makes me happy."

I left him sitting alone, pondering everything we'd discussed.

He was right, though. He wasn't my dad. A dad picked you up when you scraped your knees. A dad checked in your closet for monsters. A dad threatened to kill any boy who broke your heart.

I might've shared DNA with Knight, but that didn't make him family.

Colt was propped up in bed, shirtless, the lamp on the bedside table casting a warm glow across his golden skin. Seeing my name in ink settled me in a way I couldn't explain. It was like Colt's arms were around me, giving me silent, solid comfort.

He looked up from his phone. "Hey."

"Hey." I shut the door and then padded my way over to the bed, falling face first on top of the comforter.

"Long night?"

"Long night with bourbon."

He chuckled.

"I have a father," I murmured.

He paused and then said, "Yeah."

"Still trying to wrap my mind around that."

Colt lifted his arm so I could scoot closer to him. I pressed my nose into his side and took a moment to breathe him in, needing the solid assurance that he was there.

"What happened with your call to Sanchez?" I asked, my eyes drifting shut.

"He's agreed to help us. Not without a steep price though. His shit is already being distributed through the Southwest. He hasn't claimed Waco, but he is now. He also wants his product in the Heartland of the United States."

"So we're trading one cartel for another?"

"Yes, but there's one major difference," Colt said, his hand finding a way under my shirt. "Sanchez is on our side."

"The devil you know, I guess."

I wanted to ask more questions but with the comfort of the man I loved next to me in bed and the flow of potent bourbon in my veins, I fell asleep.

By the following morning, news that Knight was my father had already rippled through the clubhouse. Boxer publicly apologized for punching Knight in the face. Knight graciously accepted Boxer's apology and slapped him on the back.

The Blue Angels—Waco and Coeur d'Alene—had all gone to the shed for church, no doubt to discuss the Sanchez situation and what do about the product sitting unguarded in the storage unit.

The kids were still asleep downstairs in the theater room, but I knew it would only be a matter of time before they were awake and demanding food like angry baby birds.

The remains of last night's party were minimal. The bonfire had burned out hours ago, and all the beer bottles and plastic cups had been tossed into two huge garbage cans.

The girls and I were out back at one of the picnic tables, enjoying the morning air. Rachel sat across from me and was on her second cup of coffee. Darcy perched next to her, staring into the distance. Joni was by my side, close enough that I had to pretend not to see the whisker burns on her neck. Allison had returned from throwing up her guts due to morning sickness. She stood at the edge of the table, nibbling on a cracker.

"This is just so weird," Rachel said. "I can't believe Knight is your dad."

"I know," I said with a nod.

"How are you feeling about it?" Darcy asked.

"I don't know yet," I admitted. "He's young. Which is blowing my mind. He's not who I pictured when I thought of who my dad might be."

"He's also kind of hot," Rachel said. "Sorry, but it's true."

"You would go there, wouldn't you?" Joni said with a laugh. "What did you guys talk about?"

"Everything. My mom. How they met." I frowned.

"What's that face for?" Darcy asked.

"I just—I feel like he knows me, a little bit anyway. I told him about my childhood and growing up with Grammie. But I don't feel like, I don't—*know* him. He wasn't really forthcoming about his life and what it looks like."

"Do you want to know all those things?" Joni's gaze was curious. "I mean, it's one thing for your long lost dad to show up. Here, of all places. And a Blue Angel, too. Which, wow, coincidence much? But it's another thing for you to actually want to get to know him."

"And you won't get to know him in one night, you know?" Darcy added. "That takes time."

"Yeah." I nodded. "That's true."

"He's still a stranger," Allison said, swallowing the rest of her cracker. "Just because you share blood doesn't mean you automatically have trust and a relationship."

"And this adds a whole new layer of family ties to the Blue Angels," Darcy remarked. "Think about it. The Coeur d'Alene chapter was willing to help the Waco chapter because they consider each other family. But now Knight's daughter is the Old Lady of the president of the Waco Blue Angels. It's all meshed and intertwined."

"Blood allies," Rachel added with a nod. "Yeah."

The shed door opened and the Blue Angels poured out. They all looked alert and ready for the unknown despite the fact that we'd all gone to bed late and woken up early.

Darcy immediately hopped up from her seat and went to Gray, wrapping her arms around him. I loved seeing them show each other affection. Torque came to Allison's side immediately and whispered something in her ear. She sidled up to him and pressed her head to his chest and closed her eyes.

Reap sauntered up behind Rachel, set a hand on her shoulder, and stole her coffee. She didn't even bother fighting him over it.

I pretended not to see Zip giving Joni a long, lingering look.

"What's for breakfast?" Boxer asked, breaking the tension filled silence.

"Whatever you're cooking," Darcy said.

"Ah, come on," Boxer whined. "I'm hungry."

The back door to the clubhouse opened and Lily ran out, clutching her blanket, her eyes sleepy. She encircled Darcy's legs with her spindly arms before looking to her father. Gray scooped her up, causing her to giggle.

A gesture so simple it reminded me that I'd never had that growing up. I caught Knight looking at me, his face schooled into a blank expression.

I placed my hands on the table and stood up. "I'll make pancakes. But I need help." I looked at Lily. "You want to help?"

She nodded eagerly, scrambling to get down from Gray's arms.

By day three of the lockdown, everyone in the club-house was at each other's throats. Kids squabbled, couples bickered, and I had to pretend that I didn't see Joni and Zip sneaking off to be with one another. The inactivity had everyone on edge.

Colt and I hadn't spent a lot of time together since he was constantly talking to Knight, Mateo Sanchez, or Flynn Campbell.

The fourth morning of the lockdown, I finally broke my silence. "You have to let everyone out of here." I pulled on a pair of jeans and went to the dresser and grabbed a Blue Angels tank top they sold in the garage. It was soft, faded cotton and it felt like wearing pajamas.

Colt lounged from his spot in the bed, one arm under-neath his head, eyes heavy-lidded as he watched me get dressed. "Why?"

"I don't know if you're aware of this," I said with a wry grin, "but I'm pretty sure there's going to be a death or two —gladiator style—and soon. The tension in this place is at an all-time high."

"Huh. I haven't noticed."

"Liar. What's been happening with the Iron Horse-men?" I asked, changing the subject.

"Nothing. Dev has been silent. No blood on the streets. That doesn't mean it won't happen," he said.

"You're being overly cautious."

"That's my job. I have to look out for you and the club. Until I know for sure when Sanchez will send men to move the product, I don't want our people on the streets."

"And when do you think Sanchez will be sending men?"

"Soon."

"That's not good enough," I snapped.

"What's this really about?"

"I'm stuck in here unable to live my life. That's what this is about."

"You don't think this has something to do with Knight?"

I rolled my eyes. "Oh, please."

He shrugged.

"It has nothing to do with Knight."

"So you say. Have you talked to him since the night you found out he's your father?"

"Been kinda hard to." I wasn't actively avoiding the man, nor was I really seeking him out. There were always people around, and furthermore, what was I supposed to say to him?

A shouting match started up just outside our closed bedroom door, followed by a thump and another thump. The sound of yelling migrated down the hallway. A door slammed shut and then nothing.

I looked at Colt and raised an eyebrow. "Who do you think that was?"

"Reap and Rachel, if I had to guess."

A rapid succession of knocks sounded on our bedroom door and then, "You two better be decent!"

"He's talking to you," I said. "I'm fully clothed."

"Not by my choice," Colt muttered as he quickly reached for a pair of jeans. He didn't bother with a shirt, but headed for the bedroom door after he'd gotten his jeans buttoned.

Zip strode in. "Call the lockdown off."

"Oh good, maybe you can talk some sense into him," I said to Zip. "He won't listen to me."

I left the two of them to duke it out and went into the living room, wondering if I could pick at some of the breakfast leftovers. Meals had been on a rotation schedule, but we were all tired of cooking for the masses.

"Where are the kids?" I asked Darcy, who sat at the kitchen counter.

"Video game show down," she said. "I hate sticking them in front of the TV, but sometimes it's the only thing to do."

"They need to be running around after a Frisbee or soccer ball," Gray muttered from his spot on the couch.

The living room was fully occupied, but I didn't see Knight or Bishop, his VP, who I'd yet to really talk to. I'd caught him side-ways glancing at me, though. I couldn't help but wonder what he thought of Knight's long lost daughter.

I scraped together the last of the eggs and bacon, poured myself a cup of coffee, and stood at the counter to eat.

"Did you talk to Colt?" she asked.

"About letting us out of here? Yeah. He didn't really want to hear it."

"The charity sale for the elementary school is this weekend. I promised Laura we'd be at the park to help her."

I hadn't seen the woman who'd brought me a bunch of clothes in a few weeks. Nor had I given her a check for a donation like I'd wanted to, either.

"I feel so cut off from the world right now," I said.

"Yeah, I feel you."

"I haven't even called Shelly," I admitted. "To tell her about, well, everything."

No matter how much I tried to keep her in the fold, she wasn't part of the Blue Angel family, and therefore would always be on the outskirts. She should've been the first person I talked to when I found out about Knight. But we were on lockdown and Rachel, Darcy, Joni, and Allison were here so I'd turned to them.

"This is fucking ridiculous!" came Zip's roar.

"I've a right to be concerned!" Colt yelled back.

All movement and conversation stilled as the fight down the hall unfolded.

"Concerned, yes. But this is fucking ridiculous. We need to be able to live our lives."

"Get the boys. We'll fucking vote on it," Colt bellowed.

The Blue Angels didn't need to be gotten since they could hear everything that was going down between Colt and Zip. With a sigh, Gray stood up and headed out back. Boxer, Reap, Torque and the others followed suit.

I finished breakfast, tossed the paper plate in the trash, and then headed back to our bedroom. I was sorting our dirty laundry when Colt filled the doorway, his face dark with annoyance.

"Vote didn't go your way, did it?" I asked.

"Democracy's a democracy," Colt said, but his voice was filled with anger. "Why are people so shortsighted?"

I nudged the door closed so we could speak in private. "I think because people make most of their decisions emotionally."

"Yeah." He shoved a pair of dirty boxers into the bag. "You're right about that."

"They're right, too, though. Can't live your life in fear, waiting for something to go wrong."

He let out a sardonic laugh. "That's just it. I know things are gonna go wrong. It's just a matter of time."

"Hell of an outlook on life, Colt."

"You disagree with me? You? Based on what you've lived through the last few weeks?"

"Sure, life is one shit storm after another," I agreed. "But look what it can bring. I've got you. I've got the girls. New family."

"Knight."

"He's not my family," I protested.

"We haven't gotten a chance to talk about it the last few days, have we," he murmured. "Sorry for that, babe. Sounds like you can use an ear."

"I could use my own bed," I stated.

"Yeah?" He slowly came toward me, backing me up until I hit a wall. "What do you want to do in that bed?"

I grinned. "Sleep for hours without being awakened by screaming children or fighting couples."

"Everyone is clearing out except for the Coeur d'Alene brothers. I don't want to take you home—not while all this shit with Dev and the cartel is still a loose end."

I sighed and reached up to wrap my arms around his neck. "I know you couldn't control the outcome of the vote and everyone is taking their families home. But if you want to stay, if it'll make you feel better, then I won't fight you on this."

He leaned down and captured my lips with his. "Thank you."

Chapter 25

I waved to Shelly across the park lawn, shaking my head when I saw her outfit. Skinny white jeans, a pink and white checkered sleeveless button up, and cork wedges.

"You look like you're ready for a day at the rodeo," I said with a laugh, hugging her.

"If I was going to the rodeo, I would've worn my cowboy boots." She not too discreetly surveyed the area. "Which one is he?"

I gestured with my chin to Knight who was leaning against the fence of the basketball courts.

"Wow. He's good looking."

I glared at her.

She shrugged. "Sorry, honey, but he is."

The night before, I'd called Shelly to invite her to the charity yard sale that was being held in a public park due to the huge space, and to fill her in about Knight. I glossed over what I could, but had to mention club business because Colt had called the Blue Angels from Coeur d'Alene in for back up to deal with the Iron Horsemen. And it wasn't like I could get away with not telling her *why* we'd needed back up. But I did manage to leave out the part about a cartel being involved.

"Introduce me," Shelly said.

She took my hand and squeezed it, knowing I was nervous. I still wasn't sure how to act around Knight. He might've been my father, but he was a stranger.

"Hey," I greeted him awkwardly.

"Hey," he said, his gaze darting to my best friend.

"Knight, I'd like you to meet Shelly."

"Shelly," Knight repeated. "Good to meet you."

"Nice to meet you too," she said, clearly looking him over and studying him.

"Guessing you know who I am?" Knight asked with a smile.

She nodded. "Mia brought me up to speed."

I stood by while the two of them talked. Every now and then, Knight's eyes would dart to mine, like he wasn't sure how I was going to take his interaction with Shelly. But Shelly was Shelly and knew how to pretend awkwardness didn't exist. She was aware of social cues, she just chose not to pay attention to them.

"She's nice," Knight said after Shelly excused herself to find a restroom.

"She's the best," I said. "We've been friends forever. She was there when Grammie died. She's the only reason I got through it."

His eyes saddened. "I'm sorry you've had to live through so much loss."

"I—" Emotion blocked my throat. "I need to help Darcy set up."

I turned away from Knight. I wasn't prepared for public shows of emotion with him. My heart kicked up in grief when I saw his face fall and then close off.

The lawn was covered with folding tables and volunteers were hauling boxes of donated items from their cars and trucks. Kids ran around, laughing and having fun, and Blue Angels stood in small clusters, talking and watching. I caught Colt's eye, gave him a quick wave, and then turned my focus to Darcy and the girls who were unpacking used books.

"What can I do to help?" I asked her.

"Sort the books by genre," Darcy said. "I'm trying to create a semblance of order."

I bent down and grabbed a handful of old-school paperback romance novels and set them aside.

"Did I see Shelly?" Rachel asked.

"Yeah. She's here. She went to find a bathroom."

"Was it my imagination or did I see you introduce her to Knight?" Darcy asked. "Self-help books go on the other end of the table."

"Yeah, they met. It's just weird, you know?" I shook my head. "I don't even know how to deal with it. Oh, I wanted to ask you guys before Shelly gets back...I'm going to throw her a bachelorette party. Something small, and not a strip club situation. Maybe like a boozy brunch. Would you guys be down to attend?"

"I love that idea," Allison said. "Except I can't partake which kinda bums me out."

"Sorry, lady," Rach said with a grin. "I'm not forgoing alcohol in solidarity."

"I second that," Joni said.

"A girl can dream, right?" Allison sighed. "Aside from the no booze thing which really sucks, I have a hard time staying awake past nine now. It's like the clock strikes nine and I'm supine."

"Hey, you rhymed!" Rach said with a laugh.

"Enjoy your sleep while you can," Darcy said. "Lily still

wakes me up in the middle of the night if she has a bad dream."

Shelly found her way to our table. Rachel immediately put her to work as they gabbed. Laura came by, brown eyes surveying our work.

"How's everything going over here?" She frowned. "You guys aren't done yet? We're supposed to be ready to go in twenty minutes!"

"Relax," Joni said. "We'll be ready. Your yard sale will go off without a hitch."

Laura huffed and then turned and walked away, no doubt to berate other volunteers who weren't finished with their section.

"Why are we stuck with the books?" Rachel asked. "I wanted to man the costumes. I saw at least three boas over there."

"Ah, speaking of boas…" Darcy began as Cameron chased Lily across the grass. The little girl wore a bright pink boa that streamed behind her.

"They're cute," I commented.

"They're exhausting," Darcy said. "I've been with them nonstop, even though the lockdown is over and we're back at our house, Lily has become my shadow. And Cam can't sit still."

"I'll take them for a weekend," I offered. "Or even a couple of days during the week if you need a break. Maybe after all this stuff with the club is sorted."

"I couldn't ask you to do that," Darcy protested. "They're my children. I'm obligated to love them and therefore entertain them."

"You're not asking, I'm offering."

"You don't want to clear this with Colt first?" Darcy asked with a grin.

"He'll be fine with it," I assured her.

"You know my brother wants babies, right?" Joni stated.

"Yeah," I sighed. "I know."

"So you're hoping to use my children to scare the hell out of him and praying he changes his mind," Darcy acknowledged. "Good plan."

"Not a deterrent," I said. "But I'm not ready for all that—I want to finish my degree and not feel like the rug is always about to be pulled out from under me."

"I wish I'd brought my flask," Joni said. "This seems like a good flask conversation."

Darcy grinned. "One step ahead of you." Reaching into her back jean pocket, she whipped out a metal flask. "And before you judge me, it's Amaretto. It's basically water."

"I knew I liked you guys for a reason," Shelly said with a wink. "Drinking in a public park. My kind of ladies."

Cars started pulling up and parking on the street. People trickled across the grass, looking through the tables of second-hand belongings, discovering items they felt they couldn't live without.

By one o'clock, we had more foot traffic than we knew what to do with. Laura had "hired" a band, which was just a group of fathers with kids who attended the elementary school. They covered classic rock hits and jammed out, having a blast. There were four different types of food trucks, so there were options. Laura had thought of everything and I marveled at her event organization skills.

"Mama," Cam whined. "Can I get a hotdog? And a Sno-Cone?"

"Me too?" Lily asked. They both hung off her like little wolf pups. Darcy was in the middle of trying to sell a woman an encyclopedia collection that was missing the letters X and Z.

"I'll take the kids for a bit," I volunteered.

Darcy sent me a grateful look and then fished around in her pocket. I waved at her to put her money away, grasped Cam and Lily's hands, and walked toward the hotdog stand.

"We have to make one stop before we get food, okay?" I asked. "First one to find Laura gets their own cotton candy."

Cam found Laura, who was sitting at a folding table at the entrance of the park, holding the cash box. Lily nearly pitched a fit until I told her I'd buy her a cotton candy too. Her pout turned into an adorable smile.

I reached into my back pocket and pulled out an envelope to give to Laura. "Here."

"What's this?"

"My donation. For the clothes you brought me."

She adamantly shook her head. "Put that away. You don't need to donate. The clothes were a gift."

"Please take the money and save us a lot of time," I said.

"But Colt—"

"But Colt what?" he asked from behind me.

I turned to him. "I shouldn't be surprised to find you standing right there, and yet, I kind of am."

Colt grinned, leaned down, and kissed me quickly. Cam made a gagging noise while Lily giggled and hugged his leg.

He reached down and hoisted Lily up and settled her onto his shoulders before returning his attention to me. "What are y'all talking about?"

This man, speaking in a drawl with a cute little girl on his shoulders, had me sighing like an idiot.

"She's trying to give me a donation," Laura said, looking at me with a knowing smile.

"You gave me clothes when I had none," I protested.

"I was happy to do it."

"They've been arguing for a billion minutes," Cam informed Colt. "And I'm hungry."

"Me too," Lily added.

I folded the envelope and shoved it into the pocket of Laura's denim skirt.

Laura didn't look at me but at Colt. Colt nodded and then Laura accepted it.

"Come on," Colt said. "I'm hungry."

"How hungry?" I asked in a playful voice.

"So hungry that I don't think a few hotdogs will do it."

"No?" I asked.

"No." Colt pretended to look thoughtful. "I think I want…a Lily burger!"

"What? No!" Lily laughed as Colt lifted her off his shoulders and slung her over his back and began to nibble on her arm.

"Yep," Colt said in amusement. "I'll have a Lily burger, medium rare, with everything on it!"

"And fries!" Cam added with a grin.

"You're next," Colt warned.

"Eat him first!" Lily offered.

Colt set Lily down on the ground and playfully tugged on her pigtails. "Nah. I think it's too much trouble. Guess I'll settle for three regular burgers then."

I snorted in amusement. "Just three?"

"Gotta keep up my strength for tonight." He winked.

"Why do you need strength for tonight?" Cam wondered.

"Way to go," I muttered.

"I'm gonna be in a wrestling match," Colt deadpanned.

"With costumes?" Lily asked in excitement.

"Yeah, we'll wear suits."

"Hey, guys, why don't you run ahead to the hot dog truck and order. Colt and I will be there in a moment," I suggested.

The kids took off in exuberance, and when I was sure they were out of earshot, I looked at Colt. "Suits?"

Colt slung his arm over my shoulder and pulled me into his chest. "Yeah, suits. Birthday suits."

I let out a chuckle. "You think you're hilarious."

"I got you to laugh, didn't I?"

"Yep. You also got me thinking about you naked."

"Then I definitely did something right. I've been missing you this week."

"You've been busy," I said. "How are things with Sanchez?"

"Coming along. Knight and his boys are going to do us a solid and help Sanchez's men move the product."

"For a cut, right?" I asked.

"A cut of the game, yeah. They want in. Make it profitable for all of us if we can run shit up all the way to Idaho."

I paused in thought and frowned.

Colt noticed my pensive expression. "What?"

I glanced around at the park bustling with smiling, laughing kids, their parents, young twenty somethings buying used furniture to outfit their boho chic apartments.

"I just—drugs destroy communities." My gaze drew back to his. "Are we knowingly going to be part of something that will change the landscape of Waco? It'll have repercussions and they won't be good."

Colt scratched his jaw, obviously weighing his words. "What about pharmaceutical companies? Doctors write scripts for opiates. Do you know how long it takes to get addicted to opiates? Ten days. You know the duration doctors are writing those scripts for? Ten days. Bankers swindling old ladies out of their pensions. The world is stuffed with people robbing each other blind."

"Two wrongs don't make a right," I pointed out.

"That's true. But why is it okay for others to fuck with humanity? Because it's *technically* legal? It's bullshit. How many people die from alcohol related incidents versus pot?"

He took a step closer and wrapped his hand around my neck. "You chose this life, Mia. When you chose me."

My eyes swept up to meet his. "I know that, Colt." I sighed. "But I'm allowed to push back. It helps me process."

I reached up to cover his hand caressing my neck. "I'm not going anywhere. If that's what you're worried about. But that doesn't mean I can turn a blind eye without saying something. That money will be used to take care of our family. That money will send Cam and Lily to the college of their choice. But in taking care of our family, who do we hurt in the process, you know?"

"I know," he murmured. He paused for a moment. "You still love me? Knowing what you know?"

I smiled slightly. "Yeah, I still love you. I just have to reconcile it, okay? And this wasn't me busting your ass or naively saying, 'Oh, just do something else for money. Something legitimate.' I just don't want to be a raging hypocrite, enjoying the comfort the money will bring without at least broaching the topic of what my comfort will mean for others."

"This event is because of the Blue Angels. All under wraps, mind you, because we don't want to make people uncomfortable. We give back to our town, and maybe that's all anyone can ever hope to do, you know?"

He squeezed the back of my neck and then let go. "Can we be done talking about this now?"

"Yeah, we can be done."

He smirked. "Can we talk about when we can get out of here?"

"Not for a while yet. Oh, and when all this stuff is sorted with the Iron Horsemen, I told Darcy we'd take her kids for the weekend."

"Why would you do a thing like that?" he demanded.

I grinned. "So she and Gray can remember what it's like to be childless for a couple of days. And then I can give you an idea of what our life is gonna be like when we finally decide to go that route."

"You think you're gonna scare me away from it, but ten bucks says it backfires. You're gonna see how hot I look caring for kids and you're gonna beg me to—"

I jumped into his arms and sealed his lips with mine. Partly so he wouldn't say anything dirty in public and partly just so I could kiss him.

After we got our hotdogs and burgers, we took them to a spot on the grass. Lily finished her hot dog in record time and then asked for ice cream instead of a cotton candy.

"Let's wait a minute," I suggested, not wanting to deal with an upset stomach if I let her gorge too fast.

"But—"

"Listen to Mia," Colt commanded gently but firmly. Lily closed her mouth and crossed her arms over her chest. Then she widened her eyes and gazed at Colt.

"Don't look at me that way," he said, his voice losing some of his gruffness. "I'm immune to manipulation."

Lily dropped the act and frowned. "What's immune mean?"

"It means that look you use on your parents won't work on Colt," I answered.

"Rats," Lily said.

"Ten minutes," Colt relented. "Then you and Cam can have your dessert."

Cam and Lily high-fived. "Can I go play with my friend Brock?" Cam asked.

"Where's Brock?" I asked.

Cam pointed out a dark-haired boy. Something about Brock looked familiar.

"Okay," I said. "But you have to stay where I can see you."

Cam scrambled up from the grass and dashed after his friend.

"What about you, Lily Burger?" I teased. "You want to go play with them, too?"

She shook her head. "They don't like it when I tag along."

"We're more fun anyway," Colt said.

"Who's Brock?" I asked Colt.

"Laura's son."

"Ah."

Lily climbed into my lap and I hugged her. I pressed my cheek to her blond head and closed my eyes. There was something about Lily. Maybe it was her inherent sweetness, her trusting nature, even though she hardly knew me. But I realized how much I wanted to be around to see her grow up. To paint her toenails and give her advice. To see her go to prom with a nice boy who respected her.

An ache formed in my throat and swelled when I thought of Knight, who'd missed all of that with me. I didn't know what kind of father he would've been, but the photo he'd shown me of him and my mother, and my mother's smile...

She left him not because she didn't love him, but

because she wanted to protect me from Knight's way of life.

I glanced at Knight who was standing with Bishop and Boxer. He threw his head back and laughed, and I realized in that moment that I wanted to know him. It wouldn't make up for lost time, and all the years he hadn't been there could not be gotten back, but that was neither of our faults and it wasn't fair to punish him for my mother's choice.

It was time for Knight to be a part of my life.

"What's that smile about?" Colt asked.

"I'm just...happy. Despite all the crazy."

"Has it been ten minutes yet?" Lily asked impatiently, effectively ruining the intimacy of the moment.

"It's been long enough, honey. Let's get you an ice cream," Colt said.

I turned to Cam and Brock and yelled out, "You guys want ice cream?"

The young boys ran toward us, boisterous and full of energy, eager for sugar, which they clearly didn't need.

And then I heard the sound of motorcycles, followed by a series of gunshots and the screams of terrified children.

"Brock!" Laura shrieked.

"Mom!" Brock howled, darting toward her.

"Stop him!" I screamed to Colt as I shoved Lily behind me to shield her. "Laura! Get down! We've got Brock!"

More gunshots rang out and I heard a distant scream. Laura tucked and rolled behind one of the bushes, and Colt didn't hesitate as he ran for Brock. Cam was frozen in fear next to his friend; Colt grabbed both boys and pushed them to the ground. "Stay down," Colt commanded. "Crawl on your bellies to the hot dog truck. Get behind it and stay there. Go!"

The boys snuck off, and I gave a sigh of relief when I saw them make it to safety.

Colt took out his pistol and peered around, looking for threats. I crouched and slid across the grass, all the while making sure my body was in front of Lily's.

"Be careful," I called to him over the roar of motorcycle pipes and shots.

I continued to slither with Lily until we made it to the hot dog truck. Brock and Cameron were sitting with their backs against the vehicle, terrified, pale, and shaking.

"It's okay," I whispered repeatedly, trying to wrap my arms around all three of them, wanting to block out the noise but unable to.

"Cover your ears," I commanded all of them. Once they did what they were told, I peeked around the back of the truck to survey what was going on.

Five masked men in white T-shirts sat atop motorcycles with weapons drawn, letting off shots at anything that moved, the chrome of their bikes gleaming in the sunshine, their presence sending fear through the crowd.

I knew it was the Iron Horsemen, but why was Dev bringing this war out into the open instead of keeping it between clubs and on club territory?

He'd violated the sacred code of not bringing a war to families. Colt would kill him for it.

They reloaded their firearms and opened fire again, causing more panic and screaming. I felt Lily trembling beside me and I reached a hand out to her, but my eyes were scanning the park, searching for the people who were my family. I removed the pistol from the holster at my hip, feeling safer with a weapon in my hand. I'd defend myself and protect the children. Whatever the cost.

I saw Colt in the middle of the park, helping a woman

and her child toward the safety of the public restrooms, which left him out in the open.

The Iron Horsemen didn't waste any time as they fired off another round of shots, and I watched as Colt fell to his knees. His face was a picture of shock as his hand went to his side, covering a bloody stain on his shirt.

I opened my mouth to scream, but no sound came out.

Colt lifted his pistol and fired off a few shots toward the Iron Horsemen, but they went wide and he missed.

He dropped his weapon to his side, a look of angry resignation passing over his face as if he could hardly believe he was going out that way.

Turning his head, his eyes found mine. There was nothing but remorse shining out from them, silently apologizing for the life we wouldn't get to share.

Colt mouthed something to me and even though it was too far away to lip-read, I knew what he was saying.

I love you.

"Fuck that, Colt," I whispered, tears spilling from my eyes.

Hope drained from his face, mine going with his. I refused to look away, I refused to let him think he was dying alone, that I wasn't dying with him. Because I was. Every last bit of me that had survived the death of my mother and grandmother, would die now, too. Colt had helped me live. He'd helped me love.

More gunshots from across the park pulled his attention and a slow smile crept across his face as though he had embraced the finality of what was to come.

"Get down, you bloody fool!" Flynn Campbell yelled from behind a large oak tree.

Colt heard him and flopped to the grass, letting out a moan, his eyes closing.

Flynn yelled in a foreign tongue, which sounded very

much like a war cry. Men swarmed from every avenue, armed, ready, and firing at the Iron Horsemen.

My heart was torn in two. The love of my life was bleeding out on the lawn, but there were three children who needed my protection.

My savior came in the form of Darcy who had somehow managed to avoid the fray and snuck up against the hot dog truck. No danger would stand between a mother and her babies. She sent me an overwhelming look of gratitude for protecting her children, but then she gestured with her chin at Colt.

"I know," I whispered. "I have to go to him. It might already be too—"

"Go," she urged.

I attempted to hand her my pistol but she shook her head. "I've got one."

All rational thought for my own safety left my mind, and before I stopped to think if it was a good idea or not, I was up and running toward Colt. I didn't get far because someone tackled me from behind and I went down hard, teeth rattling in my head.

"Let me up!" I wheezed, attempting to get out from underneath a solid body of muscle.

"I'm not gonna let you die," Knight murmured in my ear.

"I'm not gonna die," I snapped.

Gunshots rang out, cutting through the screams. I managed to lift my head, enough so that I could watch more people dodge bullets and run for cover.

"Let me up," I commanded again.

Knight's hand went to my head and pressed it into the grass. "No."

"Colt—I have to go to him."

He sighed. "All right, but you crawl. You stay low to the

ground. The brothers need my help. You promise me you'll stay low!"

"I promise."

Knight reluctantly released me and then went to join the fight. I hadn't considered him my father, but he'd thrown himself over me, shielding me from the spray of bullets. It was true paternal instinct.

I crawled on my hands and knees, my pistol still in my grasp. When I got to Colt, I pressed two fingers to the pulse of his neck. It was rapid but strong.

I let out a breath.

"No, get to safety," he croaked, opening one eye.

"Hush." I set my weapon next to me and pulled up his shirt to assess the damage. Not that I had any idea what I was looking for.

"Mia, get out of here, it's not safe," he gritted as I lowered his shirt and mashed it into his side to staunch the flow of blood.

"I'm not leaving you."

Flynn bellowed from behind us and it jarred me out my stupor. I took Colt's right hand and pressed it to his left side.

"Press here, and hold tight," I said.

Adrenaline coursed through my veins. The love of my life, the last person in the world I could bear to lose had been shot by a man who was hell-bent on killing me and destroying everything I loved.

Anger, unlike anything I'd ever felt, burned inside of me, demolishing every last trace of fear.

I watched as the Iron Horsemen drove around, trying to circle Flynn and escape his men. One of the bikers approaching on a motorcycle caught my eye. It was Dev and his mask had slipped during the fight.

The bastard had made this personal.

I picked up my pistol, lifted myself slowly to balance on one knee, and locked eyes with Dev as his motorcycle roared.

The scent of bloody steel, oil, and gunpowder engulfed me in the faint stirring of the breeze.

I raised my pistol and gripped it with both hands, focused on my target, and fired.

Chapter 26

I STARED into a pair of cobalt blue eyes.

Flynn Campbell looked down at me with a gentle smile. "There you are."

"Here I am," I murmured. "What happened? Why am I flat on the ground?"

He scratched his jaw. "You—ah—might've hit your head when you were tackled."

"Twice in one day," I groaned. "Who took me down? You?"

"No. Ramsey did."

"Ramsey? Who's Ramsey?"

"For all intents and purposes, Ramsey is my younger brother."

When I tried to move, Flynn crouched down next to me and gently placed his hand on my shoulder. "Take it easy. You might have a concussion."

"Why are you here?" I asked. "I thought you and Barrett went back to Scotland."

"We went home to visit the boys, but Colt called and—"

"Colt," I demanded. "Where is he? Is he—"

"He was loaded into one of the first ambulances on the scene. Joni rode with him to the hospital."

"Take me to him, please.

"Stay down," he growled. "Until an EMT can check you out."

"Where's Knight? Where's Shelly?"

"Take a deep breath, Mia."

"Don't tell me to take a deep breath," I snapped. "Was anyone killed? Did I—please tell me I got him? Please tell me I hit Dev."

Flynn shook his head in negation, his jaw clamping shut. He didn't address any of my other concerns because his eyes strayed from mine to look across the lawn.

"What is it?"

"The sheriff is here."

"For the love of God, that's all we need," I muttered. "Fuck this." I slowly sat up and I was immediately assaulted by dancing vision. I closed my eyes to keep from throwing up.

Flynn bellowed, "Hey! We've got a woman with a concussion over here."

"Why did Ramsey tackle me?"

"You'll have to ask him that."

"Where is he," I muttered. "I'd like to give him a piece of my mind."

"Pleased to meet you," said a smooth voice, dripping with a velvety Scottish brogue.

"Mia, I'd like to introduce Ramsey Buchanan. Take nothing of what he says at face value."

The man named Ramsey rolled striking green eyes and pushed the dark curls off his forehead before squatting down next to me.

"Sorry, lass." He winked. "Had to take you from behind."

I couldn't help but laugh even though it hurt my head. "You didn't have to tackle me."

"Aye, I did. You were in danger. Quickest way to get you out of danger was to tackle you."

An EMT finally made his way over to me; Flynn and Ramsey stayed while I got the green light to move.

"If a headache comes on, get to a doctor immediately," the young EMT said. "Same for blurry vision, nausea, any hint of passing out or not being able to stay awake during normal hours."

"I'm about to head to the hospital. I'll be surrounded by doctors if I need one," I replied.

Looking around the park, I was saddened by the carnage. Books with fractured spines and torn pages littered the grass, broken toys, splintered pieces of furniture —everything that had been for sale was decimated. It was a depressing sight.

I walked toward Boxer and Reap. They were talking with a handful of men I didn't recognize; I assumed they were with Flynn. "Where's Knight?" I asked Boxer. "The last I saw of him, he was in the thick of it."

"Getting stitched up at the hospital." Reap grimaced. "He went after one of the guys that shot at you. Got himself a knife to the shoulder for his trouble."

A pang of worry went through me when I thought about my father and his injury, but he was alive.

"Just got off the phone with Joni," Boxer said, his eyes dark. "They've patched up Colt's side. He'll be fine, but they conked him out." His jaw clenched. "Cheese took a bullet to the chest. He's in emergency surgery."

"Oh God," I whispered.

Boxer looked at Reap, who nodded.

"What?" I asked. "What's that look mean?"

Boxer placed his hand on my shoulder and gave it a tight squeeze. "It's Shelly."

～

She looked peaceful.

Her left hand rested on top of the sheet, her engagement ring catching the sunbeams streaming through the blinds of her room.

The ventilator machine beeped in time with the rise of her chest.

"You shouldn't be here."

I didn't turn my head at the sound of Mark's angry voice.

This was my fault.

She wouldn't be in the hospital on life support if it hadn't been for me.

Me.

I was the one who'd chosen a dangerous life. I was the one who'd selfishly wanted Shelly to still be a part of it because she was my family. I'd been determined to meld it all; my old life with the new.

And now my twenty-five-year-old best friend who I loved like a sister, whose life had just been getting started, who'd been planning a wedding, was in a coma.

Mark's anger was palpable.

I felt it in the air.

Felt it on my skin.

I wanted Colt next to me, to hold my hand during this awful moment of my life. But he was still unconscious from the drugs they'd given him. Zip and Joni sat by his bedside while I tended to this.

This.

Whatever *this* was.

So familiar. Another loss piled on the mound of losses I'd already buried.

My mother.

Grammie.

And now Shelly.

"She wouldn't want this," I said, my tone flat.

"You don't get to decide what she would've wanted," Mark snapped.

I heard heartbreak fighting its way through rage.

"I know what she wanted." I finally looked at him.

White face. Pinched features. Red eyes, ready to burst with tears. But this was not the time for them. The tears could come later.

After.

"There's still hope." Mark looked at his fiancée and then walked to her bedside. He tenderly brushed a finger across her cheek. "There's still hope she can wake up from this."

Severe brain trauma resulting in permanent mental deficits.

Paralysis.

Feeding tube.

Colostomy bag.

The doctor had regurgitated a statistic that a small percentage of people made it back from injuries like this, but his eyes had betrayed him.

I could read between the lies.

Mark's cell phone buzzed.

"It's my lawyer," he stated. "You—"

He didn't finish his sentence. Instead, he stalked from the room, the door shutting with a soft thud.

I leaned forward and gripped Shelly's hand in mine. "Hey, girl. Can you hear me?" I paused, like I expected her to sit up and answer me. To tell me to stop being dramatic.

But nothing happened.

The sound of her respirator filled the room. Tears finally flooded my eyes.

"I hope you're on the other side already and not scared or in pain. I hope it's gorgeous there. Peaceful. I hope you're happy."

Part of me thought she might give my fingers a squeeze. Part of me thought this was all a sick joke, and that the universe had a wicked, dark sense of humor.

But when Shelly didn't move and the beeping machines continued to control her functions, I knew this for what it was.

Something cold settled in my chest where my heart beat.

Mark would fight me even though his lawyer would tell him it was pointless. Shelly may have been marrying Mark, but I was her next of kin. We had been close for years. So close that I was in charge of her medical directive. They hadn't been together long enough for her to change the paperwork giving him the power of attorney. After Grammie died, Shelly and I had made sure that our affairs were in order.

We were family, through and through.

We'd prepared for the worst because the world hadn't gone easy on either of us—hadn't ever given us a break. Even though we'd both found love, we still hadn't trusted it. Not really.

I brought our clasped hands to my mouth and gently kissed the back of her hand, a single tear falling onto her skin. I set her palm down by her side and then I forced myself to stand, taking one last look at her before I turned to leave.

Mark was pacing the hallway, barking something at his lawyer. When he saw me slip out from Shelly's room, he hung up and came at me.

"You *bitch*."

He was suddenly in my face, close enough that I felt his saliva hit my cheek as he spewed his venomous hate.

But I stood there and took it because I was guilty and deserving of his anger.

I was the reason she was in that bed, and I would stand there and let Mark hurl his vitriol at me if he chose.

Boxer had other plans.

I hadn't seen him coming down the hallway, but he was suddenly there and forcing himself between me and Mark.

"You fucking touch her and I'll kill you."

Mark had once been uneasy around the bikers who I now called family. None of that unease was there now. Mark straightened his spine.

"Try it, fucker. You're scum. You both are."

Mark stomped away, his phone out of his pocket and to his ear in the span of a few seconds. His steps echoed across the floor and then disappeared as he turned the corner.

"Hey," Boxer said, wrapping his arm around me and pulling me to his chest.

I stood there without saying a word.

"I know it's a shitty time...but Colt is awake. He's asking for you."

I nodded and then swiveled my head away from Boxer's gaze so I could wipe away another tear that had escaped the corner of my eye.

"It's bad, isn't it?" Boxer asked.

"You don't know?"

"I tried to harass the doc into telling me what's going on, but he said I wasn't family so he wouldn't tell me shit."

I inhaled a shaky breath. "She's on a ventilator. A machine is breathing for her," I said softly. "She doesn't—there's no brain activity. She wouldn't want this. Stuck in a bed until medicine finally quits on her. Mark wants to leave her on the machines. I don't. I'm in charge of her medical directive. Not Mark."

"Fuck."

I nodded.

"I'm not sure I should be the one to give you more shitty news, but I don't know if Colt knows yet or if Zip is filling him in..."

"What?"

"Cheese died in surgery."

His words didn't even penetrate.

Not the way they were supposed to.

"Mia?" Boxer pressed. "Did you hear me?"

"Yeah," I murmured. "I heard you. I just don't know what you want me to do about it."

He looked at me with a frown, but said nothing more.

We arrived at Colt's hospital room and both went in. Joni and Zip were sitting next to each other in plastic chairs. Colt's glassy eyes found me immediately.

"Babe," he whispered.

I arched an eyebrow, shooting him a cool expression. "Always the hero, huh?"

"If I remember it right, I wasn't the only one in the line of fire." He licked his lips. "What does a man have to do to get his woman to kiss him? Almost die?"

Out of the corner of my eye, I saw Joni's spine snap straight. Zip looked at his lap. I couldn't see Boxer since he was behind me, but even he wasn't cracking a joke.

"Some of us have died," I said quietly.

Colt's eyes turned somber and he nodded. "I heard about Cheese. Joni just told me Shelly's here? How is she?"

"She's on life support."

"Fuck. Come here and let me hold you—"

"No," I stated coolly. "I don't want to be held right now."

His brow furrowed in confusion and then his gaze shot over my shoulder. I turned to glance at Boxer who was shaking his head and shrugging.

"Maybe I need holding," Colt stated. "You ever think of that?"

"That's the morphine talking," I said.

Colt looked to Zip. "You guys mind giving us a few?"

"Take all the time you need, brother." Zip got up and came toward me. He stared at me and then before I knew it, he was enveloping me in a tight embrace.

I didn't hug him back.

He released me and then followed Boxer out of the room. Joni was slower to leave, first going to her brother and leaning down to whisper something in his ear. Colt nodded at whatever she said. She stood back up and squeezed his shoulder.

When Joni's gaze darted to mine, I couldn't detect the emotion in them when she looked at me. She sailed past me without a word or a touch. I wondered about her for a moment, before dismissing her from my mind.

"You're still standing over there," Colt said after the door shut. "When you should be over here."

I walked to him and took a seat on his bed, close enough that I could feel the heat of him.

"What's going on inside your head right now, Mia?"

"What's going on inside your head right now, Colt?" I parroted back.

"Right now, I'm on a lot of drugs. I can't even feel where they dug the bullet out of me, and I'm wondering why you're acting the way you're acting."

"I tried to shoot Dev for you, Colt. And I missed. Do you know how fucking angry I am that I missed?" I swallowed. "Do you know what it was like for me? Thinking you were dying?" I didn't pause to give him a chance to reply. "Do you know the fucking *terror* I felt about losing you? I watched you take a bullet, Colt. I had your blood on my hands."

His face darkened with his own anger and impotence. "You don't think I know that? Shit, Mia. My last thoughts before I passed out were of you. And the guilt I felt about bringing you deeper into this and not being able to protect you."

"Your guilt is no match for mine," I stated. "I got pulled into all of this because of Richie. I chose you because I wanted to. But Shelly?" I shook my head. "She's not getting married, Colt. She's not going to wake up, ever, and it's because she chose *me* as her family. Cheese died today. Shelly may as well have. Her body is still here but only for now. You got shot. How many more people will get hurt because of me?"

"What are you saying, darlin'? Because it sounds to me like you're trying to walk away. But it's too late for that now."

My gaze slid from his to stare at the wall. A white, sterile hospital wall that gave no comfort to its patients or the people that came to visit loved ones.

"I'm not walking away," I replied, my tone faint. "You're right, it's too late for that. I'm in too deep." I reached out and grasped his hand—the one with the IV needle—and linked my fingers through his.

"I'm sorry about Shelly," Colt said, his tone mournful. "I don't know what else I can say."

I nodded, tracing his knuckles. "This is the life, isn't it?"

"Mia—"

"Just…can we sit here? And not say anything for a few minutes?"

He pulled his hand away from me and raised his arm to create a space next to him. I gently crawled in beside him, nestling myself at his non-injured side. Colt draped his arm around me and I pressed my head to his chest, listening to the sound of his breathing, grateful that at least one person I loved was still alive.

～

I awoke to the sound of Colt's hospital door opening. Dying sunlight filtered through the blinds. I had somehow fallen asleep despite everything that had occurred.

Though Colt was warm next to me, I felt numb.

"How's he doing?" Zip asked, his voice low.

"Okay, I guess. I don't know. We fell asleep." I gently sat up, careful not to jostle him. "I don't want to leave him, but I have to…Shelly…"

"Right." Zip nodded and rubbed the back of his neck. "Look, shit is bad right now. Reap'll be here with Colt. He'll be taken care of."

I blinked. "You think the Iron Horsemen would come to the hospital?"

"I wouldn't put anything past them. They went after women and children. They broke the code. They are out of their fuckin' minds."

I looked at my hands and then back at Zip. "What happens now? Reap shadows Colt while he's recovering. What do we do about all the other stuff? The mess we have to clean up from the park. The sheriff showed up…"

"Flynn is handling it."

"Of course he is," I muttered. "What about Darcy and

the kids? What about Cheese's funeral—"

What about Shelly and what I'm going to have to do?

I pushed that thought down as far as it would go so I could focus on the here and now.

"Zip will act as president," came Colt's raspy voice. "Lockdown is back on. You'll go back to the clubhouse and—"

"Like hell I will," I replied.

Colt didn't take his eyes off me when he said to Zip, "Give us a minute, will you?"

Zip wasn't one to make a snarky reply; that was Boxer's territory. The Blue Angels VP nodded and quietly exited the room, leaving Colt and I to duke it out in private.

"I can't sit and wait, Colt," I said. Though my tone was soft, it was threaded with steel. "I sit and I wait, and I worry. Do you know what it's like to feel useless? To go from complete independence to not being able to make a single move without your boyfriend's approval?"

"Dev is on a rampage," he said, his tone laced with pain and anger. "He'll stop at nothing now. Don't you get it? He went after the innocent. He doesn't give a shit now what happens. He started a war."

"Yeah, and he made that war personal for me." I pointed to the door. "Shelly is lying in a hospital bed and I have to—I have to sign the forms to let her go."

Colt's dark eyes brightened with intensity. "I get it, Mia. If anyone gets it, I do. I lost a brother today. We're burying a twenty-five-year-old man who was as loyal as they come. You know what Zip told me? You know why Cheese died? Because he dove in front of his brother."

My heart stuttered and then thawed a bit when I thought of Silas, Cheese's younger sibling. Then my heart re-froze because I *had* to be cold. I had to stay clear headed.

"Have you cried?" Colt asked, pitching his voice low. "For your friend?"

"Cried? What good will that do?" I demanded.

He leaned back against the pillows and stared at me. "It'll hurt worse, you know. Shoving it aside and dealing with it later."

"I'll deal with it when Dev is dead."

He suddenly looked tired. In the span of a few minutes, Colt went from robust, iron fisted president to a man lying injured in a hospital bed.

"I'm not going to like what you're about to tell me, am I?" Colt sighed, like he knew what was coming.

"I have to help get rid of him, Colt. I have to."

"The truth, Mia. I want the entire truth."

"That is the truth."

"Is it? You just feel obligated to help get rid of him, or is there more to it than that?" he murmured.

I paused and then said, "He's trying to take everything from me, Colt. My family, my freedom, my life. I have to… I *want* to…"

"Say it," he growled. "Say it to me now. Tell me what it is you know you have to do or you'll never be able to look at yourself in the mirror."

"I have to see him die."

The words slithered out of me like a snake hiding in the brush.

Foul, angry words.

Truthful words.

"It won't bring Shelly back," he said.

"No," I agreed.

"I'm not sure it will make you feel any better, either." He leaned his head back against the pillow and his eyes were glazed with pain. "But I guess you'll have to wait and see."

I slid into an empty pew and breathed in the silence of the chapel.

Boxer stood by the doors, guarding me without interfering with my private time. I'd waited until Colt had fallen asleep before leaving his room. I'd gone and sat with Shelly, despite Mark's hostile glare pinging me from across her hospital bed.

Lost in my own thoughts, I didn't hear the chapel doors open.

A large body sat down next to me and stretched out long legs in worn jeans. The smell of cigar tobacco permeated Knight's clothes, but it wasn't unpleasant.

"I didn't take you for the religious type," Knight said.

"I'm not. But it's quiet here." I looked at him. "Thank you."

"For what?"

"Saving my life."

He nodded slowly, but said nothing.

"How's your shoulder?" I asked him.

"I'll live."

We fell silent for a moment and then he said, "I heard about your friend. I'm sorry, kid."

The word *kid* slipped out of his mouth. Like it was normal, natural.

With a sigh, I leaned my head against his uninjured shoulder. I felt his muscles tighten for a moment and then relax.

"What happens now?" I asked. "It feels like we're scrambling."

"Gotta ask Colt. He's the one leading all of this."

"Colt is passed out in a hospital bed. Zip is president for the time being."

"You should go back to the clubhouse and get some sleep."

"Will you sleep tonight?" I asked, lifting my head so I could stare at him.

"Point taken," he said darkly.

"Besides, I won't leave while Colt is here. While Shelly is here."

"I saw what you did. Firing a shot at Dev, wanting to avenge your man. You're true Old Lady material, Mia. And I'm proud of you."

His words washed over me, but they weren't a balm to my battered soul.

I looked up at the ceiling. The chapel was serviceable, a place one could sit and ponder, pray, curse, but it wasn't a spot of beauty. The room was built for function, not frivolity. It didn't have the elegance and craftsmanship like those gothic cathedrals with huge stained glass windows. In a hospital that wasn't what was needed.

"I didn't think I'd be doing this again," I whispered.

"Doing what?"

"Saying goodbye to someone else I loved. I feel powerless. Useless." I threaded my fingers through my hair, wanting to reach out and strangle something just to combat my feelings of impotence. To kill my inability to change the circumstances.

Knight didn't offer any platitudes, not that I expected him to. He was a rough man, made rougher by the life he'd chosen to live. But his presence was a comfort anyway, and maybe, words were stupid and useless.

Maybe all we had were the people we chose to be our family. Maybe they'd be our strength when we were ready to fall.

Chapter 27

We buried Shelly and Cheese three days later.

I'd asked Mark where he wanted her laid to rest. He told me I should make the choice because she was my sister. Sister in all but name and blood.

I'd squeezed his hand in gratitude.

Though Shelly wasn't a Blue Angel, Colt had made it possible for my best friend to be buried next to Cheese.

"She's got family looking out for her," Colt whispered, his arm around my shoulder while we stood at the graves laden with freshly turned dirt.

Mark's eyes were wet, but it was the slump of his shoulders that told me of his defeat, of his brokenness.

Flynn, Ramsey, and a few of their Scottish brethren, stood by our sides and mourned with us.

Silas, Cheese's brother, stared at his brother's grave, tears streaking down his face. I wanted to go to him, but what was I supposed to say? How could I offer a child any sort of comfort when it felt like I was choking on broken glass?

It was an intimate affair; Shelly hadn't been close to

many people. A few friends from Dive Bar showed up to pay their respects, but they left quickly, clearly uncomfortable with the men in leather and tattoos.

Everyone was piling into cars to head to the clubhouse where we'd have a wake of sorts. We all wanted to get drunk and forget about what had happened for a night, but no one wanted to let their guard down. Not while the Iron Horsemen were at large.

The Garcia cartel hadn't yet struck out in violence, and when I asked Colt about it while he'd still been in the hospital, he'd explained. The Garcia cartel was not yet wise to the missing shipment and Dev had enough cash to make it look like he was still selling product. It was a stopgap, and it was why he'd escalated the war. He was desperate.

One by one, the cars started to disappear from the lot. Mark took out his car keys and unlocked his black Mercedes. He wasn't a flashy man by any means, but he enjoyed nice things and had been willing to give Shelly everything she would've ever wanted.

"Mark," I called out softly. His name carried on the breeze.

He turned. His face was somber, but there was no hostility in his gaze so I took a hesitant step toward him.

"Where are you going?" Colt asked, his hand still linked with mine even though he was conversing quietly with Zip.

"I need to talk to Mark," I said.

Colt squeezed my fingers and then let me go.

I approached Mark cautiously, like I would a feral animal that had been beaten one too many times.

"I'm sorry." It was a stupid thing to say to him, but it was all I could muster.

He nodded. "I know."

My apology was all encompassing. For getting Shelly killed. For being the one to determine end of life care. For being the one Mark had to look at over Shelly's prostrate form when she took her last breath. Mark and I were now eternally linked by death when we should've been linked by celebration and marriage.

"I'm leaving Waco," he said finally.

"Are you?"

He nodded. "I'm gonna go stay with my mom for a bit." He swallowed. "I've never loved anyone like I love Shelly."

She'd want Mark to be happy, to find love again, to have a family. But he knew all that, so I didn't have to say it. Because that was Shelly. She loved people fully. Wanted them to be happy, even at her own expense.

"I—be well, Mark," I said with finality, knowing I'd never talk to him again.

He opened his mouth to say something, but nothing came out. Instead, he nodded. I took a step back so Mark could open his car door and leave.

I watched as he got in the driver's seat and started the engine. I knew he'd never be able to put this behind him. Shelly's death would haunt him forever, casting darkness over every happy moment he managed to find.

My heart was heavy with sorrow and guilt. I turned so I didn't have to watch Mark drive out of the cemetery parking lot.

I saw Silas, Cheese's brother, wipe tears from his cheeks with one hand, and reach down to his bike's handlebars.

"Silas!" I called out.

The eleven-year-old boy didn't appear to hear me. He gripped his handlebars, but made no move to actually climb onto his bike and pedal away.

Colt caught my eye and I nodded my chin in Silas's direction. Colt looked over, a frown covering his forehead.

I jogged over to Silas, my low black heels getting stuck in the grass.

"Silas?" I hesitantly placed my hand on his shoulder.

He stiffened, but made no move to get away.

"Did you ride your bike here?" I asked even though it was rhetorical.

He nodded.

"Where's your Mom? Your Dad?"

"Mom left. After she heard about Chester. Dad is where he always is."

On the couch. Bottle in hand.

I'd been encased in a fortress of grief—but Silas's words were a hammer of anger, cracking through my exterior, finding their way into my heart. My cheeks heated with rage.

When Silas threw his leg over his bike seat, I placed a hand on the bars to stop him. "Come with me."

He looked up at me with tears in his eyes. "Why?"

I reached out and threaded my fingers through his silky brown hair. "Because I'm going to make it better."

He swallowed. "You shouldn't make promises you can't keep."

The boy had lost the only family that had ever given a damn about him. A brother who could no longer look out for him, protect him from the cruel world he had grown up in. Like hell I was going to let Silas go home to an alcoholic father and a now absent mother.

Abandonment and death would not be this boy's life. Cheese had been doing everything possible to ensure that Silas knew he had someone who cared about him, and I would not allow that love to die with Cheese.

Silas wheeled his bike along side of me as we walked

to Colt and Zip. Colt's face was pale and I knew he was dying for some serious painkillers, but he adamantly refused. My first thought was to roll my eyes, but I quickly realized that it wasn't Colt trying to show off his manly bravado. It was because he didn't like anything clouding his judgment. It was about control, so all he allowed himself to have was over the counter anti-inflammatories.

"Hey, Silas," Zip said.

"Colt? Can I talk to you a second?" I asked.

He looked down at me and nodded. Zip stayed with Silas while Colt and I slowly made our way to the crop of trees about fifteen feet away so we could have some privacy.

"He can't go home," I told Colt without preamble. "I mean, it's not really a home. His mother left when she heard about Cheese. And his dad—"

"Yeah." Colt sighed. "Cheese told me about his old man once. Useless piece of shit."

"Silas needs a real home. Some place secure. Where he knows he's got people who won't leave him. Who won't bail when shit gets hard." I took a deep breath. "I think—I think Silas and I might need each other, Colt."

Colt stared at me for a long moment and then he reached up and cradled my head in his hands, his thumbs skimming across the apples of my cheeks. "You've finally got some color in your face. Is this you coming back to me?"

I blinked. "Coming back to you?"

He swallowed. "You shut down. I didn't know if you'd snap out of it." He looked away from me to stare at Silas. "I'll give you whatever you want, babe. Whatever you need."

"I want Silas," I said, surprising myself.

"You, who didn't want kids yet?" His smile was teasing, his eyes creasing at the corners.

"The heart wants what it wants, right?" I tamped down the flood of emotion threatening to overwhelm me. "I want to be better, Colt. I want family. I want to be happy. I *choose* it. Because if I don't, then the weight of Shelly's death—"

He pulled me to him, mindful of his injury. "All right, darlin'."

~

I parked Colt's truck in front of the trailer Silas pointed to. The blue paint was flaking, the tin roof looked like it had seen far too many hailstorms, and the lawn in front was more weeds than grass.

The rumble of Boxer and Reap's bikes came to halt.

Colt turned off the engine and climbed out of the truck. The two of us followed Silas up the worn dirt path to the steps. Silas showed no hesitation whatsoever about reaching for the door handle, but Colt stopped him by placing his hand on the boy's shoulder.

"I'll go first," Colt stated.

"Why?" Silas asked, brushing hair that was too long out of his eyes.

"Because," Colt said with a rueful smile.

Silas smiled back and I breathed a sigh of relief. The boy had spent enough time around the Blue Angels not to be afraid of them. For that, I was grateful.

I gently urged Silas back to stand in front of me. Colt went inside first, pushing the door open wide. The smell of stale cigarettes and sweat filled the air, and I instantly breathed through my mouth.

Silas's father was sitting in a recliner, staring at the television, a bottle of whiskey in his lap. He raised it to his lips as he briefly looked in the direction of the door.

His eyes scanned the three of us in confusion, but he said nothing.

"Silas," Colt said, his tone soft. "Why don't you show Mia your room. Pack your things, yeah?"

"Okay," Silas said, latching onto my hand and dragging me to the back of the trailer, through a kitchen with peeling linoleum and warped, mildew-stained walls.

Silas pushed open a door and waved me inside. I stepped into his room, which was nothing more than a twin mattress on the floor. It was surprisingly tidy and I wondered if that was Silas's doing, or if Cheese had been the one to clean it.

There was a tin bucket by the window and half of it was filled with dank water.

"What is this?" I asked, pointing to it.

"The roof leaks," Silas said.

I inhaled a shaky breath, trying to keep my anger contained. Silas didn't need that. I looked around for a suitcase or a bag. Silas was tossing action figures and a few comic books onto his bed along with a few clothes.

"No suitcase, huh?" I asked.

He shook his head.

"Garbage bag? In the kitchen?"

He nodded. Silas bent down to crawl into his closet and I noticed that his pants lifted to show his ankles. Too small, I realized.

I didn't tell him not to pack his clothes even though we'd be getting him new ones almost immediately. Even little boys had pride.

I slipped out of his room and headed back into the kitchen. Colt was sitting on the stained brown couch, not even a foot away from Silas's father, his body turned toward the man who hadn't even bothered to greet his son.

I couldn't hear what Colt was saying and I didn't want to know. All I cared about was getting Silas out of this place.

I rooted around underneath the sink, letting out a startled squeak when my hand brushed something furry.

"Fuck this," I muttered.

I slammed the cabinet shut and high-tailed it back to Silas's room. He looked at me with questioning eyes.

"Er—all out of garbage bags."

He smiled in genuine mirth. "Did you meet Murray?"

"Murray?"

"My rat."

"Like a pet rat?" I asked.

He shook his head. "No. I sort of adopted him though."

"You won't be devastated if he stays here, right?"

"No. I never really wanted a rat for a pet."

I saw the pile of belongings on his bed and used his sheet as a makeshift satchel.

"Mia?"

"Yeah?"

"I'm okay leaving Murray behind, but can I bring Captain?"

"Who's Captain?" I asked nervously.

"I can't believe I let you talk me into this," Colt said as he slowly moved to the bed and pulled back the covers. He slid between the sheets and groaned in relief.

"You saw Captain. There was no way I could deny Silas."

Captain, as it turned out, was a medium-sized, black and white speckled mutt with one ear that flopped down and another that stood straight up. And Captain only had one eye. After a bath and a meal, Captain was now conked out with Silas and the other Blue Angels kids in the clubhouse theater room.

By the time Colt and I had made it back to the clubhouse, it was nearly dark. The wake had been going for hours. The mood had been somber—until we'd arrived with a one-eyed dog.

"He needs new clothes," I said.

"Hmm," Colt said, his eyes closing, exhausted from an emotional day. "We'll get it sorted."

"Did Cheese ever say anything to you about Silas's living condition?"

"No. I had no idea it was that bad. But Cheese had his pride and I know how much he loved his brother, so I know he was trying to get Silas out of there."

"I wish he'd said something. It would've been so much better if we could've helped sooner."

"Hmm," he murmured in agreement.

"Silas is going to need his own room at the house."

"Obviously."

"I think we should let him pick out his own furniture and paint. Maybe that will help ease his transition."

"Mia?"

"Yeah?"

"Can't all that wait?"

I let out a breath. "Yeah, it can."

"He's okay for now, right? He's got his dog. He's got his friends. He's sitting downstairs with Cam and Brock. He knows these people. He's known them for years. I'm willing to bet he's more comfortable here than he ever was at home. Let it be for right now."

"All right." I lifted the covers, wanting to tuck him in. I'd helped him change his bandage and I'd blanched when I saw the angry red wound in his side. He'd griped and cursed, but I'd somehow convinced him to take a pain pill, so at least he could sleep. Sleep would help him heal.

"What did you say to his father?"

Colt's eyes were half-mast and I knew the potent drug was dragging him into sleep, but he still found the resolve to answer me. "I told him I was taking his son and giving him a better place to live. I told him he had two choices. I'd give him a thousand bucks a month for him to sign the paperwork for guardianship and for the schools, and then he'd keep his mouth shut, or he'd disappear and I'd get Silas's guardianship in court when he was gone. He chose not to argue."

"We did the right thing, getting Silas out of there."

"Yeah, we did." He paused, his breathing evening out.

I thought he'd fallen asleep and was on my way to the door when his words stopped me.

"I'll call the club lawyer in the morning. We'll make sure we are Silas's legal guardians as fast as we can, okay?"

My eyes softened and the tears that I felt threatening were in danger of spilling over.

"Okay, honey. Sleep if you can. If you need anything…"

He didn't reply and I knew he'd passed out.

I closed the door and headed down the hallway to the backyard. The wake for Cheese was still going strong. I planned on having a drink in his honor. And a drink for Shelly. And then I'd find a secluded place and cry. Let out all the bottled up emotions that were still sitting somewhere inside of me.

The girls swarmed me, enveloping me in their arms. They didn't offer empty platitudes, just their silent comfort and the knowledge that they were there if I needed anything.

"Did you eat today?" Darcy asked, pulling back.

I shook my head. "I haven't had much of an appetite."

Rachel handed me a bottle of Irish whiskey. "This'll do you right."

"Thanks." I took a sip, enjoying the warmth of it as it settled in my belly.

"Amazing thing what you're doing for that boy," Joni said.

"Anyone would've done it."

Allison raised her eyebrows. "No, not anyone."

"He was Cheese's family," I said with a raw throat. "Cheese was *our* family. It was the only thing to do." I raised my bottle in the air and yelled, "To Cheese!"

Echoes of my toast resounded across the yard as people drank to their fallen brother.

"To Shelly," Boxer called, his eyes meeting mine.

"To Shelly," everyone chanted.

We continued to drink and then the guys lit a massive bonfire. Flynn and his boys were not at the clubhouse, but out on the streets of Waco, sniffing out all they could about the Iron Horsemen. Knight and the Coeur d'Alene brothers were seeing to our safety, guarding the clubhouse entrances so we could mourn and drink, though no one was getting sloppy.

The club was on total lockdown. No one would harm us tonight.

I wandered over to Boxer who was sitting on a table by himself, his face expressionless. He didn't bother to crack a joke or try to lighten the atmosphere. Tonight, we'd let the mood be dark. Tomorrow, when the sun rose, we would face it all again, but for now, we kept to the shadows to mourn the spirits that would haunt us.

"Shit day," Boxer stated.

"The shittiest," I agreed.

I drank from the bottle of whiskey, no longer feeling the burn of it.

"How's Colt?" he asked.

"Down for the night."

He chuckled, but it sounded rusty and forced. "What did you have to promise him to keep him in bed?"

"That's between me and Colt."

My comment had the effect I wanted; it caused Boxer to throw his head back and shout with laughter. He draped an arm around my shoulder and dragged me close to him.

I sighed thinking maybe we'd be okay. Maybe we'd all get through this.

"Can I ask you something?" I asked.

"Shoot."

"Have you ever hated someone so much that you wanted to kill him? Actually close your hands around his throat and choke the life out of him?"

"Have another sip of whiskey," he suggested. "And ask me what you really want to ask."

I drank and then wiped my mouth with the back of my hand. "I want to kill Dev."

"I know."

"I mean, I want to,"—I swallowed—"hurt him. And then I want to be the one to end his life. I'm not joking. I am dead fucking serious."

Boxer rubbed a thumb across his lips. "Have you talked to Colt about this?"

"Sort of. When he was in the hospital. I want your thoughts, though."

"Why mine?"

"Because underneath that carefree exterior beats the

heart of a savage." I looked at him and raised an eyebrow, daring him to deny my assessment of him.

"A woman who sees me for what I am, and who's bloodthirsty for revenge. Damn fucking shame Colt got to you first."

"Boxer," I said quietly. "Please."

He paused for a moment and sobered. "Revenge is a beast that stands alone, Mia. You get it, thinking its gonna make you feel better, thinking it will replace that thing you lost. Sometimes it is that way. You get revenge and it's all you need to sleep well at night. Feel like you did right. But other times...other times, living with what you've had to do to even the score?" He shrugged. "That might haunt you worse than the losses." He looked at me. "You wanna be the one to put the gun to Dev's head and pull the trigger? Do you have what it takes to end a man's life?"

"I took a shot at him in the park," I said.

"So I heard. Were you actually trying to kill him? Or wound him?"

"I don't know," I admitted.

He scraped a hand across his whiskered jaw in need of a shave. "From what I heard, if Ramsey hadn't tackled you, you'd have been successful."

"Huh. That's an interesting piece I didn't know." I paused. " I'm consumed with rage and I've never felt like this in my life."

"People are complex, Mia, and the world is gray. Our actions are sometimes dark and sometimes light. What you did for that boy? That's all good. It's the light in you that makes you a good person. Will killing a man take that away from you and make you dark? No, but thinking about murder and committing murder are two very different things. I'm guessing you already know how I know that.

One thing I will say though, I won't be the one to take the choice away from you."

"You didn't answer my question. Do you think I could end a man's life?"

"Yeah, I do. There's strength in you, Mia. But Colt would never let you pull the trigger."

"Why not?"

"Because it's his right as president to execute the man that killed one of our brothers. Plus—well—he would never want you to have to live with the weight of that decision. That is his cross to bear."

"He'll take away the choice from me so I don't have to worry about it? That doesn't work for me."

He shrugged. "That's between you two. Though, I'm not gonna lie, I kinda wanna be there when you give it to him."

I took a sip from the bottle. "Can I change the subject?"

"Really wanting to bend my ear tonight, aren't ya?" he asked with a wink.

"I haven't cried yet."

"No?" he asked.

"No."

"Why do you think that is?"

"I don't know," I murmured. "I thought it was because I was numb. Just a cold block of ice." I absently rubbed the spot on my chest over my heart. "But I got angry today. Over Silas. I got protective and sad, and I wanted to bawl my eyes out thinking about that little boy without his brother, wearing jeans too short for him, living in a trailer with a father who couldn't give two shits about him. I just —it was like all the ice around me melted. But when I think of Shelly, I can't—there's no sadness there. No well of emotion to feel from. Just blackness and hate."

"I'm sure you've got a theory about that." He reached for my bottle of booze and drank from it. He didn't offer it back and I didn't take it from him.

"When my grandmother died…it sent me into this…I don't know—not a depression—I wouldn't let myself be depressed. I worked all the time, I barely slept. I'm afraid that," I swallowed, "if I break down and grieve for Shelly, I'll be grieving everyone I've lost in my life. Does that make sense?"

"Makes sense," he said softly. "But I gotta tell ya, if you don't find a way to process, to mourn, you'll think you're fine and then one day something will come along and break you apart. And there will be no coming back from that. You took in Silas, a little boy who needs boundaries and parents, and someone to tuck him in at night. What will happen if you fall apart on him too? He's already learned that his parents are shit and his brother is dead. Don't be someone else who fails him."

I looked up at the stars, wondering if they would give me answers.

"Grieve, Mia. We'll be here waiting for you."

I crept into the silent and dark clubhouse. I checked in on Colt, who was still sound asleep. I then went down to the basement to look in on the kids and to see if Silas needed anything.

A nightlight lit the way.

Darcy had told me that her children had had nightmares the past three nights and crawled into bed with her and Gray. Tonight was the first night that they'd wanted to sleep with their friends in the basement. Not wanting to smother them, she stayed upstairs in Gray's clubhouse room.

I didn't know if Silas had nightmares since he'd been at the trailer with his father. Silas and I hadn't yet talked about his brother and the day at the park. I was suddenly overwhelmed with the thought of getting to know a long-lost father as well as getting to know a boy who'd I claimed as mine.

Silas was sleeping in a pile with Brock and Cam, with Captain sprawled across his legs. The dog lifted his head to stare at me and then snuggled back down when he realized I was a friend. I gently scratched his ears and he let out a noise as he yawned and stretched. It made me smile.

I took a moment to study Silas and then brushed his hair from his face. He stirred, cracking one eye open. He didn't look surprised to see me and even let out a little sigh before closing his eyes and falling back asleep.

I moved to the couch, careful not to step on any pockets of sleeping children. After I got settled, I pulled a blanket from the back of the couch over me, including my head. Closing my eyes, I focused on breathing, but the more I sank into it, the more shaky it became. Before I knew what was happening, I was crying silent tears not three feet away from a group of children who'd been traumatized by a psychopath.

I cried until there were no more tears, and then I fell asleep, dreaming of revenge.

Chapter 28

"You son of a bitch!"

I shot up on the couch, instantly awake. The blanket still covered my face and I hastily pulled it off my head, looking around for the direction of a man's yell.

The children were awake and Captain was sitting up on his haunches. He let out a little woof, but he calmed the moment Silas placed an arm around him.

"What's going on?" Lily asked, wiping sleepy eyes.

"I don't know." I looked toward the stairs that led to the main floor.

Cam yawned. "What time is it?"

"Late," I said. "Or early. Do you guys think you can go back to sleep?"

Silas shook his head and I noticed he was dragging his hand across his cheeks.

Tears.

Had he cried silent tears too?

"You fucking prick!" came another shout.

I jumped up from the couch and headed for the stairs.

The kids trailed after me. "Er—you guys should really wait down here."

"Captain has to go to the bathroom," Silas said, looking at the dog.

"And I'm scared of the yelling," Lily said.

"I'm gonna get your Mom," I told her. "Silas? You want to come with me and let out your dog?"

He nodded and stayed close on my heels—close enough that I almost tripped up the stairs. The door to the main floor was cracked and I pushed it open, sticking my head out into the hallway…and heard the unmistakable sound of a fist hitting flesh.

"Run out back with Captain," I told Silas. "And then find Darcy and tell her about Lily. Will you do that for me?"

He nodded, trying to look around me toward the living room where the fistfight was clearly taking place.

"Go on," I urged him.

Silas looked like he wanted to argue, but then Captain pawed at his leg.

"Come on," he told the dog, and the two of them headed to the backyard. As soon as they were out of sight, I dashed toward the living room and came to a complete stop.

My jaw dropped open.

Colt was on top of Zip, pummeling him into the ground. From what I could tell, Zip wasn't even fighting back. My gaze darted to the kitchen to see Joni gripping the counter, her face pale.

Her eyes met mine.

Understanding dawned on me.

"Should I stop them?" I asked.

She shook her head. "This is how they do things."

"I don't care that this is how they do things. Colt's injured."

"I know." She sighed.

"How did he find out?"

"He caught us."

I blinked. "Like in the throes of it?"

"God, no! Can you imagine? He caught us kissing."

"Where?" I demanded. "I thought you were trying to be all discreet."

"We were. But I—look at him. I can barely keep my hands off him."

I looked back at the two grown men who were on the floor. I hadn't planned to say anything, but then I noticed the splotch of red seeping through Colt's T-shirt from his side wound.

"Enough!" I barked.

Colt stopped pummeling Zip for one moment to look at me over his shoulder. His eyes were dark with irrational rage.

"This is between us," Colt rasped.

I pitched my voice soft but firm. "You're bleeding. It has to stop. Now."

He glanced down at himself. "Tore my stitches."

"Fantastic," I muttered. "Do you think you can possibly wait to beat Zip up until after you heal?"

Colt climbed off Zip, whose head was lolling back. He appeared to be in danger of passing out and I grimaced, thinking about how hard Colt had been hitting him.

When Colt moved away from Zip, Joni rushed to his side, squatting down next to him and cradling his head in her lap. One eye was already swollen and I knew it would be black and blue by tomorrow.

Colt watched his sister tend to Zip and with a labored sigh, he stalked back to our room. The door slammed shut.

I glanced between Joni and Zip.

"What does this mean?" I asked.

"I claimed her as my Old Lady," Zip slurred through a swollen mouth. No doubt he had a few loose teeth. "Took my punishment from her brother. It's over now. He won't interfere from here on out."

Joni stroked his hair and looked down at him. "You sure you want me for your Old Lady?"

He smiled up at her. "Yeah, babe. No other woman is worth getting my ass beat for."

She gently kissed the end of his nose and let out a feminine sigh.

"My nose is not what needs kissing," Zip stated.

I turned and left them alone in the living room, not needing to witness Joni tending to Zip. As I was making my way back to the bedroom, I saw Silas standing in the hallway with Captain by his side and Darcy closing the door of Gray's clubhouse room.

"Silas told me the kids are awake?" she asked with a questioning look.

I rubbed the back of my neck. "Colt and Zip had an altercation."

She raised her eyebrows.

"Joni."

"Ah. So that finally happened?"

"You knew?" I asked with a surprised smile.

She grinned. "Not a lot gets past me." Darcy set her hand on Silas's shoulder. "Should we get you guys back to bed?"

Silas nodded and hastily brushed his too long hair off his forehead. "Will you come back and sleep downstairs with us, Mia?" Silas asked, his eyes wide with trust.

"Colt isn't feeling well," I said. "I need to make sure

he's okay. And then I promise I'll tuck you in. Is that all right?"

"That's all right," he said.

Before I knew what was happening, Silas lurched forward to wrap his arms around my middle, giving me a hug.

I looked at Darcy who stared at me with a slight smile.

I embraced Silas tightly and then dropped a kiss to his forehead.

"I'll be downstairs in just a minute," Darcy said. "There's ice cream in the freezer down there. You guys need a bowl before you go back to sleep."

Silas's face brightened and with the promise of ice cream, he ran down the stairs, Captain at his heels. When Darcy was sure he was gone, she said to me, "Being a mom comes pretty naturally to you."

"How do you balance it?" I asked her. "Wife and mother? I feel guilty as hell for wanting to tend to Colt when Silas is clearly the more fragile one."

"Practice. You'll make mistakes along the way, but you get better at the juggling act." She peered at me. "Just don't forget to take time for yourself." She embraced me quickly and then went downstairs.

I could hear the rowdiness of the kids who'd been awakened in the middle of the night—and now Darcy was going to give them sugar. Maybe it wasn't the best idea, but these weren't normal circumstances.

I thought about Shelly, my heart heavy. She would've loved all this. The crazy, the fighting, the laughing children, these people who loved hard and fast.

I didn't know how I was going to get through any of it without her. We were supposed to be there for each other, through marriage and kids. Now, she'd never be able to offer me advice with a margarita, tell me I was doing a bang up job or tell me when I was failing and help me pick up the pieces like a true friend would.

The world was a darker place without Shelly in it—*my* world was darker without Shelly in it.

Mark and I had barely spoken at the funeral, a quick greeting, and an even quicker goodbye. But he'd given me something that had belonged to Shelly, her favorite piece of jewelry. It was a gold plated necklace with a heart shaped charm. It was worthless, and it had turned her skin green, but she'd won it at the county fair when we were in high school and kept it all these years. She'd worn it every day until the chain had broken, but she'd kept it anyway because she was sentimental.

"It's good luck. It's going to bring me my true love," she had said with a twinkle in her eyes.

We'd giggled and fantasized about what our true loves would look like. We were teenage girls who were bound together by loss and grief, who found solace in friendship because we were soul sisters.

"Love you, girl," I whispered.

Colt was sitting on the closed toilet, grimacing as he tried to bandage his side.

"Need some help there, tiger?" I asked leaning against the doorframe.

"Would you think less of me if I said yes?"

I pushed away from the doorjamb and came to his side. "Let me see what you did to yourself."

He reluctantly pulled the bandage away from his wound. It was angry and red, and reminded me that he'd been in a hospital bed not that long ago.

"Oh, that looks like shit," I told him. "Let me wash it and bandage it."

"Did you know?" he asked.

His question stopped me in my tracks. "Yeah. I knew."

"You knew and didn't tell me. Why?"

"Because Joni is my friend and I kept her confidence." I looked him in the eyes. "Are you mad at me for that?"

"For loyalty?" He shook his head. "No."

"You really didn't know anything was going on between them?"

He rubbed a thumb across his stubble. "I knew something was going on between them. I didn't know it was serious, but I knew."

"You pretended like you didn't." I bent down to his side with a warm, wet washcloth and gently cleaned his wound.

He gritted in pain but didn't make a peep. "I thought they were just fucking around."

"You sound disappointed to find out that it's more than that between them." I set the cloth aside and blew on his skin before slathering on antibacterial cream and concealing it with a sticky bandage and tape.

"I wasn't happy with either scenario. Fucking around meant that one of them would lose interest and then they'd go about their business. But making her an Old Lady? That's serious shit. And that fucker went behind my back and defiled my little sister."

I was pretty sure Joni had defiled Zip first, but I wisely didn't voice that thought.

"What was he supposed to do?" I asked instead. "Come to you and tell you he wanted to screw your sister? And Joni didn't want to tell you until she knew there was something to tell."

"I've got no beef with my sister. But Zip and I—"

"You beat him into a pulp. That's not enough?"

"He went behind my back," Colt said again.

"I get it. You feel betrayed. But this isn't about you."

"You're right." He slowly stood up. "This is about the Blue Angels and brotherhood."

"Did he fight back?" I pressed. "Did Zip defend himself? Or did he know he did wrong and he was willing to let you knock a few teeth loose so you didn't lose face?"

"I'm pissed as hell at him," Colt growled.

"But you still trust him, right? He made an honest woman out of your sister. Whatever was going on between them under your nose or behind your back, the end result is good. They're together, they're committed, and Zip doesn't want any bad blood between you two."

"I need a fucking pain killer," he muttered.

"I'll get you one."

I helped him into bed and then grabbed him a pill and a glass of water.

"Why are you awake?" he asked, settling back against the pillows.

I took the cup of water and set it on the bedside table. "*You* woke me up."

"You weren't sleeping here. So how did you hear me?"

"I was in the basement with Silas. Your voice carries, you know."

He grinned. It was lazy and sleepy. "After a fight I usually like a good fuck. All the adrenaline. But damn, I'm just wiped out."

"Yeah, it's called healing from a bullet wound." I leaned over and brushed my lips against his. His hand came up to grasp the back of my head.

"What if you get on top?"

"I don't think that's a good idea." I pulled back, but Colt's grip on my wrist stopped me.

His eyes were dark, hazy with pain meds and lust. "You need a good fuck too, Mia."

"Why?"

"To remember that you're still alive."

I swallowed. "I'm not—I'm not ready, Colt."

"All right, darlin'." His eyes were drifting closed. "Just sleep next to me. That's enough for tonight."

"What the fuck happened to you?" Boxer asked the next morning when Zip came into the kitchen.

"Colt," Zip said. "For Joni."

Brothers sat on the couch and recliners, some held up the walls, eating breakfast. Colt hadn't yet made an appearance—it was slow moving for him. All eyes turned to Zip, waiting for him to explain.

"Joni's my Old Lady now."

"When the fuck did this happen?" Reap asked in surprise.

"Last night, I guess." Zip shrugged. He ambled to the coffee maker to pour himself a cup.

The bedroom door opened and a moment later, Colt appeared.

Tension filled the room.

Colt glared at Zip but said nothing.

"You hungry?" I asked Colt.

"I could eat," he admitted.

I fixed him a plate of scrambled eggs and bacon that Darcy had made in bulk with Rachel's help. The kids were currently outside, playing in the sunshine with Captain. The girls were out there with them, but I hadn't yet seen Joni.

"Fuck, boys," Boxer said, glancing out the window.

"Looks like we've got trouble."

I frowned in confusion. No one was reaching for a pistol, so I knew it wasn't Iron Horsemen trouble.

A few minutes later, there was a knock on the front door of the clubhouse.

Boxer opened the door. "Sheriff Valenti, to what do we owe the pleasure of your visit?"

Ice chilled my veins as I saw the sheriff standing with his deputy and another officer, and three squad cars parked at the front of the clubhouse.

"We have warrants for arrest. For discharging firearms in a public space and within city limits." He read off the legal names of Acid, Zip, Boxer, Reap, and Colt.

Torque and Gray stood by, their gazes alert as we watched the other Blue Angels get cuffed and shuffled to the squad cars.

Colt's gaze met mine, but then slid to Gray who nodded. I tried to step forward, wanting to go to Colt, wanting to say something to him, but Gray's hand on my arm stopped me. It wouldn't be prudent to say anything in front of the Sheriff. Colt and I were committed, but we weren't yet married.

And just like that, they were gone.

It wasn't until I heard the squad cars peel out of the gravel lot before I was steady enough to ask, "What the hell just happened? I thought Sheriff Valenti was on our payroll."

"He is. But the Iron Horsemen went above the Sheriff and paid off the mayor," Gray stated. "That's the only reason our boys are in cuffs."

"How do you know that?" I demanded.

"Not our first rodeo," Gray replied.

"What do we do now?" I asked, trying to stem the flow of panic. I'd just watched Colt being carted off to jail. Was this the first time of many to come? I didn't want to think about it.

"We call Vance, the club lawyer," Torque said.

"And we get Knight and his boys back here," Gray said. "Because most of our club is in lockup and we don't have the manpower to defend our shit if the Iron Horsemen show up."

"Guess it's a good thing you and I didn't go to the park that day," Torque said with a grimace. "Otherwise we'd be locked up too."

Gray scratched his beard. "Gotta get the women and children to the cabins."

"Cabins?" I asked. "What cabins?"

"Colt didn't tell you about the cabins?" Gray's eyes pinned me, his brow furrowed.

I shook my head.

Gray and Torque exchanged another look.

"The club has cabins in the Kisatchie National Forest in Louisiana. About six hours from here. So if shit ever hit the fan…"

"This is shit hitting the fan, isn't it?" I asked.

Gray nodded.

"We get all the women and kids and we send them to the cabins," Torque said. "Gray and I will stay here. Get Knight and his boys back. Call Vance. Get shit sorted as fast as possible."

"Need to call Flynn, too," Gray added. "Let him know what's going down."

My mind was in overdrive. What would happen to the club with most of the boys locked up? At that moment it seemed like the Iron Horsemen were going to take over Waco, regardless of whether or not Sanchez and his men came to our aid. I didn't like the idea of Colt behind bars. And I especially didn't like him injured and behind bars.

"How long will it take to get Colt and the others out?" I asked. Fear ran deep. "How do you know Dev doesn't have guys waiting for Colt and the boys in jail?"

"We don't know, but those boys can handle themselves," Gray said. "They have to now. It's gonna at least be a few days before we can get them out."

"A few days," I murmured. "We need to act and we need to do it fast."

Torque frowned. "You're not part of *we*. You're part of the women and children."

"I'm not leaving town," I protested. "All this shit started because of me. Dev made this personal. And now he's got my man behind bars so he can wreak havoc? Pick us off one by one? I don't fucking think so."

"We can't involve you in club business, Mia," Gray said. "Even though I enjoy your spunk, we don't put women into the line of fire."

"Have people forgotten that I took a shot at Dev in the park? I'm made of stronger stuff."

"Darlin'," Torque began. "I don't want to be a dick, but I'm gonna be a dick. You might have shot at him, but you didn't get him."

"No one else got him either," I muttered under my breath.

"Safest place for you is with the others," Gray said, clearly not having heard me.

"Fine," I said. "I'll go with them."

"I'll call the lawyer," Torque said.

"I'll call Knight," Gray added. "Mia, get Darcy. Tell her everyone is going to the cabins and to get people ready."

"Sure, I just need to use the restroom real fast. Then I'll head out back and talk to her."

Gray didn't say anything since he was already pulling out his phone. Torque did the same.

I went into our bedroom, struggling to keep my shit together, praying Colt had left his cell phone on the nightstand.

Bingo.

I picked up the burner and scrolled through the numbers, finding the one I wanted. He answered on the first ring.

"It's Mia. I need your help."

"I don't want to go to Louisiana," Silas complained as he buckled himself into the back seat of Darcy's Range Rover. Captain was nestled between him and Lily, who sat behind the driver's seat. Cam was riding shotgun.

"It'll be fun." I forced a smile. "You get to be outside and sleep on a bunk bed. I bet if you ask nicely, Cam will let you have the top bunk."

"But then how will Captain get up there?" Silas inquired.

"You're a smart kid." I grinned. "Maybe the bottom bunk is better."

"Why aren't you coming?"

"Because I have to run some errands," I lied. "Trust me. You won't even notice I'm gone."

"Why isn't Colt coming?" His voice sounded panicky and not at all like normal kid panicky.

"Hey," I said softly. "Look at me."

He reluctantly turned his gaze to mine.

"When you get back from your fun trip, do you want to pick out a paint color for your room?"

"Really?"

I nodded. "Yeah. We'll paint it whatever color you want. I promise." I bent down and hugged him. "You're stuck with us, kid. Don't think of leaving us."

He let out a nervous laugh, but I could tell it was laced with fear.

I pulled back, scratched Captain behind his ears, and then shut the car door. I went to help Darcy who was still loading the back of the Range Rover with sleeping bags, food, and clothes.

"Thanks for looking out for him," I said.

"No problem." She peered at me. "You sure you know what you're doing?"

"No."

She smiled slightly. "The boys are gonna be pissed when they find out you didn't get in my car."

"They will thank me when all this is over and our boys are out in the world again."

"Promise me you'll tell me everything that goes down?"

"I'm not supposed to talk club business," I said with a wide smile.

"So you'll tell me and the girls at our next girls' night?"

I hugged her. "Can't wait."

"Be safe." She embraced me back hard and then let go. "And if you can, keep my husband out of trouble."

I held my tongue, not divulging that I had plans to use her husband and his skills. I knew what I had in mind would work, but I didn't know if I'd be able to convince Gray and Torque to help me.

I went to Joni and Rachel to say my farewells. Allison was already gone, having said goodbye to Torque earlier. She'd taken her younger sister and gotten out of Waco fast. Joni looked pale and shaken up, despite Rachel attempting to crack jokes. Even she looked worried.

"It'll be okay," I told Joni, my voice soft.

"How can you be sure?" she demanded.

"Because I won't let anything happen to any of them," I vowed.

Maybe it didn't mean a lot coming from me, the woman who had brought wreck and ruin with her to the club and nearly destroyed their way of life, but the Blue Angels were family now and I would be damned before I let anything happen to them.

I was the daughter of an MC president. I was related to the O'Banions as well as the Capones. My bloodlines did not lie and I was born for this life.

By choosing Colt, I accepted it.

I squeezed her hand and then stood back so she could get in the passenger seat.

I waved to them as they drove out of the gate to Louisiana.

To safety.

I sat at a large wooden table in between Torque and Gray.

The other seats were occupied by Flynn and Ramsey, Knight and Bishop, Sanchez's man Franco, and the Jackal club president, Pike. We were in a private room at The Rex in Dallas; Flynn had graciously offered to host the assembly. It was fairly neutral ground for all concerned.

"Why is a woman sitting in on our meeting?" Pike asked, his glare directed at me.

It didn't make me balk or sweat, or sit up any straighter. Gray had warned me about what I was getting into. Men still governed the criminal underworld and it didn't matter that I was Colt's Old Lady.

But I wasn't speaking for Colt.

"She sits with us," Torque said in solidarity.

He wasn't any happier about having me in the room. His jaw had dropped open when he'd realized I hadn't gotten into Darcy's car. I was a wrench in his plans and Colt would pummel his ass if anything happened to me. No one wanted me involved in any of this, but we were a united front.

I caught Knight's eye. He'd never say it aloud because he wasn't a Waco Blue Angel, but he was a warrior, a savage, and I was his daughter. His look said it all; he was proud of me.

I still hadn't processed that he was my father. There hadn't been time to process much of anything, really. Not even Cheese and Shelly's deaths. Not even the fact that I'd taken a child out of his home and decided he was going to be my family. Add in Colt's arrest and I realized most women would be sitting at home under the covers, broken and terrified.

But I wasn't most women.

If I'd learned anything from Grammie's death, it was that the world continued to rotate, and it was your choice if you wanted to move forward and live your life or let your past destroy you.

"Who's orchestrating this discussion?" Franco asked, his Spanish accent thick and sultry.

Everyone spoke at once, all trying to talk over each other. I was in a room stuffed with criminal alpha males, all with different stakes in the outcome of a cartel and biker drug war.

Franco spoke for Sanchez who wanted his product distributed through Waco and then through the Heartland of the country up to Idaho. Knight wanted to lay the foundation to be part of the distribution for the northern territory and see to it that the Blue Angels of Coeur D'Alene were the only source to buy from. Flynn's bottles of scotch were being used to hide the product for international shipments. Pike and the Jackals weren't allies of the Blue Angels, but they hated the Iron Horsemen, too.

The enemy of my enemy is my friend.

I let everyone talk until finally they all fell silent—no one took the lead because there was no lead, just a common goal.

"May I say something?" I asked, treading lightly, not wanting to piss off Pike any more than he already was.

Franco didn't appear interested in what I had to say and I could tell that he, like Pike, was merely tolerating my presence.

Flynn nodded for me to continue.

I took a deep breath. "We've got to get the Iron Horsemen off the streets and destroy the Garcia cartel's stranglehold on our territories. That is our singular objective. I'm sure you can all agree on that."

After several nods of agreement, I went on, "I know for a fact that Dev has some weird personal vendetta against me." I swallowed. "He thinks I'm involved in what Richie did and that I know where the shipment is. I wasn't involved and really did know nothing, but that's changed now. I know where the shipment is kept. We need to set a trap for him, and I'll be the perfect bait."

No one spoke for the first few seconds after I closed my mouth. Then Knight jumped in, protesting vocally, followed by Gray and Torque. Both Flynn and Ramsey tried to speak over them. The only two people who didn't object were Franco and Pike.

Shocker.

I wasn't going to fight to be heard, and when the room finally quieted down again after the commotion, I took a chance and spoke out for the second time. "Dev is desperate to find the shipment Richie stole before the cartel kills him. He crossed the line when he opened fire on women and children at a public park. It was a fucking charity event to raise money for an elementary school. Two people are dead, ten are injured. Decorum be damned. He's out of control and not playing by the rules anymore. We can't sit idly by and wait for his clock to run out with the Garcia cartel and for them to kill him. How many of us will die between now and then?"

"We are not using you as bait, lass," Ramsey voiced. "That's not how we do things."

"I'm also not supposed to be at this table," I pointed out. "And why is that? Because I'm a woman? I'm not trying to change the way you gentlemen do things. Frankly, I don't want to be involved. But Dev has been after me for weeks. Why shouldn't we use his own desire for me against him?"

"Have you ever had a gun put to your head?" Pike asked.

I frowned. "What does that have to do with anything?"

"Do you panic? Or do you keep your cool under stress? How would you react if a gun was put to your temple and there was a real chance that you'd die? You could actually die, you know? With this plan that's not even a real plan. It's an idea."

Pike didn't like me sitting at the table, but he was being honest and levelheaded. He wasn't saying anything that the others were disagreeing with, either.

"Barrett would approve of this," Ramsey said, his voice low, his comment directed at Flynn.

"Of course she would," Flynn stated. "Because my wife likes to be in the thick of shite."

"And if she were in town, she'd be at this meeting," Ramsey added.

"Aye. What's your point, Ramsey?"

"My point is," Ramsey paused, "Dev would never see a woman coming to take him down. Men never do."

The black cloud of Dev had been hovering over my head for far too long. He'd taken my sense of security, curtailed my independence, killed my best friend, and wounded the love of my life.

I'd never be able to look over my shoulder as long as the Iron Horsemen president was breathing. He was wreaking havoc, destroying a city and tearing apart families, all in the name of violence, greed, and power.

Dev wanted the product Richie stole from him.

And he would have it.

Night had fallen. I listened to the sound of cicadas beating their wings in the otherwise quiet evening. I slapped at my skin, trying to kill a buzzing mosquito.

Looking up at the stars, I thought of Colt and the boys who were currently in a jail cell. I thought of the rough, thin blankets they had to sleep with and the men who might try to shank them in the night, or strangle them with their bare hands. It was a fight for life for them.

No one did well locked up, but I knew it was worse for Colt and his brothers. They rode on motorcycles so they could feel the wind on their cheeks, breathe in the fresh air as their bikes ate up miles of road and they believed in their souls that authority figures had no right to rule over sovereign men.

Lawless brothers penned in by laws.

The back door opened and my solitude was interrupted, but I didn't mind. I hadn't liked the direction of my thoughts, knowing any moment they'd slip from gentle musings to downright melancholic.

Knight pulled up a lawn chair and sat down beside me. I glanced at him, noting his exhaustion. Tension lined his mouth.

I silently handed him the bottle of Jack. He took it and drank.

"You don't bother with cups?" he asked with a wry glint in his eyes.

"Just another dish to wash."

He handed the bottle back to me. I'd never been the type of girl just to drink liquor straight from the bottle, but things changed.

I changed.

"He's not going to be happy when he hears what's about to go down—with you involved," Knight said, his tone deceptively mild.

"Yeah, I don't envy Gray being the one to tell him tomorrow."

I'd wanted to visit Colt myself, but Gray and Torque quickly nixed the idea. Saying it would be worse for Colt, who didn't want me to ever see him confined like a caged animal.

Oddly enough, I hadn't pushed against the edict. My mind wandered through a weird state of limbo. It bounced around from past, to present, to future. To outcomes. To a time when we were all together, and this shit with Dev was a vision in the rearview mirror.

"I have no right," he said softly, "to tell you what you can or can't do. I have no right to tell you I wish you weren't involved in any of this. I have no right to tell you that I think you should've taken Silas and run like hell of out Waco."

I slowly turned my head to look at him. "But if you did have the right? Why would you tell me to run? This is my home. My family." I paused. "My legacy."

"This is also your life we're talking about." He leaned over and placed his elbows on his knees, his gaze dark, questioning.

"Say whatever you want to say," I commanded. "Even if you don't think you should."

"I just met you, Mia. I just found out I have a kid. You don't need a dad. You're an adult. You grew up fine without me." He swallowed like something painful was lodged in his throat. "But I *am* your father. And my job is to protect you. I can't—I don't know what's going to happen with you being involved with all this shit, but it's got me thinking the worst."

I paused. "That I won't live."

He nodded his head in agreement. "If you die, it'll break them. It'll break us. Colt. Silas. Me."

"Don't put any of that on yourself. It's not your choice." My tone wasn't forceful or even angry. It was flat, cool, like river water over pebbles.

He ran a hand across his face and then held out his other for the bottle, which I gave him.

"This is my shit to clean up," I told him. "For Cheese. For Shelly. But most of all, for me. Dev will keep taking people from me unless I stop him. It's more than that, though. I need to see it. With my own two eyes. I need to know he's been put down and he can't hurt me anymore. I can't—I haven't been able to grieve Shelly the way I need to. It's like,"—I looked away from him to stare once again at the night sky—"there's a wall and she's behind it. There's no door, no handle. She's blocked off, and I can't get to her to grieve until I do this."

"You think being part of Dev's death is the dynamite that will blast that wall down?"

I nodded. "I can do this. I *have* to do this. Or I'll never find a way to be at peace with her death. Does that make me crazy? Does that sound insane?"

"No. It doesn't sound insane," he said softly. "But I've got news for you. You never really get over the pain of losing someone—you just figure out a way to live around it."

I paused a moment. "Are you talking about my mother?"

"Maybe. But Scarlett didn't die. I let her go. It's different than what you're going through."

I nodded, getting lost in thought again.

"Do you want to be left alone?" he asked.

"Yeah. I do."

"I'll leave you to it, then." He stood and walked toward the back door.

His hand was on the knob when I called out, "Dad …"

Knight turned slowly. "Yeah?"

"You're never too old to need a father." I lifted the bottle to my lips and drank deeply. Knight waited another moment and then with a creak of the screen door, disappeared.

Chapter 29

THE NEXT EVENING I walked into an Iron Horsemen club wearing a little black dress. And because I was a biker's woman, my little black dress was made of leather. It was a halter, and it clearly showed off the ink on my shoulder.

I'd paired the dress with leather ankle boots with silver metal studs and spikes and a matching black studded clutch. Unfortunately, the purple cast on my wrist detracted just a bit from the bad-assery. But Ramsey assured me it would absolutely make Dev think I was weak and incapable of taking him down. The cast, he said, was an asset.

There was no room for any sort of weapon on me anywhere, and though I didn't like going into a wolf's den unarmed, I knew I'd have to in order to set my plan in motion.

I passed the bar and ignored the writhing bodies on the dance floor. I glanced up at the second story of the club and saw two Iron Horsemen lording over their holdings.

I quickly found the stairs and slowly approached both

men wearing leather cuts. Every square inch of skin that I could see, aside from their faces, was inked.

There was a door at the other end of the balcony, which I knew— thanks to a hacker friend of Flynn's who got us the floor plans—was Dev's private green room. An office and a place to play cards where he could kick back and relax.

The two men slid around me, halting my progress.

"Where do you think you're going?" the one standing behind me purred.

"I've got a meeting with your president."

The oaf looming in front of me clucked his tongue. "They've already got entertainment for the evening."

"But we don't." The one behind me reached out to grasp my hip and pulled me back into his hard body. I felt the evidence of his enjoyment, but I didn't react.

"He'll want to see me. Tell him it's Mia." I looked at the peon in front, watching his eyes widen in understanding. The goon behind me released me like he'd grabbed a hot poker straight from a fire.

The thug turned to stride down the hall. He knocked once on the door and then entered, shutting the door behind him. A few moments later, the door opened again, this time all the way and he gestured for me to come forward.

Adrenaline pumped through my veins as I walked into the wolf den.

I stepped through the doorway, careful to keep my face blank.

"She's alone," the criminal behind me said.

"You pat her down?" Dev asked without looking up.

"She's wearing a tight, slutty dress. Where would she be able to hide a weapon?"

Dev sighed like he was tired. "Get the fuck out."

Duly chastised, the half-witted criminal slunk from the room and shut the door.

Five men, including Dev, all sat around a card table. Each of them had a scantily clad woman sitting on his lap, but none of them paid their toys any attention. Dev hadn't even glanced up when I entered the room.

Women were nothing here.

With a quick scan of the table, I realized they were playing Texas Hold 'Em and were at the turn card.

I took a moment to study each man playing. Dev was the only one wearing leather, the other four were all of different nationalities and wore suits. International businessmen?

Criminals for sure, if they were associating with Dev.

I watched them hold their cards and examine them, and when the Asian man shifted in his suit, I recognized his tell and knew he had a stellar hand before the river and there was no bluff about it.

Dev placed a five hundred dollar bet. The Asian man matched it and raised another five hundred.

The other three folded.

The dealer dealt the river card and both men checked after a moment eyeballing each other. Dev gestured with his chin at the Asian man who showed his two cards.

Royal flush.

I couldn't stop the smirk that fell across my lips when Dev cursed and threw down pocket aces.

Considering the cards on the flop, it was a bad hand, thought strong only by weak-minded men.

"Fuck," Dev cursed before lifting his eyes to mine. He said nothing, but instead chose to rake his gaze down my body. I forced myself to stand completely still and act like it didn't feel like a million little insects were crawling across my skin.

He smirked. "Nice cast."

"What's the buy-in?" I asked ignoring Dev's dig. My gaze flitted away from Dev to peer around the room.

One man—the Slavic—stared at me in curiosity, but barked something out in his native tongue. It was grating to my ears.

"You don't have the kind of cash to buy in to one of my games, darlin'." He leered, leaning back in his chair, his hand palming the backside of the blonde perched on his lap.

I opened my clutch and tossed out a packet of cocaine.

It landed in the center of the card table with a soft thud.

"What about now?" I asked softly. "Is that enough?"

His eyes darkened. "Everyone out." He lightly smacked the girl's butt, making her squeal. She jumped up and sidled around the table and then out the door. Her compatriots followed suit and so did the men who'd been sitting at Dev's card table.

The door closed with finality.

I took it upon myself to pull out a chair and sit, spine straight, legs crossed.

"You've been holding out on me. I knew it." He reached for the packet of cocaine and then took the next few moments to sample it.

"Does your business partner know about your love of his product?" I asked mildly.

Dev's eyes were hazy. "How's your friend? The pretty blonde with the stellar rack? Oh, that's right." His smile was cruel. "She's dead."

My rage was icy and intense. My blood froze and it was all I could do to control myself. But it wouldn't do me any favors to let Dev under my skin. I couldn't let him cloud my judgment with emotion.

"I guess we're done here." I placed my hands on the table and stood. "Good luck explaining to your business associates that you nearly recovered their massive shipment of cocaine, only to let it fall through your fingers."

His hand lashed out to grab my right wrist and squeeze. I felt the bones crunch underneath his relentless grip. "Want me to give you a matching cast for the this arm, you fuckin' bitch?"

I didn't answer, and I didn't wince even as the pain intensified.

"What's your angle, darlin'? Because I know you didn't walk in here with a packet of coke to dangle like a carrot in front of my face. You're up to something."

"Damn right I am," I said mildly. "You mind letting go of me?"

He squeezed it one final time and then released me. "What the fuck is this? Why are you here?"

"You brought the cartel to Waco," I said. "Let's pretend I give two shits about that. I don't. What I do care about is you fucking with me and my livelihood and shooting at women and children in a park." I cocked my head to the side. "You seem awfully calm for a man who owes millions to the Garcia cartel. You're still alive, which tells me they don't know that Richie stole the shipment from you. But the window is closing on how long you can bullshit them. Once they realize what's going on, you're fucked."

"So you have it all figured out, do you?" he murmured. "You don't know shit."

"No?" I nodded. "Okay." I turned to leave.

"You want something. What is it?" Dev demanded.

His words made me pause and slowly turn around to face him. "Richie left Dive Bar to me. I want you and your boys to fuck off, and stay out of it."

"Dive Bar doesn't exist anymore. Your man had it burned to the ground."

"I want to rebuild and reopen it. And I *do not* want the Iron Horsemen attached to it. Clean slate. You will also forfeit your territory on the East side. In exchange, I'll take you to the warehouse tonight and you can recover your shipment. And hopefully keep your head before Alejandro Garcia removes it."

I placed my hands on the table and leaned over. "I know who you're in bed with. I know what they're capable of doing. Your shipment for my bar and your club stays the fuck out of the East Side of town, that's the deal."

"You've got to be shitting me," Dev said with a rusty laugh. "I'm not giving you the East Side. Why don't I just kill you now and be done with it?"

"Simple. My guys have moved the shipment. I no longer know where it is and won't find out until I'm safely out of this building and call to confirm you've agreed to the deal. Only then do you get an address. You can show up heavy if you don't trust us. We just want the bar. We don't want shit to do with the cartels and the bar provides us clean money. Fuck with drug muling if you want, but keep us out of it.

"Besides, I can't imagine you're down for what Alejandro will do to you if he finds out you've crossed him by involving Richie. He certainly won't care that Richie is dead. But if you don't care about yourself, then maybe you care about your club?" I shook my head. "You know they won't stop at just killing you, right? You know what they do to men who fuck them over. What do you think they do to women of the men who fuck them over?" I cocked my head to the side. "How is Sydney, by the way? She's a freshman at A&M, isn't she?"

His jaw tightened but he said nothing, his eyes glittering with suppressed rage. "Why did Colt send his Old Lady to negotiate for him?"

"Kinda hard for him to speak for himself, what with him being in jail and all. And you and I both know, none of the Angels could walk into this club and make it out alive."

He smiled, but said nothing.

"Once we get outside I'll get in my ride so my guys know I'm safe. Then I'll give you the address to the warehouse and then you make a call to get Colt and the others released from jail. We all know who pulled the strings to get them locked up anyway."

"I don't trust you not to fuck me over," he stated.

"That's the pot calling the kettle black," I seethed. I reached into my clutch and pulled out a set of keys and tossed them at him. "As soon as I give you the address you can go and see for yourself."

His eyes gleamed. "Do you think I'm stupid? Do you really think I'm gonna go to an address that I haven't scoped out yet. It could be a trap. You're coming with me."

"As what?" I asked, brows raised.

"Collateral."

"I'm not going to a storage unit in the middle of the night with you. What's to stop you from getting your entire shipment back and then putting a bullet in my brain?"

He grinned. "Nothing."

I stared at him. "You kill me, and you start a war."

"Darlin', are you stupid? The war has already started."

His eyes lifted to the spot over my shoulder.

I turned.

And then everything went black.

∿

My head throbbed and something warm trickled down my temple.

The goon who clubbed me into unconsciousness had thoroughly enjoyed putting his hands on me. That much was obvious when I finally opened my eyes and met his gaze.

I was in the back of a van; my limbs and hands were free. Even if I was able to get a good kick at the asshole, rendering him inert, there was no way I could get through the metal safety screen between the front and back of the van.

Better to wait.

My heart beat frantically in my chest. I'd prepared for Dev to hurt me physically. We had discussed this possibility at great length while solidifying the plan. Still, it was one thing to mentally brace yourself for pain, quite another to actually feel it. Nausea churned in my belly as we went around a curve.

"Bitch is awake," the Iron Horsemen thug in the back of the van said.

His friend who was driving said nothing, but passed a phone to Dev, who was sitting in the front passenger seat.

"Mia, darlin', what's your ride's number?"

I told him and he put the phone on speaker.

"You know who this is. We've got your girl and need the address for the pickup."

I heard mumbling on the other end of the line but couldn't make out what was said.

"Oh, that's simple. If you don't give me the address, I'm gonna bring her back to you in about five different garbage bags. Give me the fucking address! Now."

I heard a delay, then a response, and then Dev hung up and I shut my eyes to keep my headache from spiraling out of control.

They'd moved the shipment from a storage unit to a warehouse in a deserted, blue-collar part of town.

Twenty minutes later, the van came to a stop. The door flew open almost immediately and Dev was there, hauling me out, a pistol trained on me. He was taking every precaution and it was clear he assumed he was walking into a trap. But the fact that he came at all proved how desperate he was to get his hands on the missing product. I'd been fishing for information when I'd said I knew the cartel didn't yet know the shipment was missing and I'd struck a nerve.

His clock was ticking and time was almost up.

The full moon lit the sky and there wasn't a cloud in sight. A bead of sweat rolled down between my breasts. My mouth was dry and I was in desperate need of water.

Dev jabbed the pistol into my lower back. "Move."

My vision was spotty and my head ached, but I forced one foot in front of the other. I couldn't see the two men that were with Dev, but I assumed they were surveying the area.

"All clear," one said, confirming my suspicion.

"Yep, I don't see anything," his friend added.

"Look around," Dev barked. "I don't trust this bitch."

"Smokey and Mac checked it out as soon as we got the address and they didn't see anything. It's been a while now and nothing. They're watching from across the street but no one has come in or out."

We trekked toward the warehouse and when we arrived at the door, one of his boys pulled out a bolt cutter and cut off the lock.

"You first," Dev said, prodding me with the pistol.

I opened the door. "I'm going to turn on the light, okay?"

"Do it."

My hand slid across the wall and the lights flickered on, showing the stacks and stacks of cocaine in plastic bags. Dev reached into his leather vest pocket and pulled out his phone and dialed a number. He placed the cell to his ear and then said, "Back the van up to the door. We're loading up." He ended the call and then moved us farther into the warehouse. His grip on my arm was slack, but he was clearly strong enough that I couldn't overtake him. Regardless of the movies I'd seen, I knew that small women didn't beat up massive bikers.

The light overhead flickered before sputtering out.

We were pitched into darkness and a sliver of the full moon managed to peek its way into the warehouse, illuminating Dev's harsh features. I could smell the acrid stench of fear seeping from him.

There was the sound of a distant crack like a massive whip had flicked through the air, and then the thud of something striking the exterior of the warehouse followed by a shout. Another bang a split second later accompanied by a thump, and then there was nothing.

"What the ever loving fuck," Dev snapped. His slack grip suddenly became like a vice as he hauled me toward the door.

When he yanked me toward him, I twisted an ankle, causing me to stumble and fall toward the floor.

Dev jerked me up easily with one arm as though I weighed nothing and made sure to keep a firm grip on his pistol, as he marched us out the door of the warehouse.

The two men who'd accompanied Dev were leaking blood onto the ground in pools around the stumps of their lower jaws and necks.

They'd had their heads blown apart.

A sudden wave of nausea assaulted me as the smell of

blood, like old copper pennies, hit my nose and I began to breathe through my mouth and hastily closed my eyes.

Gray had done his job.

"You lying bitch," Dev seethed as he pulled me in front of him and stuck his pistol under the base of my skull at the back of my head.

"Come out, fuckers! Come out now or she dies!"

When no one made a move, he pressed the weapon more firmly to my head and made a guttural sound like he knew he was going to die.

The bite of metal against my skin made my heart pound, but it suddenly felt like everything was happening in slow motion.

I knew Gray's general position on the roof across the street, but like any good sniper he was impossible to see. Dev didn't know Gray was out there, for all he knew it was two men on foot down below, but Gray hadn't taken a shot at Dev yet. That told me he couldn't hit Dev without injuring me.

Out of the corner of my eye, the light in the warehouse suddenly turned on, causing Dev's gaze to stray.

I took advantage of the distraction and in one quick breath, I lifted my arms into the air, balled my fist up tight and elbowed Dev in the solar plexus as hard as I could.

"Fuuuck!" Dev screamed, firing off a shot in my general direction as he lost his grip on me.

I rushed forward to escape him.

He stumbled back, tripping over one of the bodies of his men. When he fell, he dropped his pistol and his eyes darted around in search of it, reminding me of a trapped rodent searching for an escape. He was without his men, and now he no longer had a hostage to ensure he'd leave alive. Desperation had set in.

I kept waiting for Gray to take his shot, but it didn't come.

Something was wrong.

I felt it deep in my gut.

Had Dev's two men—Mac and Smokey—who'd been watching from the distance found Gray? Was he fighting on the roof for his life, or was his existence already forfeit?

Dev started to laugh when he realized I was alone and unarmed, that he could now finish me off and there wasn't anyone to protect me.

I'd been right on one account.

Dev had followed me into a trap, but the trap failed.

I had no idea where Flynn was, or if Gray was still alive.

I was on my own—facing off with a madman who would stop at nothing to kill me.

My only shot in hell was making it to the van and praying his man had left the keys in the ignition.

If not...

I took a step forward only to have pain lance its way up my leg.

I looked down and realized I'd been hit when Dev's pistol fired. A river of blood poured from the wound, trickling down my calf and into my boot. I became light-headed.

"Where's your boyfriend now, you fuckin' cunt?" Dev taunted, rising from the ground with a pistol he'd found by the body of one of his men. "You think his name on your shoulder is gonna protect you?"

I hobbled toward the van, my hand to the wound on my leg. But my palm kept slipping off because of the blood.

The air smelled of gunpowder and death.

"You don't think I knew this was gonna be a set up? Of course I knew."

"Then why did you let my guy kill two of yours?" I asked, feeling faint.

"Sometimes you have to sacrifice a few for the many," he stated. His eyes took on a deranged glint in the moonlight.

Spots marred my vision and my breathing was already labored as my heart tried to pump more blood and oxygen to the wound in my leg.

"You didn't think I knew about your alliance with Flynn Campbell? Or your boys' meeting with the Jackals. The Jackals would be idiots to pick the losing side in a drug war."

It was on the tip of my tongue to ask how he knew. But I realized it didn't matter. He had been one step ahead of me and I was going to die for it.

"I know all, darlin'. I own this city."

I reached the van and grabbed the door handle as Dev slowly approached from behind, not at all concerned that I was attempting to escape. The door was locked and my hand slid off the metal, leaving behind a bloody trail. I whimpered, even as I felt myself sinking to the ground.

As I rested against the wheel of the van, Dev crouched down to get into my face.

"I admire your balls." He grinned. "For a woman. Still, you're just a woman."

He caressed the side of my face, almost tenderly, almost like we were lovers. Lovers entwined in blood.

My vision was hazy and I refused to let Dev's face be the last thing I saw before I bled out. I focused on the warehouse behind him, a slight smile curving my lips when I saw the tendrils of smoke curling out from the warehouse.

"Guess you don't know everything," I wheezed.

Dev frowned and then looked over his shoulder, following my line of sight. "No," he whispered, rising from the blood-soaked pavement beneath us.

He repeated the word over and over as he watched the warehouse of cocaine slowly become engulfed by fire.

"How? How did this happen?"

I wanted to tell him. I wanted to gloat. But I was having trouble staying awake. And just before I passed out, I swore I heard the faint rumblings of a motorcycle.

I was being lifted off the ground and pressed to a warm, solid chest. The cotton T-shirt smelled familiar. Like my favorite detergent—and Colt. I would've snuggled closer, but everything felt heavy. My head, my limbs, my entire body.

"Fuck." The voice sounded very much like Colt's. Which was impossible because Colt was in jail.

And I was dying.

Maybe it was an angel with Colt's voice escorting my soul to heaven. My internal voice snorted at the thought. If anything, it was the devil shepherding my soul to hell. For the things I'd done. For the wrongs I'd committed. For the life I'd chosen.

I felt something cinch around my thigh.

"Brother," came another voice I recognized.

Zip.

Why was Zip with the devil taking me to hell? Did devils work in pairs? Deranged thoughts. Thoughts from deprivation of oxygen.

"I can't lose her." Colt again.

Bleak.

So, so bleak.

I wanted to tell them that I was still here and I wasn't ready to leave yet. I wanted to tell them that I had more living to do, more loving. I'd just found my father. I'd just unofficially adopted an eleven-year-old boy that I had no idea how to raise. And Colt. I couldn't leave Colt.

I finally found the strength to open my eyes and stared into Colt's intense brown gaze.

And then I died with a smile on my lips.

Chapter 30

Hell looked very much like a hospital room.

I blinked heavy eyelids, staring at light blue walls and a white ceiling. The IV in my arm tingled with pain when I moved my hand.

Colt was sitting next to my bedside, his head lolling to his shoulder as he slept. I thought about calling out to him to wake him up, but I didn't want to disturb him.

Cottonmouth had me doubting I could even form a word.

I slid my finger back and forth across the sheet that was covering me. My nail on the cheap fabric made a sound, causing Colt to jerk upright in sudden alertness.

We stared at one another and then Colt was out of the chair and at my side. "Darlin'."

"Water," I growled through a parched throat. "Please."

He grabbed the pitcher and poured water into a plastic cup. When I had my fill, he set it aside.

I had so many questions I wasn't sure where to start. So I began with the most obvious one. "How long have I been here?"

"Brought you in last night. They rushed you to surgery for the bullet wound in your thigh. They dug it out, transfused the fuck out of you, and here we are."

I looked out my window and saw the fading sunlight.

"Gray? He was—"

"Fine. He's fine. Reap and Boxer found him wrestling one of Dev's men on the roof. Gray managed to slide his knife into the other one."

I breathed a sigh of relief that Gray was alive.

"He feels guilty as fuck, you know. Since he was supposed to pick Dev off."

"Nothing goes according to plan, right? Dev told me he knew about the set up. Is that true?"

"Yeah."

I peered up at him, feeling drugged and loopy, my brain and words struggling. "Piece this together for me, because I have no idea how you're not in jail and I swear, while I was bleeding out propped up against the van, I thought I heard your voice."

"You did hear me." He raked a hand through his hair and grimaced at the sudden pain from moving his side and feeling his own wound.

The irony, that we both had bullet wounds, courtesy of one insane MC president.

"Vance—our club lawyer made a call to a high-profile judge, who made a call to the mayor, who called the sheriff."

"Interesting chain of command," I murmured, wondering what that conversation had sounded like and how the hell a judge was ordering the mayor to do anything.

"Anyway, Flynn and Ramsey met us at the station with our bikes. On our way to the warehouse, we got caught up in a firefight with Dev's men. It was an ambush. If it hadn't been for Knight and the Idaho boys, we wouldn't have been able to get out of there."

"I don't understand."

"There was a shooting. Knight and his boys took over the fight. Most of them are former military, remember? They covered us while we rode to the warehouse and they killed a few of Dev's men. The Jackals were supposed to be riding with us, but they had an issue on their own turf. Someone in their club ratted us out to Dev, probably hoping to get in tight with the Iron Horsemen. Dev knew the rest of the Jackals would ride with us against him, so he created a diversion to keep the Jackals close to home. We lost them as backup.

"By the time we got over to the warehouse, we found you bleeding out by a van, the warehouse was on fire, and Dev was gone."

My breath caught. "He escaped? After all of this?"

"For now."

"Are you—" I exhaled. "Are you going to track him down?"

Colt shook his head. "Mateo Sanchez has Franco on it already. They'll find Dev and then hand him over to the cartel and let Alejandro decide what's to be done with him. He's no longer our problem, and with the coke all gone, he'd be stupid to ever come back to Waco. Once Alejandro finds out that the coke is missing along with Dev, the entire crew is history."

I shivered. "What about their wives and children? I know what cartels do. They murder entire families just to make a point. They've even killed people's dogs before."

"I've already asked Sanchez to negotiate for their safety."

"What will that cost us? The price has been too high already!" I cried, hysteria rising in my tone.

Colt placed his hand on my shoulder. "Easy. Take it easy."

"I can't."

"You need to take a deep breath for me."

When I felt like I was calm, I had to ask, "Will Alejandro come after me? Us? We were the ones who burned his coke to the ground. It was worth millions…"

"Only after Dev let it slip through his fingers. No. Alejandro won't come after us because Sanchez's men are sticking close to Waco to ensure the peace. Even a few million dollars in cocaine isn't enough for Alejandro to take on another cartel head to head. Especially not in the States. That's bad for business. It's better for him to wipe out the Iron Horsemen so his street cred stays valid and leave out the details that we're now working with Sanchez. It will look like the Iron Horsemen fucked with a cartel and got obliterated, which is true. All the other shit will be swept under the rug."

I wasn't sure that gave me any comfort.

"How's your pain?" he asked suddenly.

"What pain? Morphine is kind of swell."

He didn't smile at my light tone and I was instantly on my guard. "You're going to yell at me, aren't you?"

"You think I'd yell at you while you were lying in a hospital bed after having been shot because you willingly placed yourself in danger even though you had no business being in danger in the first place?"

I paused, pretending to look thoughtful. "Yeah, I think you'd yell at me."

"Well, you're damn fucking right I'd yell at you," he bellowed. "What the fuck were you thinking?"

"I was thinking," I replied, tone calm, "that you guys were in jail and I had no idea when you'd be getting out. I knew this stuff with Dev was a time sensitive issue and it needed to be dealt with."

"What else," he demanded. "What are you leaving out?"

"This was personal for me, and if I didn't have a stake in taking him down, I knew I'd always regret it. And I'd never find peace with Shelly's death. But you knew all that. So why do you seem so surprised?"

"Surprised doesn't even begin to express how I feel. I was scared shitless knowing I couldn't protect you." He hung his head in near defeat. "You can't always go charging into dangerous situations."

"I didn't charge. I sat down and planned with Gray, Torque, Flynn and the others."

I closed my eyes, not because I was finished with the conversation, but because the morphine was flowing and I felt myself slipping away from consciousness.

"We're not done with this discussion," Colt whispered in my ear.

"You haven't told me you loved me," I mumbled.

"I thought that was a given."

"I told you I loved you after you got shot. It's courteous to repay in kind."

His lips brushed my forehead. "I love you. Losing you would devastate me. My life has no meaning without you. There. Are you happy?"

I smiled, my eyes still closed, "Your delivery needs work, but yeah, Colt. That made me happy."

The next time I woke up, it was late at night and Colt was standing by the window, staring out at the hospital grounds.

He must have heard me stir and turned back to look at me. There was hardly any moon or starlight, and I could only faintly make out the outline of his big, brawny body.

"How are you feeling?" he asked, stalking toward my bedside and reaching for the pitcher of water.

"I don't know." I pressed my tongue to the roof of my dry mouth. "Will you flip on the lamp?"

He did as I requested.

"How do I feel," I repeated. "Like down is up and up is down. Like my emotions are all scrambled and I don't know what I'm supposed to feel."

"You're supposed to feel whatever you want to feel."

I frowned, taking the glass of water and bringing the straw to my lips. After I had my fill, Colt took it from me and set it aside.

"You haven't kissed me. You've barely touched me," I said.

"You're in a hospital bed. Did you kiss or touch me when I was laid up in bed?"

"I think I did touch you. And I think you wanted me to touch you. Why won't you touch me now? I'm not talking carnal—just gentle intimacy. I know something is going on with you. What is it?"

"I'm fucking livid with you," he said, his voice dispassionate. "I've had hours to think while you've been asleep and I just—haven't figured out how to wrap my head around your actions."

I watched him pace the room as he vented.

"I can't believe Gray and Torque didn't have the good sense to keep you out of this."

"Out of this," I repeated. "Where have you been the last few weeks? This was all because of me."

"It wasn't all because of you."

"Fine. I was the catalyst that got it all moving." I swallowed. "What's the opposite of the Midas touch, Colt?"

"I don't follow."

"You know, Midas. Everything he touches turns to gold? Well, everything I touch turns to ash."

His gaze softened in understanding. "Ah, darlin'."

"No, don't." I held up my hand to stop him. "I'm not looking for sympathy. Okay? I was just—I had to help clean up the mess I brought into your life. To the Blue Angels' lives. For me. For you. For Shelly."

Saying her name out loud hurt me. Saying her name felt like summoning a ghost. A fissure of emotion erupted in my body shoving away the numbness that had enveloped me.

The tears were gentle at first and then they turned into a cascade. I became a careening, mourning woman who sounded like a deranged animal in pain.

Colt sat down on the bed next to me and held my body as I shook and broke apart.

"He killed her," I hiccoughed the words, my eyes nearly swollen shut. "He killed her and I couldn't even make him hurt. I couldn't even make him hurt one bit of what I feel."

Colt crooned against my hair, brushing away my greasy locks, not caring that I needed a good scrubbing to remove the smell of hospital, the smell of death.

Would this eat away at me my entire life? Not being the one to end Dev?

When I quieted, I pressed my nose to Colt and inhaled. He smelled like Colt, like freedom and light. Like the air in summer. Like life itself.

"No one asked me to help," I said when my tears had abated. "I volunteered. No one wanted to involve me. Torque nearly lost his shit when he saw that I didn't get in the car to head to the cabins." I pinned him with a stare. "Cabins, Colt. You never told me you had cabins."

"I don't have cabins. The club has cabins. And don't change the subject. How did you get Gray and Torque to let you sit at the table?"

"I asked." I shrugged. "You have to understand—none of them were okay with using me as bait, but they knew it would get the job done. It was supposed to get the job done, anyway. But we failed. I failed."

"What is failure, though? You didn't get to look Dev in the eye and pull the trigger? Okay, so maybe that's your version of failure. But we succeeded overall."

"We don't have Dev. He's still running around—pissed as hell, ready to set more fires."

"Franco found Dev."

"He did?" I gaped. "When?"

"A few hours ago. Franco already handed Dev over to Alejandro's men. The deed is done." He reached out and laced his fingers through mine. "You're cold."

"Yeah."

My gaze dropped to the bed sheets.

"Do you know what this means?" he asked finally.

"It means I had no part in ending Dev's life, and that doesn't sit right with me. I'll feel like he's always out there, somewhere."

"You'll have to make it right within yourself. I know you think pulling the trigger and killing him would ease your grief, but it would turn you into someone else. Someone you might not like." He shook his head. "More importantly, now that Dev is with Alejandro's men, we get to go home. They're professionals, in what they do. Dev is as good as gone. We're safe."

I looked up to meet his somber gaze. "We get to go home."

He nodded. "You get to recover in our bed. Silas gets to pick out colors for his room. We get to step outside and not have to look over our shoulder and wonder if Dev is gunning for us. It's over."

It wasn't enough.

I didn't get my revenge.

I didn't get to watch the life fade from Dev's eyes.

All the pain and suffering I'd endured at his hands didn't have an outlet.

Colt stared at me, his dark gaze intense. "This is life, Mia. Sometimes things don't play out the way we want them to." He squeezed my hand. "You've gotta find a way to let this be enough. Otherwise…otherwise, it'll eat away at you and there will be nothing left worth living for."

The next morning, Boxer and Zip paid me a visit. After Boxer made a few jokes about my appearance, he stared at Zip and said, "You tell her."

"Tell me what?" I asked.

Zip and Boxer exchanged a look, having one of those silent bro conversations I was never privy to.

"Come on, guys. Tell me what's going on."

"Colt left," Zip said.

"He left?" I asked, mouth agape. "What do you mean he left?"

"I mean he's gone. As in not here. He said he'd be back in a few days," Zip added. "But he didn't tell me where he was going."

"Why would he tell you?" I pressed. "You guys were at each other's throats."

"They made up in prison," Boxer quipped. "Not like *that*, but they're brothers again."

"Glad to hear it," I murmured.

I glanced out the window. I'd only just woken up an hour or so ago. A nurse had come to take my vitals but then had left quickly. Colt hadn't been in my room when I'd opened my eyes. I thought nothing of it, thinking that he might've gone for coffee.

But he was gone. Without a word.

"I got a theory," Boxer said slowly. "You wanna hear it?"

"I think you'll tell it to me whether I want to hear it or not," I said, dragging my eyes away from the window.

"I think he went for a ride," Boxer said. "To clear his head. To put it back on straight. He…"

"He what? Spit it out, Boxer."

"God, you're fucking cranky," he stated.

"I'm about to get fucking crankier," I muttered.

Boxer sighed. "Colt might've punched a wall while you were in surgery. He's been off ever since. Riding is the only thing that clears out the cob webs."

"I can't believe he left me."

"He didn't leave you," Zip said. "He went to go find himself."

"Find himself. What the fuck is that? He has that luxury, but I don't?" I gestured to my leg. "I've got months of physical therapy to look forward to. Basically being bed-ridden. And I never got to pay back the man who killed my best friend. *Find himself?*" I sounded like a banshee, screaming and caterwauling like a wounded animal.

Hell, I was wounded, and it wasn't just my leg.

"What about me? How the fuck could he do this to me? We're supposed to be a team. You don't just—he really took off?"

Boxer and Zip both nodded.

I leaned my head back against the pillows. "This is unbelievable."

I wished Joni was here so she could shed some light on her brother. "When is everyone coming back from the cabins?"

"Not for a little while," Zip said. "We wanna make sure all the shit is wrapped up here before we bring them home."

"What other shit? Dev is gone, apparently. What else is there to handle?"

Boxer scratched his chin. "Alejandro's men are cleaning the streets looking for the Iron Horsemen. It's not a bright idea to be riding around Waco wearing a cut right now."

"Don't watch the news," Zip said. "They're reporting solely on the crime wave. It's bad."

"So it really is over," I said in amazement. After weeks of fear and terror, of being on lockdown and the losses, it was done.

"Yeah, it is," Boxer said with a nod.

"Have you talked to Joni?" I asked Zip. "How's she doing? Is everyone okay? Silas?"

"They're fine. The kids don't know anything that's going on. Silas is doing well from what Darcy said."

I breathed a sigh of relief. One less thing I had to worry about.

There was a knock on the door, followed by Knight popping his head in. He looked at me in concern. I nodded for him to enter. He walked through the door and held it for Zip and Boxer who moved toward the exit. Boxer grasped my big toe and gave it a tweak before leaving.

Knight came all the way into the room and sat down on the edge of the bed. He examined me for a long moment and then said, "Christ."

"I'm okay."

He shook his head. "You're not the one who's supposed to be reassuring me. I'm supposed to do that for you. I sat with Colt, you know. When they brought you back from surgery. The both of us sat by your bed waiting for you to come out of anesthesia. Your boy was a real wreck."

"And you?"

He sighed. "Same. Boxer and Zip…did they tell you about Colt?"

"About how he's gone? Yeah. They said he went for a ride to clear his head."

"I don't know you well," Knight said slowly. "So I'm gonna need you to be honest with me."

I looked at him in confusion. "Okay."

"What's your mental state? I mean, how fragile is too fragile?"

"You know where he went, don't you?"

After a moment, he nodded. "I followed him to the parking lot. We had some…words."

"You had some fists, you mean?"

He smiled slightly. "It might've come to that. I got protective over you. He landed a punch. I hit him back. Then I made him tell me where he was going."

"Where did he go?"

His eyes met mine. "To get your revenge for you."

I dreamed the devil climbed into bed with me.

He held me in his arms, kissed my lips, tasting of violence and seduction. He smelled like gunpowder and leather, woodsmoke and man.

He felt solid and real, but I knew he was a figment of my morphine-induced imagination. I cried tears of bereavement because I knew once I opened my eyes, he'd be gone and I'd be alone again.

So for the time being, I gave into his touch, I gave into the feeling of not being so alone.

And when I came in my sleep, his lips were there to steal my cries.

~

I cracked an eyelid, taking a moment to get my bearings. My head was not resting on a pillow, but on a warm male chest.

"Colt?" I whispered.

"Hmm." His fingers played with my hair.

"Where did you go?"

He paused. "I thought Knight told you."

"He did." We were silent a moment and then I asked, "How?"

"I asked Flynn for his help. Cost me a bit. To be there at the end."

"What did it cost you?"

"Alejandro Garcia is still going to have some jurisdiction in Waco through the Jackals. They'll take the East side. We'll take the North side. Garcia will branch out east toward Louisiana when he wants to expand. Sanchez will branch out north toward Idaho."

"Divide and conquer, eh?" I asked.

"Criminals gotta eat too, babe."

I huffed out a laugh. "Yeah, I guess they do." I paused. "You think Alejandro and the Jackals will keep their end of the bargain?"

"I don't know. I guess time will tell."

"What about the bloodshed? Waco's seen enough, don't you think?"

"We stay on our side, they stay on theirs. I've talked to Franco. He's assured me that Sanchez doesn't want to see the loss of innocent lives. Can't say the same for Garcia."

I traced the warm skin that peeked out from the collar of his T-shirt. I couldn't worry about that now. There would always be unknowns. Danger would continue to lurk around the corner. I was an MC president's Old Lady. It came with the territory.

I didn't ask if he got to be the one to pull the trigger, or if he was just there to watch Dev's life come to an end. Not that Colt would tell me, anyway. And it had nothing to do with the fact that we weren't married and I wasn't protected under spousal privilege. He wouldn't want it to weigh on me.

"Were you mad when you found out I'd left?"

"Yeah."

"Are you still mad?"

"I don't think so."

"No?"

I tilted my chin up to look at him. "Thank you. For making sure it's truly over. Thank you for being there for me."

His gaze softened. "You're welcome."

I rested my head against his chest and snuggled up against him.

"Mia?"

"Yeah?"

"Marry me."

Epilogue

One year later…

"Silas," I said into the phone. "Silas, take a breath."

"Sorry," he said. "I'm just excited. You and Colt will be back in time, right?"

"Yeah, honey." I looked at my husband, who was naked from the chest up and slowly undoing the button of his jeans, a wicked glint in his eye.

"We'll be home. First place in the science fair. Like we'd miss watching you get that big blue ribbon. I'm proud of you, Silas."

"Thanks," he said. "It was all because of Ramsey. He helped me."

"You should call and tell him you appreciated his help." I grinned at his enthusiasm, even though I wasn't terribly excited that Ramsey Buchanan had taught my son how to rig delayed timers for bombs and disguised them as heat lamp timers for chicken coops in an agricultural setting. Hopefully winning first place at the science fair meant that Silas was on a solid, academic path instead of a criminal one.

"Where are you guys now?" Silas asked.

Out of the corner of my eye, I saw Colt strip off his jeans, quickly followed by his boxers. He gave himself a few pumps and leered at me.

I turned to him and gave him a sharp glare, which only made him laugh.

"We're in Florence, Oregon," I said. "Tiny little town off the coast. There are sand dunes here, Silas. Do you think Captain would love the beach?"

"Yeah, he would, definitely!"

"Then we'll have to bring you both here for a visit. I'm sorry we couldn't bring you this time."

"Mia," he said, sounding like an adult instead of the twelve-year-old-boy he was. "People who get married go on honeymoons. It would be weird if you'd brought me. You don't bring kids on your honeymoon."

My hand absently went to my stomach.

I'd just entered my second trimester and had only recently started to show. Joni had caught me throwing up on my wedding day and had called me on it. I'd finally come clean with her—the only other person who knew was Colt. I hadn't been ready to share it with the Blue Angels. I was superstitious; whenever anything good happened in my life, someone or something came in to shit all over it.

"Mia? You still there?" Silas asked.

Colt came up behind me, placed a large palm on my belly, and yanked the phone from my ear. "Hey, Silas," Colt said. "How's it going?"

I looked up at him and caught him smiling and nodding.

"Atta boy. Knew you could do it. I'm about to take Mia

out for a really romantic dinner. Can we call you tomorrow? Great. Take care, kid."

He hung up and chucked my phone aside.

"He's twelve," I said. "Not an idiot. Pretty sure he knew you wanted to get into my pants."

"You're not in pants. You're in a dress. And I can't wait to get you out of it." Colt quickly stripped me of my blue sundress and flung it aside. And then he tossed me on the bed.

I landed with a gentle bounce, and before I knew it Colt was gripping me by my legs and dragging me down to the edge.

He got on his knees and grinned.

His mouth devoured me, his tongue lapping at my center, making me thrash and moan.

"Damn," he muttered between my thighs. "You're more sensitive now than you were before you got pregnant."

"Shut up and keep going," I commanded.

He laughed and then did as he was told. His hands slid to my thighs, his palm grazing the scar on my thigh. It was hardly visible now that it was covered by a tattoo. I'd put a lot of thought into the artwork and had decided on a dandelion with its seeds blowing in the wind, and Shelly's name spiraling up the stem.

Colt knew exactly what to do to make me scream his name, and while I was still crying out for him, he slid up my body and slipped inside me.

He was gentle, yet relentless in his thrusts. I could feel him everywhere as our open eyes locked on each other. He reached underneath me and held me against him. He ground into me, hitting all the right places, filling me up.

"Colt," I whispered.

"I know." His lips took mine in an insatiable kiss and

didn't stop plunging into me. Not until I was coming again. And then he was shouting my name. My heart felt like it was going to burst out of my chest from happiness.

After, he rested his head against my naked breasts, entwining his fingers with my left hand, his thumb grazing the ring finger tattoo. He'd given me a wedding band, which I never wore because I hated how it felt against my skin, but the tattoo…that was forever, something that couldn't be lost.

I'd lived so much life in the past year.

I'd finished my degree. I'd rebuilt Dive Bar and renamed it Shelly's. It was turning a profit—and not just because the Blue Angels used it as its unofficial headquarters to do business and launder money.

Once the smoke had cleared from Grammie's house, I'd assessed the damage and realized it could've been so much worse. I'd lost a few mementos in the fire, but not all. Grammie's teacup had survived, along with my favorite framed photographs.

I'd remodeled the house entirely and bought brand new modern furniture and then had Laura and Brock move in. They'd been living in less than stellar conditions because of a shitty slumlord. The Blue Angels had taken care of that problem, but I'd wanted her to have a home. A real home. With flower bushes and a roof that didn't leak. Grammie would've been happy the house had become a home once again.

"Are you happy, darlin'?" Colt looked up at me, resting his chin on my breastbone.

"Yeah, I'm pretty happy." I grinned.

"What about the baby?" His hand stole across my stomach. "Are you happy about that, too? For a woman who wanted to wait to have children, you adopted one and then got knocked up with another within a year."

I laughed and wrapped my arms around his neck. "Someone told me it was bullshit to live by society's rules and standards."

"Who told you that? Sounds like a very smart guy."

"One the smartest men I know," I said softly. "One of the kindest, strongest, most beautiful men I know."

"You're not talking about Boxer are you?"

"Get off me," I said with a laugh, pushing against his shoulders.

He chuckled and moved off my body. My stomach growled.

"You did promise me a romantic dinner tonight," I told him. "But can I tell you something? All I want is Huckleberry ice cream."

"I can make that happen," he said, reaching for his shirt. "I blame your father for your new Huckleberry obsession."

A few months prior, Knight had sent us Huckleberry jam from a local farm in Coeur d'Alene. My addiction to it only seemed to grow in tandem with my pregnancy.

"Speaking of your father," Colt began as he pulled on his jeans. "He's bringing Bishop down for a meeting with Franco and Ramsey."

"Yeah, he told me."

"When did he tell you?" he demanded.

"A few days ago when I talked to him. Are you guys finally going to expand?"

Colt nodded.

It had been a prosperous year after the war, and there had been very little bloodshed in the streets of Waco once Dev had been dealt with. The cartels were making too much money to let their men get out of control, the MCs were protecting the city from any outsiders who might try to edge in and cause anyone harm, and it seemed like everything was smooth sailing. Still, I didn't expect it to always be like this because I knew better.

My phone vibrated from somewhere under the bed. I crouched down to grab it and saw Joni's name flashing across the screen.

"It's your sister," I said to him.

"Answer it."

I pressed a button and said, "Hello? Joni, you're on speaker phone."

"I'm engaged!" she shouted.

"Ow. And oh my God, congratulations!" I looked at Colt, whose jaw had dropped open. "Your brother can't say his congratulations right now because he's just had a stroke."

She laughed. "Bachelorette party as soon as you get back. The wedding is a week after that."

"Why so sudden," Colt demanded in true brotherly fashion. "Are you pregnant?"

"No, you asshole. Some of us use protection. I'm a nurse, remember? I actually know how to put a condom on a man."

"I don't need details," Colt muttered. "And for the record, it was Mia who went off her birth control and let me—"

"Oh, wow, hate to cut this short, but Colt promised me dinner. We'll see you in a few days," I said.

I hung up on her and glared at Colt. "Maybe you don't tell your sister we have unprotected sex."

He sighed. "Mia, babe, you're four months pregnant. How else do you think you got a bun in the oven? Huh? Besides, I've walked in on a girls' night. I know what goes down with you all and a bottle of tequila. Men have nothing on you gals."

The last girls' night had resulted in Rachel getting

pregnant. She still hadn't forgiven me for it since I'd been the one to make the margaritas. Virgin for me, of course.

"Our girls' nights are going to be pretty tame for the next few years. Allison has a newborn, Rachel's pregnant, I'm pregnant, and ten bucks says Joni will be pregnant within a month of her wedding."

"A month? No way. Three—maybe."

"She's thirty five. Her clock is ticking. And she's wanted little tiny Zip babies forever."

"Great, now I'm nauseous. Thanks."

I grinned at him.

He grinned at me.

"Are *you* happy, love?" I asked him, gently running a finger down his cheek.

"Yeah, babe. I'm happy."

He took my hand and we walked out of our bed and breakfast out into the misty sixty-five degree weather. We got ice cream and then strolled barefoot along the beach before sitting on the sand to watch the sunset. Colt scooted in close behind me, nestling me in the cradle of his body.

I thought about how nothing good lasted forever, but it was the same for the bad. Life was volatile and mercurial and it liked to kick me while I was down. But it also had the power to lift me up and give me everything I ever needed. And things I didn't even know I wanted.

As the sun sank into the ocean, I thought of Shelly.

I thought of her smile and her laughter. I thought of Grammie and Mom and Cheese. I thought about them all —the people I'd lost who'd imprinted themselves on my heart.

Life was a journey. Like a river. Always changing course.

Family.

Family got me through the hard times and celebrated with me during the joys.

Family didn't have to be blood, I realized.

I had chosen mine.

"What are you thinking about, darlin'?" Colt asked, his chin resting on my shoulder, whiskers prickling my skin through my clothes.

"I'm thinking about how lucky I am."

"Really?"

"Yeah." I turned my head so I could brush my lips across his stubbled cheek. "Let's go home, Colt. I'm ready to go home."

Additional Works

Writing as Emma Slate

SINS Series:
Sins of a King (Book 1)
Birth of a Queen (Book 2)
Rise of a Dynasty (Book 3)
Dawn of an Empire (Book 4)
Ember (Book 5)
Burn (Book 6)
Ashes (Book 7)

The Spider Queen

Writing as Samantha Garman

The Sibby Series:
Queen of Klutz (Book 1)
Sibby Slicker (Book 2)
Mother Shucker (Book 3)

Additional Works

From Stardust to Stardust

About the Author

Emma Slate writes on the run. The dangerous alpha men she writes about aren't thrilled that she's sharing their stories for your enjoyment. So far, she's been able to evade them by jet setting around the world. She wears only black leather because it's bad ass…and hides blood.

Made in the USA
Middletown, DE
25 May 2022